PRIME MINISTER BY ACCIDENT

An uplifting tale of relationships, intrigue and power

Jim Reay

First published in Queensland, Australia in 2019

Copyright © James E. Reay

The moral right of the author has been asserted.

Disclaimer
All characters and events in this publication, other than those clearly in the public domain, are fictitious and any resemblance to real persons, living or dead, is purely coincidental.

ISBN   9780648473916 (paperback)
       9780648473923 (eBook)

A catalogue record for this book is available from the National Library of Australia

Edited by Patrice Shaw (www.psediting.com.au)

Page layout and cover design by Kirsty Ogden (www.epiphanyediting.com.au)

Printing and distribution by Amazon

Available worldwide on Amazon books

www.jimreaywriter.net

Dedicated to our young clever visionaries
who see the world as it might be!

Visit Jim's website

www.jimreaywriter.net

About the Author

Jim Reay is a former high school principal and senior public servant; now a writer of crime mysteries and short stories. He is based in Brisbane, Australia.

Born a Scot, he brings a range of perspectives to his stories; from Europe and Australia – as well as his love of history, learning and culture.

Other titles by Jim Reay

Fiction:
The Guanaco Affair (ISBN 9780994377890)
The Napoleon Curse (ISBN 9780994377821)
Roller Coaster (ISBN 9781875872930)
The Chess Board (ISBN 9780994377807)
Searching for Siobhan (ISBN 9781875872893)
The Run (ISBN 9781875872916)
Catching Legends (ISBN 9781875872886)

Non Fiction:
The Most Avoided Questions (ISBN 9780994377845)

Humility, not hubris

**'If we are victorious in one more battle with the Romans,
we shall be utterly ruined.'**

After the Battle of Ascalum in 279 BC, Greek general, Pyrrhus,
despite being the victor on the day, lost so many troops that he had
to retreat from the war – hence the term, *Pyrrhic victory.*

in Parallel Lives, Pyrrhus. 21.9

Plutarch (46-120 AD) Greek biographer

**'It is the certainty that they possess the truth that
makes men cruel.'**

*Anatole France (1944-1924) novelist, essayist, Nobel laureate for litera-
ture 1921*

'It always seems impossible until it is done.'

*Nelson Mandela (1918 -2013) anti-apartheid activist, Nobel peace
prize 1993, President of South Africa 1994-1999*

Chapter 1

Brisbane

Justin

Justin Kipps can only laugh.

The way this land is governed is lunacy on so many levels – a tragic comedy, if it wasn't so serious. No wonder Justin's generation scoffs at the gridlock of politics and those who profess to be experts in it.

Self-important media commentators endlessly trawl through each other's political opinions – as if by stirring and re-stirring the mud on the bottom of the pond, they might somehow bring clarity to the water.

And yet to solve it all is hardly brain surgery. They just have to stop doing *same old, same old.*

As a soon-to-be history/economics honours graduate, Justin Kipps feels somehow qualified to tell them there is no future in the past – only the past. Not even the present is the same as the past, let alone what it might become.

He is strolling in the direction of his parents' house – not where he lives anymore but a place of belonging nevertheless. Then he stops, puzzled – jolted from his thoughts. He is sensing a rolling thunder. He can't hear it but he feels it ominously moving towards his youthful frame.

Justin looks normal, as he should; like a fairly conventional twenty-one-year-old Australian – if on the favoured side of normal.

1

Perhaps that is why he gets twinges of guilt, why he questions the way the world is organised, why he gets so frustrated at the mindless theatre that passes for political or mass media *entertainment* priorities.

He has a suburban upbringing. Comfortable parental home. Executive secretary mother taking time-out until all the children finish school, while managing to squeeze in a game of bridge once a week to stay mentally sharp. Accountant father, who is a member of the golf club; younger brother and sister still in high school, while Justin himself is just waiting to graduate from uni.

They are a family who discuss issues and tell him to follow his dream. *You can be whatever you want to be* is the mantra. He knows it is just aspirational bullshit but they keep saying it and seemingly think that anything is possible. Or is it just the devil peeking over the window sill, winking, *If you believe it, it can't be a lie,* before ducking back like a chortling puppet-show character?

He glances up at the sky – is the atmospheric pressure changing?

Back to his thoughts. Political charades. Maybe he should stand for parliament – show them how it could be done. Maybe he should go all the way and become Prime Minister while he is young enough to see the answers. Actually it doesn't seem that hard – at least from the outside looking in.

Meanwhile, in Canberra …

Chapter 2

The man's body looks peaceful, just pulled from the water at the base of the Scrivener Dam and shielded from any prying eyes by police privacy screens.

Detective Sergeant Sarah Power from Australian Capital Territory Policing, Criminal Investigations section, watches the pathologist, Dr Barry Cotter, make a preliminary examination.

Beside DS Power, newly appointed Detective Constable Luke Dexter, experienced in general policing but fresh from detective training college, asks, 'What do you think, Sergeant? Suspicious?'

'All deaths like this are suspicious, until proven otherwise,' comes the DS's over-the-shoulder reply. 'Just watch, listen and look around. Tell me what you see.'

'Caucasian male. Dark hair. Around 180 cm, at a guess. In a water pool at the base of the dam that holds back Canberra's huge lake. Clearly broken neck from the misshapen angle of the skull. No obvious wounds on the face or front. Clothes not cheap by the look of them – leather jacket, quality leather shoes, dress trousers, designer shirt, gold chain on neck, no rings.'

'So, how did he get in the water?'

'No flow over the top of the dam from Lake Burley Griffin, so he wasn't washed there from the lake. Given the broken neck – a fall from the pedestrian walkway above seems likely.'

The doctor turns the body over ... to reveal the back of the skull significantly distorted by an impact.

DS Power nods at the revelation with a wry smile. She gives a pointed look to the walkway above, where police motorbikes at each end have closed off public access. Forensic specialists in white overalls check the railing for possible evidence. She turns to Dexter. 'So, when?'

'By the look of the body, no obvious significant decomposition ... and near a lookout with a well-used car park. If it was here yesterday, in daylight, surely it would have been noticed. So, overnight?'

'That Lady Denman Drive going along the dam top would have cars crossing regularly during the night. He would be obvious standing waiting to jump, don't you think?'

'CCTV? Dash cams?'

DS Power nods again. 'Entering or leaving the bridge area in the past twenty-four hours. Anyone driving through, with or without dash cams. We need whatever we can find, to rule things in or out.'

The body bag is loaded into a police van to go to the morgue, the Forensic Medicine Centre in the suburb of Phillip. Dr Cotter moves towards the detectives, slowly pulling off his rubber gloves.

'First impressions, Doctor?' DS Power asks.

'Suspicious, I'd say, Sarah. I'll know more after an autopsy. No identification in any of the pockets. That's unusual. The wound at the back of the head looks too specific to be caused by hitting one of the concrete teeth in the spillway, even with water flowing from any normal release. That scenario is possible ... but the injury could just as easily be caused by a blunt instrument ... like a hammer, perhaps.'

Power turns to look at the watching DC Dexter to acknowledge the suggestion. 'And then falling or being pushed over the rail of the walkway, Luke. What do you think?'

'Curious ... a puzzle.'

Chapter 3

Brisbane
Wheels in motion

'What have you done, Justin?' his mother asks. 'They were talking about it at the bridge club. "Is that your Justin that was mentioned on Sydney talk-back radio?"'

'Sydney?' A long way from his Brisbane home. 'What are you talking about, Mum?'

He can feel it again – coming for him; like a road-train rolling down a dusty track, sensed but not seen for the cloud of dirt enveloping the apparition. Would it emerge like the *Horsemen of the Apocalypse*; dramatic, inspiring, threatening?

'Dai Evans – only the most influential right-wing commentator in the land – has been going ballistic about what a Brisbane youth has written on social media. Justin Kipps. So, is it you?'

'I posted a blog about greed and human nature. That's all. A political statement.'

'Was it called *The Manifesto?*'

'Yes. But …'

'Oh, Justin. What have you done?'

'It's only a blog, Mum. Just to get people to think outside the square. What's the fuss?'

'The fuss is that *The Voice of Australia* is gunning for you and broadcasting your name all over the land. Oh, wait till your father hears about this.'

'Slow down, Mum. Cool it. It was just a blog. That's all.'

'Did you use your own name?'

'Yes. I'm not ashamed of my name. Should I be?'

A chatter of lorikeets heads like a cloud of darts from the tree in the back yard, screeching loudly, easily heard even through the kitchen window pane – spooked by something, as mother and son vaguely focus on the outside distraction. Justin can grasp it, the sense – it isn't just the birds.

'Mum, have you read what I wrote?'

'No. Let me read it. Can you find it for me on my computer? I don't follow anybody's blogs – but maybe I'll be reading yours. Do you know what *manifesto* means?'

'Yes, Mum. I know what it actually means – and I'm not hung up by all the connotations others choose to put on the word. There ...' He passes the seat at the computer over to his mother, who adjusts her glasses to focus on the text.

'Yes. It is definitely on your blog,' she says, as if checking her sanity before she starts to read. 'It has your name on it ... Justin Kipps. I don't believe this is happening. I just don't believe it. And that you would use your own name. Oh, Justin ...'

The Manifesto. **Part 1a – Economic Security**

It is just unchecked human nature.

If there were no social rules and you said to people, 'Take what you like.' They would go through the place like a plague of locusts.

No rules – no checks and balances.

Greed – wanting more.

Fighting – for the scraps or to prove who is most powerful.

Sick – minds and bodies out of balance.

These are consequences. Even in nature, animals have social rules to survive. But man can often ignore the rules of survival evolution.

Isn't this what history teaches us?

That the strong and brutal conquer and colonise the weak. **It continues because it can.**

The catch comes when the wealth of the Earth has been squandered; and when the land turns into a wasteland unable to produce more sustenance. No?

In the wider modern world, it is more subtle.

The powerful make the rules and spin the narrative so that we are all led to believe that our place in life is just the natural historic order of things.

Progressively, we extract the finite resources of the planet and stuff the productivity. We are on a spiral of mindless destruction, heading like lemmings for the cliff.

I have a dream for lifting us out of the rut.

It has three planks: economic security, physical security and social security.

Let's start to peel the onion layers off the first part.

There seems to be less and less left to plunder; not wealth, not resources, not even space. So unhealthy scenarios take over – pillaging the remains of the fossil fuel and uranium resources which have the potential to wreck the planet. **You can see polluted skies with your own eyes.** In many of the countries around, people are walking with filtration masks. **I want clean air and uncontaminated water.**

We have to break that cycle of dependency on finite fuels.

It is just like a narcotic; we have been led to believe that there is no other way – that we can't escape from its addictive clutches.

Logically, electrical power will eventually have to be generated in a sustainable way from recyclables and by using natural power: falling water, wind, sun, temperature and tides. This is not rocket science, but it *is* science.

It is just that the powerful vested interests who control the fossil fuel industries mount massive publicity campaigns to stifle all other commentaries and to control the decision makers.

Shock jocks spout sensational rhetoric as if it were true. The peddlers of that line cannot be allowed to ruin our lives.

We must call them out!!

These dealers tried the same technique with tobacco and asbestos, even with the African slave trade – and they lost all those arguments, eventually.

Their style is to ridicule and marginalise the objectors.

Wait for it to happen.

This is just the first onion layer of the first plank.

Watch this space for the next installment of *The Manifesto*!

Sally Kipps lifts her eyes from the screen and slowly shakes head. 'I love you, son, but you're too young to understand the complexities associated with this.'

'Mum, I'm about to graduate with an honours degree in history and economics. I'm twenty-one, nearly twenty-two – an adult.' He looks at his mother with accustomed peaceful eyes. 'I've done my homework. I know what I'm writing about.'

'Justin,' she shakes her head again. 'I'm not talking about economics or history. I know you are extremely bright but this is not like being president of the students' union or debating for Queensland. I'm talking about power – nasty power. Politics is a dirty business. Your unflappability will not be enough. They will soon be investigating you – us – and even what your grandparents were like. You said it yourself in your blog. You don't understand what they are capable of. They are dirt diggers … and the public will be happy to suck up any salacious rubbish that they write or speak. That's what you don't understand.'

'Hey, Mum. It's just a blog. What's the worst that can happen?'

And he stiffens to the ominous sense.

Chapter 4

Brisbane

Dai Evans

'Justin, you're on the breakfast show. Some dude called Dai Evans …' The voice of his sister carries up through the house.

'Pause it, Jenny. Be down in a minute.'

Justin Kipps rubs his eyes. He hadn't really intended to stop the night at home, but the evening conversation had needed some working through. His brother, Harry, had been right with him. He'd read the blog and had seen no big deal. He'd even suggested that Justin should run for parliament – a joke, of course. 'You'll have my tick in the box,' he'd said, 'when I'm old enough to vote later in the month; and I'll get the footy team on-side, and the Year 12s, when they've all passed the magic birthday, too.'

His sister, Jenny, had just screwed up her face as fourteen-year-old girls can do, with 'Hey, have you ever watched that parliament stuff? Drab men in suits either talking to empty green leather benches or else they're shouting like some primary school rabble at break.'

His father hadn't been aware of what had been going on when he'd eventually come home after a long day at work, but he'd picked up quickly on his wife's waves of dread. 'Can I read what you've written then, Justin?'

The sheet of A4 paper was flicked across the table – it had been printed out for maternal and filial analysis.

'So, what's wrong with that, then?' his father had asked at last, with a puzzled frown.

'Dai Evans is what's wrong, Howard,' his mother asserted. 'He was ranting away on his talk-back show yesterday about this upstart Justin Kipps and young kids bagging the fossil fuel industry.'

'Did he know anything about Justin?'

'Only his name – but since when have facts mattered to him? I found out from Joan Wilkins at bridge. She'd heard it on morning radio and asked if it was our Justin who was being talked about. Kipps isn't a common name.'

''Tis in this house,' Harry quipped, as his father gave a tolerant wince.

Howard turned to Justin. 'Can he tell where you live from your blog?'

'Only that I live in Queensland and that I'm a uni student.'

This drew a paternal laugh. 'Well, that would get him going for a start. But your mother's right. You have to watch that this doesn't blow up into something bigger.'

'I didn't expect the shock radio or the tabloid TV to pick it up. I was just trying to write something to get people thinking and discussing. I thought maybe two men and a dog might give it a passing glance.'

'But why do you have to write it at all, Justin?' his mother had asked.

'Because *politician speak* scores 10 on the BABS scale.'

'What's the BABS scale?'

'Boring as Bat Shit. A ten point scale where 10 is the highest.'

'That language is not appropriate, Justin,' his mother had said.

'It is more meaningful to my generation than the meaningless babble that comes from politicians.'

'No, Justin. Many politicians work very hard and know what they are talking about.'

'So why do they put the talking robots on mainstream media then. Okay. I accept what you say. You are probably right, Mum … about some of them.'

His father intervened, 'Maybe just stop at this blog and it will all pass over.'

'But I've already posted the next one, Dad.'

'The next part of *The Manifesto*? Oh. Right. Okay. Well, we'd better read that one too.'

'I'll print it off.'

* * * *

It is back in Justin's brain – just pressure building – but, as he looks out onto a blue morning sky, it doesn't make any sense. The others are moving … and heading for the stairs. This is today.

'Well, are you all coming?' shouts Jenny from downstairs. 'I don't want it stuck on pause for ever.'

Justin's brain clicks in.

'On our way,' Harry calls from the next room and his brother rumbles down the stair.

'Let it roll, Jenny,' Howard Kipps instructs, looking his usual business self in a long-sleeved blue shirt and dark pin-striped suit trousers as he tousles Harry's unkempt sandy hair at the breakfast bar. 'Still half asleep, son? All well, Sal?' He looks across at his wife, who is steeling herself, with the arm of her big son Justin now round her shoulders, for whatever is about to emerge on the television.

Well, what's your beef with The Manifesto, Dai? the presenter asks.

Just start with the title. If that's not the club colours of commies and lefties then I'm not a fair dinkum Australian. He's a student, for goodness sakes – hardly out of nappies and purporting to tell our business leaders that they are some evil horde of plunderers, drug dealers even, narcotics peddlers, when they are the very backbone of the standard of living that whelps like Justin Kipps take for granted …

'Hardly out of nappies! A whelp!' Sally Kipps' anger burns in her eyes. 'How dare that opinionated creep make comments about my son? He doesn't know any of us. Why does he get air time?'

'Easy, Mum,' Justin soothes, his arm cuddling her shoulders. 'I'm not bothered.'

'But I am,' his mother asserts. 'How dare he? Howard? How dare he?'

'I agree. It's not on. That's tabloid TV at its worst.'

Let them get a job before they start commenting on how the world works. We don't need such ill-considered undergraduate piffle floating out on this social media, as if they were giving us intelligent facts. Someone might be tempted to believe this lunacy. That's the weakness in this whole social gossip thing. It is a very dangerous phenomenon. Anyone can write what they like. There's no editorial oversight…

'Who's overseeing **him**?' Jenny calls out. 'He's just shooting his mouth off … and through those pouty lips. He's just miffed.'

'Jenny, Jenny.' Her father's voice is always measured. 'He's paid to provoke. That's his job – unpalatable as it is. So that people will want to watch the show – waiting for the next blow-up. Controversy sells. That's the way it works these days – and people must fall for it, if you believe the ratings.'

'Bogans, maybe,' his daughter replies with a snort.

And his second blog questions our fundamental values and about how to sort out Australia's revenue stream. Where do they get off, these young ones? They haven't lived and suddenly they are experts on tax law and revenue streams …

Well, thank you, Dai Evans. We're out of time this morning. We'll save the tax dodgers for another time. I'm sure many of the viewers will be listening in to your talk-back later today to hear how this story develops. You should get Justin Kipps on your show – to see what your listeners would think …

'I've had enough.' Sally Kipps' tone is instruction enough to mute or kill the program – and perhaps all who are involved in it. 'How dare he?'

'Are you going on his show then, Justin?' Harry asks, pretending to shadow box. 'I'll be your protection team.'

But Justin says nothing. He is listening to a rumble that no-one else can hear.

Chapter 5

Canberra

Hetty Fry and Malcolm McGlashan

The Prime Minister's chief of staff, Hetty Fry, phones from her office in the House of Representatives to Liberal Party headquarters in the Canberra suburb of Barton. She wants to draw the matter to the attention of the organisation's leader, Malcolm McGlashan.

'What? Some kid's blog on social media? Haven't we got more important things to do?'

'Usually, yes, Malcolm. It's called *The Manifesto*, Part 1a. That got Dai Evans going. He spoke about it as only he can on his talk-back show in Sydney yesterday – and he was on breakfast TV this morning.'

'And?'

'And … there's a lot of interest in the matter.'

'So, something and someone that no-one had heard of has become an issue because bloody Dai Evans gave it some oxygen?'

'That's what it looks like.'

'He should know better. I'll speak to him. It'll be old news by the time the next drama hits. We'll come up with something to distract.'

'Perhaps not, Malcolm. The blog is linked to a Twitter feed – not the boy's personal account. After yesterday's talk-back, there were 23,000 retweets.'

'These are just phantom followers. It's the way Twitter is set up. It'll pass.'

'And after Evans appeared on the breakfast show this morning, the retweets have hit 500,000; that was in the next three hours. That's hundreds of times more than the numbers of followers the kid had on his personal account. That's big. It's going viral.'

'Damn. Damn. Damn. What's the kid's name?'

'Justin Kipps. Student from Queensland. That's all we know at this stage. His personal Twitter and Facebook have been made inactive.'

'Alright. I'll contact Peter. He'll do some work on the kid and get some alternative comments jamming his blog.'

'That's the catch. There is no provision on his blog to make comments. It's just a website. The word is spread only by Twitter and Facebook – and the youth grapevine. You can't comment on his inactive personal accounts, either.'

'What? Okay. It's a flash in the pan, Hetty. But thanks for the heads-up. Peter and his team will neutralise this annoyance. Oh, do I need to be aware of what the kid is writing? Is there anything in it?'

'I'll copy them over to you as attachments. Malcolm, he may be young and naïve but I don't think he's an idiot. Even now, the international protest organisations are taking an interest. Peter can see it all if he goes on Twitter.'

'Bugger!'

* * * *

Malcolm McGlashan finishes reading *The Manifesto* Part 1a while he splutters in confused annoyance, 'Undergraduate piffle, alright! Why the fuss? Damn Dai Evans for giving air time to this rubbish.'

He opens the second blog. *The Manifesto* Part 1b Economic Security.

The Manifesto 1b – Economic Security
Our value system is all wrong!

When accumulating money is the desired end point of so much social activity, we have missed the plot.

'What is this? Some set of leftie uni discussion topics?' McGlashan mutters.

When **your value** is determined by how much money you can get, we have serious value problems.

Have we become prostitutes – being sucked into a seedy world by the lure of lucre?

There are many other human and social values like **decency, honesty** and **helping others**. Can't we learn to be content with sufficiency – not to be greedy?

Where are our role models?

Politicians, lawmakers, chief executive officers, business directors, church leaders, sports people, media hosts … What values are they promoting?

Certainly, we need to collect revenue or money to pay for services – and we need to collect more than we spend.

That is just arithmetic!

How it is done needs to be **equitable** – not equal, **but fair**.

A fundamental underpinning principle of Australian life is *the fair go*.

It is conventional wisdom that every earner should pay a fair level of tax. But it has also been another type of conventional wisdom in Australia that people should find legal ways to minimise their tax bill wherever they can.

The underlying implication is that governments are ripping off people's hard-earned.

To change an attitude, we need to stop the rip-offs, starting with public representatives using shonky rules to behave without moral integrity.

Book it up to the company or the government has been the get-out for centuries.

But the government is actually **us**, the tax payer – and it is us, the other tax payers, who are being ripped off … not some anonymous government.

And the irony appears to be that the laws actually allow global corporations to minimise their tax contribution to next to zero – but there are no rules like that for you and me.

It is arithmetic.

The more rip-offs, the more the rest of us have to pay.

Now, I'm a rebel. I freely admit that the stifling blanket of the status quo does nothing for me.

The attitude must change, starting with politicians perks, as an example to us all that no-one is getting special treatment. Follow that with removing legal loopholes on companies and people who avoid their fair level of tax.

Ah ha! The critics will cry. If you take away perks and loopholes, no global corporation will do business in Australia.

Twaddle (I'm being polite).

They do business here because they can make a fortune from resources and a cashed-up market.

The reason the loopholes exist is because weak-kneed lawmakers from the past and present have given into **lobbying intimidation**.

It is bribery, dressed in business suits and carrying legal briefcases.

Let them know that we won't put up with being conned
any more.

Do what I suggest and then see how the revenue part of
the ledger balances up!

Wait for more in the next edition of *The Manifesto*!

And McGlashan picks up his phone, 'Peter, we have an issue
for you to fix.'

Chapter 6

Canberra

Power and Dexter

DC Luke Dexter pops his head into DS Sarah Power's open office doorway at the Winchester Police Centre, the ACT Policing Headquarters in the Canberra suburb of Belconnen. 'There's been a reaction to your press conference already. Well done.'

Luke fully understands why the superintendent had asked his DS to brief the press herself. She has both the face and the encouraging personality to get her words straight onto the news channels. They have all been broadcasting an appeal for anyone to contact Crime Stoppers immediately if they have seen anything strange overnight on Lady Denman Drive above the Scrivener Dam, particularly anyone walking in the area.

'Dash cams?'

'No. None of that yet. But one driver reports a recollection of a man on the walkway around 2 am. He didn't give it much thought at the time – he was returning from a party. Another, travelling south, thought she saw a man and a woman together on the walkway around the same time. She was a lane across. It is just a vague memory in the periphery of her headlights. No description, just shapes. We have a third, travelling north, reports a couple of car headlights waiting to cross in front of her into the zoo car park, on the north side of the dam.'

'Two cars? Time?'

'They are all around 2 am. Nothing too specific yet. But two cars – yes.'

'Type of cars?'

'Just headlights at this stage.'

'Okay, Luke. Forensics have just sent through their preliminary. There is definitely blood on the railing. Their samples are off for testing already. And they found a distinctive large earring.' She shows a photograph on her screen. 'There is blood on it. Perhaps, they will get DNA too. It might have been torn from an ear lobe.'

'So we have a woman there, too?'

'Or a man could have worn the big earring. I'll get in touch with Barry Cotter to see if he has anything preliminary on the body. His people are flat out – not just ACT cases but a chunk of the NSW suspicious deaths, west of the range, come to his team too. He won't get to a full autopsy until late this afternoon. Do you want to attend? See what they do?'

'Potentially.' Dexter smiles as he turns to leave. 'I'll get back to my screen in the meantime.'

Dr Barry Cotter sounds tired as well as professionally in control as he answers Sarah Power's phone call.

'I have the full autopsy scheduled for 4 pm if you can be here. But I'll send you my written preliminary over within the hour.'

'Thanks, Barry. Appreciated. DC Dexter and I will be with you at 4 pm.'

'Okay,' Cotter says. 'Here's the basics of my findings so far. We have a Caucasian male, dark hair, brown eyes, 181 cm tall, 98 kg, early-to mid-30s, well muscled – possible gym candidate. Some dental capping on front upper teeth. Scarring on eyebrows, consistent with repeated boxing hits, for example. Recent skin abrasions on knuckles of right hand – they would have bled recently. What appears to be a healed, stitched knife cut on the right rib cage.

'Clothes are good quality leather jacket, shirt, trousers and leather shoes. I'll get the photographs of the fashion labels sent over to you. No name identification for the owner. There are blood traces on the back collars of shirt and jacket, although diluted by water contact. I've sent them for testing.

'No wallet, phone, keys or other ID in pockets. Only a water-congealed blob of tissues in the right trouser pocket. Is he right handed?

'Now, the body has had a high impact on his left shoulder, which is broken to a shattered level and displaced; fractures to clavicle, humerus and several left-side ribs. There is a long fracture of the left scapula – shoulder blade. The C5, C6 and C7 vertebrae are significantly displaced – broken neck.

'That would all be consistent with a fall from the walkway into the water of the spillway. The speed of the fall would probably mean that he impacted underwater with the concrete base of the spillway, albeit slowed slightly by the water.'

Sarah Power scribbles brief notes as she listens for the *but* that she knows must come.

'But, Sarah. The first wound was probably a forceful blow to the back of the skull by a blunt instrument. To my eyes its shape seems like the rounded-back head of a ball-peen hammer. Do you understand what I'm describing?'

'Yes, Barry. A metal-working hammer. Got you. Was that the fatal blow?'

'If it happened on the walkway, he would definitely be unconscious on the way down. Some force involved.'

'What about time of death?'

'This is an imprecise science. The body has been in cold water, probably turned around by the gentle flow, and superficial blood has been washed away. I would estimate within twelve hours of the body being found – so overnight. I can't be more precise, at this stage. We'll know more when we do the full autopsy. Questions?'

'We are definitely ruling out suicide?'

'Even if he tried to deliver the blow to the back of his head while leaning over the railing, it would be an impossible feat to get the force required … in my opinion.'

'Can we rule out that he was hit by a vehicle and tossed over …
or flipped by a motorbike on the walkway?'

'No, we can't. But very unlikely. Any type of bike on the
walkway would be unlikely to knock a big man over a railing. In
my view, there has been another human's deliberate intervention on
whatever has happened to this man.'

'Okay. Thanks, Barry. See you this afternoon. I'll await your
preliminary report in due course.'

She has had only a minute to reflect after the call to the doctor,
when Luke Dexter brings in more information.

'The Canberra Zoo reports that a black Audi was left in their
car park overnight … and it is still there, locked – in the entrance
parking bays. A uniformed patrol is checking it out as we speak. I'm
getting the vehicle registration information.'

'Good, Luke. Have the vehicle brought in for full forensics. We
need a clue, a name for the victim and more evidence. Oh, and 4 pm
for the autopsy at FMC, the Forensic Medical Centre. I'll drive you
over. The doctor is sending over his preliminary. His initial suggestion seems to be still the best explanation.'

As the detective constable leaves, Sarah Power looks at the
photograph of the earring – African? … calabash shaped with inter-
laced hoops pecked into the silver – and she ponders. Not a small
woman who would wear such an earring. Not a cheap ring. Is the
woman strong too? Strong enough to tip a 98 kg man over a railing?

Chapter 7

Brisbane

Forming the plan

Dai Evans' dismissive comments are really pissing off Justin Kipps but also steeling his resolve not to be distracted in his quest.

Twitter has gone mad; Facebook too. Kipps is starting to understand more fully – a quick look online at the mushrooming cloud of contacts shows the response to Dai Evans has gone viral. His website is safe – simply a place to post his manifesto. It isn't the traditional interactive model, inviting direct comments. He is grateful that he took Frank's advice to protect the blog page.

Frank Willis is his flat mate in their Capalaba share house – he had warned Justin of some sort of challenge if *The Manifesto* got up the ribs of the powerful. But he wasn't sure what the reaction would be like.

The site only provides hashtag links into non-personalised manifesto social media accounts, set up for the purpose by Frank. Even so, most of the early texts and tweets have been flooding in from people who actually know him and they have been getting contacts from their networks. The retweets are going crazy.

Still in his parents' house, he is just coming to terms with his morning and he needs some outside wisdom.

He picks up his ringing phone.

'You have struck a chord, Kippsy.' Frank Willis sounds confident and encouraging. A year older than Justin, Frank studies arts/

law, as well as having a sympathetic appreciation of Justin's political and philosophical priorities. 'Bloody well done.'

Justin deflects the praise with, 'Where are you, Frank?'

'Lying back on my Capalaba bed. How are your folks taking it?'

Kipps pauses. 'They're angry at Dai Evans' comments and they're wary of where this might go. I sense we need to be more than a bit smart about this. Big wheels could get involved, not just talk-show mouths.'

'You're right. Twitter is on fire; serious national blogs are interested in what you're saying.' Frank's energy bursts from the phone. 'They want more – and permission to republish on their websites. Good on old bullshitting Dai Evans for stirring the pot. We're on a roll. What do you think? We need a strategy to move forward so that we can get *The Manifesto* out there. I think you're going to be in demand very soon.'

Justin's mind is rolling. What are they to do? Surely his blog is not that controversial? It is only a concocted media frenzy.

Should he get up a town hall meeting to argue his case? No way. Rent-a-crowd wouldn't let him get a word across and the media would just beat up the ridicule angle. Should he go on the plethora of political chat shows to defend himself? No. Definitely not, on so many levels – to be ambushed, encircled by smiling assassins all armed with the faceless people's gotchya questions.

Open up the website blog to impulse comments? Same answer – worldwide trolls and professional spoilers would just saturate the feedback, to squeeze out intelligent views and dilute any sensible messages. It is more effort for the trolls to follow hashtag links and they probably wouldn't bother.

No! He knows that *the forces of darkness* already have the superiority in weaponry, training and experience. Their social control systems are set up to stymie any head being poked up above the parapet with alternative or critical thinking. They have killed off any and all threats to their power before – and they would be intent on doing it again.

But ... what Justin has been doing has cut through for some reason. No-one can argue against that. The blog entries have been read. The tweeters have spread the word. Dai Evans is having apoplexy and doubtless many others behind closed doors are cursing, fuming and frothing at the mouth that another voice can be aired in the ether and in cyberspace.

'Frank, I never expected that it would take off like this. Totally bizarre. Let's get our tight group together – away from the uni. What about a coffee house somewhere? Maybe where you, me and Zoe meet down at Manly, near the esplanade. I have thoughts, but I wouldn't mind refining them a shade – a bit of legal perspective would be good too, before *the armies of doom* descend on us. Dad's off to work now. Harry and Jenny are at school. Mum's getting ready for her volunteering later today – she's only working two days a week just now. But she's hurting more than the others. I want a bit more time with her before I leave.'

'Two o'clock? We can meet, like you suggest, at the usual place at Manly. So who do you want?'

'Well, those who understand – Graham, Janet, Zoe for sure. Maybe, someone who is not as carried away as we are – an alternative voice.'

'Karen Porter, perhaps? Her father is a barrister, isn't he? We might benefit from knowing more of the rules and the legalities than I know yet.'

'Do we know anyone who has been a politician – beyond our student stuff?'

'Somebody with a family member, you mean?'

'Yes.'

'Brandon Jones. He's a Young Liberal. His uncle, on his mother's side, was a senator once, so I believe – maybe a great-uncle. I've heard him skiting about it in a seminar. But, would you want him? He wouldn't necessarily think like us.'

'What do *we* think like? I've never joined *the young anythings*. A bit like religion – I listen to them all but don't buy into any. We just want a more effective and responsive system of government.

What we have isn't working well enough. Too entrenched. That's all. Surely, ideologies aside, that's what we all want. I think, sound him out – what harm can it do?'

'He could disclose what we're doing.'

'So could any of us. We're not doing anything illegal. We are just trying to get a message out and we seem to have a vehicle which is being read. We're not in anyone's camp.'

'Okay, I'll set it up with as many as I can from your list. See you at two. Maybe you should get your next blog up online – keep the interest going.'

'Sure. They're all written. I've just been letting them out in readable doses. I thought maybe two men and a dog might have bought into it but Dai Evans has lit a whole bonfire of interest. Amazing. I'm really surprised.'

Willis pauses before, 'Tell your readers, that if they will give you their support, you will stand for federal parliament. That'll stir some interest and old Dai Evans will probably blow a gasket.'

'That's a big call, Frank. It's one thing to have ideas. It's a whole different ballgame to step into the machinery of government. But maybe …? Your idea, I mean. Not actually doing it. You could be right. We might as well capitalise on the interest. It probably won't last long. And the next election is ages away. I'll get back to the house in an hour or so and cadge a lift with you to Manly. Cheers.'

Chapter 8

Canberra

Detectives

'The car is a late model Audi, leased to a courier company, based in Fyshwick,' DC Luke Dexter says.

'Right. Fifteen minutes away. Let's get over there.' DS Sarah Power is on her feet and grabbing her car keys.

* * * *

The duty overseer at the courier company greets them with eyebrows raised in confused query.

'I just deal with the vans and the courier cars. That Audi is nothing to do with us. You'll need to see the manager.' He points to the office at the side of the warehouse.

'What sort of packages do you courier?' Power asks.

'All sorts,' the overseer replies. 'Customers book and pay online. They print out the packing labels at their business or home. Our people pick up and deliver ... or if going interstate, packages are brought back here for trans-shipment. My job is to organise the logistics – the drivers, the routes, the vehicles ... but that Audi is not in my inventory.'

* * * *

'I'm sorry, the manager is not here for a few days,' the manager's secretary advises. 'He's in Melbourne.' In answer to the querying look from the police officers, she continues. 'The head office is in Melbourne. The manager goes there for a few days every month.'

'We need to contact him,' DS Power says. 'Please give us his mobile number and address in Melbourne.'

The secretary looks distinctly uncomfortable as she writes the number on the back of the company business card … and hands it over. 'That's his private mobile number.'

'Now, this black Audi car?' Power continues. 'It's leased as I understand it. Correct?'

'Yes. It's a courtesy company car.'

'Who is the current driver?'

'A Mr Wilson from Melbourne. I only saw him when he was given the car about four weeks ago.'

'You would have a photocopy of his driver's licence then?' Then, to the secretary's nervous nod, 'We need to see it, thanks. Now.'

After shuffling through a cabinet, she presents the police with the filed record. Power shows the page to Dexter.

'Victorian licence. Desmond Wilson. 32 years old. 181 cm. What does Mr Wilson do for you that he needs a company car?'

'I'm not sure. I think he is some sort of auditor … time and motion studies, maybe. We have had a few over the years. That's what I was told in the past. But, like I said, I haven't seen Mr Wilson since the day he picked up the car.'

'Do you have his home address?'

'It's not in the file for the car. I don't deal with these people – only to issue the cars. I imagine Melbourne does the bookings for accommodation.'

'The car hasn't been returned, then?' Power asks, disingenuously.

'Oh, no. The keys would come to me and the car would be on the warehouse floor.' She looks out the window to confirm.

'Thank you for your time. Please give us a photocopy of Mr Wilson's licence.'

* * * *

28

Dexter listens on loudspeaker phone as Power contacts the courier company manager, a Leo Clarke, in Melbourne.

'Mr Clarke, this is Detective Sergeant Power and Detective Constable Dexter from ACT Policing. We wish to know about a Mr Desmond Wilson who has been driving one of your courtesy cars.'

The police exchange glances as they both recognise the hesitation and nervous vibrations in Clarke's voice as he replies, 'Has he been in an accident?'

'When did you last see him, Mr Clarke?'

'I don't really see him at all. The loan of the car is a courtesy for business acquaintances.'

'What sort of business acquaintances?'

'Like directors of associated companies. We're part of a larger business group. They support us financially and we look after their occasional visitors to Canberra with a courtesy car.'

'What was Mr Wilson doing in Canberra?'

'I'm not privy to that. Sorry. This is a business arrangement at a higher level than me.'

'Who is the contact for this higher level than you?'

'I'm not at liberty to divulge that information over the phone.'

'You are talking to the Canberra Police, Mr Clarke. It takes one phone call to have the Victoria Police talking to you in an interview room, very soon. Do you have Mr Wilson's address in Canberra?'

'Can I call you back, please? I don't have that information to hand.'

'Mr Clarke, we require Mr Wilson's address in Canberra and the names of your superiors who have made the arrangements for Mr Wilson. I'll have the Victoria Police contact you within the hour. Thank you for your assistance.'

As Power clicks the phone off, she asks Dexter, 'Well, what do you think?'

'He's very nervous. Mr Wilson is unlikely to be a company auditor on that basis. And Clarke doesn't yet know that Wilson is dead.'

'Right ... or not letting on, perhaps. This part is a job that needs to be passed to Victorian Police to check into Desmond Wilson's background. We need to know if there are any relatives to advise. We also have to brief the Australian Federal Police in case this *larger group* that Clarke mentions has its tentacles into overseas connections and perhaps organised crime. That goes through our superintendent.'

Luke Dexter's eyebrows rise as he takes in the process. To which, Sarah Power responds, 'This is the system here, Luke. Most of your policing has been in New South Wales. But you have to understand Canberra. This is a place of wheeling, dealing, lobbying, favours given, favours owed and the potential for significant corruption and crime. We will follow transparent procedures. Now we need to be out at Phillip by 4 pm for the autopsy. Are you still right for it?'

Dexter nods, without bursting enthusiasm.

Chapter 9

The Manifesto 1c – Economic Security

An economic theory based on continued growth is doomed to failure.

The resources that are being used are finite and they are being divided among an ever-increasing population on an ever-degrading planet. There is less per person to go around. It is just simple arithmetic.

Am I pessimistic? Not a bit. I am young enough to visualise a better future.

We are still only with the economic plank because, if that one doesn't work, the rest is unlikely to happen.

Let's start with education.

It should be about developing multi-literate young people who can think critically; who can analyse information from many frames of reference and find solutions to the world challenges without being caught up in the sticky web of past-practice politics or being brainwashed with 'this is how it is done'.

In the current version of democratic government, **we are being sold out to the lapdogs of global vested interest** coupled to a gobsmacking arrogant indifference to any sense of social justice; and delivered with a sleight of hand of practised conjurors.

A high-quality education system for the future is **an investment in intelligence, not a cost** – and, indeed, it should be free for all, with progress at higher levels based only on merit. (I will return to what universities should be doing in a later blog.)

Clearly, this is a much bigger topic than can be handled in this short space.

Suffice it to say that the current schooling system is a relic of when powerbrokers, industrialists and global vested interests wanted mass labour trained to a useful level – basic literacy, numeracy and the capacity to follow instructions blindly.

An elite few were filtered through to a higher level to become the next generation of manipulators – **the puppeteers who pulled the lawmakers' strings.**

But, in a finite world, that old model is unravelling. Why?

Conventional economic theories were, and are, based on an infinite supply of cheap inputs which could then be on-sold with a mark-up to an ever-growing consumer market.

In the new technological world, the repetitive manual labour jobs of the old industrial factories will be rare. The new workforce must be technology-literate and able to think beyond dogmatic practices.

The future is about reasoning and being aware of wider issues, philosophical concepts and about recognising when we are being duped by the manoeuvring of slick

powerbrokers who specialise in pulling secret strings and feeding crap to the masses.

We can see through the con – the three-card trick.

Clearly we need to change the way that political process works.

This is not about revolution – it is about working within the Australian Constitution to bring moral honesty back to the legislative process.

Put up or shut up, you say.

I will.

If necessary and if supported by you, I, Justin Kipps, will stand as an Independent voice for the federal seat of Killen at the next election.

I need you to spread the word because you can be sure that vested powers will do all they can to belittle me, scandalise my past, ridicule my intellect as well as satu-rate traditional and social media with their bile.

But, **you** can educate people beyond that storm of lies and misrepresentation.

You can help people see it for what it is.

Watch this space for the next stage of *The Manifesto*!

* * * *

As Justin finishes re-reading his new blog post, he can feel the pres-sure in his head. Can he slice through the storm of misrepresentation?

Nerves? Or is he prescient?

He prefers to think that it is the latter, as a peaceful clarity wafts through him – and the pressure dissolves away. The cerebral challenge is suddenly exciting … his readership seems to be moving with him …

The older generation focuses too much on the peripheral stuff, the distractions of social expectations, and miss the issues that actually can make a difference.

And yet …?

Chapter 10

Brisbane
The team

Justin sits next to Janet Chou for no other reason than she is an extremely good-looking, happy woman who he met in an economics seminar a year before – and they seem to click. No other agenda … and she is a smart thinker too.

Frank has been as good as his word. Graham McGrady, from Moree in NSW, is a mate from the student union meetings. He has graduated in some communications course, attended all union functions and spoken about doing some law and media units later – an honest straight-talker. Zoe McAllister has been a long-time *friend* of Frank's – and is a couple of years older than him. She is sitting alongside Karen Porter, of the barrister father. Brandon Jones is the surprise. How Frank got him on-side is a mystery – but they are all there as the coffee orders are taken.

'This is impressive, Justin.' Zoe gives him a beaming smile. 'I've just read your third blog. Are you really going to stand for Killen?'

Graham gives Justin a victorious knuckle nudge, with a whispered, 'Good on yer, brother.'

'I've only suggested it. This whole thing could be dead in the water by this time next week. Just floating the idea.'

Brandon Jones is grinning. The Young Liberals are a group unto themselves. He is rarely seen at student union functions – and then probably only to see what is going on. 'What do you know about being a member of parliament?'

'Bugger all – but I'm eligible. I'm Australian with no dual citizenship issues at least as far back as my grandfathers on both sides. But we are probably descended from English convicts, if we go back far enough.'

'Isn't there a deposit required?' Karen asks.

'It used to be a thousand bucks. Might be more now.' Brandon's grin is getting smugger and smugger. 'And you don't get it back unless you get four per cent of the vote.'

'How many is that?' Graham queries, with a shrug.

'Killen?' Jones appears to be delighting in exhibiting his expertise. 'Eighty-two thousand electors, roughly. Been Liberal for the last two polls at least.' The smirk again. 'Labor has had it once, maybe twice, in its history – different boundaries then, of course. Round figures. Three thousand primary votes needed, maybe a bit more. That's more than the family and a few friends. And that isn't winning the election. That's just getting your money back.'

'Shit, Justin,' Graham says. 'You'll need forty-one thousand to get over the line. Dream on.'

Janet gives Justin an encouraging nudge. 'Don't let them put you off. You have hundreds of thousands following your manifesto. Stay with it.'

Kipps' face is serious but he gives a delayed smile back to Janet as her words register. 'I'm really not expecting to stand for the parliament. I'm just trying to keep the interest in *The Manifesto* ideas going – to get the message out while it's still in people's Twitter feed.'

Karen has been sitting and thinking. 'But, you don't need forty-one thousand primary votes, do you? If you can get preferences, you might do a lot better than you think. Brandon, who would be the Libs preference?'

'Not the Greens or Labor. Crackpot Independents will be slipped in wherever they might cause mischief.'

'So would Justin's manifesto match with Lib priorities? Not as a crackpot Independent, mind you.'

'I've only seen his first couple of blogs on economics. He might get some cred for at least addressing revenue. What else is in your manifesto? Border protection, for example? National security. Defence forces overseas? Small business? Lower taxes? Less government interference? Come on, Justin. This is just a joke.' Brandon Jones laughs this time.

Justin looks calmly back at him. 'The ideas are not a joke … and people are responding to them. Border protection comes up under the *physical security* plank. It is part of the Constitution – defending the nation. While refugees are hardly attacking forces, there are implications if they start to come in waves again. I've no problem with temporary protection – Labor stuffed that up and let it become politicised. The Coalition just entrenched the problem. Certainly, I don't like the idea of automatic permanency when there are many others waiting through due process.'

'That's Liberal policy, more or less.'

'But I wouldn't be demonising them, Brandon. They need to be treated with respect and dignity, not as anonymous illegals who should be shunned. That's divisive fear politics. Same with the defence forces operating overseas. It is an alliance action against terror, criminal elements; not against religion or *evil* foreigners. Some of them are Australians, after all.'

'Liberal policy too – more or less. It's the other side that lifts the ante all the time. You could put a case to State Liberal HQ and they could take it up with Federal HQ.' He shrugs. 'It's possible, if it came to that. But I think you might just be laughed away.'

'So what lines up with Labor?' Frank prompts.

'Most of it, I hope.' Zoe speaks earnestly. She has a maturity about her, perhaps because she has been out in the permanent workforce – working as a project manager in the entertainment industry, events management; as Justin vaguely understands it. 'Not killing off the Arts or pricing degree study out of the reach of most of us.'

'Excuse me.' Janet interjects with an ingrained politeness. 'If Brandon is right and Liberals would be expected to win, it won't be their preferences that are important at all. Labor, Greens and other Independents will be the first to be cut, won't they? They will have the least votes in the first count. Their votes will be the ones to be redistributed.'

'You're spot on, Janet,' Justin agrees. 'How do you see the demographic of Killen, Brandon?'

The dismissive chuckle is back. 'Retirees, or soon to be. Small business people. Upward aspirants battling in the mortgage belt. Southerners who want to smell the bay breezes. There's precious little of your Green or Red voters there. The margin was around five percent to us, the Libs, at the last election. Pretty safe, I'd say. Tony Maynard is our very popular member. He'll be elected for as long as he wants to be.'

The group falls silent, lost in the enormity of an Independent's task, as the coffees arrive.

Finally, Justin seems to have collected his thoughts. He speaks quietly, with the confidence that has seen him elected student union president and able to chair sometimes quite rowdy meetings.

'I'm not advocating *same old, same old*. I want something new. It's an uphill battle however you look at it; but it is still just arithmetic – forty-one thousand votes or preferences. We have seven here, three in my family. That's ten. We get out and muster ten each – that's a hundred and ten. They get out and muster ten each and we are at one thousand, plus the original one hundred and ten. Those eleven hundred go out and muster ten each, and we are over twelve thousand. Once more and we have the whole electorate.' He smiles at his caricature of simplicity, before continuing. 'But Brandon's right. We can't compete with the major parties on money, offers or advertising. All we have is a small group and a blog that is being well read.'

'And not by people in the electorate, I should add.' Brandon Jones seems to be thoroughly enjoying his spoiler role. 'Those blog numbers are worldwide.' He grins again. 'I couldn't guarantee to be voting for you. It's a two-party system. You're either with the power or you're not in business at all.'

Janet bristles, 'Are you always such a knocker?'

'Just playing *devil's advocate*. Frank said you wanted another point of view.'

'And Frank's right,' Zoe intervenes. 'However, aren't we actually trying for higher standards, a vision for the future? Isn't that what the blog is trying to achieve?'

'Well, Zoe, that's all admirable.' Jones is undeterred. 'But in the hard world of politics, it's not a forum for faint-hearted fantasists.'

'Justin is neither faint-hearted nor fantasising,' Janet rebuts.

The quiet voice of Kipps, the potential candidate, breaks the banter. 'I don't want to be the expert on politics nor the giver of gifts to those who ask for more. I want a process with integrity, to dig us out of our complacency and intolerance as a nation. I have no intention of fitting into any party's boxes or being the foil for political commentators to get headlines.

'My appeal, if I have any, will be to get beyond the self-interest – to show a vision of who we might be and where we might be heading. I don't want to be a career politician, but I do want to make a difference.'

As Janet nudges him again in support, Karen suggests, 'You'll need some pretty clear headlines to cut through and you need to get your manifesto out for discussion, quick smart.'

'Be controversial, brother,' Graham adds. 'Rip into them on the breakfast shows.'

'No.' Kipps speaks quietly again. 'No. If we just engage in the debate like everyone else does, we'll be run over by their well-oiled armies and spin doctors. We need to be so different that people will stop, look up and say, *What?*'

Zoe sounds like a master spy as she whispers, 'I don't know if you have been noticing but there's a woman on the other side of the street – don't all look at once. She's on the phone … but she's not. She's videoing us. And there was a man there doing something similar only a few minutes ago. We're being stalked, surveilled.'

'They wouldn't hear what we are saying, though – not from there.' Frank seems offended that his organised meeting might be compromised.

'Who knows?'

'I'll go and bail her up,' Graham suggests, with his country directness.

Justin can sense a rumble. He looks up at the blue sky – no clouds, no sound; but it is there. 'No. What's done is done. Let's meet somewhere less public next time. I thought gathering in plain sight would have been a good way to hide, but maybe I was wrong.'

Karen gives a quiet laugh. 'Anyway, Brandon, you could be in trouble now – consorting with the enemy. You'll be struck out of the club.'

The others grin as it seems some of Brandon's bluster evaporates. The Young Liberal tries to parry the last comment with, 'She's moving off now. Maybe nothing at all. You're all paranoid. If you're like this now, how would you be if Justin actually got elected and had to go to the bear pit in Canberra. Privacy would be nil then.'

And Justin's mother's words floated through his mind. *You don't understand. Soon they'll be investigating you – us – and even what your grandparents were like. This is not like student politics. This is about power.*

'Let's split.' Zoe is the real-world practical voice. 'Like Justin says, *What's done is done.* Frank will get a room somewhere for the next time. I have some contacts who owe me a favour. In the meantime, get your manifesto out for consideration and comment, Justin. I think Karen is right.'

Karen Porter raises her finger to emphasise her point. 'Just stick to Twitter though for the comments. If the enemy is weak, it's through social media. They can't control what happens there – but on an open blog, they could; they'd saturate it with trolls and paid hacks.'

Brandon Jones has regained his composure. His chest is puffed, almost condescending. 'You've put big wheels in motion now, Justin. But I'll give you credit. At least, you're shaking the branch. I'll see what I can glean from my mother's uncle. Did you know he was a senator in the past? Forewarned is forearmed.'

Frank grins at Justin.

'Good on yer, Brandon. That's the way.' Graham's earthiness is a reminder to them all. 'Empower the people. That's how this started.'

'We might even write to Dai Evans and thank him for the free profile,' Zoe suggests.

Frank is back to being all business. 'Okay. Keep *The Manifesto* coming out in bite-size stages. Zoe and I will manage *The Manifesto* Twitter account. We'll block any trolls, send replies and note any good ideas. The rest of you, give the whole business some thought. We need to think *election campaign*, a few key points and a host of policies developed from Justin's proposals. Thanks for coming.'

Graham is chirpy. 'I've never been spied on before. We must be important.'

'Or a threat.'

'I'll text when we have a room somewhere.' Frank seems to be taking over the role of campaign manager.

'Texts are all being recorded too,' Karen notes pointedly. 'It's all held by service providers – metadata – just as long as you know that someone could be reading it. Face-to-face is how important things should be discussed.'

'And then in a whisper,' Brandon goads. 'You're all becoming paranoid. I told you. Thanks for the invite. See you around.'

'Likewise.' Karen gave everyone a hug, saving a special one for Justin. 'Keep thinking it through, Justin. I think you could be on a winning track. I'm just not sure what it looks like yet – but you'll get it. See you.'

'Got to move on. Apologies. Pre-season footy training, mate,' Graham says. 'Gotta keep my face known if I'm to get a run in the first team, off the bench. Keep me in the loop.'

And then there are four. 'And, Justin,' Zoe adds pointedly. 'I'd cancel your personal Twitter and Facebook accounts, at least for the moment. That will channel feedback where we want it to go.'

'Already done.'

She smiles at Justin's reply and waves them all to follow. 'My flat. It's not far – bit of a mess but say nothing. My flatmate's at work. It can be private.'

Janet stays close. She is definitely going to be part of the scene. And that rumbling – what is it?

Chapter 11

Canberra

Autopsy

Forensic autopsy rooms are probably quite similar across the developed world but nothing quite prepares the novice for the chilling temperature, the cold naked body on the slab and the slow, methodical performance of the pathologist as he or she checks to verify the cause of death.

Sarah Power is well aware that this is likely her new detective constable's first experience and she offers him a position just behind her left shoulder and near the exit door.

Dr Barry Cotter, resplendent in green theatre wear, says, 'First time, Luke? I'll explain what the external examination shows and what it might mean for your detective work. Then, I'll tell you what I will be looking for with the internal examination. You don't need to stay for that, if you choose. Oh, this is John, my assistant.' He nods in the direction of a man similarly clad in a green theatre gown, gloves and hair cap. 'This is not a fast process like on the TV crime shows. Okay?'

He glances at Luke Dexter for a confirming nod. 'In my preliminary report, I've already noted all the physical characteristics, the damaged left shoulder, arm, ribs and shoulder blade. The damaged neck vertebrae also – broken neck in common parlance.' He points out the damage for the observers' benefit, 'Note also the scar on the right rib cage. To me, it looks like an old knife wound, sutured fairly roughly – perhaps not by a medical person. Note also the scar tissue on the eyebrows and cheeks. That's common where the skin has been frequently split – as with boxers. Now, the nose. The nasal passages show significant inflammation. I will check with blood tests but I suspect that this man was a habitual cocaine snorter. It is likely then, in this day and age, that he was a user of other drugs too – amphetamines for example. We will check.

'Now, while he's in this position, let me explain the internal examination. I will cut a Y incision from about the armpits to the xiphoid, the front base of the rib cage and then down the centre of the abdomen. Then I'll check, weigh and sample each of the major organs, particularly the stomach and intestine to establish when the last meal was ingested and whether any foreign material is there.'

Cotter turns to his assistant. 'Let us turn the body now, John, so that Luke can see the back of the skull.' The two men roll the corpse with practised efficiency using rubber blocks to hold the position for viewing. 'There now, Luke and Sarah, can you see, even amid the general distortion, how this part,' he points, 'at the back of the skull has a circular indentation with about a 5 cm diameter? That's a deep wound, fracturing the skull and causing significant bleeding. And that's what I mean by being caused by something like a ball-peen hammer – although how that might have occurred is a job for detectives.'

The pathologist smiles at both the detectives. 'Now, that is the general part that should assist you as police officers. The next part is slow and methodical, checking for normality or abnormality in the organs and then sending samples for testing. At the end, we put it all back and sew it up for the undertakers.' He gives a dismissive grin and shrug. 'Given your workload, you may choose to leave now and solve the mystery. I will have my next results in several days. Try not to send me too many more, in the meantime.'

With exaggerated thanks, the detectives leave.

Outside Sarah asks, 'Well, what do you think, Luke?'

Luke moves straight into serious analytical mode. 'I think we need evidence from the Audi and then we need to match it with

44

what we already know. It would be good if some dash-cam videos appear. It will be important to visit Desmond Wilson's accommodation here in Canberra and it would be nice if the Vic Police can fill in some background.

'I don't think he's an auditor of any type – but he has expensive clothes. I think he's some form of enforcer … who has just been enforced by someone else.'

Sarah Power smiles. 'A fair starting summation. I bet you topped your detective course at the AFP College. Let's check with forensics on the car results. Are you okay or do you want a drink to settle yourself?'

'Just a quick one, maybe.'

Chapter 12

Brisbane

Setting standards

'I have some priorities, Zoe. I won't bag my opponents' person-alities.' Justin glances at the other three in Zoe's crowded flat as he speaks. 'It's important that we start by modelling the grace and dignity that we want to pervade political debate.'

Frank is taking notes. He has agreed to be the campaign organ-iser, with Zoe's wise counsel and assistance. Janet sits close beside Justin, giving supportive smiles.

Together, they have established that Justin's first initiative should be to organise a students' union meeting at a pub in the Killen electorate. It wouldn't be advertised beyond the union members. Frank assures them that the pub room would be given free, with the establishment making its money on the sale of refreshments. The police would be advised but Frank is sure that the pub security will handle any public nuisance issues.

Janet has suggested visiting old people's homes – places where people might not have normal access to computers and social media – with flyers outlining the main points of the campaign. She has volunteered to set up a list.

'Okay.' Zoe accepts Justin's condition. 'Principled behaviour is good, Justin. Now, to the campaign; Brandon is right. The Libs would expect to romp it in at any election – probably with a high margin; so, we wouldn't be getting Liberal preferences anyway. We have to convince Labor, the Greens and the other Independents to preference us second on the *How to Vote* cards. How do we get to them?'

'Start at their party meetings.'

'They'd just try to get us to jump to their ship.'

'No.' Zoe seems wise in such matters. 'This is just a business arrangement of preference swaps. They'll benefit too, if you get culled early, Justin.'

'Aw! That's a bit harsh,' Janet complains, with a grin.

'How are the blogs going, Justin?' Frank asks.

'Number 4, the last on economic security is there now.'

'Super ... because the feedback is asking for more. Half-a-million retweets again.'

'What is the feedback saying? Read me a couple.'

'Sure. Quite a few rough ones. *Peng, Dude. Tell it as it fuckin is.* Or *Yaaaass. Bout time. Up that freakin Evans cringe.*'

Janet's eyes widen, 'What?'

'*Peng* means cool, Janet, and they don't like Dai Evans,' Frank replies.

'Jeez,' Zoe says. 'Any non-slang comments? These ones wouldn't be old enough to vote.'

'Someday they will be; but most are good ... like*: Keep your festo coming, Justin* or *You'll get my vote* or *Good Argument, Justy.* Some ask questions like *How'll you encourage small business to employ disabled people?* or *What's your approach to climate change?* I can field these okay.'

'Frank, do you understand this phenomenon?' Justin asks. 'I haven't invented the wheel. Plenty of others have written similar views. Do you think this is all down to Dai Evans making such a scene about it?'

'Probably. Don't knock it, Justin. It's working. Let's ride the wave. Even if most of it is coming from lots of young ones. Revolution has sprung from stranger beginnings, like tea on ships in Boston.'

Zoe grins as she glances up from her phone. 'I'm just looking at your next post. You're heating it up, Justin. I think this suggestion to run for Canberra is getting people in – maybe even people of voting age.'

'And making the Dai Evans's of this world even more pissed off.'

The Manifesto **1d Economic Security**

We are a trading nation and there are a number of international trade agreements in place.

Let's not call them Free Trade Agreements because they are anything but free – and most are time-delayed for over a decade.

They look after particular lobbied interests and totally ignore others. Both major parties are complicit in that cute play on words.

So what does a country like Australia do, into the future, to promote economic security in a sustainable manner?

The first is to audit all the deals: subsidies, perks, concessions and tax breaks currently in place – and conduct an evaluation of the logic behind each of them. Many represent the ideologies of their time – and, invariably, they exist to make already-wealthy people even more comfortable.

The second task is to wipe all the perks out of the statute book, UNLESS there is a transparent rationale to support particular practices over others. I suspect that vigilance over tax collection, coupled with removing these subsidies, might balance the ledger very favourably.

Then, stimulate the employment of the population in meaningful work – to give ALL individuals a sense of purpose, dignity, independence and the capacity to be creative.

Why not let everyone share in the wealth?

'Really?' they will say. 'The shareholders take the risk and risk needs to be rewarded. The sky will fall in because no-one will invest.'

'Not true,' I reply.

The puppets are voicing false truths.

The people's House has become an insiders' club, engaged in so much self-congratulatory rhetoric that few outside can be bothered listening; which leaves media commentators salivating at each other's irrelevant opinions.

Why, I ask, when there is a Speaker or President to maintain the standing orders of behaviour, is Question Time such a cacophony of personal abuse, catcalls and puerile grandstanding?

Wit would be just tolerable, occasionally. But bullying and hectoring should surely have no place among our representatives, many of whom carry the archaic title of *The Honourable* when clearly, at least some are far from that.

Hansard is the official documentation of parliamentary decisions – law-making. It is the record of speeches by parliamentary members, often made to almost empty chambers.

What is the point of that practice of speaking to empty chairs?

The real debates and discussions – compromise deals, if you like – are done behind closed doors with the chamber only being the venue for votes, divisions and making an official record.

Politics has become its own self-serving industry with many parliamentarians making a lifetime career out of this wheeling and dealing.

These issues affect all the population and yet are largely controlled by **faceless party people and even more faceless powerbrokers behind that.**

I hope they are reading this!!!

How many of you have read Hansard?

How many of you have seen a media report of what is written in Hansard? The media stories are about gotchya sensations or leaked whispers or fabricated distractions or misspoken gaffes. Yet, Hansard is available on the web very quickly after each sitting day.

Maybe, the record is just boring rather than edifying.

The irony is that Hansard will be preserved forever, while the smart insider headlines will be lost in a few days, as recycling – or wrapping for the garbage.

An elected Independent member can shine a light into dark corners.

An Independent member is **inside** the parliament and can influence – he or she has a voice, a media profile and an ability to present rational arguments inside and outside the parliamentary chambers.

Independents are not sealed in a box, unable to stray from the party line, living in fear of the Whips – and doesn't that say it all?

Next time, I'll get to the physical security plank of this *manifesto*. Keep up the energy.

In a democracy, **your** view should be as important as anyone else's.

A combined view can influence an electorate.

An electorate can change the course of government.

Watch this space!

Chapter 13

Canberra

Background checks

'So what have you got on that new blogger, Peter? What's his name?' Malcolm McGlashan asks of Peter Connell, his chief go-to investigator.

'Kipps. Justin Kipps. We've had him followed and checked out. He's the university students' union president this year, about to graduate in history/economics. His supporters are students mainly. I think this is just a student rush of blood that Dai Evans gave an unfortunate brief flash of notoriety to.'

McGlashan agrees with a sigh. 'What a dickhead he can be. Go on!'

'Kipps' father, Howard, is a company accountant – financial projections and compliance monitoring. His mother, Sally, was an executive secretary before the children. Now she works two days a week in the office of a brass fittings company, just to keep her hand in till the kids have all left home, and to train the young office staff. Two siblings: brother, Harry, about to finish Year 12; sister, Jenny, finishing Year 9.

'Mother plays bridge and volunteers on some of her days off. Father plays golf on weekends when he's not needed for kids' sport. Kids are into touch, swimming and netball.

'Kipps, himself, doesn't seem to be very sporty – a participant rather than a star. Very high grade-point average at uni, though

– Dean's top medal standard. Seen as a moderate union president. He was school captain and head of the debating team. He debated for Queensland at a national level so he's no mug. Rather the opposite, in fact. Lions Youth of the Year district finalist.'

'How do you get all that so quickly?'

'A lot of it is online. The rest comes from quiet questions from locals. It's all about how you ask, Malcolm, without frightening the pigeons. People say he is very calm, organised – which is probably why he put his considered thoughts into a blog. I don't understand the fuss. Heaps of kids do that blogging.'

McGlashan rolls his eyes skyward but continues into the phone, 'But they don't have half-a-million retweets on whatever they write, each time they post something.'

'Malcolm, Malcolm. Seriously, the whole family seems like our sort of people. This is just a beat up from that shock jock. He's just a mouthy prick. I hope you sent a rocket up his clacker.'

Ignoring the expressed hope, the party president replies, 'Okay, we'll file Kipps away for future reference. Your people up in Brisbane? Are they ours or contracts?'

'Contracts. Investigators for most media outlets. Social pages. They'll be paid off.'

The Manifesto 2a – **Physical Security**

The fundamental premise underpinning this principle is that none of us had a choice in when we were born, or where or to whom.

Skin or eye colour, height, size, gender or first language are not things about which we have a choice. Nor is the culture or the belief systems or the family circumstances – wealth or lack of it – that are part of those early years.

So, **I object to people being picked on or devalued or raised onto a pedestal about things over which they have no control.** No-one is inferior or superior because of the lottery of birth. What they have chosen to do with those attributes can be a matter for critique or revision.

People then should be entitled to go about their peaceful business without being bullied, intimidated, sidelined or enslaved; or profiled into social or education boxes.

Ideally, Australians should feel safe in their own homes, in the protection of the family, the village, the community, the state and the nation.

That is the purpose of social rules and regulations, which are created and endorsed by elected representatives. That is the process for resolving disputes or aggression. The police enforce those rules and the courts decide the cases on the balance of justice. **The responsibility of citizens is to abide by the law or to challenge inappropriate laws through the elected political lawmakers.**

Under Australian law, everyone is innocent until proved otherwise by the rational analysis of evidence by judges or peers. Long gone should be the lynch mobs, vigilantes or inquisitions which used irrationality, group think or hysteria to take the role of the police or courts.

That's the system and it is workable until the subtext uses double-speak, weasel words, legal obfuscation, repetition of obvious lies and dog whistling to send subliminal messages of division.

Divide and conquer is a good mantra for creating fear. It breaks up organised opposition and drives the bewildered towards the security of confident hope-peddlers.

So refugees, you ask? What's your view on that, if everyone is to be treated with respect?

Australia is a large continent with a relatively small population – a wealthy per capita population. As a target, it is the bullseye. The world population is projected to reach 8 billion in 2025. It reached 7 billion in 2013. In 1950, it was 2.5 billion. **That is the elephant in the room. Wake up to it!**

Think of your house. Comfortable? Able to manage children and the visits and sleep-overs of friends? Good people care about others.

I agree.

What if social media then gave out your address and said, *Head there and you'll be looked after.* You wouldn't be prepared for the scale of the challenge.

You would call the police for protection – the challenge is too large and too dangerous for you to handle alone.

Likewise, in an invasion scenario, the government is entitled to defend its population and manage danger-ous influxes even by waves of fleeing people. **It is in the Australian Constitution.**

By all means, we should offer temporary sanctuary to people in need, as happens to millions around the world. **Fleeing people should be treated with respect, dignity, without any negative profiling or dog whistling.**

Such physical protection challenges our moral conscience.

We need significant global drivers to reduce both the growth of population and the displacement of refugees.

The first duty of any parent, who brings a child into the world, is to nurture and protect.

This opens a whole new topic of debate – **human rights and human responsibilities.**

None of this is easy.

Watch out for the next installment of *The Manifesto*.

Chapter 14

Brisbane

Safety for all

The house is quiet as Justin lets himself into the family home. He finds his mother in a reclining chair, feet up, eyes closed. He glances at the clock – three in the afternoon – his noisy siblings will be home soon, unless there is training on.

His mother looks so peaceful. Her voluntary work might have been exhausting – he can't remember which charity cause it is, this week.

He pads through to the kitchen to pour a glass of milk and the chinking causes his mother to say, 'Is that you, Jenny? Was practice cancelled?'

'No, it's me, Mum. Justin. Only a quick visit. You okay?'

His mother appears in the kitchen doorway. 'Good to see you.' And she envelops him in a big hug. 'Has your day been alright?'

'Yes, easier than yours by the look of it.'

'I'm fine. Just closed my eyes for a minute. Any developments?'

'About what?'

'About Dai Evans and your manifesto.'

'No, Mum. I caught up with a few friends for a coffee on the esplanade. We're just hanging around after the exams, waiting for the final results to be posted. Frank sends his regards.'

'Did you tell them about all the fuss?'

'They already know, Mum. They're sweet with it all. We're doing nothing wrong. It's only that shock jock who's excited.'

'And a few hundred tweets.'

'Yeh, the publicity has rocketed the retweets into a few hundred thousand. But it'll die down. That's just social media for you, Mum. They have short attention spans. It'll all be fine. No worries. Aren't you pleased that I'm challenging corruption – shining a light on them? Didn't you bring me up to stand up for good values, to help the less fortunate? That's why you do your volunteering, isn't it?'

'I *am* proud of you, Justin ... and how you speak up for worthwhile causes. It's just that you have always been cut from a fearless mould. Do you remember when you chased the wild dog that was worrying Grandpa's sheep out on the Goondiwindi property? And it turned on you? That nearly ended very badly. Good that Grandpa got there in time.'

'I was fourteen, Mum, and I saved the sheep from being mauled. I only got a few scratches when I tripped, running away.'

'It was closer than that and you know it. Sometimes you need a little fear ... for personal safety. You're good at lots of things but you don't always see the danger that could appear. It is a mother's right to worry. And politics has some nasty people in it. We want you to be successful ... not hurt. Just graduate and get an economics job for a while.'

Justin gives a calm smile. 'Don't worry, Mum. It's all cool. I only want to light a fire under our politicians and get my generation activated. This is theoretical politics – not the real thing.'

'Like I said, these things can get out of hand. You can't always control it. Big wheels start moving when power is threatened. Take care.'

* * * *

The Manifesto **2b – Physical Protection**
The laws of our land are made by politicians.

They give the parameters to the police forces and security agencies as to how they should protect citizens. We have largely delegated authority to the police and the defence forces to go into harm's way on our behalf.

To manage that process, **there are checks and balances to prevent corrupt behaviour or abuses of that delegated power.**

Courts make judgements about breaches of laws and what penalties should be appropriate to meet the social norms. **There is a clear separation of power between the legislative, executive and judicial functions of governments.**

And, in full circle, the politicians – who are ultimately responsible for the quality and scope of the laws which govern our behaviour – can be thrown out of office at the next election. That process, in the macro sense, should ensure protection within our borders.

Like-minded nations enter into alliances to protect each other. Warfare in the twenty-first century is unlike many of the pitched battles of uniformed armies from the twentieth century. Guerrilla and terrorist movements have been more like the present patterns of aggression **– frequently using the excuse of religion or a persecution cause to mask their true motives of power plays.**

To that extent, **Australia should be a secular society that tolerates all belief systems and religions. It is stated in Section 116 of the Constitution of Australia.**

Belief systems should not determine national policy nor laws; no matter how well organised they are.

Why not? Because policy and laws should be determined by reason and logic – by the **certainty of doubt.**

If the laws are guided by inclusion, fairness and a rejection of the superiority of one group over another, then several of the major arguments of the dissidents are immediately diffused.

Raise these matters with your politicians. Challenge the expert shock jocks who use fear to inflate their importance.

At the end of the day, the votes of an educated public will overcome the negativity.

The power of doubt is also the power of thinking and reasoning logically.

Don't follow the herd. Look out for the next installment on social security.

Chapter 15

Sarah Power has been at work for an hour in her Belconnen office – fired with enthusiasm to solve the apparent murder of Desmond Wilson – when Luke Dexter sticks his head into the open doorway.

She glances at him, eyebrow raised in question, and then breaks into a welcoming smile. 'Luke, you're going to tell me that we have definitive dash-cam video to solve this Desmond Wilson crime?'

'Sorry, Sarah. Not that. But the city CCTV has picked up the black Audi appearing to pursue a blue Toyota Camry. We couldn't get the number plate of the Camry clearly but they were both heading along Lady Denman Drive on the north side of the lake at 1.53 am. That would get them to the zoo car park turnoff around 2 am.'

'Good. Progress. See if the technical boffins can get even a couple of letters of the registration plate. Any identifying features would help.'

'I'm asking. They're busy but there is good will.'

Sarah nods. 'I have the preliminary report from forensics who have been checking the car. They have a fingerprint match with Desmond Wilson all around the driver's seat and door. So, it is his car and he was the last driver.' She pauses. 'The passenger side is more complicated. Someone has attempted to wipe fingerprints from door handles but they missed a couple of things.

'One, there were a couple of long fair hairs, probably female, on the head rest of the passenger seat. Two, there was a recent drop of blood on the door sill, to the left of the passenger seat. They say it is like a drop from a bleeding nose.

'That is the evidence so far. Our challenge is to work out what it all might mean. It does suggest that a woman with blonde hair was sitting in that seat at some time. Who tried to clean the door handles?'

Luke squeezes his forehead as he ponders. 'The timing becomes very interesting, doesn't it? We have a witness suggestion from the public appeal that there was a man and a woman on the walkway around 2 am. We have two cars arriving at the car park around that time ... or before. The blue Camry is not there in the entrance car park but the black Audi is. We need to identify and find that Toyota.'

'Have you got a scenario in mind, Luke?' Sarah gives an encouraging smile.

'Blonde-haired woman arrived in the blue car, Wilson in the Audi. She sat in the passenger seat of the Audi at some point. Then they are both seen on the walkway. We know where the man ended up. Presumably the woman left in her blue car ... with the contents of Wilson's pockets ... which would include his wallet, phone and car keys. She could have opened the passenger door and tried to wipe away any evidence that she had been there.'

'And then locked the car again, Luke. It was locked in the morning. Which puts her in the frame for a murder. Let's prioritise. Back to the CCTV of the two cars. We have nothing closer?'

'No. The camera for the public lookout on the south side of the dam focuses on its own car park. Wrong angle. The zoo, on the north side, has no footage of the area where the car was found in their entrance car park. They have checked.'

'Right. Let's see what other vehicles were on the road when the two target cars were spotted. We may find some other passing driver with some memory of events. How busy was that road at 2 am? And we want more ID on that Camry. I'm expecting a brief from the Vic Police in an hour and from the forensics about the walkway – confirmation of blood, maybe two types if something comes off that ear ring. I think I'll call another press conference before the trail gets too cold.'

'Sarah, am I being naïve? But I find it hard to believe that a woman could clobber a fit man like Wilson with something like a ball-peen hammer and tip him over the railing. That takes some strength.'

'Let's see how the evidence unfolds. Routine police work will bring clarity.'

Chapter 16

Brisbane
The Green Man Hotel

The Green Man Hotel is a new pub in the district, serving the burgeoning housing estates near the bay and looking for a bit of exposure. Even Darryl Hope, the proprietor, thinks it is an interesting choice to host a city university students' union meeting, but he is excited. Even allowing for the short notice, he's seeing a potential regular customer in the making.

There hasn't been time for posters to advertise the event but Frank Willis has assured him that people would be contacted on social media. He said that the union president, Justin Kipps, would be giving some type of address about the future – and that name rings a bell from somewhere.

Hey, a crowd is a crowd as long as they buy a few at the bar and are well-behaved. He hasn't been given a definite indication of how many would attend, but Frank Willis thought they might get up to fifty.

* * * *

The large room is bulging as Graham and Frank cart extra chairs from the neighbouring function room.

'That's a hundred chairs now,' Janet notes. 'Well done. The rest will have to stand.'

The two security guards look just a shade nervy – new hotel, new customers and most of them are students – but they are making their bulky presence very obvious around the doors.

The word has indeed been out – clearly not all student unionists are young. Twitter has been in a controlled frenzy. Half-a-million retweets didn't happen every day in the bayside – people want to see what it's all about. And the man of the moment is hopefully going to tell them.

'Thank you for coming.' Justin Kipps speaks quietly, urging his audience to listen for his next word. 'Apart from the sensation that Dai Evans has caused, I want to speak to you about *The Manifesto* that is progressively appearing on my website.'

He pauses as he notes that even Brandon Jones is standing against the side wall.

'I am passionate about lifting the calibre of political debate in this country – not to mention performance – out of its self-congratulatory malaise. I want to bring some vision and good management to the country.

'Having said that, I am still only twenty-one with a lot to learn. That will be seen as a handicap in some eyes. But I've just finished my degree in history and economics so I have a few perspectives which are not the same as you hear from our politicians. And I'm not a product of the party system. I have never been in Young Liberals, Young Labor, Young Greens or Young anything. I'm an independent thinker. That's why I wrote *The Manifesto* and posted it – only a few days ago in fact. I am putting it out in small bites so that readers can get a chance to digest the essence and respond on Twitter or Facebook, or in person through meetings like this.

'A particular opinionated radio provocateur has chosen to highlight my blog in the mass media in a way I never intended. The publicity aside, my hope is that from the bare bones of the three strands – economic, physical and social security, as well the nine key themes or points – I will get feedback to improve this declaration of policy and aims.

'So let's mention the nine points which are not yet on the website. The first is *the certainty of doubt*. As thinking people, you would realise that doubt is part of everything we do; it is the scientific method – and yet, as I listen to national leaders, they speak with a confidence and certainty which can only come from ignorance, mindlessly following an ideology or blinkered dogma. They ignore science and, to me, they are spruiking the mistruths of their sponsors. Self-righteous know-alls are a real challenge to this country, especially when they get into positions of power. A bit more humility and listening would be much better assets.

'I pledge to you that I will never knowingly speak down to you, or anyone in Australia. The vast majority of Australians are very smart people and don't deserve to be lectured by public officials – as one famously misquoted, no-one is the repository of all knowledge – or by half-smart TV commentators, the eunuchs of the whole political process. And that's just saying it as it is.

'I'll whizz quickly through the eight others because I want to give you a chance to react or question. Next is the need to be *content with sufficiency*. Why do we need to be greedy? The advertising industry feeds that. Third, *It's arithmetic*. We can all count. Economics, at its heart, is nothing more than arithmetic, wrapped up in some theories. It is money in and money out. You want to collect more than you spend. But there's a huge load of global corporations and very wealthy individuals who pay less tax than any of you – and it's legal. Ask yourselves who makes the laws... and why that has been allowed to be.

'We need *equitable revenue raising* – that's four – with *common sense put back into salaries and perks* – that's five. Let's get out of the attitude that you can just book it up to the government – because that is *you* in the end, the taxpayer, who is getting ripped off by people who can afford to pay their way.

'Six, seven and eight are investments in the future of our people and nation – *free health* and *disability care*. Let's look after those who need help. It could be you or your family, next. *Free needs-based education*. We don't all start with a clean slate. For years, the feds have been pumping massive dollars into wealthy elite schools, creating a *haves and have nots* scenario. We all know that. So, let's draw a line in the status quo and not just pork-barrel the dollars out to the lobbyists but, rather, really attach the dollars to the student rather than the school, based on their needs – isolation, disadvantage, disability et cetera.

'Eight is *free bachelor-level university education* to students who qualify on merit. It was the Whitlam government of the seventies who brought it in – to replace the selective drip of bursaries to a needy few, who also happened to fit the mould. In concept, university education is an investment in developing the expertise of our people, which then flows into innovative business practices and expanding productive employment. The reintroduction of fees came about because the program was so badly managed in the early Whitlam days. Yet all of Scandinavia, Germany, Scotland, France and even Argentina, among many others, have free university education for their citizens, based on merit. Australia, sadly, has followed the model of the United States where their universities are primarily businesses and that effectively prices out many of the talented potential students. Bursaries and grants only go so far – you know that. Let's not run businesses and pretend that they are halls of tertiary research and advanced learning. That would be selling out the young people who are starting from scratch.

'Finally, *the peace of physical security*. Everyone has a right to feel safe, not to be discriminated against or bullied or attacked. That is both a cultural education program as well as a policing one.

'So those are my priorities, along with the three planks.

'What do I seek from you? Protests from *outside* parliament can only achieve a little. By having an elected Independent member *inside* parliament, you can have a much more potent voice. But the party machines have had the process stacked for decades. They buy the advertising and control the media – and they are controlled by their vested lobbyists. Except, as this week has demonstrated, there is an even greater advertising power … in social media.

'I need you to spread my manifesto – not as *a sermon from the mount*, but as a proposal for serious rational debate. No doubt there will be changes – I expect improvements – that's what quality democracy and representation is all about.

'To compete against multi-million dollar political machines with their global backers is hard to do from my back patio in Capalaba. Many of the electors in Killen are older people, without access to computers. This is arithmetic. If each of you here tonight was to persuade ten people who you know personally about the merits of *The Manifesto* and the process we are following, then a thousand would be on-side by tomorrow. If those thousand, buy into the need for positive change and they get out and speak to parents, grandparents, bowls clubs, golf clubs, sailing clubs – any-where where people can think for themselves, then we would get to all the electors in Killen – eighty-two thousand, I'm told – and we could see change for the better.

'So, over to you.'

A loud male voice from a group at the back of the room. 'We get all your planks and points. You sound like a bloody carpenter. Are you aiming to do a better job than the last carpenter who tried to be a world leader?'

Amid the varied cries of 'Shame' and 'Get out, you prick', Justin's amplified calm tone carries over them all.

'I'm asking for opinion. That's alright. Let's not silence anyone or ridicule. That's how parliamentary Question Time happens now – and you couldn't say it works well for anyone. So, Sir, up the back. No, I'm no evangelist and I certainly don't have all the answers. But, rather than wit, I'm looking for ways to improve policy, to debate issues. Did you want to come up and share the microphone with me? Or suggest improvements? I'm happy for that.' To the sound of enormous guffaws, 'No? That's okay then. Well, feel free to talk to some of the others, or to me about your constructive suggestions. Pardon the pun.' He gives a small smile which some in the audience understand.

'When are we going to see the whole manifesto?' from the front.

'I'll post the last part tomorrow. Rightly or wrongly, I wanted it to come out in bite-sized portions. So you'll have it all; but bear in mind that it's just the bones of possible policy. I expect there will be lots of refinements.'

'Do you have any flyers or posters that we could give to others?'

'We're on a student budget. We have some. But Frank will shoot colour flyers out electronically to everyone who gives an email address. That's Frank up at the back door with his hand up. See him? Good on you, Frank.'

'How do we contact you? We can't leave comments on the blog.'

'That's to discourage politically motivated trolls. We're trying a new way, given our budget. I'll visit as many meetings in the electorate as I can over the months ahead till the next election – that could be a year or so. Frank and Zoe will set up email trees to send out and receive information. You all have Twitter, Facebook, text and email. Those links are on the blog site. We have only done preliminary tests so far but you should get responses to your ideas fairly promptly through one of those several methods. But we can't compete with the machinery of the big parties. Nor do we think we should have to spend money like that to win an election. Yes, the lady in red in the middle; you have a question?'

'My arithmetic says that you will need forty-one thousand votes to win in Killen. Surely that's impossible.'

'I'd agree that number of first preferences would be impossible but if you are talking to Labor people or Greens or Independents, then they could give their second preference to me. That could be enough – all that it needs. Our quick research has shown that Killen hasn't ever been won on first preferences, certainly in the past thirty years. If the Libs are as strong as they claim to be, it would be the preferences of all the others that we would need to get us over the line.'

'So it's possible, then?' the lady in red persists. 'This isn't all just wasted energy.'

'It's arithmetic and a lot of energy on your parts. But absolutely, it's possible Thanks all. I'll come down and share a beer with you.

Frank, Zoe and Janet will collect your contact details for those who want to be on the email trees. Let's keep the energy and challenging going. This is about the future.'

* * * *

The Manifesto **3a – Social Security**

One of the roles of good government is to assure the security of its people and its evolving culture.

It follows that those in society who genuinely need support will receive it from a caring structure of policies.

That would include such universal matters as access to health care, equitable education, and support for people challenged by disabilities.

It also includes support for **communicating the national narrative though the Arts – dance, music, drama, writing, poetry, art, cultural stories, languages – as well as the honest history of the land, personalities who made a difference and the character of typical attitudes of progressive eras.** This is part of securing the culture of the society as it evolves.

Under the Australian Constitution, the federal government has an obligation to look after the elderly with pensions. Under 1970s government legislation, **health care – Medicare, is available to everyone – and it is free.** This is a proactive investment in maintaining community health. It saves on the federal government's budgetary need to provide restorative medical procedures.

The 2013 Australian Education Act speaks of all students in all schools being entitled to an excellent education, allowing each student to reach his or her full potential so that he or she can succeed, achieve his or her aspirations, and contribute fully to his or her community, now and in the future. Further, the quality of a student's education should not be limited by where the student lives, the income of his/her family, the school he/she attends, or his/her personal circumstances. **Education is another investment in the social security of our nation because an informed critical-thinking public can make intelligent assessments of candidates for parliament;** as well as make considered policy recommendations for the Houses of the people.

Consequently, **quality education should be free for all students through primary and secondary schooling and … into tertiary institutions, with the latter based on merit for selected courses, rather than any background of privilege or influence.**

It is a form of *soft infrastructure. Hard infrastructure* includes things like roads, rail, airports and power generation.

But, we are still working on the economic models of past centuries. There are NEW sustainable models of economics which don't involve plunder and greed – models which can secure our social security with realistic optimism within a democracy.

Watch this space!

Talk to your politicians.

Chapter 17

Canberra

Detectives

DS Sarah Power turns her large computer screen round so that DS Luke Dexter can see it in real time – the Victorian Police feedback on their meeting with Leo Clarke and their advice on the background of Desmond Wilson.

'It would appear that Mr Clarke has been cooperative with a little visit from our colleagues in Melbourne.' Sarah Power smiles. 'And there is Wilson's Canberra address and his mobile number. Try it, Luke.'

It takes less than a minute. 'Message bank. To be expected.'

'Okay, on your priority job list, contact the technicians to see if they can get a track on the SIM card for that number, before and after the man's demise.'

Dexter makes a note on his own phone.

Power continues. 'We'll work through this information and head over to Wilson's apartment in Narrabundah. I'll speak to the superintendent. We'll need a locksmith to open the place. So, who was this Wilson man?'

They start to read the dot points.

'Wow! He arrived on the Vic patch from Western Australia. Worked as an assembler at the Altona Toyota site in Melbourne for three years,' Luke says in astonishment. 'Left well before it shut down in 2017. Then worked in security.'

Sarah laughs. 'Not the accredited kind, though. Interesting note. I love police humour. He has been a strong arm for some mob or other. No charges on record but he has mentions in submissions for suspected criminal involvement. Hardly auditor material.'

'And well paid. He was well-dressed and driving an Audi.'

'True. Probably on someone else's tab though. I'll get over to see the superintendent to arrange our official entry to his apartment – just to see if all his clothes are expensive. Can you check if anything new has come in from our appeal for public assistance?'

* * * *

Sarah Power returns from the superintendent with all the approvals for the apartment access.

As she passes Luke Dexter's desk, he puts down his phone with a fist pump and a controlled throaty call of 'Yes!'

With a sparkle in his eyes, he looks at his detective sergeant and says, 'Sarah, I need your wisdom. We have a dash cam. A lady driving north over the dam at a little after 2 am. She has saved an image of a dirty white Mazda 3 entering the zoo car park. No sign of the Audi or the Camry in shot. The uniformed men have just brought it in. The techs have it at their workroom.'

Scarcely breaking stride, she wheels. 'Let's go to their workroom, Luke, and see what they have.'

The technician's screen shows the car approaching the turnoff to the zoo car park. The time on the video shows 2.04 am. Sure enough, there is a small white car, a Mazda, facing the camera and indicating to turn right into the car park.

'Can you get the rego, please?'

'Just doing that,' the tech zooms in, 'There.' He reads out the registration. Luke Dexter calls Vehicle Registration immediately while Sarah stares at the car. 'Can you see the driver?'

'Not clear. The light is wrong.'

'Scroll forward to when the headlights of this car hit the windscreen.' She watches as the image inches forward. 'There. Can you screen shot that, please?'

'Okay.' The tech looks back at her feeling satisfied. 'It looks like a woman to me, by the size and the bunched hair. Not clear. Too much glare distortion. What do think? Or a man in drag?'

'Mmm.'

Luke Dexter puts down his mobile. 'Adla Bello. Address in Bruce, not far from here.'

'Okay. Woman, then? We want a copy of her licence. See if we can get the uniformed branch to pay her a visit and see what she was doing turning into the zoo car park at that time of night.'

She turns back to the dash cam. 'Can we reverse the recording slowly as the dash-cam car is advancing over the dam wall, please? At that time of night, I'm looking for two people who allegedly should be on the downstream walkway, just metres from the car.'

The technician slowly reverses the image until he stops. 'There. Could that be two people huddled down?'

'Hiding?' Luke suggests.

'Or wrestling, perhaps,' Sarah says. 'Can you run it back and forward slowly?' She pauses. 'They are flat on the walkway ... and not close enough to where the fall occurred. I think they could be scuffling. That's a man's back. You can see the leather jacket. Mmm. It could just be one man hiding. Can you actually see another person?'

'Too blurred. The car would have been doing 60 kph, at least,' Luke says. 'The 2 am timeline was just a rough guide from the previous witnesses. It could be a few minutes later that they got further out.'

'Mmm. That time at least is on the recording. Is there any way to check that it's accurate?'

The tech gives a despairing glance. 'Given the car, the dash cam and the time for testing, we can produce miracles. But these machines are usually pretty accurate – satellite timing. This is a good dash cam – not a cheapy.'

Luke says, 'The lady switched it onto *save* when she heard your press conference but she couldn't see anything particularly odd initially – hence the delay in contacting us.'

'Right. Let's get her interviewed and checked out. Meanwhile, we'll get over to Wilson's apartment in Narrabundah.'

* * * *

The locksmith and the uniformed patrol open the door to let the detectives enter, suitably gloved and with their shoes in protective disposal covers. The uniformed police remain outside.

It is a two-bedroom apartment. There is an unmade double bed in one – with ruffled and tangled sheets perhaps indicating a sleepless night – and a made-up single bed in the other. The kitchen is neat with a pizza box in the recyclable rubbish, and with other takeaway detritus in the other bin.

'Not much cooking done here,' Luke observes.

The bathroom is bleak – two towels, one soap, razor, aftershave, spray deodorant, toothbrush and toothpaste.

In the living room, the television is set into a wall unit with adjacent, fairly bare shelves and sets of drawers beneath.

Sarah takes a range of photos in each of the rooms as she goes through. 'Something's not right. It's not a lived-in place. I just want to reflect on it, later. Look for the unusual.'

One odd observation is the presence of cigarette packets in each room – saucers acting as ashtrays in the bedroom and living room. Clearly, Desmond Wilson does not respect the *no-smoking in the rooms* policy, clearly indicated by stickers on the front door and living-room window.

A yellow Post-It notepad is on the bedside table, under the light and beside the ashtray. *Ring Peter* is handwritten on the top page. Sarah photographs the page and the bedside table layout. Forensics can check it all later.

A photocopy of the car lease from the courier company is folded and tossed on a side table. No phone, wallet or keys are visible anywhere in the apartment.

'Let's check his clothes,' Sarah says.

The wardrobe has a dinner jacket and dress trousers plus a range of formal and casual clothes, all of high quality.

'What's that for?' Luke asks at a waiter's dress outfit.

'Check the pockets in these jackets.'

Dexter hits pay dirt quickly. A bundle of one-hundred-dollar bills in one and a bundle of fifties in another. 'Interesting hiding place.'

Sarah Power photographs them and places them in clear plastic evidence bags.

'There's a safe in here, with a jumper lying over it. Locked.'

'Get the locksmith in to bypass it.'

The dress catering jacket has an accreditation pass in the inside pocket. 'Have you seen one of these before, Sarah?'

'A pass to get into secure meetings. Secure catering? Mmm.'

The locksmith opens the safe in seconds.

Pills in zip-lock plastic bags with codes written in felt pen. More bundles of cash ... and several more passes.

Luke passes them to his detective sergeant for photographing and explanation.

'These are press and political party accreditations. They look genuine. Mmm. Perhaps, excellent forgeries or real passes with names changed for Desmond Wilson. We'll bag all of these, Luke.'

'So who is this man? No carrier company auditor, that's for sure. Drugs. Protection rackets?'

'More than that, Luke, I think.' Sarah Power has a puzzled expression. 'These are passes into select meetings – political meetings, access to government ministers and their advisers. I'll take all this to the superintendent. He will perhaps want other sections of the Australian Federal Police involved.'

'It puts a new light on the courtesy car for powerful people in Melbourne, as yet unnamed.'

'Indeed. Let's leave with our bags of evidence. We'll send the forensic team to check for things we can't see.'

Chapter 18

Brisbane

Shady Rest

Shady Rest has been Zoe's recommendation and she has set up the meeting. Justin Kipps is the entertainment for the morning tea; and as he casts his eyes around the room, he is assessing – eighty percent women, many alert and cheery, only a few with heads down having a snooze; nearly all moving with the obvious incapacities of age.

The manager or matron, whatever her title, introduces Justin as the new social media sensation and someone with ideas for the country's future – and most eyes zone in slowly on the well-groomed young man in dark trousers and open-necked mauve shirt. He smiles as he makes eye contact. With polite charm and old-fashioned courtesies, he gives an impression of gentleness, of confidence – of caring.

His quiet voice explains that he is disappointed with the manners and lack of respect that is being shown to Australia in the way parliament is presented in the media. 'There needs to be a sense of honour and dignity in the way people speak to one another. Don't you agree? It seems that telling lies and twisting words just becomes, *I misspoke*, followed by an insincere apology like *If anyone was offended or misunderstood what I said.*

'You wouldn't have accepted that behaviour from your children, would you? But complaining to each other ... what does that achieve? Who would be listening?'

To the growing smiles and gleams of interest, Justin Kipps works through his three planks of policy and the nine points he wants to address first. He does it quickly because, as he says, 'I'm sure you are so much wiser in these matters than I am.'

As more members of his audience grin, chortle and nudge neighbours, he says, 'I need you to help me get to parliament as an Independent Member for Killen. I know many of you will have voted the same way all your lives. I understand that. If you can't change, I respect your view but would you please then honour me by putting my name, Justin Kipps, as your second preference?

'Also consider that I need to get into parliament to change it from the inside. You have to be in the room to be heard when the decisions are made. Things will only get worse if we don't nip it in the bud – a stitch in time saves nine.' And he stops the clichés there. 'Over to you for questions. And then, for those who don't mind, Zoe, Frank and I might come round in case there is anything you want to say to us quietly.'

And they wait.

Eventually, a lady with beautifully permed hair adjusts her hearing aid and raises her hand. 'Young man … Justin is it?' she looks at her neighbour for nodding confirmation. 'I have voted Liberal all my life. My father would turn in his grave if he thought I would do otherwise. But, if I heard you right, you want to be an Independent in parliament. Have I heard you correctly? Then who will listen to you, a lone voice down there?'

'Thank you. Several things in reply. Are you hearing me okay?' Justin smiles at her as she nods, her face serious with concentration. 'The major party representatives all have to vote the same way as the party decides. Agreed? No-one is actually listening to *them*. They are puppets to the will of the machine. But we've had times in recent parliaments when Independents have held the balance of votes in the House of Representatives and the Senate. So the party bosses, Liberal and Labor, have had to talk to them; and to compromise. Do you remember that?' He waits for a slight nod.

'Next, this is a new world. In your day, most of your information came from newspapers, radio and television – and hasn't that deteriorated in recent years? They're all controlled by monopolies – even overseas people; with money being a more important interest than doing the right thing by Australia. But today, computer websites and social media can reach thousands and millions of people, in seconds. If people in parliament are doing the wrong thing, an Independent member can highlight that straight away – and they *do* listen. Of course, it cuts both ways.

'You can see me. I'm just an ordinary person with a strong desire to clean up politics and make this an even better land for the future. I wrote a blog, a story on my own website – mainly what you've heard from me today – and within hours, Dai Evans, the shock jock from Sydney, was on the air calling me for everything under the sun. That sort of bullying attack has to stop. We have to clean up the way our public life has become. Don't you agree?' He waits again and looks at the listening expressions. 'So, if you must vote the way your father would have wanted, at least put me second on your list … please.'

* * * *

As the questions die down, Justin is called across to a small group of two men and three women – two in wheelchairs.

One woman in a wheelchair beckons Justin close so that she can whisper. The other four heads crane in for support.

'Justin, we're not all Liberal voters in here. I've voted Labor most of my life. But we can't get to the polling booths – we vote postal. Can you make sure you have a poster around to remind us of your talk this morning – we're getting older and forgetful.' She smiles. 'And others get picked up in a Liberal bus and taken to vote. We need to be able to put something else in their hands.' And the others share a conspiratorial grin.

'You can vote however you wish no matter who takes you to the polling station,' Kipps assures, to the grimacing annoyance of people who don't want to be underestimated.

'I know that, Justin,' she replies, as her wince remains. 'I may be old but I'm not silly. You'll get my vote to try to clean up politics – maybe many of our votes. You seem fair dinkum. I hope you are.' She looks at the others, nodding either through agreement or infirmity. 'But you need to keep reminding people. When's the next election? Years away? Get us some flyers and we'll keep everyone here remembering what you are standing for. And get round to other places like this. People need to see your face and hear your voice. You're a nice lad. Your parents should be proud of you to put yourself forward like this.'

'Thank you for your advice. I'm new at this game. I appreciate your wisdom.'

* * * *

Heading toward Zoe's flat with Zoe at the wheel and Frank in the front, Justin feels energised and supported by the meeting at the retirement home. Certainly, they have given him thoughts to ponder – and lots of work to do in the months ahead.

In the meantime, he'll have to get a job. As soon as the final uni results are posted, that will be the holiday over for him – Janet and Frank still have at least a year to go. The graduation will come in its own sweet time. He's had a number of offers, including a traineeship with Cassidy Economics; not Deloitte, but a start and a regular income. Given his current quest, he'll have to avoid any associations with political parties or unions or any of the partisan institutes. His mother is right – they will use any tenuous link to devalue his opinions. But, at least Dai Evans has died down.

'Holy stapparonies!' Frank is studying his smart phone.

'What?' Zoe queries. 'Less of the excitement when I'm driving, please.'

'Holy stapparonies! I don't believe it.'

'What?' asks Justin from the back seat.

'Have you heard of a Pieter Goosens? A Victorian?'

'Yep,' Zoe replies. 'Attack dog for the right of politics. Another shock jock with a website and blog. What has he done now?'

78

'Better pull over for minute, Zoe.'

Frank is continuing to scroll on his smart phone screen. 'Wow! This Pieter Goosens is claiming that the current social media sensation, Justin Kipps, is using token Aboriginal and Asian people on his campaign committee …'

'What …?'

'There's more – lots more. There's a photo of us at the esplanade coffee shop to back up his claim.'

'Those bloody stalkers. I knew she was videoing us.'

'And … he's running a story of people ejected from the students' union rally where Justin Kipps was speaking. "Is this just like the Brownshirts of 1930s Germany – storm troopers intimidating people out of free speech?" he asks.'

'What … channelling the Nazis; a rally,' Justin splutters. 'That's all lies. No-one was ejected. The hotel will verify that. And I'd never even thought that Graham was Aboriginal or Janet Asian. Why would it matter? Isn't this all illegal – to spread malicious hate talk?'

Zoe is quiet for a few seconds before, 'Yep, Justin. It probably all is – if there aren't loopholes for the barristers to claim innocence. That's why we need to get you down there to Canberra. But the reality is that his story is out now. Newspapers and TV news will pick it up and run with it, as if it were true.'

'Jeez, I'll need to get home to Mum so that she's forewarned. Is this all worth it?'

Frank's jaw is set firm. 'This is exactly why it's worth it. This is their technique, every Independent, every beacon that's shone out as being different … a challenge … they have gone for them all. Sure, we could take them to court. We could check with Karen's dad if you like – but, by the time we get there, all the damage has been done. Even if we won, it would have cost us two mortgages in legal costs. That's what they bank on – that the little people won't try.'

'But,' Zoe adds. 'We have a new ace to play – social media. We can rebut there, show the liars for what they are. What do you think, Justin?'

'Maybe. Maybe not. Is this just another of their traps to draw us into their type of slimy battle? As soon as we use demeaning language or bad mouth them – then that becomes the new story. They double down and we are victims twice over.'

'Only if we play it their way,' Frank argues. 'The backlash won't come from us. Just as they are using other people as their attack dogs – people who are many stages removed from the real culprits – our rebuttals won't come from us. Indeed, we must work very hard to retain our dignity and decorum.'

While Justin nods in agreement, Zoe comments with a cynical headshake, 'So who are the adults in this business?'

Justin is still quietly unruffled, as he nearly always is – but he can sense the rumbling. It has returned. 'Mmm. I'm just wondering what these people in the retirement home will be thinking when the news hits tonight.'

Zoe smiles encouragingly. 'C'mon, I'll drop you home, Justin.'

Chapter 19

Canberra

Background machine

Hetty Fry is on the phone to Malcolm McGlashan even as Goosens is still fielding and provoking his callers on the radio.

'Malcolm, this is totally over-the-top. It's too blatant to even be called dog whistling. The PM will be furious when he returns from Europe.'

'I know nothing about this, Hetty. But I've got Goosens' website up on the screen now. I see the photo. Look, just plead ignorance. It's nothing to do with us. Goosens is a freelancer who has lost the plot. We'll cut him. Got to go. Thanks for the heads-up. I have Peter Connell to speak to.'

* * * *

'Peter, where did the photo of these Brisbane kids come from? They're the ones you've been investigating for us. Have you seen it before?'

'Yes, the contract investigators in Brisbane sent it through. But we haven't passed it on. *They* must have done that deal of their own volition. Bloody last time they'll get any work through us.'

'And the connotations of storm troopers? Any truth in that?'

'Unless they spoke to security at the hotel? They didn't get any of this from us, Malcolm. Like I said, the Kipps family seem like our sort of people.'

McGlashan pauses. 'What's in it for Goosens? So, he apologises in a week's time, says he was misinformed. What's he after? He wouldn't think we'd pay him for stirring the bees' nest that we had just settled down.'

'He loves the big-noting, Malcolm – promotes his business profile. Unless … unless, of course, it's a dirt team from the other side – fomenting mischief at barge-pole distance, in the hope of damaging us, as well the young Brisbane kid.'

'Peter, I sometimes wonder about all this character assassination stuff. Research into background is one thing. Dirt? I don't like it. At the end of the day, does it actually achieve anything?'

'Let's see how this plays out, Malcolm. Most times we can turn it to our advantage – and, hey, it's costing us nothing to watch the fight.'

'You must have ethical ice in your veins. Do you even have a heart?'

And he disconnects the call.

Chapter 20

Brisbane

Frenzy

It's been an hour since Zoe dropped Justin at his parents' house where he is now tracking the escalating Twitter frenzy.

Frank and Zoe are following developments at the Capalaba house.

A local journalist has issued a police statement saying that there had been no disturbances at the students' union meeting.

Another report quoted a member of the crowd asking the speaker, Justin Kipps, if he was comparing himself to Christ.

The hotel said a hundred people had a meeting with some question and answer. No-one had been ejected.

Goosens claimed that an unnamed participant was intimidated by a mob and forced to leave after an innocent question. According to Goosens, the victim felt threatened.

However, the security guard tweeted that he remembered the incident and said the patron left of his own accord. He wasn't thrown out either by the crowd or security. He had been making smart comments and annoying the audience. They'd told him to 'piss off'. And he had.

Twitter continues to ask questions.

The photo at the coffee shop is of a group of friends? Yes? WTF? Dozens leap to Kipps' defence. Since when has it been illegal to be

Aboriginal? Not for half-a-century at least, is a half-smart rejoinder. Or Asian? Not for over a century.

And then retweets go viral as they hit the wider market. A wave of condemnation pours towards Australia, swamping any who try to argue for free speech. The implication is stark – Goosens had better back up his slurs or face the withering fire.

* * * *

Frank turns on the one-o'clock ABC news to see if any of this is in their broadcasts – but there's nothing. He flicks over to FM whose take is that a shock jock had indeed shocked the Twittersphere. More to follow.

By three o'clock, a statement from the shadow Attorney-General's office condemns the spreading of such vile inaccurate poison in the strongest possible terms and calls on the Prime Minister to do likewise.

At four o'clock, the commercial TV networks announce a Twitter backlash against Pieter Goosens' comments. They report that social media has condemned the radio commentator for attempting to beat up fallacious stories into a sensation – and they compare it to a lynch mob mentality.

The commercial network also report that their investigations into the 'Brownshirts' at the union meeting can find no substance to the story. As to the innocent photo of a group of friends at a bayside coffee shop being posted on Goosens' website, they report that it has been referred to the Internet carrier, the government and to the police.

The six o'clock news reports that an outspoken Melbourne radio shock jock has been suspended while the station investigates the matter around that morning's show. They wish to apologise for any offence that has been caused or taken and assure all listeners that the station promotes the highest integrity in its presentations.

At eight o'clock, a pay-TV political commentary team ponder who had put Goosens up to presenting information which not only seemed to be wrong but was also damaging to the credibility of talk-back commentary. Veiled aspersions were variously cast towards the major political parties but then, 'Why would either wish to be involved in such murky business?'

And the apparently innocent party, Justin Kipps? He's not a political candidate, nor a public official; just a student with a website … what of Kipps? The consensus seems to think he is undamaged … because he is clearly an innocent victim. But some mud might stick.

And what of the dog whistling about ethnicity? 'Oh,' they wail, 'we thought that was all in the past, that the country had moved on from that.'

Not so, the Twitterites flood back. Wake up to yourselves. Don't allow these vermin to spout their malice.

At midnight, newspaper websites report the next day's headlines – the villain is definitely Pieter Goosens and a new wave of support is flooding in for the social media sensation, Justin Kipps.

* * * *

As the new day dawns, Frank, Justin and Zoe make it their business to invite Graham and Janet to breakfast – at the same coffee shop on the esplanade.

Passers-by recognise them and give them the thumbs-up, accompanied by supportive smiles as well as mouthing derogatory comments about shock jocks and a few other parts of the social fabric.

But hurt has definitely been caused to both Janet and Graham – they are very quiet. The out-pouring of public support appears to soothe them a little – enough for them to give courteous smiles.

Graham has a determined set to his body. 'We're used to it. Can't change the past but we won't cop it now or in the future. Now I'm even more determined to see you get to Canberra, Justin. All this rubbish is motivated just by you writing *The Manifesto* – and they don't like being challenged.'

Janet sits close. 'Justin, would you like to meet with some Chinese business people in the Killen electorate? They contacted my parents yesterday, when they heard what was happening. It would be at a Chinese restaurant. I would be with you as interpreter if you wish – not so much to help with language, because they all speak English quite well – more for customs and culture, translating meaning for them and you. I think they would like your message.'

As Justin is agreeing to that opportunity, Frank is noting from his phone, 'And the Greens have agreed to a meeting about establishing common ground. I expect to hear from Labor today or tomorrow. I've delegated getting a meeting with the Libs to Brandon Jones.' He laughs at the thought.

Justin appears genuinely grateful. 'It's happening, isn't it? Thanks to all of you. It's some roller-coaster we've embarked on.'

It is then that Frank picks up the first headline on his smart phone – about an accident on Moreton Bay.

'A private fishing boat appears to have run straight into the mangroves on Peel Island. A police helicopter is on the scene.'

Zoe frowns. 'Strange at this time in the morning. He must have gone out for dawn fishing. Hardly had time to wet a line – and then straight into the mangroves. Must be a medical situation.'

* * * *

They are just finishing their coffee as Frank announces the next headline.

'The speculation is that a prominent local identity was the person in the boat and he is dead.'

'Very sad.'

* * * *

As they are walking to the cars, Frank stops them all with a hand signal and a gulp.

'There is speculation now that the person who died in the Peel Island fishing boat incident is believed to be the local Member for Killen, Tony Maynard. That news site is checking with the electorate office. An official statement is expected soon.'

The five stare wordlessly at each other as the implications are absorbed.

86

Chapter 21

Canberra

Detectives

'Gee, forensics are doing a great job, Luke,' Sarah Power says as new information pops onto her computer screen.

Luke Dexter waits patiently as the DS continues. 'The blood on the walkway railing is, for the most part, Desmond Wilson's. But there is a different smaller blood spatter at two places on walkway – where the fall might have occurred and another sample of the same blood type about 20 metres closer to the car park. Wow!' She checks her reading of the report again. 'That blood spatter matches the blood smear on the single earring.'

Luke shakes his head and takes a few seconds to think. 'Perhaps … perhaps … where the dash cam showed the leather jacket bent over, some blood was spattered, not from the leather jacket but from the wearer of the earring. Does that fit?'

Sarah Power looks at Dexter with a proud smile. 'And then she – let's make it a she until otherwise proven – made it further along the walkway with Wilson to the place where the earring was dislodged …'

'It was ripped out of her ear, wasn't it?'

'That's the hypothesis. Then whatever happened next caused Desmond Wilson to bleed from a blow to the back of his head and then fall over the dam.'

'Is there more, Sarah? On the report?'

'Yes. They have a partial DNA profile from the earring as well. And more, the spot of blood on the Audi passenger door sill matches the second blood spatter. They are working on the hairs from the headrest to check for a fuller DNA profile.'

'It's falling into place. Any more from Doctor Cotter from the autopsy – like drugs, for example.'

'Only one comment until the organ tests are finished. He says the last meal was taken about six hours before death … and it was probably a Hawaiian pizza, given the pineapple, meat, tomato paste and flour base. So, how are you at generating an updated working hypothesis, Luke?'

Dexter grins as he senses the encouragement of his detective sergeant. 'I'll give it a go.

'Desmond Wilson had a pizza at his apartment around 8 pm – we have found the used box – six hours before death. Then, close to 2 am, he is in his black Audi pursuing a woman in a blue Toyota Camry. For reasons not yet known, she pulls into the zoo car park and he follows. We would have to assume that he knew her.

'She ends up in the passenger seat of the car. There is no indication of sexual activity. Indeed, she was probably there for no more than a few minutes … because she has fled along the walkway with Wilson in close pursuit.'

'You are going well, Luke. And about 2.04 am, Wilson catches her, pushes her to the ground and punches her to draw blood. How do we know?' Sarah smiles, in question.

'The white Mazda was turning into the car park and we have the two incidents locked in place on the dash cam. Grazed knuckles on the right fist may have been caused then.'

'Right,' Sarah agrees. 'So that is the first spatter of blood from the woman. Perhaps a bleeding nose … to generate a spatter. Go on.'

'Okay, but she got up and ran farther along the walkway – maybe twenty metres and the man caught up with her again. He has punched her again … and torn the earring out of her ear – hence the second blood spatter … or her nose again, as well.

'And then …. and then we hit a brick wall, figuratively speaking. How did she hit him with a hammer, empty his pockets, push him over the edge? Who carries a ball-peen hammer in her handbag, anyway?'

'Okay. Then she returns to *his* car, opens it with *his* keys and wipes the handles to get rid of her fingerprints.'

'But a drop of blood from her bleeding ear lobe or nose falls onto the door sill.'

They both pause and look at each other.

Sarah Power says, 'Then she coolly locks the Audi and drives away in her Camry, having killed a man? What is missing, Luke?'

He grins. 'The woman in the white Mazda would have been in the vicinity … probably even in the car park. I haven't seen the report from the uniforms interviewing her. I'll get right onto it.'

'And the other big question, Luke, is why? It would appear that the two knew each other but not in friendly way … judging by the fighting. Then we have Wilson's flat with bundles of money, accreditation passes into sensitive meetings or gatherings … and drugs in bags. This is politics, Luke. This is Canberra and there are lots of dirty tricks here.'

'I need to check on Adla Bello, the owner of the white Mazda.'

'And *I* need to brief the superintendent. No rest in this business … but we are going well, I think.'

Chapter 22

Brisbane

Tony Maynard repercussions

The sudden death of Tony Maynard is shocking news. Fifty-two years old. Well respected Liberal member. Married with two adult daughters. The cause was apparently a heart attack with the boat throttle jamming as Maynard collapsed against it. The boat rammed him into the mangroves, before the revving and grounded boat was noticed by other craft.

The funeral was a sombre affair with many moving eulogies, televised on every local channel and a few national grabs. Dignitaries and celebrities smiled and made suitable muted platitudes to nourish the media coverage.

Justin didn't attend. A courtesy; to not distract from family grief – he had never met the deceased man or his family.

A by-election would be called at some time. Insiders teased the media with their speculation. Don Finucane was the man likely to be preselected – his grandfather had been a former Liberal member for the area, when the electorate had a different name in a previous distribution.

The date would be announced in due course by the Prime Minister. Would it be before the end of the year or would it be delayed to the new year? There was a window of opportunity to fill the position quickly.

* * * *

It is a busy time for Justin and his team – just getting themselves familiar with the rules of federal elections. The slow, planned build-up has now become a frantic research project – just as well that it's downtime for most university students.

The date has yet to be announced and a writ issued for a by-election. Then the electors would have until 8 pm, seven days later, to get registered on the roll. Harry and all his Year 12s would need to get organised.

Frank gets the social media purring into action with the urgent need for the youth of Killen to support Justin Kipps' bid, and to get their names on the roll.

With the loss of the Member for Killen, the government's effective safe margin in their own coalition right could potentially be reduced to one only – if it also provided the Speaker in the House.

Zoe is all business. 'The Libs will throw everything at this one. They have no other distractions and a fair voter margin from the last general election.'

* * * *

The Prime Minister, just back from his Europe trip, wastes no time. Clearly, the Liberal Party machine wants to press home its advantage with no delay. The date for the close of nominations is set for fourteen days away.

The system is cutting down the time for others to get organised. Polling day is to be four weeks after the declaration of nominations. It will just fit in before the Christmas holiday season.

Six weeks is not long to change a gentle learning process for Justin's team to a full-on election strategy; to get his name and profile known, to answer the questions and to become competitive.

* * * *

The publicity has announced, 'Come to the leagues club. Hear Justin Kipps tell you the real story about his vision for Killen and Australia – not the hype from the southern shock jocks.'

And they are rolling in the door.

Frank has been worried about rent-a-crowd stacking the meeting with hecklers and abusers but Justin's solution seems simple enough – he will be on the stage, out the front, with a microphone and Frank would have the roving mike. The volume would be set so that the amplified voices could carry over, drown out, any others.

Zoe's concern is about the press, but again Justin is Mr Cool.

'Let the print media in. Who knows, anyone could be recording the meeting on their phones, anyway. No doubt the TV channels, if they choose to turn up, could be jammed up the back – but they could grab someone's phone video anyway.'

'Abusers?' Janet had asks.

'Leagues Club security at the door; police, if they persist. This is an orderly meeting to exchange views. We don't want to exclude anyone – and we actually want to hear what they have to say. We need them to listen to what we have to say, too.'

Chapter 23

Brisbane
The Leagues Club

The leagues club manager seems impressed at the turn-up – there will be a few dollars to be made, for sure. He gives a smiling thumbs-up to Justin on the stage as he closes the doors at the back of the room. A security man is inside with, presumably, another placed outside.

Justin gives a seven minute summary of his key points and opens it up for questions to the roving mike.

Whether they are surprised at the brevity of the address or surprised to be asked to contribute isn't immediately clear but a large man, prop forward material in his day, offers to go first.

'No disrespect, Justin, but you're still a kid – what; fresh out of uni? – and you're talking in visions and dreams to improve Canberra. What's in it for me, here in Killen, Justin? We have a port, an airport, a tourist mecca on the bay – what are you going to do for us – tax breaks? What?'

'Thanks for your question. I'm nearly twenty-two. I had no say in when I was born.' It raises a few chuckles. 'Old enough to vote though, old enough to serve in the Australian Defence Forces if I choose, and old enough to be elected to federal parliament. I don't stand before you with a bagful of goodies or with all the answers. I'm certainly not going to make promises about what's in it for you. If that's what you want, then honestly, don't put me as your first preference.

'I won't be part of any political party. Frankly, I want to go down there to Canberra to lift the game of politics; not to be a passive follower or a bearer of gifts. I'll only serve at the most for two terms – six years. Then I'll pass the baton and get on with my own life. But I will have given some of my best years to this public service.

'Let me give you one particular answer to your question. In a nutshell, the finances of the country are as simple as arithmetic. Revenue must be greater than expenditure – and every earner must pay. We can't have it being legal for global corporations or the super-rich to dodge their responsibilities by using tax havens. The politicians and commentators will tell you that it can't be done – that all the companies will pull out of Australia – mind you, their contribution at the moment is mainly to fleece us and pay back less tax than *you* pay. But that aside …

'I'm a soon-to-be graduate in economics. I know a bit about a few things. The fiddles that are dudding you and me are legal. Fair dinkum! They are legal. Politicians of the past wrote the laws to allow this cheating of ordinary citizens to be part of normal business. Did you know that?

'Stopping those rorts is as easy and as simple as changing the laws. Having the cooperation of the tax havens countries would be good, but they are hardly going to frighten off their own golden goose; and we don't need that anyway. That's just a politician's get-out clause – to do nothing, while looking as if they might be.

'We are a sovereign nation. We make the rules, as a country in our own right. If you do business in Australia, then you pay your tax here and it will be illegal to be making any smart within-company resource shifting. Bingo. The loopholes have gone and the budget is able to be balanced. Suddenly there is no crisis and you can get the infrastructure you are asking about. How's that for a start to your question?'

The big man looks shocked and he turns to his mates to ensure that he has heard properly before asking, 'Are you fair dinkum? It's as easy as changing the laws? Why hasn't this been done in the past?'

Justin Kipps gave a sympathetic shrug. 'Ask the other candidates. Ask the political parties who have allowed this scam to pass through parliament. I *am* fair dinkum – and that's just one of many loopholes in everything to do with all those business subsidies and deals with government – because the country has been run by faceless lobby groups – and frankly, the general public has been conned. Okay?' The shocked man nods dumbly. 'Another question, anyone? This lady down the front, Frank. The microphone is coming, Ma'am.'

She is well-dressed in fawn pressed trousers and a teal-blue top, shoulder-length dark hair and white-rimmed spectacles. 'Education, Justin? Your flyer says you want free university education. Whitlam tried that and it collapsed in a few years. Will this be another unstoppable drain on federal finances?'

Justin lowers his microphone and takes two deep breaths. 'My degree will leave me a debt of around $25,000. My parents could have paid it at the outset but they believe in me developing my own financial responsibility – and my political nous. I will pay it back in stages when I am earning but it will take time – years.

'In simple terms, we are all being sold a business model, not a national investment in quality education, as the federal act requires.

'Even if the current cost of university courses never increases, as any profitable business would require, tertiary study will still be beyond the aspiration of many talented youngsters who may well have other responsibilities in life – like looking after family members. Not everyone is born as lucky as me and, perhaps, you.

'So, my first concern is that universities have become businesses who will sell you a qualification for a price – and that filter will exclude many meritorious students. These businesses want students who are able to pay, or who are prepared to take on huge debts for courses, some of which may well lead nowhere.

'Don't fall for the statistical claptrap that university graduates, ON AVERAGE, will earn more than others without a degree. Any intelligent person who has studied arithmetic can see that half the graduates must be below that average. And, the students' reward for buying the snake-oil pitch? They have a significant debt and poorer earnings. Half of them have been sold a pup. How anyone can stand up with a straight face and spout that stuff is beyond me. Even more insidious is why the media doesn't question such bizarre distortions.

'Sure, universities or charities will offer bursaries – but that is throwing crumbs to the chooks. There are so many unknowns that don't show up in the types of statistics that are spouted – because they expect that you won't check the underlying assumptions. And why should you have to? But really, you'd want to read the audited books to see what impact bursaries actually make – and you'd need to know how many of the bypassed meritorious students would have asked to be enrolled if they or their families could have afforded it.

'My second concern is they say that the market will determine the courses which will be offered. That has given us a huge surplus of primary school teaching graduates for whom there are no vacancies in the schools – but they fill up the course numbers – billed to the government – and that is *you*, the taxpayer, footing the cost in the long run.

'At the same time, we have shortages of medical research scientists, doctors, high school maths teachers, solar energy innovators, who can develop the household battery technology to make houses self-sufficient, makers of electric cars and trucks … The list of community priorities is long.

'There are huge challenges on the planet. Tertiary education should be about investing in the intellectual capital of the generations who will take Australia into the future. Shouldn't the debates in university be about ethics, morality and justice? It's about nourishing our collective minds through the Arts and Science – giving context, challenge, being certain about doubt and promise.

'Free university education could lift the awareness of the general public so that they could all be confident enough to distinguish spin from reasoned programs – or, indeed, the meaning of averages. But, as you know and I know, anything free needs to be managed well and regulated, if it's to provide the long-term benefit for the community.

'Universities will tell you that they will collapse in the competitive world market, unless they can charge huge fees. Rubbish. Quality will always be in demand. But the free component should be for Australian citizens only, not for the international payers. And, free entry should be on merit only – no shortcuts through influence or dodgy bursaries. Extra places should be made available to the financially-flush overseas market only after the locals have been catered for. And that is what is worrying the business culture of universities.

'I'm happy for tertiary institutions to be elite by performance but not by excluding our own talented people. And, for every free place, there should be a bond so that the recipients stay contributing to Australia for a period of time – *giving* back if you like, rather than *paying* back. The government makes the rules. This can happen. It writes the laws. That's why I want to influence it.'

The dark-haired lady smiles and seems to ponder what has been said. But she is interrupted by a shout from a blond man standing at the side. 'But they are not going to listen to you – either in universities or in Canberra!'

Kipps doesn't miss a beat. His voice has a quiet timbre despite the amplification. '*You* are here, listening to me! Aren't you? Why wouldn't they? I have a weapon which is actually bigger than theirs,' he raises his hand as if holding a club, 'thanks to the shock-jock publicity. My name is now known by thousands of Twitter followers. I will publish government deliberations – on social media. I will report back in person to you, in this electorate. I have an audience and readership. And it won't take them long to realise that.

'So, yes. I think they'll listen. It's about shining a bright light into the dark nooks in the corridors of power – the places where faceless puppeteers lurk and scurry. Corruption commissions have been highlighting their dealings for years – and they don't like the exposure.'

Frank stands looking isolated with his roving mike as a large woman roars,

'What about the disabled then?'

Kipps nods again and takes his time to answer. 'None of us can choose how we were born or what ailments might afflict us throughout life. There needs to be an insurance scheme that looks after people in need.

'The challenge is to ensure that it is manageable; that it works for those who actually need it most; and that they are treated with dignity. And that is not just respecting *their* dignity, it is about respecting our *own* dignity in how big we are in dealing with sensitive and difficult issues.'

That last comment drew a few *hear, hear* mutters from the crowd.

Justin continues. 'Governments, sadly, have a poor history in managing such large programs,' – more *hear, hears* – 'so there needs to be good processes for diagnosis and treatment. It is possible to apply rigorous procedures with care and empathy – otherwise, in two decades it will get so slack that we'll all be diagnosed with a disability. And that's not what this is about – it would completely defeat the purpose. No. It is for the fair dinkum needy ones.

'Likewise, with health treatments – the funding is not a bottomless pit. Medical care schedules need to be negotiated with the profession; and managed to avoid the temptation to rip off the system. It is a priority but it needs to be well handled. Okay?'

The large woman gives a grudging nod.

Frank calls, 'Justin, I have a question here.' And he hands the mike to a man in navy-blue work clothes. He has a deep voice. 'That leads into something else on your website – you want to change the notion of it being alright to behave irresponsibly. Dodging tax is just one, but there are lots of other rorts going on. So is this about responsibilities rather than rights?'

Justin smiles. 'Thanks for going to the website. Again, I have to acknowledge that I am young. But it seems to me that we need to elect a government that is worthy of honesty and straight dealing. And then that government has a responsibility to treat its citizens with respect, within the law. We all want our rights but it's a two-way street. I hope I'm never reduced to making a personal attack on anyone – even a shock jock.' He eases a grin out. 'I hope I can contribute to improving the quality of debates in parliament. It's a big ask but you have to use manners and treat people properly. I may fail – but they will know that I'm there, like a nagging conscience, not letting them get away with dishonesty as if it was some larrikin form of virtue. No smart answers for you, I'm afraid, but the behaviour we accept is the behaviour we don't challenge.'

'Good on you, young fella,' the navy shirt replies. 'That's the way. Good luck.'

The prop forward up the back has his hand up again and Frank rushes across to him. 'Justin,' the big man sounds puzzled, 'you fair took the wind out of my arguments before. I've never met a political candidate who didn't promise upgraded roads, railways, tax cuts and more jobs. You're not offering anything like that. Have I got that right?'

'You have it right. Firstly, I don't want to promise what I can't deliver. I'm not the government and I don't control the dollars. But secondly, I am independent of the party conferences, conventions and the caucuses which control the thinking of the big parties. If you put me first on the ballot paper, you can be sure that Canberra will know that I am there, representing everyone from here – but also promoting the aspirations for a better Australia.'

A spontaneous applause rolls round the room with a lot of mumbled *okay* and *good on yer* comments.

Frank senses his opportunity and speaks through the mike.

'Given such a good crowd, perhaps we can mix and mingle for a while. Justin and the rest of us will be here to listen to your suggestions and to answer your questions. The leagues club here has donated a few plates of savouries. Would you all look after the club too and buy a drink or two? They have provided the room at no charge because we're poor students.'

Almost on cue, the smiling manager opens the back door to usher his waiters and waitresses in with their silver platters.

As Justin leaves the stage, a tall earnest lady with a notebook rushes up to collar him.

'I'm Ann Fletcher from *The Bay News*. Thanks for your talk. Very good and a big crowd for midweek. Do you mind if I ask you a few questions?'

'No, I don't mind, Ann. Good to meet you. I should tell you that I would like you to report what I said from the stage, with the questions and answers from the crowd. Will you be doing that?'

'Oh, yes. But I'm also interested in you as a person. It is rare for a twenty-one year old to stand for federal parliament and, as you pointed out … as an Independent. So, what does your family think of it?'

'Do you know, Ann, my family is not standing for election.' He waits until the notebook is lowered. 'I really want to lift the level of media commentary to the issues and debates about policy.'

'But I'm sure they also want to know about you as a person – your hobbies, your past – schools, clubs … you know, to fill out the personality. That angle?'

'Perhaps, they would, Ann. However,' his voice is slow and deliberate, 'I would just like you to report the discussions of this meeting – straight reporting, nothing subjective or speculative. That's the part of my personality that people should understand; that I am seeking to be considered as a serious candidate for Killen, with a manifesto published on a website. I don't want any celebrity beyond my candidacy and arguments. I think that is much more important than my hobbies. Will you take that angle for me? You have a recording of what was said?'

She gulps. 'Yes.'

'Then I'll look forward to reading your report in *The Bay News*.'

Chapter 24

Brisbane
Offers

'Justin, we're getting requests for interviews from all the main TV channels.' Frank is staring at his screen spreadsheet.

'What are they offering?'

'Sky wants you on their *Agenda* program for half an hour ... and they have volunteered to sponsor a debate with the other candidates, televised on their multi-view channel. ABC have a slot for you on *The 7.30 Report*. Channels 7 and 9 will feature you on their Sunday evening flagships if you choose and will pay you well, for the privilege – their words, not mine – they didn't disclose a fee. Channel 10 will give you four minutes on *The Project* – light comedy but to a large audience. Oh, and ABC local radio, Brian Miller of breakfast radio fame, is setting up a debate opportunity with all the candidates after nominations close, at the Wynnumdale Shopping Centre – morning radio, that is. What do you think?'

Justin laughs. 'I've never been so popular. But these offers are all about them and their ratings. Can you just tell all of them that we will think about it. There's weeks till the election and their forums are not our battleground – that is the system's comfort zone. We live and grow on social media. I think I'll dodge all of them, except perhaps some of the written media. I want to see what the lady from *Bay News* writes ... and whether or not she passes it on to the mainstream papers.'

'What are you expecting?'

'I'm hoping that she will report the leagues club meeting fairly. If she does, that's a good thing for her – that she has understood the message. Perhaps, she will be a person we can trust into the future. The big outlets will all have agendas and editors who could do anything with what we give them. I'm just a bit wary – maybe that's some of my mother's genes in me. Meanwhile, we've got more than enough to keep us out of mischief.'

'That's for sure. Mind you, the email trees seem to be working well. They're getting the message out. That's a particular demographic, though. I've got contacts now in most retirement homes; people who will keep the name up in lights.'

'Thanks Frank. You are doing a brilliant job. Zoe and Janet too. All good.'

'Are you still going to the Chinese dinner with Janet?'

'Yep, tomorrow in fact. I have my mother's car for the evening. She's not needing it on the next day either – having a day off from volunteering for others.'

'Mmm. Hope the meeting goes well. I'll be over at Zoe's that night so you'll be on your own.'

'Really.'

Chapter 25

Canberra
Adla Bello

Sarah Power has the forensics team leader on the phone from Desmond Wilson's flat.

'Sarah, the place is wrecked. Drawers pulled out. Clothes all over the floor. Safe door open. What were you doing here?'

'What was *I* doing? What are you talking about? The place was immaculate when we left.'

'Well, it isn't now.'

'I'm stunned. Photograph it and send the shots to me. I'll send you my photos from when we were there.' How glad she is that she'd had the foresight to take photographs of every room.

The photos come through in a matter of minutes, followed by the phone call from the forensics team leader.

'I see what you mean, Sarah. So, someone else has been in here and trashed the place.'

'Has the door been forced?'

'No. Someone with a key must have come in.'

'They must have been looking for something. Probably the evidence that Luke and I bagged and is safe in your secure store back here at the station.' She pauses. 'Is there a yellow Post-It pad on the bedside table beside the unapproved ashtray?'

'No.'

'Photograph that table for me … as it is now and beam me the photo. Thanks. The superintendent would like to see the differences.'

'Done. It's on its way. What do you want us to do here?'

'Usual examination for prints and the like. Otherwise, leave the mess as you found it. I'll handle it from this end.'

* * * *

'Luke, someone with a front door key has gone through Desmond Wilson's apartment searching, probably, for the things we removed … and left the place trashed.'

'Wow! Trashed? Who?'

'Perhaps the person who leased the premises for Wilson … or the person or persons he was reporting to.'

Dexter sighs. 'I see. You're right, Sarah. There's a lot more to this than meets the eye.' He refocuses. 'Now, I have another matter to do with the case. I've arranged an interview with Adla Bello, the owner of the white car. We can meet her at her place in Bruce.'

'Good. Not far. I'm still reeling from the trashed apartment. What was her – Adla, you say – what was her story to the uniforms?'

'She was out for a drive because she couldn't sleep. When she approached the dam, she realised that she had travelled far enough … so she turned into the car park to circle round and go back the way she had come. No, she didn't see any cars or other people. She often can't sleep. She works with a catering company, long evenings, she says.'

'Really. Catering? Let's talk to her. You drive. I need to think.'

* * * *

Adla Bello's apartment is on the second floor of a long apartment block. The police are clearly expected as she answers the door at the first knock.

Adla stands about 170 cm tall, slim, with dark frizzy hair lifted in the African style. The vivid colours of her yellow-patterned smock dress contrast with the dark tones of her skin.

She politely welcomes the two detectives into her living room and invites them to sit on her couch.

While DS Power explains they are following up on her statement to the uniformed police, DC Dexter's eyes scan around the room – wall hangings in what look like African-inspired designs as well as a featured antelope skin shield with a cross of a short wooden spear and knobkerrie club fitted behind – a tribute to her heritage perhaps.

'You are the owner of a white Mazda 3 which, we understand, you told the uniformed police that you drove into the car park at the Canberra Zoo a couple of days ago, in the middle of the night. Is that right?'

'Yes. I own the car. I just used the car park to turn around. I told the police that.'

'Why were you over there, driving, at that time of night?'

'I don't know. I drive a lot in the dark. It's relaxing. My brain free-wheels and the streets are quiet … after midnight.'

'You work for a catering company. Is that correct?'

'Yeh. It's hard to unwind sometimes. I find driving helps.'

'Which catering company is it?'

'It's just a contractor out at Fyshwick. There's always plenty work. We are busy most nights.'

'Does the contractor have a name?'

'Yes. Mario.'

'Does Mario have a business name?'

'I'm not sure. He would have but he says he doesn't need to advertise. He has heaps of work.'

'How long have you been working there?'

'A few months. A friend got me the start.'

'Are there many people in the business?'

'I'm not sure. Probably a dozen or so that I've seen. I just do the waiting on table and drinks. We work in shifts. I don't how the business runs. It's a job … it pays and I often work odd hours.'

'Okay, so you drove over to the zoo and turned there. Have you done that before?'

'Yes, I have. I'm kind of on auto pilot. When I saw the glisten off the dam, I thought it was time to turn around.'

'Could you see across the dam wall to the south side?'

'It was dark. I wasn't paying attention to things like that.'

'So, you drove right into the car park?'

'Far enough to turn around. It's hard to do a U-turn right at the entrance.'

'I understand. What did you see when you drove in?'

'Like what?'

'Were there other cars parked in any of those entrance parking spots?'

'I didn't see any. I was just turning around.'

'But you drove into the entrance car park?'

'Yes. At that time of night, like I said, I'm on auto pilot. I wasn't thinking about what else was there.'

'About what time were you turning in the car park?'

'Some time after midnight. Like I told you, I was just driving to get myself ready for sleep.'

'The police visited you earlier because your car turning was picked up on a northbound car's dash cam.'

'Look. What's this all about? I've answered your questions. I can't tell you what I don't know.'

'There was a black Audi car in one of those parking spots inside the entrance. It was still there the next day. You didn't see it?'

'No.'

'Have you been watching the news updates? A man was found dead in the spillway of that dam in the morning after you turned your car at the top. That's why we are interested in piecing together all the parts of what people might have seen.'

'I didn't see anything. I've told you. I didn't see a man there or a black car. Is that all now? I'm sorry I can't help you more.'

'Okay. Thanks.'

As the detectives rise to leave, DS Power turns and asks, 'Did you drive straight back here after you turned your car?'

'Yes. I suppose I did. I haven't thought about it. I didn't know I was going to be quizzed about it later.'

'Oh, one more thing.' DS Power shows Adla a photo of the earring, on her phone. 'Do you recognise this earring?'

She glances away. 'Never seen it before.'

'One last question. Have you ever met a man called Desmond, through your work?'

Adla stiffens, annoyance in her stance and says, 'That's enough. I've told I don't know people or their names.'

'Okay. Thanks for your time.'

* * * *

Travelling back in the car, Sarah Power asks Luke, 'Well?'

'She's lying and more than a little angry at us. There's no way she could have driven into that car park and not seen the Audi parked there.'

'It *is* black. It might be possible to miss, if she was as distracted as she claims.'

'But, at the time we know she was there – 2.04 am – there would be a blue Toyota Camry parked close by … and she didn't see either of them. No way.'

'So, hypothesise some more, Detective. You're on a roll.'

Luke Dexter takes his time before replying. 'I think we have a man and *two* women involved in this. If Adla arrived after the other two were on the walkway – which the dash cam suggests – she could have followed the distracted people along the walkway …'

'And then what?'

'Just a random thought … but did you see the display on her wall … of the shield, wooden spear and club?'

'Yes.'

'The end of the club is a rounded shape like the back of a ball-peen hammer.'

'Are you suggesting that she went out for a drive with a short African club on the passenger seat?'

'I'm hypothesising, Sarah. But it is possible. Safety for a woman driving alone at night.'

'That club looked pretty fixed in the display.'

'It might not have been that particular one but something similar. Goodness, we surely don't believe she drove there by accident.'

'Now you are really hypothesising. Are you suggesting that she knew Desmond Wilson and/or the other woman on the walkway?'

'She froze when you asked her about the name, Desmond. I'm sure she knew someone of that name. She was either angry or frightened. It would make sense in explaining why she was there at the car park and the chain of events that the evidence is suggesting.'

'Good. Did you notice her earrings?'

'She wasn't wearing earrings.'

'Then, did you notice her torn ear lobe?'

'No. I didn't see any torn ear.'

'Good again, Luke. Nor did I. There were no marks on her ears. So she's not the person who had an earring torn off her ear, so viciously that it bled occasional drops. But she did recognise the photo of the design, don't you think? Did you note her body language as she denied it?'

'Yes. I saw her eyes and how she looked away.'

'Not conclusive … but certainly an indicator of her discomfort. Then, add in the political mix. She is working in catering of some sort for a man called Mario out of Fyshwick. Desmond Wilson had a catering dress uniform as well as accreditation to get into discreet private parties. Desmond's leased car came from a courier company in Fyshwick.'

Luke's eyebrows lift in question. 'Does Adla have similar accreditation to get into these parties? Are all these connections linked?'

'Welcome to the intrigue of Canberra, Luke. Now, I need to keep the superintendent updated. I'll see what approvals I can get.'

Chapter 26

Brisbane

Preparations

Justin looks out at the sky. No clouds … and no sound. But he can sense it. He is visiting his family's home again – just keeping them in the loop. His mother is there with his brother and sister.

'A thousand dollars?' Jenny Kipps says, gasping at the thought. 'Really? Just to put your name forward. How can that be fair?'

'I suppose it's to discourage flippant nominations.' Justin has a new sense of confident purpose. The death of Tony Maynard, coupled with the Prime Minister's seemingly hasty wish to jam in a by-election before the Christmas break, has given him a focused serenity – an ability to separate the important from the unimportant. He has read of Formula One racing drivers whizzing round race tracks in excess of two hundred kilometres per hour but their minds have become so attuned to the speedy experience that they are seeing things as if they were travelling at only sixty kilometres per hour. Justin is sensing a similar gentle transcendental feeling. 'Anyway, if I get four per cent of the vote, I get my money back.'

'But that's still a hell of lot of money just to put your name forward.'

'I have it – from all my part-time jobs. I was planning to go to Europe in a couple of years. That was part of my savings. Maybe, I'll just see less of Europe or go to Asia instead, if I've done my dough.

And I'll need to get a car soon. Better to have tried and lost, than to sit wondering about what might have been.'

'So you are nominated now?' Harry asks.

'Yes. Are all your eighteen-year-old mates on the electoral roll yet?'

'As many as we could contact. I even contacted the school's "Old Boys" to spread the word.'

'To the "Old Girls" too, I hope.' Justin glances at his sister to see if there is any reaction.

'You knew what I meant.'

Jenny only shrugs, but asks, 'So what happens now? For us, who are denied a vote through the accident of a birth date?'

'Frank is the campaign manager. He and Zoe are handling the Twitter feed and the email trees. Some others, like Graham McGrady and Karen Porter are getting flyers out to old people's homes and all the clubs – footy, netball, bowls, sailing, golf …

'Janet is doing the service clubs and the Asian communities. It's all very busy. We have no money to employ an office staff. Some of the student union have put their hands up to help. This is all voluntary and happening from our Capalaba verandah and Zoe's share-flat in Wynnum.'

'We can help.' Jenny's eagerness shines in her wide eyes and inspired smile. 'Fourteen-year-olds can volunteer too. Can't we advertise at school?'

'No. Definitely not. Schools are supposed to be safe from all that stuff. You can use your personal contacts through Twitter outside school though. But you have exams to think about as well.'

'It's not every day that your big brother stands for parliament.' She squeezes her forehead before coming up with her next light-bulb inspiration. 'What about other ethnic groups? It's not just Asians. A lot of Somalis and Sudanese have arrived … here in this electorate.'

'Do they have a vote?'

'They're old enough. I don't know if they can enrol.'

'They have to be citizens, not just residents.'

'Some would have citizenship surely. There are Sudanese girls in our year level at school. They are much older than us and some of them might even be eighteen – and their home language is Arabic. Couldn't we just talk to them – just explaining the process so that their families could get enrolled?'

'There are only four days left, if they are already citizens. Can't do any harm. They could maybe translate my policy platform into Arabic.'

'Swahili, too,' Harry adds helpfully. 'Well done, Sis.'

* * * *

Justin is listening to Frank on the mobile. 'It's flat out, Justin. The commercial channels have all been back on to us, wanting to know what it will take to get you onto their programs. National ABC TV can't be bothered. They can handle rejection, it seems.'

An unflappable Justin responds, 'Maybe we are too local for that show.' It is as if he refuses to get excited by the usual hysteria.

'Well, the local ABC radio can't handle rejection. They are really pissed off with you. Brian Miller? Have you heard of him? You are the only potential Killen candidate not going to his broadcast of the much-vaunted shopping centre debate in two days. He took great trouble to tell me how terrible it would look that you wouldn't be there – clearly he's not used to being snubbed. He'll milk your absence.'

'No problem, Frank. It's our indifference that gets to them. Maybe they'll stop their outrage long enough to think about why we're not jumping through their hoops. They're not used to being unable to control the agenda – to show how important they are. We're not playing to their song sheet. At the moment they're part of the problem, not the solution.'

Justin can almost imagine Frank shaking his head in the silence over the phone; before his campaign manager eventually concedes. 'Well, it's certainly an interesting tactic you're using – but I'll go with you. It's your nomination. Zoe thinks your strategy is a winner too – but I don't know. You could be kicking a grizzly bear who will come back with big teeth and a munch. I don't like stirring things up when we don't need to.'

'Thanks, Frank. I appreciate your support and doubt. But I think we actually do need to stir them up. We have to get forty-one thousand votes in a little over a month – from people who never usually think of Independents as a viable option; and people who have never even heard of me. What about the meetings with the parties about preferences?'

'A strange way to go about it, nevertheless.' He pauses. 'Yes, the Greens are scheduled for tomorrow, if you are free. If not, Zoe and I will go. It's just a business meeting with a deal to be made. Labor is two days away. I'm still waiting for Brandon Jones and the Libs.'

Justin laughs. 'The election could be over before Brandon pushes that meeting through. They wouldn't lower themselves to talk to us. They are going to win, by a substantial margin. Isn't that what Brandon said?'

'That might be what the arrogant ones think but I'm not so sure. We are getting a lot of good vibes back on our sites. Some water has flowed under the bridge since the last election.'

'I hope you're right, Frank.'

Chapter 27

'The superintendent is happy with our update on the Scrivener Dam death and that the body is the man whose driver's licence identifies him as Desmond Wilson from Melbourne. But he's not happy about Desmond's apartment being trashed,' Sarah Power explains to Luke Dexter. 'Fortunately, I was able to show him the before and after photos – so he knows that we didn't do the damage.'

'What made you take those photos, Sarah? That's not our normal role.'

'Something didn't smell right. It was gut instinct. I wanted to look at it all again in my own time because I'm missing something. I've done it before ... and will again when I have that uncertain feeling.' She pauses. 'Maybe it was the yellow Post-It note or Wilson's cavalier attitude to smoking in a non-smoking apartment.

'We found no alcohol in the flat. So, he's not a drinker, presumably. But, there's an arrogance about him.' She looks at Dexter. 'And the note said *Ring Peter*, and that note is now gone. We need a clue to take us further.'

Dexter shrugs and he thinks the problem through. 'I was thinking of seeing if our spotters in the traffic section can find the blue Toyota Camry on the city's CCTV network. How many blue Camrys are there in Canberra?'

Sarah Power nods. 'Yes, Luke. The priority has to be to find the woman on the walkway … with her torn ear lobe and, I imagine, a bashed face. The hospitals and GP network might turn up something. What else are you thinking of?'

'Could we track Wilson from his pizza box – a Hawaiian pizza. It would have been delivered. I'm pretty sure the company and phone number was on the box. If they have a record of the mobile number that Wilson called from – which they must have, surely – then we can get a warrant to study the phone records and see who he's been talking to. Like *Peter*, perhaps?'

'Good thinking. You're going to be a fine detective. That's routine police work that the team can progress. Any word on Desmond's SIM tracking from the boffins?

'Yes. It went from his Narrabundah flat to where he died. The timings were around 2 pm. Then it moved back into the Braddon area and it's now somewhere in Canberra's landfill site at Mugga Lane on the southern city boundary.'

'So, the woman dumped the phone in a waste tip, maybe putting the SIM in one and the phone in another … and all wiped for prints. What's your opinion on our priority now as we wait for post mortem results?'

'Adla Bello. She is lying. She knows what happened. Who is Mario? Where exactly does he work from? Can we get authority to search Adla's apartment and car?'

'Aha, Luke. Finding out her work location and a background profile will be fine. We have evidence enough for a magistrate to approve that type of search. We can detail one of the team to find out what is available about Adla Bello – and checking more with Vic Police for the person who told Leo Clarke to lease Wilson a car. The Victorians will know how the land lies there and I smell organised crime – rolls of bank notes, accreditation passes, quality dress requirements for all occasions. And do we know any more on his relatives? Parents? Children? Partner?'

'Nothing more on that yet.'

'Any more from the appeal for dash cam of other info from the night?'

Before Dexter can answer, an electronic signal beeps on Power's computer. 'Yippee!' she shouts. 'Wish and ye shall receive. The boffins have found CCTV footage of the white Mazda at 2.28 am in the suburb of Lyneham on the morning in question – not where Adla lives ... and not on her direct route home. But there's more, there is a blue Toyota travelling thirty metres in front of it. The boffins are trying to get a shot of the registration plate. Ms Bello has definitely been lying and certainly will have more questions to answer.'

'Progress, Sarge! I'll get on to Vic Police and see what we can dig up on Adla's background.'

Chapter 28

Brisbane

The Noble Peony

In his mother's blue Mazda 3, Justin pulls up at Janet's parents' home in the growing eastern suburb of Wakerley.

She must have been waiting inside the door because she emerges as soon as the Mazda hits the driveway. Her parents step out behind her, apparently to see their daughter off properly. Andrea and Charles Chou come across as very happy people who seem genuinely pleased to meet their daughter's friend from university – the one who is going to stand for federal parliament at the next election.

With smiling introductions, followed by quick goodbyes and waves, Janet tosses her soft bag on the back seat and Justin drives off round the corner.

He casts a quick eye back to the soft bag. They are heading off for a community meeting at a Chinese restaurant.

'For the sleep-over at Zoe's.' She winks.

'Aren't your parents coming to the meeting?'

'No. I asked them not to. They'd make me nervous. I will be interpreting. My mother would want to give too many alternative translations. I can't concentrate on them and the task at hand, at the same time. My parents are not silly. They understand.'

Justin drives on, wondering what exactly the parents understood – because Zoe isn't attending the Chinese dinner meeting. One of the challenges of his life has always been getting the significance of cryptic comments that women sometimes make. Easiest just to let it all pass at the superficial level.

* * * *

'The Noble Peony' is the classy Manly venue for the meal. The peony is a red flower, apparently very important in Chinese culture. 'Ong Moodaan' is the way Justin hears Janet say the word peony – known as the king of flowers; protected under successive dynasties. Its meaning is nobility, value and peace.

As Justin enters the large dining room with circular tables, chandeliers and some thirty well-dressed Chinese men and women, he feels as valued and noble as the peony would suggest.

Sam Fong and Lily Tso are the elders of the organising committee who greet Janet and Justin at the door; escorting them into a room of smiles and clear respect.

Seated at the round table, with the 'lazy susan' rotating the various dishes of Moreton Bay crab, Kung pao chicken, Mongolian beef and prawns, snow pea leaves and niangao rice cakes, it is clear that the community wish to make Justin feel honoured.

As Lily explains, it is traditional for Chinese people to eat as they talk business or politics. They would all like to listen to Justin's words casually but they would also like him to address the group more formally for a short address.

'Maybe you'll be able to enjoy the food more once you have spoken,' Sam suggests tactfully. 'We like a lot of your manifesto on your website, particularly your references to arithmetic. It is so important to get the accounts correct. But, in speaking to us all from the dais, we wonder if you would speak about your concept of the certainty of doubt. It sounds very interesting. We would like to understand your thoughts.'

With Sam's formal introduction, Justin takes the microphone off its stand so that he can have some movement on the small raised stage. Janet sits discreetly to the side.

'Thank you for your welcome and this lovely banquet. I appreciate the opportunity to speak with you and, just as importantly, to listen to your views. I may not get all the nuances of your culture but Janet assures me that she will help me with the interpretations.'

At that, Janet stands up, grinning and bowing, to translate *nuances*; but there is no way that Justin could hope to replicate the subtlety of that musical whispered language.

He can see the appreciation in the audience as they get the meaning – and he vows to keep his English very understandable. 'Thank you, Janet.' And he turns back to face the group.

'To take up your request to speak of doubt, let me start by speaking about language. I am concerned about lots of English phrases,' he notes the smiles as he continues, 'which seem to me to indicate a sense of superiority. When television commentators or reporters say, *of course*, it usually means that they are telling you something that you already know – and, if you don't, then you should feel inferior about your lack of knowledge. Other words like that are *obviously*, when it is not obvious; or *as you know*, when the speaker would be quite sure that you don't know. To me, these are *put down* comments that are so internalised in our daily habits that Australians wouldn't normally notice them.

'Well, I see people who speak with certainty in a similar light; when they are sure that they are absolutely right and everyone else is wrong. Sometimes this comes from a blind acceptance of religious dogma – that they are chosen to be superior, while others are on the outer. Sometimes, it comes from being born with advantages that others don't have – and they take that good fortune as being normal or how the world is supposed to be.

'Sadly, too often it is used as an excuse to play divisive power games or to alienate good people because of circumstances beyond their control.

'It is as hard to reason with a person who has no doubt as it is to conduct a rational conversation with someone high on drugs.' His comic head shake and hand gestures draw polite laughs. 'They have convinced themselves that whatever bandwagon or hallucination they are on is absolutely correct – and that you, therefore, must be absolutely wrong.

'On the other hand, scientists always accept the certainty of doubt. Every thesis has to be tested rigorously to give any degree of confidence that it might be correct. Even then, the rational mind is always open to further evidence adding to our knowledge and perhaps modifying our current understanding.

'Take that to politics and government. Every elected politician comes to parliament with a core set of understandings and beliefs. In an ideal world, they've been developed from multiple frames of reference, lots of questioning and listening to the experiences of their own communities and of the past.

'In a parliament, ideas must be debated and frequently compromises have to be made to allow progress to occur. So, absolute certainty has no place in that pot of discussions.

'Doubt is part of life's experiences – and indeed, is it not the surprise of doubt that brings us the joy of a new piece of music, or of new art or drama, as well as from new ideas, new cultures – and for me this evening, with new food tastes?

'Thank you for reading my website. As you will note, my policy is about being inclusive and tolerant of ideas, cultures and a wide range of experiences.

'But I am very disappointed in the way politics is conducted at present. I want to get it changed for the better.

'There appears to be a lack of respect for other people, not least towards our elders. Mannerly conversation is essential to allow people to listen, think and come to considered conclusions. That sense of order – manners – is part of being a respectful society and that will be a major priority for me if I am elected to represent Killen in parliament.

'I may stop there, to allow Janet to check what I've said with you and if I've understood you correctly.'

Janet stands to answer quick questions in Chinese from Justin's short talk. He takes in the nods as the meaning is transferred. Eventually, Janet acknowledges that the cultural understandings have been explained. She indicates a question from an elderly man at one of the front tables. He speaks slowly in English.

'Mr Kipps. Thank you for your thoughts. I, like many here, am pleased to see what you look like. And I like what I hear you say. I am an old man now. I have seen lots of changes in this land – many people with good ideas. They come and they go. My observation is made without any negative suggestion. You are young. My question is: Will you have the strength to stand up to the pressures that will be applied in federal politics – lobby groups, abusers …?'

'I've had some of that already from Dai Evans and Pieter Goosens – but I also have strong support from social media.'

Another voice from the same table asked, 'But what happens if social media turns against you? They build up heroes and then knock them down.'

'Good question. Social media is not like the mainstream media in that they're not controlled by owners with vested interests, or editors who want to channel opinion. Indeed, the experience with social media is that it is proving to be the ultimate market regulator because when abusers go over-the-top of normal protocols or when they spin malicious lies, they stir the reactions of many others – and, so far, they get pulled back into acceptable guidelines.

'At this stage, I'm trying to avoid much of the mainstream media hype – and that is apparently annoying them intensely. My strength and support comes from meetings like this in Killen and from the wider audiences of Twitter, Facebook and email. Time will tell whether they will turn on me or how resilient I will be. You see, I don't intend to be a career politician. I intend to improve what is there and help set a course so that it can continue after I move on to the rest of my life – to set up my own business.'

There are nods. He hears the word, *Business*, being muttered with reverent understanding.

A middle-aged lady in a beautiful Chinese-design silk dress raises her hand to speak. 'Mr Kipps, our Chinese culture has always respected the family and the elders. Indeed, it has been the family ties which have enabled us to care for each other through often difficult times; and to be successful. We also place a high priority on our young people being well educated and multi-literate – I note that you have made priorities of those too. We take your point about the language of superiority. Even teachers must be respectful of the students. So I thank you. I think I will vote for you to represent me in Canberra.'

Lily comes onto the stage as Justin bows to the middle-aged lady's endorsement.

Lily Tso clearly commands instant smiling attention as she says, 'Thank you to Mr Justin Kipps for speaking to us, this evening. He will need to enjoy his food now. He and Janet will be here for the evening to answer your questions. And, he would like your first preference vote at the election if you believe he can represent you well. Please show your appreciation by a round of applause.'

* * * *

The evening proves to be a profoundly supportive and enlightening experience as Justin and Janet receive advice, suggestions and encouragement while they visit each table.

* * * *

For a breath of fresh air after the intensity of the meeting, Justin drives Janet away in the Mazda from 'The Noble Peony' and heads straight for the esplanade. There, looking out over the darkened bay with the twinkling lights of slow-moving boats, they breathe in sighs of relaxation and recovery from the attention of the dinner.

'Thank you for all your help, Janet; organising the meeting – and the interpreting. It was a good learning experience. A lot to take in.'

She smiles in response. 'You made a good impression.' And she leans her head across to rest on his shoulder. It is an instinctive natural reaction and his head reclines gently on her hair – as scent fills his nostrils.

'It's a peaceful view, Janet.'

'Lovely.' She twists her head to look into his eyes. 'Romantic.'

Eyes lock, smiles slowly curl their lips.

'Are you relaxed?' she whispers. Their lips move close. She doesn't wait for a response but touches him with a fluttering kiss – inducing an immediate responding coil of arms and locking of mouths.

The startled squeaking of fruit bats flying overhead eventually draws them apart. 'That was very good, Janet. Okay?'

'Okay.' She smiles back and they kiss again for extended seconds.

As they sit back for a break, both grinning with euphoria of the moment, Justin's eye catches the soft bag on the back seat.

'Are you really staying at Zoe's tonight?'

She chuckles. 'Frank is there tonight. It wouldn't be appropriate?'

He must have been too engrossed in making a good impression at the dinner – so slow. 'Will your parents check with Zoe?'

'I told you; they're not silly. Don't you have an empty house at Capalaba?'

'The lady's wish is my command,' and he turns the key in the ignition.

* * * *

The bottle of cabernet sauvignon and nibbles seem to complement their earlier meal. The quiet jazzy voice of Madeleine Peyroux sets the tone. The couch is soft and private – a double bed lies waiting and inviting in the next room.

'I'm loving this, Janet. You're a beautiful woman. Are you sure this is where you want this to go?' Romance is not Justin's forte. He has always had difficulty believing that he can be attractive to attractive women. 'I can offer you little. Broke, and I could be gone in a month.'

She smiles and nuzzles tight. 'Who knows what tomorrow will bring? I'm fine with this. There are no strings. You are pretty good looking yourself. I'm interested in what tonight might bring.'

And, arms around each other, they stagger happily into the adjoining room.

Chapter 29

Canberra

Dr Barry Cotter

Dr Barry Cotter gives a tired smile to Sarah Power and Luke Dexter at the Forensic Medical Centre.

'You are not bringing me more work, I trust?' he asks.

'No, Barry. Just passing by. Thought we could take you away for a coffee, if you can manage it. Give you a little break.'

Cotter's tiredness seems to lift as his smile widens. 'Can't go far. Another job scheduled in twenty minutes. Downstairs. They make a tolerable cup for a government building. I take it that you are solving a plethora of crime mysteries by the day.'

'We're working away. We're still trying to solve that Scrivener Dam murder, at the moment. We think we know when, how and some of the participants involved. We just have no idea about the why.'

Cotter merely nods. 'Let's get a bit of caffeine sustenance in us. I'm interested in what you might be able to tell me.'

* * * *

As they carry their coffees to a discreet table, Cotter says, 'I see that the MP Tony Maynard up in Queensland has died and a by-election has been called for the House. That'll get all the hangers-on in a frenzy.'

'Elections are normal, aren't they?' Luke Dexter asks. Five years' experience as a uniformed policeman in NSW plus his half-year of training in the Australian Capital Territory to become a detective has not yet equipped him to understand all the subtleties of the political world.

'You're clearly fairly new to Canberra, Luke. This place is a bubble of a few hundred people who are elected to make laws and fifty times that number of paid public servants and twice that again made up of a nefarious mob of lobbyists, shysters, dirt diggers, manipulators and journalists looking for their first big break, who will gravitate round a new member like blow flies around a cowpat.'

'Really?'

'Yes, really. They will want his or her ear ... and to claim the actual vote in parliament. Or they might be angling for a sensational scandal to make their names ... or a lot of money in pay-offs. It's big business for some. Especially when the House of Reps has such a small margin. It doesn't take much to block or change legislation ... or even to bring a government down.'

'Do we know who the candidates are up there in Queensland?' Sarah asks. 'I haven't been across it and I don't have time to watch the TV twaddle.'

Cotter smiles again. 'The seat is Killen. I'm told Don Finucane is the front runner. Lib, of course. They're saying that his grandfather once represented that electorate. Labor and the Greens will not be a show ... and I think there are a handful of Independents that no-one will have heard of ... except one.'

'Who is that?' Luke asks.

'There's an Independent candidate who's been getting a following on social media thanks to a couple of shock jocks. I'm not across his name. It might be Kipper.'

'Kipper?' Luke says and laughs. 'The name would get him noticed alone. Kipper for Killen. What are the shock jocks concerned about?'

'Who would really know? Look. It's Dai Evans and Pieter Goosens. Probably someone has paid them to be provocative – their usual schmuck. But this time it's taken off on social media – viral they call it – for reasons only followers of that pastime might understand. A million retweets each day, so I'm told. Goosens has been suspended and Evans has shrunk back into his shell at the flack. But that won't last long. They'll rise again like a smell from a leaking sewer.'

'Is there really that much money involved in smarming up to politicians?'

'Some pollies would like it, I imagine,' Cotter answers. 'And if you get laws and regulations to be made in your favour, it is probably worth millions or billions to large corporations or business interests. Every new parliamentarian is pretty raw – susceptible to a whole range of charming entreaties. However, enough about this world of madness. What can you tell me about the dam jumper?'

Sarah Power grins at the dark humour. 'He might well be one of your hangers-on set, Barry. His name was Desmond Wilson. The parent company of a Fyshwick courier service had put him up in a Narrabundah apartment and given him a leased Audi for the month that he was here. What more do you know about him?'

'He was a smoker and a cocaine user,' Cotter says. 'The habit of those with too much disposable money – and some amphetamine was in his blood. He might have been quite high at the time he died. No pun intended with him falling off the dam. His liver has some damage and his pancreas is in poor nick for someone of his age – I'd guess from past serious alcohol imbibing at some stage. His general appearance and muscle tone however suggests he works out regularly. No alcohol in the system now, though.'

'Yes.' Sarah gives a tolerant grin. 'We didn't find any alcohol in his flat.'

'He might have had a scare and been warned off the grog. He has replaced one drug with others.'

'It wouldn't have helped his boxing either, if that's how he got the eyebrow scarring. What else? Lots of good quality clothes in his wardrobe, Barry. Dress outfits too – tuxedo and formal catering uniform. I suspect he might have been an invited guest at private parties.'

'In what role?'

'We don't know. But he might have looked quite sharp, given his build.'

Cotter is not impressed. 'He's an ex-boxer with a knife wound on his ribs. His only role at such functions would be as an enforcer.'

Sarah continues. 'We have a woman of interest. African. Driving in the vicinity at the right time but wasn't the one on the bridge. She claims to be in catering too. Works late.'

'That sounds like a euphemism for something else,' Cotter responds.

Luke Dexter asks, 'Are you suggesting that she is one of your hangers-on, too?'

The doctor adopts a patient face. 'Luke, this town is packed with embassies, with their quaintly titled attachés. They are mainly agents for their countries – all trying to get information of one sort or another or to influence players in the market. Throw in the political and research assistants – often another euphemism for many things – who are all intoxicated by what they perceive to be power. It doesn't take much to lead to some pillow talk or into some compromising situation which can be used to control others.

'So, yes. There are select parties, confidential meetings and gatherings every night, and they need catering … for food, drink or proclivities … as well as discretion, if you take my drift.' Dexter nods in an understanding appreciation while the doctor asks, 'So what do you need to close the case?'

'The woman on the walkway,' Sarah says. 'The controllers of Wilson. His agenda in Canberra. Something he's done has led to his death – probably, on the evidence, at the hands of two women. We don't have the proof yet but we're making progress.'

'So I have to hang onto his body for a while longer?' Cotter says.

Luke asks, 'If he has no relatives claiming him, who owns the body?'

'The coroner will make a determination after a period of time. If there is still no claim by a relative, the body will be cremated at the cost of the state, unless there is a likelihood of needing the body at a later date. Not common in this sort of case, though.'

'So you are up-to-date, Barry. When do you expect the tissue test results?'

'Soon-ish. But I don't think they'll have anything substantial to add to your deliberations. You know my side of the story. Must fly. The dead call me again. Good luck with closing the case.'

'Cheers. Thanks for the chat. Always good to talk through the evidence. It often throws up new points of inquiry. We'll keep in touch.'

As the doctor returns to his next autopsy, Luke observes, 'That was a handy conversation.'

'Yes,' Sarah replies. 'There aren't too many people who we detectives can talk to about work matters, outside the station ... and know that it will be kept confidential. Barry's a good man as well as being a good pathologist. Right, back to the office to see what the team has produced for us ... like a registration plate for a blue Camry.'

Chapter 30

Brisbane

Greens and Lions

Sunlight and a bird chorus waken Justin, as he realises that the dark-haired head next to his is Janet Chou. Her breath is wafting that perfume over him again – and the memories of the blissful night flood back. She is sleeping gently under the single sheet, her naked breast nudging gently against his arm and her thigh pressing against his.

If he was to move, she would waken.

Instead, he listens to the birds singing and watches her, relaxed and happy, beside him. How lucky is he?

And he can feel himself arousing at the thought.

She must have sensed him because she nuzzles closer and, seemingly without thought, her right thigh slides over him. Still eyes closed, she moves silently over him until her hips lie astride him. With barely a planned move, he can feel himself slide deeply into a familiar and ecstatic sensation – and their bodies move with a dreamy synergy.

* * * *

The Greens meeting is in Windsor, on the northside. Frank and Zoe are waiting in their car outside Zoe's flat as Justin arrives in the Mazda, five minutes after dropping Janet back to her home.

She had been the picture of innocence for her family but holding a magical aura of euphoria for Justin.

It was just a night – no strings. But her scent is still in his nostrils as both cars drive across the Gateway Bridge. Maybe, at another time, there could be more such *no strings* nights.

His heart rate has just about returned to normal as the three go in for their meeting with the Greens.

Frank has printed out *The Manifesto* and has highlighted – in pale green – the parts which coincide with Greens policy.

It is soon clear that they're right on-side with sustainable energy and just about agreeing with *The Manifesto* suggestion for treating asylum seekers with respect; though the Greens are unhappy with only temporary protection.

They could live with the logical arithmetic of the economic plank, particularly as it would fund free universities, medical care and disability insurance.

Their *How to Vote* cards will have Justin Kipps second. It is agreed.

Frank gives a commitment to place the Greens near the top. He couldn't commit because they still had to speak to the major parties – unlikely that either of them would get second spot but they were at least owed the courtesy of being listened to.

That draws another nod of respect for the new Independent candidate.

* * * *

Standing beside both their cars outside the Windsor meeting, Frank is reading his text messages. 'The ABC are on at me again. Brian Miller definitely wants you there on his program. The debate is tomorrow, in our electorate.'

'No, Frank. Tell them, no.'

'Okay, I hear you.' He shrugs.

Zoe breaks the mild tension. 'Have you read *The Bay News*, Justin? They have actually reported the questions and answers from the union meeting, almost verbatim. And the national dailies have each picked up bits of it.'

'Excellent. I'll grab a copy on the way home.'

'Here.' She passes her phone across. 'You'll get the gist on the screen.'

Justin scrolls through. 'Good.' And to both of them. 'Let's give Ann Fletcher another scoop then. I'll call her tomorrow and offer her another opportunity. But I'll pick up *The Bay News*, anyway. Have to support those who support us, without any obligations required.' He hands the phone back.

Frank is back to his agenda. 'Now, we have the Lions Club this evening – a chance to get your message out to a wide range of the community. Is that still okay? How about you, Zoe?'

'I'll leave that to you two. I have enough on my plate tonight. I've still got to hold down my day job.'

'Okay. And Rotary is scheduled a bit later. That's for the business heads.'

'Fine.'

As they head for their respective cars, Justin calls out, 'Oh, and Frank, I've just been thinking about it. When the debate is actually over on the ABC tomorrow morning, ring Brian Miller, would you? See if he wants to interview me at breakfast on the following morning. That'll test his reaction. I'd bet he'll blow – but he won't be game to say no!'

Zoe looks at Frank and simply raises her palms in disbelief.

Frank replies, 'Will do. Remember the munching bear.'

* * * *

The Lions Club make a colourful welcoming sight in their brightly coloured club shirts with the big 'L' on the pocket. Large white circular badges announce their names and classification – their work in the community.

It's another dinner meeting with all the usual updates, reports, comedic tail-twisting for charity … and Justin's talk.

After all the repetitive pre-dinner prattle, albeit friendly, Justin is pleased to get a seat next to the club president. How often can you hear, 'Good to put a face to the name on the news' and 'Why don't you go on the telly – then we'd all get to see you? Lift your profile, wouldn't it?'

Frank is on the other side of the room spreading the message to a different part of the crowd as Justin ponders which words to use for this talk.

Introduced as a past Lions Youth of the Year district finalist, at the bash of the president's gavel, Justin starts with, 'My manifesto is on my website.

'Essentially, it has three planks – economic, physical and social security – and nine main points. I won't insult your obvious intelligence by going through things that you can easily read for yourselves. Rather, let me handle something that might be a bit more contentious and closer to you in the Lions Club – so that you can answer questions that others might put to you.

'Let me talk about a different approach to charitable works. That approach stems from the arithmetic of balancing a national budget in a world which can no longer rely on expansionist economic growth. Secondly, it is derived from a philosophical position that all legislation should be based on reasoned argument. Would you all agree with that? Rational argument?'

Justin waits until everyone in the room realises they are being asked a question. 'Do we all agree that our laws should only be based on reasoned arguments which can be freely debated in parliament?'

Nods all round – and everyone is now paying close attention.

'My position is that quite a number of the laws in Australia date back to the attitudes and practices of colonial times – but they are still on the statute books, as precedents. That goes also for a lot of our government practices. We do it this way because it has always been done this way.

'So here's the start of the contentious part. I would like to see a secular Australia where all religions can be tolerated, indeed respected – that is in Section 116 of the Constitution – but no particular religious dogma should influence the political agenda, let alone the actual laws of the land.

'I want to see parliament get rid of automatic tax-free status for religious groups. From what I can see, many of the exemptions around religion are used to build more churches or to invest in their own money-making ventures – at our expense.

'Tax-free status should be awarded to groups who do charitable or service work for the community. Some of those will most probably still be religious groups – such as the Salvation Army or St Vinnies but it wouldn't be automatic; and it would be subject to audit regulation.

'Other community support groups like the Smith Family, Lifeline and Veterans' networks might be among the non-religious groups; as would service organisations like Lions and Rotary.

'I am a soon-to-be history and economics graduate. I have no problem in acknowledging the historical contributions to the way this country has developed – the painful parts as well as the success stories.

'But now, in the world economic context and with the philosophical position that you all agreed to a minute ago, we have to have transparent processes to justify why some groups should have exemptions from tax – and that should be directly proportional to the help that is provided to the less fortunate or to community development projects. Lions have many programs that would easily qualify and your work is all transparent.

'Not every organisation which claims exemption or subsidy would either want or welcome such scrutiny.

'So, essentially, my platform as a young Independent representing the electorate of Killen will be to lift the level of debate in parliament, to make the deals of lobbyists much more transparent, to shine a light into lots of darkened corners – and see that the way forward from here is significantly more respectful and better than we have experienced in recent times.

'Young as I am, I'm tired of listening to patent lies and weasel words, dressed up in politico-economic speak for the media sycophants to peddle. We are being conned and it's time that the behaviours were being called out. I'll leave it there, and invite questions.'

The president bangs his gavel again. 'A lot of bold words and ideas there, Justin. Do we have any questions?'

Frank winks at Justin as the bewildered Lions glance at each other for succour or wisdom.

'Yes, I have one,' from half-way down the U-shaped setting. 'Why are you against religion? This is a free country.'

Justin bounces to his feet. 'I am not against religion. Be absolutely clear. In my view, each Australian is entitled to follow his or her religion without fear or favour. Okay?'

'Right,' the questioner replies. 'That's what I believe too.'

'Good. The key to that statement is *without favour*. We have already all agreed that decisions should be made on the basis of rational argument. So any laws must be able to pass that test. If it's only someone's belief with no evidence or reasoning, then it shouldn't have sway. Agreed?'

'Unless, it is *my* belief. This is a Christian country.'

Justin gives a tolerant smile. 'So, can you justify why your belief should be part of the law of this land? If you can, it will pass the test of rational argument. So can you argue reasonably that Australians can follow *any* religion but the laws will be formed *only* by Christian beliefs? Is that what you are saying? Because, if you are, there are a lot of Australians who follow beliefs that aren't Christian.'

'But we are a Christian country.'

'According to the last census, only 61% claimed to be Christian as compared to 96% in 1911. The country's beliefs are changing.'

'And not for the better, I'll tell you. We don't want all that extremist foreign stuff in our laws.'

'Agreed. I don't want anything in our laws which can't be argued logically, as appropriate for a developed educated twenty-first century nation. Mind you, there are lots of beliefs in the Old and New Testaments that might have been appropriate millennia ago but most people wouldn't be comfortable with them today. Do you see where I'm coming from?'

Justin takes the nod either as a grudging agreement or politeness to a guest. Whichever way, he accepts it. 'And there are lots of religions who have views inconsistent with Christian beliefs. They would have to pass the same tests of logic that you would use to justify.'

'But why do we need all of this justifying? This land has been good for a long time.'

'I could invent a crazy idea tomorrow, get a few people to back me and claim it's a religion. There's no rational test in existence to disqualify me from tax-free status, including the ability to raise money as a charity and to influence parliamentarians.'

There are a few knowing nods from members in the audience who realise that Kipps is ducking the challenge to call out the complacency of self-interest – the *why change?* – which is the last bastion argument of everyone in a comfort zone. But he's speaking again. 'There will be eight billion people on this planet by 2025. That is twice what the number was when most of you were born. Technology has made the world a global village. There are a lot more snake-oil salesmen out there now than there were years ago.

'You look to your government to protect you – it is part of the Australian constitution. Well, *same old, same old* is likely to be at least half-a-kilometre off the pace. You don't want to be that far back in a cup race, do you?

'That's why I seek your first preference vote on election day; or your second preference if you can't manage to change your habits of a lifetime. I encourage you to read my website. I've only touched on one aspect which could affect this club. But, please, come and see me. You know who I am now – a face to a name. I'll come back and report to you.'

'But you're just a kid.'

'I'm more than old enough to die in the army for my country. I'm a past Lions Youth of the Year district finalist. I have a university degree. I have competed for Queensland at debating. I haven't spent my teens getting smashed at parties. I've been listening, thinking and formulating potential policies. And, thanks to Dai Evans and Pieter Goosens going off like frogs in a sock, I have a national and international social media profile. If I was to be elected as an Independent to Canberra, I could guarantee that I would be heard, representing both the views of this electorate and ideas for the betterment of Australia. Have you ever had that from your elected representatives before?'

The president senses the mood. 'Well, you have given us a lot to think about, Justin Kipps. Thank you for coming to share your ideas with us tonight. On behalf of the club, let me present you with this Lions' spoon. Lions, on the count of three – one, two'; and he bangs his gavel on the three, as the members follow suit on the table as a salutation.

* * * *

As they leave, after post-meeting socialising, Frank asks, 'Do you think it's wise to keep provoking them so much?'

'Yes, I do, Frank – for lots of reasons. If I am elected, I don't want people coming along saying that I never mentioned all the controversial things before they voted. I would also be sure that when these members go home or to work tomorrow they'll be saying, *Do you know what that young Independent candidate said at Lions last night?* The answer will be, *Who's he?* And they will say *Justin Kipps.* Come ballot time, when they get beyond the first preference and they run their eye down the voting slip, they'll look for a name they recognise and put a 2 beside it.'

'Or a 7, because they didn't like your message.'

'True – but at least, I would have been honest with them. I have to be me. You can worry for both of us, Frank.'

Chapter 31

Brisbane

Poking the bear

Kipps can't resist it. It's a new day and his interest is piqued. Brian Miller is announcing six of the seven candidates for Killen over his breakfast radio for his shopping centre debate.

'And the seventh candidate, Justin Kipps, was unavailable despite numerous attempts by this station to get him involved. I suppose you, the voters, are the ones to miss out because you won't get to hear him answer your questions. Goodness, even prime ministers come on this show. I'll leave you to draw your own conclusions. You are the voters.'

As Justin continues to listen, he hears each candidate sledge the answers of the others in what seems to him, an uncontrolled rabble – while the host salivates at what good radio this all is.

Justin rings Frank. 'Have you been listening to it, Frank?'

'Yeh. You were better off out if it. But I've just phoned ABC radio. I couldn't get through to Brian Miller, but I got his producer. She will add you to the program tomorrow – and she did say that Brian would be ropable. I hope you know what you're doing.'

'Thanks, Frank. You are doing a terrific job. I really appreciate all the organising you're doing for me and the campaign. Trust me. I think what I'm doing is the way to go – but the only certainties in life are death, taxes and doubt.'

'How are *you* doing?'

'I'm fine. I have a union committee meeting this evening. Never a chance to be bored. I'm going alright.'

Chapter 32

'Whoopee! Luke, the boffins have a registration plate for the blue Camry.' Sarah Power rarely shows so much emotion but her fists are pumping with the sense of a breakthrough. 'Ye … es!'

'Here.' She turns her screen to show Dexter the number. 'Check it out, please, Luke. This is what we've been waiting for.'

Dexter moves quickly to phone the details through to Vehicle Registration.

Within minutes, he exclaims, 'We have it. The name is Stephanie Taylor, with an address in Lyneham – nice suburb. Wasn't that where Adla Bello was caught on CCTV driving with the blue Camry almost in the same shot? These two know each other.'

'Steady, Luke. Lyneham could have been on her way home. Bello was pretty vague about where she was driving to help her get to sleep … but she could easily be lying too. I'll let the superintendent know about this latest development. See if anything has come through from Vic Police in the meantime, will you please? We need something to get our courier man, Leo Clarke, to talk.'

'Sarah, if this Stephanie Taylor was the woman on the walkway, isn't she going to lie too … just like Adla Bello? I'm new to frontline detective work but can't we just set up some surveillance on her first – legally, of course – to see where she goes, who she meets and what she does for a living?'

'Luke, at the moment, Stephanie Taylor is an innocent member of the public who happens to drive a blue Toyota Camry which may or may not be the vehicle we are interested in. This is not a police state. We can speak to her, of course, but we need to present strong grounds to get permission to surveil. Let's just gather some of our evidence first. Patience. She may well be nursing an injured face at the moment … and have gone to ground. Neither Ms Taylor or Desmond Wilson are going anywhere. We follow proper police procedure.'

Chapter 33

Another new day and Justin is at the ABC Centre at Brisbane's South Bank.

'Good morning and welcome to ABC Breakfast. I'm Brian Miller and my first guest today will be the elusive candidate for the federal seat of Killen, Justin Kipps. Welcome Justin.'

'Hello to you and the ABC listeners.'

'Can I ask you first of all, Justin Kipps, why you didn't attend the candidates' debate yesterday in Wynnumdale Shopping Centre, where you could have debated public questions in front of a live audience of your electors and be beamed out by this radio station, region-wide?'

'You can ask; if you wish to spend the interview time on that rather that what is important to the electorate of Killen?'

'Well, wouldn't they feel like you are avoiding their hard questions?'

'Or your pointed distracting questions?'

The bristle in Miller's tone would be clear to the listeners. 'Our questions have been submitted by the public; and the other candidates could have quizzed you too, on the day.'

'Brian, that format is about the media's profile and your ratings rather than discussing policies. Those mass debates are more about a lot of red-faced pointing and personal gratification. Do you want to move to policies?'

'I think these are valid questions to ask you. We've had listeners phoning in wanting me to ask you.'

'Brian, you are beginning to sound like someone jilted – and I imagine your switchboard will soon be jammed after my previous comment. Can we move on, please?'

Miller's gasp is audible. 'As you wish. Your whole campaign so far has been carried out on social media. This is the first mainstream interview you've agreed to.'

'If that's your question; yes, Brian, that's technically correct. I've spoken at many public meetings and gatherings but not on traditional media. If you want to know why I haven't given an interview, can I point out that we have now been on air for minutes and the questions have been more about you and others being miffed, rather than issues for the election? That's the challenge with the current mainstream media, in my view. The commentators have become used to shooting hard-hitting zingers of questions at passive, compliant elected officials or public servants ... and frankly, I am neither of those. Rightly or wrongly, I doubt the importance or relevance of such media occasions in getting a rational message out.'

'Alright.' Miller clears his throat loudly. 'What do you want to say to the electors of Killen? You have two minutes.' His antagonism sounds scarcely under control.

'Thank you. Men and women of Killen, I seek your vote in the upcoming election. I am independent of political parties and I wish to represent you in Canberra. The only promises I make are to listen to you and to the others in parliament. I will not be the government but I will examine and query all the proposals that they put forward and ... I will provide information back to you through the electoral office.

'This is not a *what's in it for me* for particular lobby groups. I believe the nation is at a turning point. We have a Constitution and a system which has brought us to this stage. What is missing is morality; the ability to make decisions beyond self-interest. If all that the government is about is to give in to the wishes of particular vested interests and lobbyists then *The Lucky Country* will not be lucky for much longer. There is a need to tackle national issues, including renewing our commitment to ethical and honest practices.

'My platform is made of three planks: economic security, physical security and social security. The priorities and details are outlined on my website and through all my social media platforms.

'But, in Canberra, I also want to challenge the political process, to get away from the carping, repetitive double-speak, pork-barrelling and personal abuse. Instead, my priority is to focus on debating ideas in the interests of the nation and the people of Killen. If elected, I intend to spend no more than two terms as your representative and I would want to make a very significant difference in that time, particularly in the quality of discussion and policy formation.

'Finally, I would want you all to note that I will advocate for a secular Australia which is tolerant of all faiths. However, no faith should have a bearing on how the laws of Australia are formed. If the merit of legislation cannot be argued and agreed by logical reasoning, then it should have no place in the statute books.'

'Right. You've said your piece, Justin Kipps,' Miller says abruptly. 'Your ideas will certainly put the cat among the pigeons. Given that you have offended every religion in the land, most of your vote will probably be gone now. And you were right, the switchboard has received complaints about your *mass debate* comments. Did you want to say more?'

'Offence is only in the ear of the listener. I stand by what I said then and what I've just said.'

'But realistically, if you are elected, Justin Kipps, you'll be one lonely voice as an Independent and probably ignored. Aren't you just a young man punching above his weight?'

'Brian, I can't help either my age or being fit. An Independent can be heard in the parliament – and my platform will be clearly carried through the public address system of the House ... and recorded in Hansard. There may well be several more Independents after the next election. Who knows, we may even hold the balance of power and then, irrespective of my comparative youth, the major parties will have to deal with me.

'As to my experience, I'm well educated and have lived for nearly twenty-two years on the planet. Perhaps I haven't yet succumbed to the mordant blanket of the power players who seek to delude the people into a hypnotic state of acceptance of the unacceptable.'

'Alright. You are smart.' Miller is angry but angling for a headline. 'So what do you say to those voters who have no easy access to smart phones and computers? Is it enough to say that everything is on a website? One that doesn't give space for comment, I might add.'

'I'll tell them now, Brian. In addition to the three planks of economic, physical and social security, there are nine main points that I'll run through briefly for your listeners. Let's start with the *contentment of sufficiency*. When did this cult of greed come in? Do you realise that the richest ninety people in the world control as much wealth as the poorest four billion on the planet? Ninety people would fit in a double-decker bus. We have to return to the common sense of sufficiency on a finite planet.

'Then there is *equitable revenue-raising*. No more of rich global corporations paying next to nothing in tax – and it's apparently legal to do so. Go figure! And *let's put common sense back into salaries and perks*. Why do some CEOs earn millions and tens of millions? Plus additional bonuses and perks for doing a job. I have no problem with people being wealthy as long as they earn the money by employing others and contributing to society. Governments can't control private enterprise salaries, nor should they. But shareholders can ... and should. And for those who have been used to booking it up to the government, the days of snouts in the public trough will be gone.

'And Brian, there's the *certainty of doubt*. I can't think of anything more dangerous to public life than the zealous person who believes there is no doubt. Can you? Goodness, the whole of scientific reasoning is based on doubt and checking. Mindless dogma has no place in decision making.

'Most of what I'm arguing about in revenue and expenditure is just doing our sums. This is not some mystical complex theory. We can all add and divide. I won't speak in gobbledegook to Australians.

'We need to invest in *free health* and *disability care*. Just as none of us could choose where, when or to whom we were born, the lottery of life gives us little choice in whether we contract illnesses or suffer a disability. A good society plans and budgets to support the needy with appropriate care to let them lead fulfilling lives.

'While we are on investment … the key to success as a country and as individuals in life is a broad multi-literate *critical-thinking education*. Then people won't fall into the traps of snake-oil salespeople who deal in trickery and mind manipulation. We need thinking innovative citizens in a non-divisive system. So let's commit to *needs-based free school education*, followed by certain *free university bachelor degrees* for students with merit.

'Most of the really successful forward-thinking countries invest in their people. Some political parties argue that it's too large a cost. I don't see it that way. It's an investment, not a cost, which will return benefits to the country, far beyond any short-term expenditure.

'Finally, the peace of *physical security*. Everyone is entitled to feel free from attack, persecution, bullying and discrimination. It's part of our Constitution – our list of laws – and it's part of a moral society that believes in *the fair go* for everyone. How's that, Brian, for a short platform?'

'Well, thank you. I'm pleased that the ABC could give you the opportunity to say your piece – although I don't understand why you couldn't do that yesterday at our debate.'

'Don't you, Brian? Really? I thought we'd already covered that. All the best to you and your listeners.'

'Well, I wish you well, Mr Kipps. Perhaps we will speak again. Thank you for coming on air. Now I must break for the traffic report. That was Justin Kipps, ladies and gentlemen, the aspiring Independent candidate for Killen.'

Chapter 34

Brisbane

Labor

'Why don't you all just join us?' is the first question from the Labor Party at the preference meeting.

Zoe smiles to avoid answering that particular question. 'Frank has highlighted where our policies match. We are as one on most social justice issues – free education, health, disability care, fair treatment for all in employment.'

'Like we said, why don't you join us?'

It is Justin who answers. 'At the fundamental level, I couldn't handle the union control at conferences, the lack of democracy in pre-selections and that you can't join the Australian Labor Party unless you are a union member. That immediately excludes a significant section of the community – and they happen to run most of the businesses. Until you actually include and not divide, I couldn't be part of your party – and I'm still a students' union president. Clearly we have a lot of policies in common, but I want to be an independent voice. I am looking for you to give us second preference on your ticket.'

'And in return?'

'You will be second on our ticket.'

'Hardly a fair exchange – your few hundred votes for our thousands.'

'I should point out that Labor has only won Killen twice in history. I offer you a like mind on many issues, in Canberra.'

The laughter is raucous. 'You expect to win this election?'

'With your preferences. What have you got to lose? And, if you actually are in the final fight, my preferences could make the difference to get *you* in.'

* * * *

'You've got balls, Justin,' Zoe comments on their way back to the car, with the Labor promise of number two on their *How to Vote* cards.

Frank looks at her. 'Yeh, gutsy job, Kippsy.'

Justin takes the compliments in his stride until … he ponders on Zoe's choice of words. Then it passes, among the welter of new challenges.

'Has Brandon Jones got back to us, yet?'

'No,' Frank replies.

'Let's bypass him. Would you be able to contact the Libs direct, please? We want to have the conversation with them at least.'

'What's next?'

'Rotary tonight,' Frank replies. 'I've got heaps to do and I don't think I could take another dinner meeting. Could you handle it on your own?'

'Sure.'

'I could accompany him … you,' Zoe says to them. 'There are women in Rotary, aren't there? I'm the only one of us here who actually runs her own business.'

'Sure. Good idea, Zoe,' Frank agrees.

'I'll pick you up, Justin. You're going to need to get your own car soon. This politicking is most nights. Public transport won't cover too many of these occasions.'

'It's in the pipeline,' Justin replies. 'In negotiations with my father. It's not easy with only part-time jobs. Thanks. Until this evening.'

Chapter 35

Brisbane

Rotary

The Rotarians are the epitome of politeness and decorum.

Zoe is wowing them all in her *businesswoman at function* little black dress, heels and subdued bling. 'Events management', she says in reply to their flurry of questions. 'My own agency. Can handle Billy Joel or the Berlin Philharmonic – just a matter of scale.'

Justin leaves her to it as she charms so many for whom that world of entertainment organisation is an exotic foreign enterprise.

He gives a standard brief presentation of his platform. The dinner questions are predictable.

'How will you handle the huge advertising blitz of the major parties? What is your campaign budget?'

'I expect that we might top out at a couple of thousand. All donations are gratefully accepted. Zoe will manage that for you. But really, ladies and gentlemen, social media has changed the whole dynamic of cost structures. The message is disseminated by website, email trees, Twitter, Facebook and texts, at minimal cost beyond the normal package charges. The word appears to be getting out but I would really appreciate you speaking to your contacts, particularly among the voters in Killen.'

The president looks very prestigious in his chain of office, while banging the obligatory gavel for attention. 'I'm sure that we will pass on the word about this meeting. Any final questions?'

'Just one,' from a hunched old man on the side table. 'Why are you not on the television?'

'Simple answer, Sir. My preference is to meet people face-to-face or to link with them on social media. Free-to-air TV seems to me to be about a few seconds of sound grab – more about celebrity or sensation. Whereas, here we get the chance to exchange views. I don't know everything – or indeed as much about the mud pool of politics as most prospective candidates – but everywhere I go, I learn more and have new ideas to consider. If I just appeared on news grabs, whatever you would see would be at the mercy of the editor's chops.'

'Fair point.' The old man seems to consider the answer. 'At least I know what you look like now. Get posters up with your face on it. Let people recognise you and the name. That's my advice. Vote 1 for Justin Kipps, or second at worst.'

'Thanks, Giles,' the president calls over the chortles and then in a whisper to Justin, 'Giles is our most senior Rotarian – very sharp mind still. In his late nineties. Would you believe it?'

'Thank you, Sir,' Justin calls to the elderly gentleman. 'You said it better than I could.'

* * * *

Another successful meeting. Zoe drives Justin home and steps in to see how Frank is doing with all his organisation.

'It all went well,' Zoe says. 'Justin won most of them over as usual. Good crowd. How are you going?'

'Fine. I've had a text back from Ann Fletcher at *The Bay News*, confirming the interview at their offices tomorrow. Is that still okay, Justin?'

'All good.'

With a kiss for Frank and a hug for Justin, Zoe takes her leave.

Chapter 36

Brisbane

Bay News

In *The Bay News* office, you can smell the ozone in the air even if it doesn't actually have a clear view of the water. The morning is already hot.

Ann Fletcher makes Justin Kipps feel very welcome, introducing him to her editor, Stella Watson, while they talk through a feature interview.

'You maintained the trust last time, Ann. Trust has its rewards with most things in life. I'm happy to give you and Stella, and *Bay News*, a scoop but the deal is the same as the last time – the story has to be about policy, not celebrity or sensation. The policy should be provocative enough.'

'We'll live with that,' Stella answers. 'The national papers all wanted to carry our last story – and circulation has increased with the by-election interest. We'll see that it gets into our sister local papers too. You are in a bigger electorate than the area of our main circulation.'

'So what sort of questions do you want to be interviewed about?' Ann asks.

'Perhaps, a future after the fossil fuel industry dries up? Or … I've been speaking to service clubs about new tax rules for charities and indeed, a secular Australia where all laws have to be justified by rational argument, rather than priorities of any particular belief system. What about asking if an Independent member of parliament could ever become Prime Minister? That should give you some scope for a feature article. I'm happy for a couple of photos too, down on the esplanade or walking on a boardwalk through the mangroves.'

Both journalists seem to light up at the suggestions, so Justin settles back for the questions, with the coffee and glass of water provided.

* * * *

The recorder is on and her notebook poised as Ann Fletcher asks, 'What do you think is going to happen to Australia when China, Korea and Japan stop buying our mineral resources?'

As usual, Justin takes his time and speaks quietly. 'There was an opportunity to set up a sovereign wealth fund during the first decade of this century, as has been the case with Norway and its North Sea oil reserves.

'While the Australian government of the time did pass on a surplus to the next administration, they chose to give much of the resources-boom wealth back to the public as tax concessions, instead of setting up an untouchable sovereign fund for the future. That was an ideological decision. And it was their right to make that choice. They were the elected government.

'However, by the time the next government had spent the surplus on poorly-managed programs to defray the impact of the Global Financial Crisis, all the savings benefit of that decade and those earlier had been lost. Again, the government of the time was making an ideological decision to protect jobs. It was their choice and their right to make it but it certainly needed to be much more tightly managed.

'Meanwhile, Norway is now the third richest economy in the world due to its reserves of sovereign wealth. It survived the financial crisis with minimal impact – and it will live well off the interest of its astute sovereign fund policy for many decades to come; long after the oil reserves have ceased to be extracted. They will use the funds to generate the industries appropriate to the new era, without eating into the financial principal. It really is just arithmetic and good business practice.

'In my view, we need to tailor our economic settings for a transition to a sustainable economy, using renewable or recyclable resources. And the current account budget needs to get back into positive territory as soon as it is practicable. That's no more than good management.

'Unfortunately, our current settings seem to be based on another ambitious expectation of world growth and world demand. The arithmetic would suggest that projected scenario is unlikely to bear much fruit – demand for our resources, and therefore their value, is declining. The pressure of population and deteriorating global climatic conditions will change the dynamic negatively. Yet, for ideological reasons, the government is fixated on the economic theories of a colonial era, where there were always new resources to plunder.

'In my view, they're taking our country on an unsustainable path – and they have blinkers on for the alternatives. If I am elected as the Independent Member for Killen, I will be heard in the parliament and I intend to get the alternatives both on the record and on the agendas for debate.'

Through the open door from the next room, a listening Stella Watson lifts a wide-eyed smile from her computer screen and grins an encouraging expression.

Ann Fletcher changes tack.

'You speak a lot about revenue and arithmetic. Do you have a view about the Goods and Services Tax, currently at ten per cent?'

'I do. GST would have to be part of any overall discussion of revenue. I don't like the flick pass of saying that it is just a matter for the states.

'I come at it from some fundamental principles. First, it's a flat rate tax on purchases and services – and it applies to everyone in theory. But currently there are many exemptions, which in political terms equate to *deals done in the past*. Some companies get refunds of their GST. GST doesn't apply to food or education or health.

'The process I would advocate is to publish the pros and cons of all such exemptions. Given that a GST would take a larger portion of a poor person's money than a rich person's, a rational argument could be made to exempt the basic priorities of life which could be food, medical care and education. That case could be reasonably argued and agreed, although the definitions would need to be tight, so that tax collection is fair and not opening more lurks.

'The case for exempting wealthy companies might be much harder to sustain, I suspect. Those deals would be relics of the arrangement made when the government set up the initial scheme – the more exemptions that are made, the less the revenue that is taken.

'I suspect that if all eligible people were paying the tax, then an increase of the rate might not be necessary in the short term. There are a lot more pressing tax loopholes to be chased down.'

Justin sips from his mug of coffee while Ann makes some more notes.

'One more?' she asks.

At the nod from Kipps, she asks, 'Is there any reason why an Independent member could not be Prime Minister?'

Again, Justin takes his time. 'Constitutionally, the Prime Minister is the member of the House of Representatives who can approach the Governor-General with the assurance that he or she has the support of the majority of the members in the House.

'Given that our electoral process is set up to promote a two-party system with a Government and an Opposition, there hasn't been a case in our short history when the leader of a major party has not been the Prime Minister.

'However, we have had hung parliaments where Independents on the crossbench have held the balance of power. Then the leader of the majority can only govern with the support of a number of cross-benchers. And, in those cases, the Prime Minister has still been a leader of a major party.

'But, as I understand the Constitution, there would be no legal barrier for a party to agree to follow an Independent as a prime minister. It would take a lot of swallowing of pride and power from the party machines and their supporters – but technically, it could happen.

'And, might I add, that would not necessarily be a bad thing. It could take the heat out of chairing negotiations and focus attention on the good of the country rather than any particular party's power interests.

'How different would that be, in principle, from having an Independent Speaker of the House? Ideally, that person gives up party allegiances and administers the standing orders with impartiality. It hasn't always worked that way – but we are speaking about hypothetical ideals.'

Ann continues scribbling notes as Stella appears in the doorway.

'Finished?' she asks. 'I have a question for Justin. What might be the major barrier to such an independent prime minister ever being commissioned?'

Justin looks at Stella as he says, 'Apart from the election results, I would say – pettiness. As one prime minister of the past once said, *Parliament is no place for wimps*. Pettiness is entirely about obstructing anyone else taking power. But why should you rule out what an Independent could bring to the process?'

'You are different – very different,' Stella observes.

'If Man had always stuck with *same old, same old*, we would still be living in caves, searching for our next meal and wondering when the next powerful neighbour would invade.'

Ann has collected her thoughts. 'Thanks for this. Do you want me to run this past you before going to print?'

'I trust you to be a fair journalist – no celebrity, no sensation. Let the policies speak for themselves. I appreciate your help.'

* * * *

As he walks away from the office, he wonders if he has made a wise move in trusting so much – but the Queensland sky is blue …

Chapter 37

Canberra

Snag

'What do you mean that we've been taken off the case?' Luke Dexter's gaze is fixed on his detective sergeant.

Sarah Power is staring into space, not her usual image of the confident assured policewoman. Her lips are pursed. Now, she focuses on her detective constable. 'That's what I've just been told by the superintendent. The case is going over to a crime section with the Australian Federal Police, operating on behalf of the Australian Security Intelligence Organisation.'

'ASIO? But why? We've nearly solved the bloody thing. We will have interviewed the woman on the walkway within a day. We have the address from the car registration… or at worst, if she is hiding, we'll be able to find her after putting some pressure on Adla Bello's story.'

'Luke,' Sarah fixes her gaze on Dexter's face, 'we've been taken off the case. Hear what I say. All our notes and evidence are to be transferred across to the AFP building, presumably to be studied by ASIO people.'

Luke Dexter says nothing in response but his expression shows he is still asking the same question.

Sarah continues with a quiet measured tone. 'This case is apparently political now. Interstate. Maybe international. Maybe diplomatic. Maybe national security. Whatever – it's out of our jurisdiction. We are ACT Policing – standard criminal policing.'

'Can we not just make some discreet inquiries into Adla Bello for example, to see what she really does for a living? She lives in a comfortable apartment in Bruce. That's a fair rent for someone on a catering assistant's dollar in Canberra.'

'Luke,' her voice is still calm and careful, 'which part of *we've been taken off the case* did you not understand? The decision has been made at a level far senior to us. ASIO is involved. That could mean terrorism or international crime … who knows?'

There's a long silence during which neither of them moves, before Luke says, 'This smells, Sarah. It's crime against a shady character from Melbourne, committed by one or two women. He was pushed over a dam after stalking one of them … or being in a fight with one of them or something like that.'

'Maybe,' replies Sarah Power with a sigh. 'But this is the reality of policing in this town. It's different from any other place in Australia. Like Barry Cotter said, it has all the embassies … and possibly all the spies. Hence, ASIO is involved and probably some agencies that no-one ever hears about.'

The silence returns.

'So that's it, Sarge? *Thanks for your good work* but we'll pass it to the secret experts?' He flicks the papers on his desk. 'Well, I don't like it. Something isn't right. The pieces don't fit. Is this what they talk about outside Canberra when they say, *the fix is in?*'

'Let it go, Luke,' Sarah Power's voice is firm and in command. 'The AFP are our colleagues. Honest cops, too. They have a job to do, just like us. In this business, you have to learn to take your lumps. They don't always seem logical or just. But this is life in the bubble.'

Luke Dexter paces back and forward as if deciding what to do or say next.

Eventually, he asks, 'So what do I do with the info that Vic Police have just sent through? It came onto my computer while you were with the superintendent. They say that the company that leased

Desmond Wilson's apartment is called Bollen Investments. It's a shell company based in Panama, in Central America. Not easy to track, according to Vic Police. It would appear to be an investment company playing the world markets, while in reality scamming, laundering money and manipulating government decisions to their benefit. The name of the person who gave Leo Clarke his instruction was an Ivan Jones of Bollen Investments – believe that if you wish. And he jumped to obey? Why? What does he know?

'Leo Clarke was instructed to lease the apartment for Desmond Wilson, using the courier company's address in Melbourne and the money appeared in the Melbourne account to pay for it, the lease of the Audi and a phone. I'd bet that the info is in a private filing cabinet in Clarke's office that his secretary never uses.

'The Vic Police got a print-out of the phone numbers that Wilson called in the hours before he died. We have those numbers on my computer, as we speak. There are two numbers in particular after midnight on the day he died. Any guesses? We know where his SIM card went and where the phone was when it went missing somewhere south of Lyneham. So, do I pretend that I have slight deafness and I didn't get your instruction to cease?'

Sarah Power's expression hasn't changed. 'Luke, you are a police officer and I've given you the instruction from above. I expect you to carry out that order. I would imagine that AFP officers will be here soon. I don't want you to revisit that information from Vic Police, except to flick it through to my computer as a matter of routine courtesy. I assume they've given you no more on Wilson's possible relatives? I would need to tell the AFP that too.'

'No. Nothing new on the relatives.' Luke replies with a sullen tone and carries out Sarah's instruction with a few mouse clicks.

'Now I would like you to take a walk for thirty minutes. Go and have a coffee or whatever. When you return, we'll deal with the AFP and/or ASIO and then we will move onto the rest of our case load. Thanks.'

After a confused Luke Dexter leaves the office, as instructed, Sarah Power copies the photos from Desmond Wilson's flat onto a

USB thumb drive. Then she adds the Vic Police report, including the numbers of the two mobiles that Wilson had called in the hours before he died. Sarah expects that one of them would be someone called Peter and the other would probably be Stephanie Taylor.

* * * *

Thirty minutes later, Luke Dexter returns to his office as requested, still with a disappointed expression and slowly shaking his head.

Ten minutes after that, two AFP officers arrive accompanied by a man in plain clothes and Sarah Power's superintendent. The AFP men are in obvious possession of a transparent evidence bag of accreditation passes from Desmond Wilson's safe, plus more bags containing the bundles of money which Power and Dexter extracted mainly from Wilson's suit pockets.

'Detective Sergeant Power, the superintendent tells us that you have photos on your phone taken of a flat in Narrabundah, including these passes.' He holds up the accreditation passes. 'Is that correct?'

'That is correct'

'Please find the photos on your phone and pass the phone to the gentleman accompanying us.'

Sarah finds the photos and passes the phone over. 'These are all the photographs I took there,' she says honestly.

The AFP man says, 'This gentleman is about to permanently erase those photographs. Do you understand and agree?'

'I understand and agree.'

The gentleman pushes several keys, waits for about fifteen seconds, presses two more keys and hands the phone back via the AFP man.

'Thank you, Detective Sergeant Power. You and your team are now officially removed from this inquiry. We thank you for your work. Your final and only role will be to write up the reports of your investigations for the coroner, which will be forwarded to our team at AFP Headquarters in the Edmund Barton Building. Your superintendent has all the details. We wish you and your colleague a good day.'

They leave, with the superintendent giving Sarah a quick, sad glance over his shoulder as they go.

'What was that all about?' Luke Dexter asks.

'Welcome to the world of national security and ASIO. They don't tell you what they're doing. We just have to trust that they know what they're doing. Now, my advice to you is put this behind you, add it to your experience and move onto the future.'

'Sarah, we've nearly got the case solved.'

'You are not hearing me, Luke. I know this is hard but I've been down this path before. We're off the case. National Security will handle it from now on. We're back to standard local criminal investigation – theft, low level fraud, burglaries, standover and the occasional grievous bodily harm.'

'Alright. I do hear you. I hope they do see the case through.'

* * * *

That evening, when Sarah Power is back at her own apartment, she goes into her study. She removes some folders from the second drawer down in her desk and pulls it right out of its tracks. She turns it over and gaffer tapes the USB to the underside of the drawer. She replaces the drawer, then the folders, and slides it closed.

Chapter 38

Brisbane

Interest grows

Justin is busy in the weeks leading up to the election.

He still has a range of student union management committees to chair – which is both a requirement and a bonus, because he needs workers for the campaign and scrutineers for the election day.

With thirty-two polling booths and a minimum of two people at each – so that they can give each other a break – he would need sixty-four volunteers, minimum. And they would need to apply for registration and be trained in their responsibilities.

He has also acquired his own used car with his father's assistance – a 2016 Holden Commodore, almost the last of that model off the production line. He now has his substantial Higher Education Contribution Scheme (HECS) debt; added to his almost equally high car obligation; with his reserves of savings mostly depleted – and no job.

At least his exam passes are confirmed. He will be graduating.

The Bay News articles and scoops have been faithfully written up by Ann and Stella. As expected, other local papers have picked up some of the themes – and the thirsty national newspapers have weighed in quickly, with the heavy-duty political commentators writing their strong opinion pieces back and forward.

Justin continues Frank's schedule of small face-to-face meetings across the whole electorate, demanding daily attention but without creating major incidents.

The Bible Belt has picked up the story about a secular Australia from his comments at a Lions meeting and they have invited him out to a Christian school hall, so that the small crowd could quiz him on his views.

He gives them his standard pitch about all legislation having to be based on evidence-based reasoning; rather than tradition, precedent or particular belief systems. They reply strongly with their beliefs and values which they are determined not to lose from the legislative structure of Australian society. While Justin accepts their right to lobby, he wants to hear their rational argument as to why their religion should be considered as special, especially when they would not accept any laws promoted from other belief systems.

The *we are a Christian country* mantra disregards the original inhabitants of the land and marginalises the many non-Christians. Even accepting the historical Judaeo-Christian basis for many of the customs and legal practices of current Australia, the decline in those identifying as Christian in progressive censuses might even undermine the premise of it actually being a predominately Christian country at the next census. But his listeners are far from convinced.

While he manages to extract some grudging concessions for his other policy platforms – such as a more respectful parliamentary process, balancing the books and looking after the needy in society – he leaves the gathering with no real feeling of having won them over. But, at least he has been to see them. They now know his face and treated him with respect. He has given a commitment to return to address them in the event that he is elected by the majority.

Frank has organised a meeting at a local mosque, as well. The Muslims prove to be just as respectful an audience of men and women as the other groups he has met. The leaders state that they appreciate his stance on tolerance of all belief systems and no isolation of any groups, particularly based on matters of birth or upbringing, over which people have no control.

Perhaps it is Justin's respectful way of speaking but everyone he speaks with listens and makes sensible suggestions, without any aggression. Indeed, the only hysteria, flashing like lightning bolts over his head, is coming from the media talking-heads, who are fomenting as much mischief, division and misinformation as they can.

Janet has suggested that they might just be trying to goad Justin into going on their channels – but, for his part, he merely watches and wonders at the lightshow going on. Like billy goats bashing their heads together, they seem to exhaust themselves. Esteemed newspaper commentators, such as David Styles from Melbourne, pick up on his social justice arguments; which are then rebutted almost immediately by Sydney's Gerard Nixon, who highlights the merits of the status quo and the spurious untried nature of student idealism.

Social media rips into all of them, while Frank patiently discards the trolls and responds to genuine queries by Twitter and the email trees.

As Zoe notes, 'Justin, you are in the pages of every national daily newspaper, on every six o'clock television bulletin and most of the political commentary sessions – and you never say a word to any of them. Your name is certainly out there. If the mantra of *any publicity is good publicity* is worth anything, then you are a national leader.'

The ever-cautious Frank even suggests that he should pick a show and at least go on to defend himself. 'You'll have to do it at some stage, won't you?'

'Not before the election,' Justin replies. 'This is not a reality TV show. I'm neither an elected representative nor a public official. There is no obligation for me to jump to their tunes. Let them thrash around for air like too many fish in a shrinking pond. Without nourishment from me, their efforts and the pond will just slowly evaporate away.'

Janet agrees. 'This is what we want, isn't it? All Justin's ideas being written about, dissected in public forums and argued about. Suddenly, policy ideas that no-one had been considering are now on the agenda of most politicians and experts. And Justin's name being mentioned everywhere is the unintended bonus.'

'And we are not having to pay for the advertising,' business-woman Zoe acknowledges. 'Pretty smart.'

Chapter 39

Brisbane

The ballot approaches

Frank has managed to get action from the Liberals about preferences – Brandon Jones clearly hadn't the influence he had indicated.

As campaign manager, Frank leads his presentation with a growing, confident professional polish to the polite aloof committee. They respond that Kipps' position on religion is a major stumbling block for them. They want to align themselves with the votes in the Bible Belt.

'Fine,' agrees Frank. 'So who do you put last? And then what order above that? We have seven candidates. If the Greens and Labor are at the bottom, how many of the other minor candidates would you put higher than Justin's platform?'

Both sides agree to put each other fourth on their tickets.

Frank and Justin come out, rubbing their hands in delight.

* * * *

Karen Porter phones Justin.

'Do you realise how much shit Frank is fielding for you, on Twitter and from the media?'

It's a wake-up call … because he hasn't realised.

Frank is like a big brother to him – always reliable, resolute and supportive, even when he doesn't agree with Justin's take; and that is quite often. Yes, he has taken Frank's confident organisation for granted.

The campaign is being run on a shoe-string – just as well they are all students or recent graduates because surviving on friendship has been a way of life for them all.

A fair number of donations have been received – often from surprising sources; money and offers in kind. Justin insists that the expenses of the campaign committee be dealt with first; the fundamentals like food, fuel, office support and some breaks. 'Fit your own oxygen mask before you try to help others.'

The tired committee seems appreciative and, anyway, they don't have the energy to argue. They all understand the scale of what they are trying to do.

Justin is fronting an ambitious foray into changing something that needs to change. He is the one with *The Manifesto* and the quiet public delivery that seems to defuse most anger.

Perhaps they subconsciously appreciate that his own sanity mechanism is always to ignore the television hysterics and the derisory newspaper opinion pieces, along the lines of, *He's not even old enough to know what he doesn't know and yet he wants to represent us. He'd last a week in the unforgiving maelstrom of adult politics.*

Justin understands – but perhaps without ever fully acknowledging – that it has been the strength of his housemate that has been protecting him, giving him the space to focus on the big picture, rather than the trolls and naysayers.

'Thanks for your call, Karen. Frank is a good man. I'll be more aware of having his back too – and giving him a break.'

And then he wonders why the call has come from Karen Porter.

* * * *

'Have you had much to do with Karen Porter, Frank?' he asks innocently.

'Yes. She's been doing a lot of the procedural research around all the fine print for training our volunteers. She has her father's legal logic and that has been a great help in filtering through the mass of Twitter comments and all that media flak.'

'Have they still been giving you a hard time? Do you need more help?'

Frank gives the sardonic dismissive laugh of the soldier in the trenches. 'The media demands are constant. They can't understand why you won't subject yourself to their grilling sessions – so they get pretty shitty when I stonewall them. And they are pissed off that *The Bay News* is selected for the scoops. Hey! It'll pass. Every day we're getting closer to the ballot. They're just wanting their chance to "diss" you. It's about their egos. They're important people in their own minds.'

'So, about the more help?'

'We've actually got heaps of people giving us a hand now – dozens really, all doing their bit for a tee-shirt and the cause. Oh, Zoe's got someone wanting to give us tee-shirts. Not bad, eh? So, yeh, we've got a lot of helpers now. Most of the queries want a response from you or from me, as campaign manager. So, we do have to monitor how the team replies and what they send out on the email trees. That has taken time; but basically they're all pretty sharp tech-savvy people. Karen and Zoe have led much of the training. They're good value.'

'Thanks, mate. I hadn't realised how much Karen had become involved. Sorry that I've not been across all this support you've been able to put in place. I just want you to know how much I appreciate what you've been doing – so quietly and capably – without me really realising how much work has been involved. I've probably not said that often enough – but I do mean it.'

'No worries, mate. You've been in the zone – and you've had to be. It's all working, Justin. The polls don't suggest that; but most of our feedback is really positive. Without putting a hex on things, I really sense that we're going to go a hell of lot better than people expect.'

'Okay. Please pass on my thanks to Zoe and all the others – apologise, from me, for my being off in my own world.'

'Sure. It'll be a lot worse if you actually do get elected. I hope you're thinking through that possibility. You can't flick the media so easily then – and they'll be gunning for you after all of this.'

* * * *

Frank and Zoe handle the preference discussions with the other three candidates over the phone and gain reasonable commitments, with only one putting the Libs above Justin.

With that order sorted, Janet advises that a generous donor from the Chinese meeting had volunteered to pay for the printing of the *How to Vote* cards. It was just a question of how many would actually be needed for an electorate of eighty-two thousand – because most could be sent out electronically on the email trees, text distribution lists, Twitter and Facebook. Cleverly, the donor suggested explanations in several languages on the back and he or she is happy to pay.

The planets are starting to align.

Some polling companies suggest that the Kipps' campaign might surprise a few people by attracting a small protest vote; while others state firmly that he has a snowball's chance in hell – but Justin lets all that speculation industry just wash over him and away.

'With these polls, it all depends on what questions are asked and how they are framed,' he explains to his sister, Jenny, as she is being swept along in the confusion of the contrasting certainties coming from the media forecast industry.

'Just because a respondent is in the right demographic and professes to vote in a particular way, doesn't set in stone how that person will vote on election day. It's chicken and egg stuff – how could you tell if the poll is pushing public opinion or reflecting it? The people being polled could easily be having a joke. I would, for sure. There's no requirement to tell the truth to social interviewers who are really just feeding the entertainment industry – might as well consult the stars, tea leaves or fortune tellers.'

The Electoral Commission's random order of candidates on the ballot paper has drawn the Greens' candidate at number one, with

Justin Kipps at two and the main competition of the Liberal Party at seven, last.

* * * *

As the day of the ballot comes closer, Justin becomes more peaceful. The processes are all in place. The endless meetings are coming to an end.

Over two hundred volunteers have been amassed by the co-ordinating team and they have all been issued with tee-shirts printed with 'Vote 1 Justin Kipps. Independent for Killen'.

It transpires that the tee-shirts have been donated by an old man called Giles. He'd made the offer of three hundred shirts to Zoe after the Rotary meeting. He gave his instructions as to what he recommended be written, suggested pale yellow for the colour and asked that the invoices be sent to him – with only a couple of shirts for himself.

And Justin? He feels like a giant cartoon octopus, overlooking the whole electorate, with all the arms extending out over houses, businesses, polling booths and a host of people, most of whom he has met in different forums over the past two months.

The hard yards have been done. There is no sense that any of the tentacles are about to be threatened. And all his vibes are serendipitous.

Really, that's the way he usually is. He's been so lucky to have such a supportive family – an unflappable logical father, an organised caring mother who chooses to worry on his behalf, a younger brother, Harry, who is so different from him that there is never any real competition between them, and Jenny, who knows her eldest brother is someone who would look after her – and she reciprocates by keeping him grounded in teenage developments.

Justin's school days had been okay – pretty routine. No complaints. The teachers were fine, generally encouraging. His fellow pupils got on well with him, or left him alone. He was an average touch player, better at tennis and squash. His forte was debating.

Study was rarely a significant challenge – just a number of hoops through which to jump or dive.

They elected him class captain regularly; and then school captain – but he was always conscious that these school years were simply a transition to something else – something more important. His results would have taken him into medicine and he had a mathematical-science bent. Then, at decision time, he realised that he didn't want to be dealing in blood, diseases or with people in trauma. He didn't want to study just to get a job, like engineering or the law or accountancy, like his father. He wanted just to become more aware about the world and the dynamics of people … for reasons that he didn't fully understand.

So, off to university, which had its bright moments – but, while the learning clarified a lot of his thoughts, it wasn't hard. He doubled up history and economics – greater volume to spark ideas. He tried the bridge club in deference to his mother, even chess. Then he got involved in student politics.

That, at least, gave him the type of cerebral activity he was yearning for. At last, he had cross-campus debates and deliberations. The contacts kept him in touch with the valued occasions when visiting public intellectuals gave presentations. He was a sponge for philosophical challenges.

That was when *The Manifesto* started to crystallise in his mind.

Frank and Graham seemed to click with him early. Through Frank, Zoe came onto the scene with her wiser worldly experience … and then he met Janet Chou at a seminar. It was never more than catching up for a coffee or bumping into each other at meetings or around – but she was easy company.

And now, she has shown a whole new dimension although there hasn't been either the time or the opportunity for a repetition of that beautiful night.

Chapter 40

Brisbane

Election night

The scrutineers have been trained in their rights and obligations. The Green Man Hotel is designated as the campaign base. The manager, Darryl Hope, is aptly named. He has become a strong promoter of the Kipps' nomination and its ideas.

As he said, 'Since that union meeting, with all that silly publicity down south, business has doubled.' Hope and business success make for a good combination.

He has made his main room available for three days before the ballot and the Sunday after – gratis. 'I'll put on some platters. But if your people eat and drink here, I won't be far out of pocket, if at all. And I want you to win. We can keep this going.'

With military precision and cut lunches, the trained scrutineers leave for their polling booths. There is an almost childish excitement in their eyes. How often does a fellow student stand for election to the federal parliament?

Their task will be particularly to observe the voting process, while their pale yellow tee-shirts and identity badges will advertise who they support. If any voter has forgotten how to vote, a quick glance at Justin's scrutineers would solve the problem. How wise and generous old Giles has been.

When the polls eventually close, they will have to watch any ballots that are rejected or, indeed, invalid votes that are being counted. Then the distribution of preferences will be crucial. Those extra second votes will be critical if Justin is to end up in the top two – a forlorn ambition, according to most.

* * * *

Justin casts his vote near his parents' Belmont home, in the west of the electorate.

One news channel grabs some footage but *the man of the moment* merely smiles at the out-thrust microphones with the comment, 'Later' – and they seem to understand. Everyone has a role to play in the theatre of election day.

The rules mean that he can't personally visit the polling booths, so he bases himself at campaign headquarters – doing any menial tasks required like coffee and sandwich provision; and also responding to social media – many from interstate and overseas, he guesses. It is then that he more fully understands what a massive task Frank, Zoe, Karen and the volunteers have been doing on his behalf.

* * * *

Home for a shower and change of clothes. Then back for the start of the count after the polls close at six o'clock.

Charles and Andrea Chou have supplied pale yellow bunting along with balloons with a huge helium gas bottle for inflation. Graham is the custodian, amusing all with his transformed high-pitched helium squeak and a huge *Justin Kipps for Canberra* banner.

Harry and Jenny seem to be major players in co-ordinating the many volunteers with ladders, string and sticky tape, transforming a standard hotel dining room into a festival of lemon anticipation.

Frank, Zoe, Karen and even Graham are taking regular calls on their mobiles, from the different booths. Darryl has erected two wide-screens linked into ABC and commercial TV channels.

Janet has a smart-board linked up to her computer. She is keeping her own scrutineer feedback tally; to be ahead of the professional commentators' projections on mainstream television – at least for the first few minutes of booth counts.

There is a quiet happy tension as the esteemed ABC psephologist, Laurie Black, starts his measured analysis of the early counting. He notes a swing away from the major parties – with a scale of movement that has not been generally predicted in most of the pre-election polling.

Indeed, as the first hour passes, the usually very careful Black is highlighting the high number of first preferences for the Independent, Justin Kipps.

The platters of food, which Justin's parents have donated, continue to be replenished, as the trickle of booth volunteers start to return to the campaign base – their shifts over. Jugs of amber fluid and water, along with glasses of red and white, lubricate the tension as one by one the booths send in their preliminary results.

By eight o'clock, Laurie Black predicts that Justin Kipps will get over thirty per cent of the primary votes, and with the published preferences of the other candidates, that might be close to toppling the Liberal dominance in the seat.

However, there is still an insufficient percentage of the votes counted in the big booths. As Black points out in his clinical manner, at previous elections those booths had provided strong major party support in the end. Likewise, the pre-polls and postal votes would be strongly for the major parties, particularly the Libs.

The commercial TV channels who have been denied their personal interest stories at the Kipps' family home – no amount of coaxing or bribing is going to have their family as part of the election circus – are now arriving in force at The Green Man Hotel. Darryl Hope is a happy man as his chefs and bar staff go into overdrive catering to the new hungry hordes.

Almost on cue, Justin takes his leave with Janet to one of the rooms provided for the purpose of sanctuary. There, they can quietly and calmly watch progress on the room monitor while Graham is the ready go-between, reporting on activities in the headquarters' hall.

Apparently – judging by the frenzied media interviews from the campaign's base room – there are many volunteers in yellow tee-shirts only too happy to share their extroverted enthusiasm and to let the country know how exciting this whole process is for a younger generation.

Their predictions range from quiet optimism to 'We'll kick butt'; with a fair smattering of 'Whatever the final count says, we have achieved something here today – and it may be the way of the future'.

By nine o'clock, it's becoming clear that the early trend towards Justin Kipps is continuing. While experienced political commentators struggle to understand this unanticipated seismic shift, the cool psephologist, Laurie Black, suggests that perhaps we are seeing the first Australian election which might be won on the influence of social media and on-the-ground meetings.

Shock jock, Dai Evans, is asked for an opinion and, with his usual grace, trumpets that this could only be a one-off and that Australian voters would rue the day they by-passed the mainstream media. He protests that the public has been misinformed and duped into voting for a patently unsuitable candidate.

The commercial stations cut away from his rant with back-tracking apologies that Dai Evans views are his own and not those of the TV channels.

At ten o'clock, Justin Kipps has thirty-eight per cent of the primary vote with sixty-five per cent of the ballots counted. Even the ultra-cautious Laurie Black is prepared to declare a win for the Independent candidate, when preferences are taken into account – given that Kipps is high on the tickets of most of his competitors.

The Libs are the only possible challenge and they are languishing at twenty-nine per cent of first preferences.

Their candidate, Don Finucane, speaks with dignity at their campaign base. Clearly, this has been a great setback for the party. He thanks, and apologises to, his supporters. By implication, he invokes the enormous loss that the death of Tony Maynard has been. 'But, it's still not an impossible task to win,' he states. 'The party will not concede until all the postal votes have been counted, checked and rechecked.'

* * * *

Meanwhile, the waves of change flood the TV commentaries from former politicians and experts. They have already given the win to Justin Kipps while acknowledging that the solid Finucane is just giving the party line, albeit gracefully.

The calls from the main room at The Green Man are reaching a crescendo – *Justin! Justin! Justin!*

The media are all poised and, at 10.24 pm, Justin Kipps at last stands on the decorated stage, microphone in hand, gently soothing the crowd as he has done throughout the campaign.

'Thank you. Thank you.' His amplified voice is controlled and quiet, under the circumstances. 'Voters of Killen, men and women of Australia, we won't know the final result tonight – there are many pre-polls and postals still to be counted – but, whatever the outcome, clearly the people of Killen have given an enormous vote of confidence for a change in the way politics should be conducted in this land.

'This has been a vote for economic, physical and social security; but also for a rejection of the cult of greed, of misinformation, of petty distractions and of divisiveness.

'Rather, the wise public actually get that it is actually about arithmetic, that we can be content with sufficiency, that the certainty of doubt is a quality to be admired and valued.

'It's about understanding that governments must raise revenue equitably, fairly – and that there needs to be common sense in the comparability of salaries and perks across this land.

'They appreciate that investment in the development and welfare of the people of Australia is not a cost to the nation. It's a long-term benefit.

'Access to free basic health care and needs-based education actually saves money for the country, over time.

'Quality bachelor university education in the key courses should be free to all Australians who can demonstrate the academic merit.

'It is about a safe Australia where persecution, marginalising, bullying and abusing are not acceptable.

'It is about accepting that we will get the government that we deserve – that *you*, the people, are in control. If the government's role is to provide the services implied in the Constitution, then the government is actually *us*, not them.

'Ripping off the government is ripping off *us*, not them.

'Boorish behaviour in public life is setting the example to *us*, not to some external *them*.

'If this election teaches us anything, it's that Australian electors appreciate being spoken to like adults – and not being addressed as if they were some ignorant mass who can be fed patently misleading information with the expectation than nothing can ever be changed in politics, other than the faces sitting on the parliamentary benches.

'This election has shown that people appreciate civilised discussion, reasoned debate, tolerance of other views and that they will not be hectored by people who believe they have the power to talk down, to reframe and to presume to know what is best for us all – when in reality, there are powerful vested interests controlling most of these mouthpieces and avenues of giving out information.

'The power of social media only exists because of the rejection of the quality of the alternatives.

'Now I have some very important *thank you*s to make. First to Frank Willis, my campaign manager, to Zoe McAllister ...'

* * * *

The TV coverage flicks back to the host commentators who appear stunned by the acceptance speech.

'What do you make of that, Laurie Black?'

'As Justin Kipps suggests, and as he has demonstrated by his win in Killen, it is time for many of those in positions of authority to rethink *same old, same old*.

Something significant has happened here tonight.'

* * * *

It is well after midnight when the crowds finally disperse. Darryl Hope's late licence has certainly been needed. He's even arranged courtesy buses to take people back out to each part of the electorate or to public transport hubs; and he has hired two security guards so that the remnant young casualties of campaign euphoria could sleep off their excitement in the safety of the main HQ room.

Sally Kipps had arrived in time for the speech. 'What an achievement, Justin. Well done! I wouldn't have believed this could happen when you started your blog. Just take care, though. Your world has changed.'

* * * *

Two hours later, she asks her son, 'Are you staying here or shall I drive you safely home?'

Frank and Zoe have one of Darryl's rooms. Janet has gone home, exhausted, with her parents. The other rooms have multiple snoring sleeping workers. Even the main room still has several dozen drained volunteers lying smilingly asleep, among the detritus of balloons, bunting and banners.

'Yes, Mum. Thanks. It's been a big night – and a big few weeks. Tomorrow and many tomorrows look as if they could be getting busy!'

As they move out to the car, Justin looks up at the starry sky. 'Do you hear anything?'

'It'll be a train somewhere. Sound carries at night.' Mothers are still allowed to talk to adult sons as if they know nothing. But Justin knows that what he's sensing is no train.

Chapter 41

Canberra

Detective frustration

Luke Dexter joined the police force in New South Wales and later in the ACT because he has an in-built sense of justice, of right and wrong … and he wants to serve the community.

He has dealt with being an early responder to scenes of crime, with fatal traffic accidents, with the trauma of violent domestic relationships … and always following due process in policing so that he can ensure the integrity of the evidence for later court cases.

He was selected for detective training and came second in his class at the AFP Training College.

Now he is out in the field and thoroughly enjoying being a regular offsider to Detective Sergeant Sarah Power. She has an encouraging way of guiding him through the on-the-ground skills necessary to solve complex criminal cases.

And here he is, right in the middle of trying to solve a tricky murder case when, to his absolute frustration, a blanket of national security has been dropped over their inquiry and the investigation has been taken out of their hands.

He has no doubt that his colleagues in AFP will do a good diligent job, following both due process and the evidence that he, Sarah, and their team have collected. The niggle comes from his suspicion about some hidden agenda, perhaps political or international, which might see their work just fade into the dust of the cold-case files.

Now, this evening, he is sitting in his humble, single-man's apartment in Belconnen – just walking distance from his base in the Winchester Police Centre – sipping a cool beer and listening to gentle *in the bar* background music through his iPod and speakers. Television is rarely on in his flat. Luke is a reader and a thinker, rather than a watcher – everything from historical biographies to classic detective writers through to thrillers and mysteries. He follows world events online, covering multiple sources and avoiding opinion dressed up as fact.

He is not a party-scene man. He plays tennis once a week – he has a fair B-grade game and is keen to join a local orienteering club, for the challenge of map reading, fitness and finding the markers in the bush. Also, these are places to meet people of like mind, who are busy with life but have the freshness to engage cheerily with people – perhaps even with a man who works in the often difficult hours of being a detective. Somehow, he seems to inhabit a world not compatible with the compromise of long-term relationships – short-term experiences have been fine but, always, the need to work in time-consuming situations has curtailed any longer term commitments.

Sarah Power, from his observation, might well be in a similar situation although she would be a dozen years older. She hasn't ever discussed her private life with him – why would she? – but she would appear to be a career policewoman. She has all the personality attributes to be a terrific partner for someone in life but she is also perhaps police commissioner material in the making.

Tomorrow is a day off for Luke and this is early evening. His mind turns to Adla Bello, working late hours supposedly as a catering assistant. He looks at his watch and wonders when she would set out.

On impulse, he decides to go for a drive over to Bruce. He knows where her apartment is. He is a private citizen, not at work … and he rolls past her apartment in his car to see a light still on in what would be her living room. He pulls in to the side of the road just to watch and ponder.

He is well-skilled in the theory of multi-vehicle surveillance methods but at this moment, he is sitting in his solitary grey Mitsubishi Lancer, listening as a simple member of the public to his quiet selection of iPod music.

At the back of his mind, he feels that ACT Policing has been dudded and that Adla Bello is not what she claims to be. He is not on the case anymore. He knows that. He is just interested in his community. Suddenly, the light goes off in Bello's apartment and then there is a flash of light from the front door opening and closing.

She will be going down to the basement garage to collect the white Mazda 3.

He waits with his eyes on the garage exit …

Sure enough, in a few minutes the car emerges and heads east through Lyneham onto the main arterial carriageway of Northbound Avenue.

Luke is three cars back as the Mazda heads south, through the City Circle, over the bridge towards Parliament House – round the State Circle, into Brisbane Avenue and then Canberra Avenue.

She is heading for Fyshwick, Dexter surmises. He draws closer in case he might lose her in the Fyshwick streets.

But she is driving on at a steady pace.

Dexter follows her at a discreet distance.

He watches as her car pulls up at the large door of a warehouse. At a toot of her horn, the door rolls up and the white car drives in.

Dexter cruises by. There is no signage on the door or the walls. It must be a very quiet catering company that Mario runs.

He circles the block and settles in to wait, with his eyes on the warehouse door. Five minutes later, a red car pulls up with a blonde female driver. Same procedure – a toot, the lifting door and the car driving in.

Ten minutes later, the door lifts again and a black Mercedes emerges. With the ambient light, Luke can see two men in the front seats and two women in the back – a blonde and the dark distinctive hairstyle of Adla Bello.

The car moves smoothly back out onto Canberra Avenue with Dexter again a few cars back. They are heading towards the round-about at Manuka Oval ... and then onwards into the leafy streets in the suburb of Forrest.

As Dexter follows at a distance, the black Mercedes disappears into the driveway of a secluded large house. He cruises by and checks it out on Google Earth on his phone.

Presumably, this is where Adla Bello and her companions will be *waiting on tables and delivering drinks* for the evening.

He settles in to wait, listen to music and to ponder the complexities of life.

* * * *

About three hours later, Luke Dexter has had enough.

His adventure has been a kind of therapy for him. In the morning, he will be a new man. And he'll have the day off from all the mystery solving.

As he moves to start the engine, a car starts to emerge from the *catering* house. It is not the Mercedes but it is black and large.

Decision made. He will follow it to see where some other participants at the party might be going.

Round the hill on Arthur's Circle and into Griffith. The large black car moves steadily and surely.

Murray Crescent into Evans Crescent ... the vehicle disappears with a left turn, through a gate into a row of trees.

Luke drives by but there are no signs to say what the place might be. A gate has just been closed by a man in dark clothes.

As before, he pulls in and checks his Google Earth ... it's a back entrance to the Embassy of the Russian Federation in Australia.

Chapter 42

Brisbane

Post election

It takes over a week for the returning officer to declare Justin Kipps as the official winner of the election for the seat of Killen. The tiny number of any remaining postal votes could make no difference to the final count. In the end, he beat the Liberal candidate with a primary vote of 37% which after preferences translated to 52%.

Laurie Black's analysis of the booth results suggests that perhaps the preferences from religious lobbies have flowed to the Libs rather than Kipps. Nonetheless, it is a significant victory for the young man, particularly since he has run as an Independent.

And, like the drunk arriving late and noisily to the party, Dai Evans continues to froth at the mouth about how ludicrous it is that an untried *whipper snapper* could be elected to a serious parliament on such a platform of nonsensical negativity. 'What sort of hopeful undergraduate frippery have those comatose Queensland voters believed?' And with no sense of irony in his tone, 'How could they fall for such a blatant distortion of all that is known to be true?'

His sycophantic fellow talk-hosts follow quickly with, 'He will be torn to shreds in Canberra and retreat into useless anonymity, licking his wounds'.

* * * *

To defray the avalanche of requests for an interview, Justin releases an only partially cynical statement.

'Thank you to the press and other media for all your kind wishes and statements of support.

'Given the closeness of the election to the Christmas break and the need to refine our approach for Canberra, I and my team will be honouring the festive season vacation and will be available for media access closer to parliament returning in the new year.

'Kind wishes to you all and may you have a refreshing time with family and friends.'

* * * *

Justin is keen not to lose his learning impetus. There's so much that he doesn't know and he certainly doesn't want to give Dai Evans the opportunity to exploit it.

When Ann Fletcher phones to congratulate him, she asks if the feeling is as good as he'd dreamed it would be. What is it about journalists, always wanting the touchy/feely impressions?

Channelling a former US Masters Golf champion, he replies, 'I didn't get this far in any of my dreams.'

And that just about sums it up. It has been a journey; heading in a direction – similar to an interview for a job with no real expectation of even being short-listed, let alone being selected.

Now, suddenly he *has* been chosen and the pot of gold is a glary indistinct image that he doesn't actually know nearly enough about.

And everyone still wants to claim fame by association. Brandon Jones appears out of the woodwork. 'So delighted in your success. Doubted that you could do it – but well done, anyway', and he doesn't offer his uncle or great-uncle to give advice.

Keeping busy, Justin bodgies up a header for correspondence – Justin Kipps, Member-Elect for Killen – and he writes personal letters of thanks to the Rotary Elder Giles; to the Chinese donor for the printing, to the clubs and community groups who had made him welcome – and, very deliberately, to those who haven't been his fans.

'Just good manners,' as his mother would say.

He handwrites notes of thanks to all of his campaign committee, personalising how each have contributed so well.

Then, he starts applying himself to the email and text trees as well as addressing the swathe of Twitter followers.

Ann and Stella publish his appreciation to all the electors of Killen as part of another story, featuring *The Bay News'* positive perspective on the enormity for democracy in a young local Independent winning in such a safe government seat.

Reflecting on the many pieces of advice he's been given in the campaign, he starts to refine his *manifesto*, so that it will be more representative of the views he's heard expressed at the meetings – and perhaps less of the naïve undergraduate idealism.

Within a day, he is getting feedback, because the givers of the advice have seen, and appear to be grateful for, his timely changes on the blog website.

He is stunned that his activities are being so closely watched. This is supportive feedback – they've been heard and acknowledged – but he'll need to be wary because others will also be watching.

That rumbling returns but disappears quickly with a shake of his head.

Hard-working, loyal Frank has needed a few days for recovery. Then, after some thought, he accepts Justin's offer to keep working for the cause – paid work this time. He isn't fussed about going down to Canberra but, yes, he will be happy to oversee the electoral office functions back in Killen, with the people he has already come to know so well.

Can he have a part-time role? The office could be manned by a receptionist with him being on call. He could defer some of his uni for a year to see how things go. He has never being overly bothered about being a lawyer – for a while, anyway – and the campaign work has been more exhilarating and satisfying than he'd expected.

Chapter 43

Canberra

New experience

There is so much to learn. Justin has no idea how much of an allowance he will get for an electoral office in Killen. Tony Maynard's office has always seemed well staffed – but perhaps party funds were going towards that.

But Frank doubts that Liberal funds would be used for anything except electioneering. He has become more hard-line through the experiences of the past weeks but his toughness is more about the political process than the actual politicking. He realises that he doesn't have Justin's flair for philosophising and persuasive charm. Horses for courses.

'The Canberra pollies will have set it up to have money to employ staff.'

'But,' Justin is doing his arithmetic, 'if you stay here in the electorate, I'll need people to assist me, when I'm in Canberra – help with the protocols, the media, reading the draft legislation, drafting changes to procedures or Bills, committees, listening to delegations … No?'

'Yes,' Frank agrees.

'And I'll need a sanity base back here too. I know what I want to do. I know the direction and the tactics. I know I can make a difference. The devil is in the detail though, as someone wise once said to me. There'll be a lot of snipers out there. You really have run cover for me very well through this campaign. I appreciate it more and more each day.'

'No worries. Just make it count down there in the big league.'

* * * *

The package arrives in the new year from the House of Representatives – all the information about who to see for security clearance, access cards, who would explain the procedures, where his seat would be in the chamber, where he could be based with the other cross-benchers, sitting dates, committees he could apply to be on, Comcars; allowances for travel, for Canberra accommodation, for electoral offices ... the list goes on and on.

'There's enough there to keep you out of mischief for months.' Frank laughs.

'Or in mischief. Not bad allowances after living as a student for so long. I'll be able to pay off my debts in a year.'

'Luckier than some, Justin. But I think you might be earning it. And you'll need to buy armour – to keep the enemies at bay.'

And he catches up with Janet again, picking her up in his flash 'new' 2016 Commodore. Yes, she will be happy to visit with him in Canberra, help him settle in – but she has another year of uni to complete back in Brisbane; that has to be her priority.

'We'll fly down for a few days – just to check it out; a holiday, on me.'

'Sure.'

Hey, they are just friends.

* * * *

Canberra Airport seems an impressive place – the corridors where all the politicians have been interviewed seem vaguely familiar, but there is no media scrum waiting for Justin and Janet; still basking in the luxury of anonymity.

The huge welded-wire statue of the athlete in the courtyard seems a metaphor for an enormous power that we should all be able to see through.

They collect their hire car – and it's off to the apartment they have booked for a couple of days.

There are tourist sites to see, a city to reconnoitre; cool beauty after the January heat of Queensland.

While Justin clears some of the early procedures for Parliament House security, access and allowances, Janet visits the National Portrait Gallery.

Together, they wander through the halls of Old Parliament House, laden with history; ghosts of past leaders and followers. Then, to the War Memorial – for a different style of leadership.

All too soon, they are flying back to Brisbane.

In a few days, Justin will make the long drive in the Commodore and his real Canberra experience will begin.

The House will be sitting in the second and fourth week of February. Then again in the first, third and fourth weeks of March. Sitting is scheduled to resume in May and June before the mid-year break.

In all, there will be twenty weeks which require Justin to be in Canberra for debates – but there will be other times for negotiations and access to the parliamentary staff.

Chapter 44

Canberra

Gordon, Simon and Bob

Being a by-election winner, Justin is the only new member as the members return to parliament. His induction is given by the Second Deputy Speaker – his seat in the House, protocols, procedures, the bells, roles of staff, copy of the standing orders, media, advice to keep his head down to watch and listen, the process for swearing-in, something of the current personalities, best places to eat, where suitable staff might be found.

He has rented an apartment for a couple of weeks – an expensive base but close to the parliamentary hub – until a more permanent arrangement can be made.

The other cross-benchers don't seem cross at all – wise people who know where the traps are and who offer to share support staff initially. Indeed, one of them, Gordon Milne from Victoria, has a spare room in his rental house, if Justin wishes to share.

It seems like a good idea for the new man in town. Nothing to lose.

Another good idea is organised by his new housemate, Gordon. He has taken it on his own initiative to invite two former NSW Independents to dinner – perhaps to give the newcomer some sense of solidarity and maybe a survival tip or two.

Simon and Bob have been through the hard times of trying to be heard from the cross-benches – indeed, just not to be ignored, while the government and Opposition players grandstand for the media and sidle up to grey-haired journalists.

'The first thing you'll get from the established members,' Simon notes sagely, 'will be that you are young and that these friendly old hands are here to help you understand how the place works.'

Bob interjects helpfully with a grin, 'That's code for *vote with us and we'll look after you* – not really, just that nothing negative will be shot in your direction.'

'You'll be their idea of a nonentity,' Simon continues. 'Tolerated. Applauded for a good Dorothy Dix question. Don't get us wrong, though, some of them are really nice and helpful, on both sides of the House. They can and will assist in getting your local items on the agenda.'

Bob grins again. 'But everything here has its own agenda. There is nothing offered without an expectation of a deal later. Be wary of any grand offers – expect the wolf in sheep's clothing.'

Justin sits quietly listening; wondering with sadness that these two former Independents still feel so bruised. But he's grateful they've been prepared to show him where the minefields are. 'So how did you get heard?'

Bob strokes his forehead, squeezing a painful idea out. 'From being a committee chair, first. You can be heard in those forums. I was dealing with the on-going water allocations and the Murray–Darling. That had been a bun fight with the states for over half-a-century. I got some respect for keeping that agenda moving forward. And then they listened to my other perspectives – you really have to build some respect and credibility. It won't be given automatically.'

'And the other way,' Simon adds, 'is to be bloody difficult. A smart-assed Whip came up to me with his saccharine smile to get my support for a motion. They actually needed me for some reason – people away on other business. I just grinned back at him – well, you could see him coming from a mile away – and he said that there was an easy way and hard way to do this. I waited for a few seconds and quietly replied, *Let's just do it the hard way.* His smile dropped like a tonne of spuds. Worth it, just to put him back in his box. They're drunk on it – all this power playing. You are an Independent. Never let them think that they have you sussed out. Your power comes from not blindly following the calf path – and not being predictable.'

'But another thing,' Simon adds. 'Your tactic of not talking to the media worked well up in Killen. I doubt it could work so well here. The machinery of politics here is not so easy to control.'

The host, Gordon Milne, nods in agreement. 'Either be bloody good or very careful. These media guys may appear to be self-important puppets but there's a lot of faceless power behind them. You'll be a target. In some ways, the media can be your friend – but you'll have to be very smart about it.'

'And watch out for the three-card trick,' Simon warns. 'The deal is done but the Bill presented is different in the fine print from the agreement you thought you'd made. They will try to play you for your inexperience.'

'But haven't we got the public service for advice?' Justin queries. 'Surely, we have to have some trust. They can't all be manipulative Sir Humphreys.'

'Most of them are good – and you do need good advice,' Bob adds. 'Share Gordon's people initially – and follow your principles. I'm afraid you'll need to use experienced people in this Canberra scene. Your Frank Willis might be great in Killen but it would take him too long to learn the traps here.'

'That's fine, Bob,' Justin agrees. 'Frank is happy to stay in Brisbane. I'll take your advice. You've lived in this place.'

Simon says, 'Yep, my strength was having an old media man, a broadcaster who understood the political juice. What committees do you want to be on?'

'With my experience, the only one I'm really passionate about is the Speaker's Panel. I want to be across all the standing orders and why they don't work. I want to make a difference to how the public sees Question Time and what passes for debate.'

'Good start – but they won't let you on that one. You don't have parliamentary experience. Try for the Procedures Committee.' Bob gives an encouraging thumbs-up. 'Oh! and watch out for the parties – the cocktail kind, especially the ones in hotels. Don't drink. Carry a glass as a prop. Tip half in a pot plant. Put it back on the table and do the same with another.'

Justin laughs. 'What a charade.'

'No, seriously,' Bob continues. 'It's not unknown for someone to slip a mickey in your drink and the next thing you know, you'll be waking up in a hotel corridor without your trousers on.'

'Or to a camera flashlight with a naked prostitute grinning beside you,' Simon adds. 'Oldest tricks in the book, just to give them leverage; to threaten embarrassment or disgrace if you don't comply with them.'

'I'm single, free – not much could embarrass me.'

'Not you, maybe … but your family and your supporters. Take your time and don't let them grind you down. They'll try. Gordon will look after you … or he'll answer to us.' Simon roars and beams a huge grin.

* * * *

'Mr Kipps, welcome to Canberra.' The media scrum is set up at the members' entrance – no way to avoid them. Justin feels confident but nervous, resplendent in his new business suit. Graham's standard comment comes to mind – *Flash as a rat with a gold tooth.*

The questions from the media mob come in a disorganised flurry.

'How do you feel on your first day? You'll be sworn-in soon – do you have a contingent down from Queensland?'

He does. Harry has travelled down with his mother – but he doesn't want to put them into the public eye. This is about getting the media agenda over onto policies rather than people.

'Thank you for your welcome.' His quiet voice seems to carry. They are checking their voice recording levels, as he continues. 'I feel honoured to be able to represent the people of Killen in *the House of the People.'*

The questions start immediately, like a pack trying to be first at the sales. 'You haven't spoken with the media before – why is that?'

'You're the youngest Independent elected to the House, how does that make you feel?'

'Any truth that you want *The Lord's Prayer* withdrawn from the start of business?'

Kipps calmly appears to ignore their blur of excitement. 'As you note, I'm not yet sworn-in. My interest is in good national policies, good quality concise debates and a high standard of integrity. I don't expect that I will be giving too many off-the-cuff opinions on this or any doorstep – but I do expect to engage with the media over time in quite deep analyses of issues. Just be patient if you would. Thank you. Now I must attend to getting sworn-in.'

'Will that be on the Bible?'

Another adds, 'Do you really want the prayer deleted from the start of business?'

A smiling Justin Kipps leaves the porcupine of thrusting microphones behind, as the swarm turns as one to look around for its next prey.

'First time I've heard his voice,' he hears from the reorienting mob behind, as he enters the building. 'Very cool for a newcomer.'

Chapter 45

Canberra

Luke Dexter

The summer break for Luke Dexter has involved him visiting his parents in Wagga Wagga, as well as a happy time with his elder sister with her husband and young family in Newcastle – time to practise his surfing and race along the beach with the children.

Work back in Canberra has been the usual run of break-ins. He did help his detective sergeant bring a small-scale protection racket to court. There were two sexual-assault investigations and a nasty hit-and-run. He is currently working through an embezzling case. But, there's always the niggling thought at the back of his mind about what is happening with the Desmond Wilson murder.

Who was Wilson? Why was he up in Canberra, from Melbourne for a month, with a *gratis* car, apartment and a flash wardrobe – paid for, allegedly by a representative of a Panamanian investment company? What, out of all that, led to him having a confrontation with presumably Stephanie Taylor, on the walkway above the Scrivener Dam – which then led to him falling to the spillway below?

And who was the Peter he was going to ring … or Mario or Ivan Jones? And where does Leo Clarke's courier company fit into the mix?

Luke was fascinated to follow some visitors at one of Adla Bello's functions as they led him back to the Russian Embassy. And he has tracked others too – apparently embassy-associated people from Kenya, the United States and the European Union Delegation, located almost opposite the US embassy.

What are all these people up to?

Luke has been over to Lyneham several times to find out if he could see the blue Toyota Camry or Stephanie Taylor at the address on her car registration but he saw no sign. Without authority to investigate, he can't do any more. Perhaps she has left town. Understandable.

At one stage, he asked Sarah Power if she had any information about how the Desmond Wilson investigation was progressing – only to be met with a disapproving look.

So now he's learning how to 'take his lumps', as Sarah expressed it.

Chapter 46

'Speaker, Members, Ladies and Gentlemen in the galleries.' Justin casts his eyes into the high seating.

They are all there; Mum, Dad, Harry and Jenny, along with Frank, Zoe, Janet and bloody Graham – good on him for giving up his footy training. He smiles and gives a thumbs-up in acknowledgement. And Karen Porter is there with Brandon Jones. And Darryl Hope from The Green Man Hotel. Goodness! What a surprise!

Is that Andrea and Charles Chou? Who is the old man sitting with them? It can't be. Is that Giles, from the Rotary Club meeting? Wow! Bloody wow! If there has been any doubt about the significance of this moment, there is none now. Justin gulps.

'Australia is a wonderful country – perhaps the best place in the world to live. But I feel as if we are on a train, rolling along a track which was well-laid decades before, in our Constitution. The main track is fine but there have been lots of movable points along the way where the train could travel off into sidings, or roll onto parallel rails, leave on spur routes or even get right off the rails. The skill of legislators is similar to that of the railway engineers – they keep the country moving forward, safely in the right direction without getting lost on the side issues.

'My manifesto has been well publicised through social media and analysed by many commentators since. It has three planks:

economic security, physical security and social security. I don't intend to revisit those ideas in this speech.

'Rather, I want to concentrate on politics and leadership.

'When I arrived in Canberra, someone asked me to look out for what is done well. Since I've been here, I have watched and listened – and I need to tell you that I doubt that we, in this place, actually do very much well.'

He can hear the rapid intake of breath along the green benches and up into the press gallery. He sees Ann and Stella up there – they must have obtained their special press accreditation to get in there – they will report what is said, without fear or favour.

'Fundamental to the train moving along the track is leadership – a sense of direction, a vision of where the train should head. Otherwise, we are all just passengers in carriages rolling to somewhere. We are obedient, unquestioning – because we trust the drivers. But, without our critical inquiries, the train could be heading for the edge of a cliff.

'In my view, political leadership requires a clarity of thought which should come from logical reasoning, not the influence of vested lobby groups or partisan ideologies.

'How we operate in these Houses is our current interpretation of what the founding fathers devised in the Australian Constitution. Those evolving standing orders and procedures may well have served the nation successfully in its history. But now, I fear, we're in tight carriages travelling along a track laid down by masked string-pullers and influencers who would sidetrack our prosperity and promise, into a dead end, for their short-term plunder.

'Look around. I am a newly elected Independent member delivering my maiden address to largely empty benches – there are more people in the galleries than on the floor. Why is that? Are they bored? Perhaps they are busy? Their research assistants will read what I say in Hansard anyway, to see if anything might threaten their comfortable status quo.

'I have to say that, while there are many well-meaning elected representatives in the parliament, the public perception that I hear comes from Question Time which is a theatrical cacophony of ill-disciplined point-scoring and hectoring. The juvenile smirks, nods and nudges just reinforce a public's despair at a train clearly heading down a siding to nowhere.

'The structure of debate is similar. Perhaps it worked in an era before smart phones and rapid electronic communication, where the words had to be expressed aloud and documented meticulously into the Hansard record. But today, few people speak in that repetitive self-serving rhetoric. The electing public deals in a couple of hundred character communications, economic transactions in nano-seconds and visual wit rather than the hackneyed puns of former years.

'Do we need the lengthy boring sermons or can we insist on concise speeches which cover all the salient points in two or three minutes?'

He glances up as a steady silent stream of suits suddenly slides discreetly through several doors onto the green benches.

'The point-scoring game has evolved from our adversarial structure – the two-party system where the team with the majority of elected members is the government and the unsuccessful team is the Opposition – except that now we have lots of cross-benchers – cross, in more ways than one, perhaps. The government and Opposition are whipped into their roles while the crossbench has freedom of thought and expression. How can it be, any longer, that partisan role-playing is a good model for developing clear legislation? The party machines have become puppeteers and the accountable elected representative are merely their marionettes. Isn't that the cart pulling the horse?'

The green benches are no longer empty. Faces stare at Justin Kipps, listening intently. Can it be the quiet gravitas in his voice? Or is it what he is saying? Or have whips been cracked?

'The Australian electors are no longer mindlessly choosing the members of one ideology over another. Now they are electing Independent people – members who can represent, listen and think for themselves.

'As someone new in this House, I ask, *Why can't ministers come from all sections of the parliament? Don't we want the most capable people irrespective of any party allegiances?*

'Apparently not! Because this is about *power,* about *the whiff of Ministerial leather* – as someone wise once noted. And the power is coming from those vested lobby groups who are content to see the train of government get off the main track and look after their particular interests, rather than the national good.

'I look forward to progressing strong arguments to reform the operations of this parliament so that the stultifying rules of operation no longer restrict the people, the nation, from getting a higher level of vision, of direction and of governing, than has been accepted in the recent past.

'Perhaps then, the general public who are the passengers on the train of state won't feel like passive prisoners, frightened to veer from the norm, because they are being peddled a song of futile hope – an illusion. They are not on the main track; they are being side-tracked by deceit, by greed and by false aspiration.

'As a nation, each of us needs to be content with sufficiency. There is no need for a greedy accumulation, especially at the expense of neighbours and fellow countrymen and women.

'We need to respect others and treat them with grace and dignity, no matter what their circumstances are. We need to be resolute in our expectation of moral honesty and we need independent policing of all corrupt practices.

'In short, we require and deserve a forward direction based not on dogma or ideology but on rationality, on the principles of science, of fact testing, of empirical challenging … and a humble climate which accepts the certainty of doubt rather than hubris of ignorance.

'I am hopeful for the future – but some hard decisions and widespread attitude modifications will be needed along the way.

'I conclude where I started; I am not sure that this parliament is actually doing very much well. But let's be clear – Australia is not in a bad way; in comparison to the rest of the world. Many good policies of previous administrations have set up this nation's success.

'But that doesn't mean that we should ignore the parts that we are not doing well. It is just that we seem to be marking time, looking after particular interests.

'The sooner we get beyond self-congratulatory power plays and tackle the real issues, the sooner parliament will regain the community respect and relevance which it so badly needs.

'Advance the fairness of Australia and then we all can truly rejoice that we are young and free. Our land does abound in nature's gifts. And we do want to make this Commonwealth of ours renowned of all the lands. We do have boundless plains to share. But, in the words of our own anthem, *With courage, let us all combine.* That is *all* of us, no matter where, when or to whom we were born. Let's keep the train on the track to somewhere better for the present and the future of this land. Thank you.'

* * * *

The applause roars from the galleries as they stand and shout approval. Like a waterfall, the sound rolls down onto the green benches, where the dark suits have stopped looking around for permission and, instead, stand in acclamation.

Almost before the excitement quietens with the Speaker back in control, the news websites have their headlines shooting out to smart phones and computer screens.

'Kipps didn't miss them!'

'Best maiden speech for decades'.

'At last, vision and decorum is on the agenda'.

'An Independent to be taken seriously'.

'A train to somewhere good'.

And then the Twittersphere lights up.

Chapter 47

Canberra

Michelle Beech

Michelle Beech possibly doesn't like being known as a highly-respected veteran journalist, but the title does have a certain cachet – earned over several decades of fearless, accurate political reporting in a range of press publications.

And yet she exudes a disarming charm towards her interviewee, Justin Kipps.

'Congratulations on a fine maiden speech – direct, to the point, consistent with your manifesto and brief. Ticks in lots of boxes.' She smiles for a response.

'Thank you.' The polite non-committal reply comes with a smile but no more words.

She nods, indicating that her quick brain might be re-calibrating her interview strategy. 'Okay. Throughout your election campaign you have refused interview opportunities with most of the mainstream media. Why was that, Justin?'

As he has planned, pre-interview, he is not going to rush into any answers, no matter how respected she is.

'Two main reasons, Michelle.' His voice is modulated, quiet, but carrying a self-assurance. 'One is the local focus and the other is quality control.

'I gave interviews to local ABC radio and to journalists at *Bay News*. Their articles and transcripts have been used by national mainstream media. My priority in the Killen election campaign was to speak as directly as possible to people in a range of social gatherings. They'd hear, straight from me, not through the filter of someone else's take on it.

'Secondly, with respect to quality control, put simply as a citizen of Australia, I am generally disappointed with the interviewing strategies being used at present. The style is *rule in or rule out, promise or deny* or *what do you say to the aggrieved?* or some superficial interest story about hobbies. I think that approach is mainly about the short media grabs; often it's to get the gotchya question or the chance to say, childlike, in the future, *but you said.*

'The reason I'm speaking to you today, Michelle, is due to the respect that I have for you as a professional journalist over many decades.'

Her expression gives nothing away. 'But you *have* used social media. You can't get much more short form than that?'

'The chronology of my campaign needs to be understood. I started by innocently placing a low-key manifesto on my blog site. It was Dai Evans and Pieter Goosens who stirred the social media to become irate at their over-the-top characterisations. All I've done is continue to use a medium which doesn't have obligations to any owners or editors. Social media may be harsh but it tends to self-regulate, in my experience.

'If I've been treated well to the present, I would like to think it is because I am speaking and writing about issues that are important to a lot of people. I think that there's a lot of disappointment out there at the way government policy is evolving and, indeed, the way the 24/7 media outlets are choosing to portray what *they* consider to be important. I'm shining a light on it. The criticisms of my manifesto and campaign have just taken the furore to a new level.'

'Media can be fickle, Justin. Social media has built you up, as you suggest. That could change and you could be just as easily knocked down.'

'Perhaps, Michelle. But my sense is that social media's self-regulation tends to sort out its own vindictiveness. And it deals in issues. Social media decides for itself what it considers to be the major concerns of the moment.'

Beech gives him an encouraging nod. 'An interesting take. Please continue.'

'Well, the social media escalation of my issues has enabled me, a student in significant debt for higher education and car purchase, to stand for election without going through the hoops of party pre-selection or being bankrolled by billionaires. That appears to have been something new.'

'With respect, Justin, to my question; it is still a short form of communication. Where is the depth in your policies?'

He gives a small gesture of the head, in acknowledgement. 'Good question. Okay. On any topic, we should be able to write a sentence, paragraph, a chapter or a book – depending on the depth of explanation. Two hundred and eighty characters can give a concise message – and we have tech-savvy generations who are receptive to the single sentence clarity of message. Is that not similar to your media headline, short report or essay?

'So, with respect to your question about depth, it will not be lost on anyone that I'm in my early twenties. I am not the government of this land. I don't profess to be a policy expert. But I have listened, watched and considered the political animal at work. By its nature, legislation is couched in legal terminology which, to the general public, is often less understandable than advanced *Klingon* language. Fundamentally, political speakers are very poor at getting messages across, simply. They speak in repetitive legalese which turns normal people off. Speech writers try to conjure media grabs to make them appeal to the masses. The end result is an insincere politico-speak, slogans and demeaning exhibitions of talking down to a public who are definitely over such pomposity.

'I try to speak in simple concepts deliberately; because, in essence, even the complex challenges of morality, economic or social policy are able to be expressed in a sentence or two. It can be the task of legal drafters and public policy strategists to work through the details and dichotomies, using the advice of the parliament committee stages. It's their expert work which should produce a fairly polished product that can be presented to the community and to the parliament for endorsement into the law of the land.'

'So, it's not your role to provide the detailed understanding in debate?' Beech's voice is quietly persistent; demanding.

'My role is to highlight the main issues. Then I should participate in the debate, like any other person, as a partner not as a dogmatic *expert*. I acknowledge the certainty of doubt. People should be able to discuss and move positions in deliberations, without the sensationalism of *backflip* or *broken promise* or being ridiculed for working through issues. I would think that flexible thinking is a mature asset, a virtue – not a weakness – demonstrating a willingness to listen and learn. Frankly, self-righteous rigid surety would rarely be other than mindless ideology and not the way to develop public policy for a complex inclusive nation.'

She makes a note. 'You've mentioned that you want to see Australia be a tolerant secular nation. Can you expand on that?'

'I have no problem at all with people following whatever belief systems they choose – and their differences deserve to be treated with community respect. I have no desire to see religious credo of any persuasion being able to determine the laws which govern all of us. My issue is that all legislation should stand the test of logical argument based on testable evidence.'

'So what about moral or ethical issues?'

'Religious dogma by its very nature is underpinned by an unquestioning belief. That is inconsistent with a legal system which examines evidence based on reason and rational compromise.

'For me, the only certainties in life are death and doubt – it would appear that even paying taxes is no longer a certainty for some.' He waits for the smile. 'Unless a premise is testable by logic, there can be no acknowledgement of doubt. For me, the scientific method and the rationality of the Enlightenment are about improving knowledge and understanding, by continuous scholarly examination – not by some blind concession to the infallibility of any particular belief system. That is a recipe for polarisation and power plays.'

'So, how will parliament decide moral issues, Justin, given that two-thirds of Australians professed in the last census to follow a Christian religion?'

'I think the figure was actually sixty-one per cent, Michelle – and it has fallen since the previous census. Perhaps, another way of looking at it is the corollary – how we currently *dodge* moral issues. The elephant in the room of all political and moral issues is that the world's population is past 7.5 billion and will be at 8 billion by 2025. That has tripled in your lifetime. The exploitation of finite resources, including physical space, is reaching a critical phase. That context trumps most other priorities.

'If a moral issue has to be seen through the lens of particular belief systems, which were developed when there was no population pressure, then no group decision could ever be reached – because the infallibility of religious belief or edict will stymie any discussion.

'As a country and a planet, we need to move beyond that ... or the alternatives are not pretty. I am an optimist. I've come to Canberra in the hope that I can influence a philosophical rather than religious approach to inclusive debate. And it has to be acknowledged that there are questions and concepts for which no-one yet has the answers.

'Those who choose to accept a greater overall meaning or theological power, to which only they have particular access, should be tolerated and respected, but that can't be used as an excuse to abdicate policy formulation to a nebulous spirit. That cannot be the basis of serious national direction.'

Beech smiles tolerantly. 'But it has been for centuries. Much of our law has been inherited from Judaeo-Christian religious traditions.'

'And now you have other Australian citizens suggesting different theological legal systems, such as Sharia, which logically is no more justifiable than the status quo. Yet, it is a fundamental underpinning of a world religious belief system. And then, what next?

There are many religious groupings in Australia – each is fervently believed by followers and simultaneously seen as weird by outsiders. Do we have to compromise with a bit from each? That is like the platypus being the committee attempt to make a duck.

'As soon as laws are based on any premise which cannot be argued rationally and be testable other than by reference to some infallible religious text, then immediately other religious groups become alienated. And over twenty percent of Australians profess to follow no religion and another twenty percent follow religions other than Christianity.

'That process is not a recipe for a harmonious society of people from multiple cultural backgrounds. I advocate the right of all citizens to peacefully follow the religion of their choice. We should be open-minded and unprejudiced. The alternative is a formula for one group dominating all others and then wondering why all the others feel marginalised. The French aristocracy didn't see the revolution coming, either.' Justin smiles at his interviewer's small nod.

Beech closes her notebook and stops the recorder with a conceding smile. 'Well, Mr Kipps, for such a relatively young man, you do indeed seem to have the ability to discuss topics in some depth. I wish you strength here in Canberra. However, controversial moral debates have not been well handled in the past. Indeed, they have polarised public opinion. Thank you for giving me the interview. I think I am flattered. My article will appear in the weekend papers. Doubtless, you'll get a myriad of questions after that.' She stands and shakes his hand. 'And it *was* a fine maiden speech.'

* * * *

As she leaves, Justin can hear it again. He shakes his head but the sensation doesn't pass.

Chapter 48

Brisbane

Twittersphere response

Howard Kipps is speaking calmly on ABC television.

'I am giving this brief statement on the independent public broadcaster, without any fee, because our son, Justin Kipps, the elected Member for Killen in federal parliament, has apparently made a mark in the capital.

'My wife and other children are not public officials and yet we have been fielding media requests really since before the election result was announced, asking such questions as, *What sort of family produces such an eloquent son who can be elected to parliament?* or *Are his views your views? Can you comment on your son's expressed opinion? How does it feel to be the family of the youngest Independent member of parliament?*

'Let me tell you that we are a very ordinary family who do all the normal things. Justin's achievements are a credit to him, personally. Naturally, we try to support him; but he is an adult following his own path in politics.

'So I would respectfully advise that we, as a family, do not wish to be interviewed or followed or photographed or featured in any media stories. I'd ask you to respect the same privacy as should be accorded to other uninvolved people in our country.'

* * * *

'Justin Kipps wants Sharia law to replace our current laws,' Dai Evans thunders on his talk-back program.

After twenty minutes of broadcasting his opinionated bile, a caller identifying herself as Michelle Beech comes on air.

'THE Michelle Beech? Well, Michelle, what an honour to have the doyenne of the Canberra press calling in. Thanks for spilling the beans on that lunatic Kipps and his plan for our laws.'

'Actually, Dai, I phoned to let your listeners know that you are totally misrepresenting what Justin Kipps told me – and that it's easy to read the correct version in my weekend article. You are fomenting lies, untruths and social mischief.'

'What? What are you saying? It was you, Michelle, who caught the young lout out. You got his real agenda. And well done too, I say.'

'Dai, tell your listeners that Justin Kipps is arguing for NO religion to affect our laws – that all people should have the right to peacefully follow their religious beliefs without fear or favour. It's the polar opposite of what you're saying. Recant, Dai. Apologise. You are spreading lies and misinformation.'

'Not at all. Miche–'

Beech's voice interrupts. 'Dai Evans, the legal papers will be with you and your station within the hour. You are misrepresenting the words I wrote. I don't appreciate that and I intend that you admit it or I will see you in court.'

Brrrrrr …

'Michelle's phone seems to have dropped out, listeners. Here's a bit of music until we see what has happened.'

And the Twittersphere lights up.

* * * *

The TV news headline is clear enough.

'Popular Sydney broadcaster, Dai Evans, has been suspended by his radio station while the substance of this morning's talk-back is investigated. Mr Evans was apparently making erroneous statements based on a weekend newspaper article by esteemed journalist,

Michelle Beech. We understand that legal papers have been served on Mr Evans and the radio station.

'This suspension follows the suspension of Pieter Goosens in Melbourne for his erroneous comments about Mr Kipps during the election lead-up. It is our unconfirmed advice that Mr Goosens will not be reinstated.

'We await the outcome of the investigation into Mr Evans' comments.'

Chapter 49

Canberra

Checking with base

Justin calls Frank in Brisbane and his old housemate's voice is comforting music to the ears – although the message is more annoying.

'We have been fielding Twitter comments all day – mostly in support of what you've done, I grant you. Our receptionist, Carol, is doing a good job – very hard to get her flustered. You know how to stir them, mate.'

'I've done nothing, Frank. It's Dai Evans again – whipping up every base emotion and grievance in society. I appreciate your hard work, mate. Have you and Carol been getting any help?'

'Sure, Zoe has been taking some time away from the day job and soon a horde of yellow tee-shirted volunteers will gather in the small dining room at The Green Man. They'll deal with getting messages out on the email trees. We can co-ordinate responses if we're all together in the one place. Darryl has been brilliant again in giving us the room. I'll be heading over there in an hour. Janet and Karen tell me they'll try to get there soon – ducking a few lectures.'

'We always knew this time would come, Frank. Isn't it great that so many volunteers are still rallying to the cause?'

'It's a battle for sure, Justin. And one worth winning. You keep at them down there and we'll look after this end for you till you get back.'

* * * *

Ann Fletcher texts her support and wonders if she can be of any use in getting the message out.

Chapter 50

Canberra

Mike Penberthy

Justin can't realistically dodge it much longer – and he doesn't want to anyway.

The redoubtable Mike Penberthy, now in his late sixties or perhaps even into his seventies, is the premier television interviewer of the past decades; reliable, trusted and perceptive. He is brought in to ask the hard questions; he is to television what Michelle Beech is to newspapers – and he wishes to interview Justin Kipps, live on air. Flattering to be asked by that quality of person. Not an offer to refuse, if the fledgling politician is fair dinkum.

Penberthy is a large man, bespectacled, with a few too many dinner meetings under his belt. But his manner is entirely professional.

He explains quickly, and once only, where the cameras will be and the cues that the crew will use. The make-up lady daubs a few more brushes of powder to conceal a bead of sweat.

The lights come on and the scene becomes even hotter.

Penberthy's early questions are routine – about *The Manifesto* and the response to the maiden speech. Then he asks about the controversy around Michelle Beech's article.

'Why do you think your views are creating such controversy?'

'I am challenging the status quo, Mike. I can only guess at the intent of Henry Parkes and Samuel Griffith in the late nineteenth century, as they conducted the referendums to put the Australian Constitution in place. But, as I read it, they wanted a process of parliamentary democracy with a House of freely-elected representatives and a balancing Senate to review legislation; a separation of powers with the judiciary being independent of the executive; freedom of religion; separate states with their own rights and obligations – a process for government of the people, by the people and for the people – with many built-in checks and balances.

'What I observe today, and what I have been speaking about, is a progressive erosion of many of these checks and balances; along with the respect and decorum which should be built into the debating processes. Democratic government has morphed into a political machine which manipulates and disenchants the public to the extent that they have tired of the rhetoric, the platitudes, the misrepresentations and, frankly, the loss of civilised courtesies in dealing with important matters. So some people, I would suggest, don't like that sort of appraisement. It seems to come, particularly, from those who believe that their power base is threatened.'

Penberthy's eyes lift behind his thick, studious lenses. 'Aren't you being simplistic? Parliament has always been a place of robust discussions and passionate views.'

'Perhaps. As everyone has been noting, I'm not as old as most in Canberra, but I think that the accepted behaviour of our elected representatives, as seen on the televised Question Time, is appalling. It wouldn't be tolerated in any other debating forum – and I *do* have experience at that.

'I suspect that the deterioration has just crept up on us. The standard of living in this country is the envy of most other places on the planet and we haven't had an invading attack on our shores since the Second World War. We have become spoilt and complacent with our good lot in life.'

Penberthy lights up at that. 'So if it's so good, what are you complaining about?'

'Its present state is only good by comparison to other places, whose economies are going backwards, who are swamped with the responsibility of caring for millions of refugees or ... they actually *are* at war.'

'You *are* being simplistic then – and ducking the obvious. We're doing okay.'

'No, Mike. It's an illusion of okay. The very skills, attitudes and vision which have got us to this point as a nation have been replaced by a focus on self-interest. In my manifesto, I wrote about being content with sufficiency. Now, we are not even content with *far too much* – it's a cult of greed. The comfortable complacency replaces any healthy doubt – opinion has taken on the form of expertise; and few are asking the questions about vision.

'In my maiden speech, I used the metaphor of a train rolling along a track. The Constitution set the path for the tracks over a century ago. The huge visionary projects, like the Snowy Mountains Scheme, are decades old. Where is the new vision? The concept of economic growth has not changed from the old plundering days of the colonies. A new concept of sustainable growth has to be the vision for the economists to work on.'

'All very nice and theoretical, Justin Kipps,' Penberthy goads further. 'But in the real world, Australia is punching well above its weight.'

Justin smiles at Penberthy's technique of not asking a question but rather making a statement and pausing for a reaction. 'Australia has made its fortune by exporting primary resources. And where is the future dividend from all that growing and quarrying? Our train has been parked in a complacent siding while the rest of the world has moved past and ahead.

'Norway used its oil reserves to create a sovereign fund which will support its new industries for a century ahead, at least. Much of the progressive Middle East is doing likewise, apart from the combat zones.

'Australia's resources have been processed in other countries while manufacturing has declined here. When we consider the physical and economic security in this land, Australia is now very poorly placed to resist crises – as the Global Financial Crisis demonstrated a few years ago.

'Mike, we're not well-placed for the future. We are complacent. We've had it good, unthreatened, for so long. The lucky country has become the selfish country. We have let the education of our population drift and we are fiddling round the edges of visionary leadership.'

Penberthy's expression hasn't changed. 'Like I said, aren't those all just generalised simplistic platitudes?'

'No, Mike. They are symptoms of a decline in the intellectual and political health of this nation. We have become resigned to the belief that nothing can change – that we are passengers in the train; that the political drivers must know best. My first point of attack in parliament is to lift the standard of real courtesy, debate, respect and intrinsic morality. If parliamentarians aren't the exemplars, who should be? Those who are paid most? The rock musicians or sportspeople? TV personalities or the CEOs of financial institutions? Do you take my point? It is time to look out for the social health of the nation – to give people hope in the integrity of the system, that the needy can be cared for, that people can get by with sufficient, that there is a standard of morality based around *a fair go* and *social justice*; that we can provide access for everyone to get a high-quality diverse education; that we don't need to frighten people into compliance but rather inspire them to a vision – a hope that we have a real sense of direction into the future.'

'You're sounding like an evangelist.'

'No again, Mike. An evangelist has certainty about the answers. I only have doubt – and I resolve that doubt by sharing the challenges with a thinking, educated public who are saying, *Stop the train. We are on the wrong track.* The readers of my blog get it and also the people I speak to face-to-face.

'Solving the problems of families, a nation and the world is far from being as simplistic as the self-congratulatory political commentators suggest – and yet it is not that complicated. It just depends on which lens you are looking through.

'The planks of my manifesto are to consider economic security, physical security and social security. The core of the problem is that a world population of 8 billion people by 2025 means that the divisor is increasing faster than the resources numerator. It is arithmetic. And, even then, wealth isn't spread evenly.

'The issue is not about some people being wealthy. I suspect the current revenue problem of Australia could be solved by a straightforward legislative approach to ensure that everyone pays their fair proportion of tax. We are a sovereign country. We are not at the beck and call of multinationals.'

'Okay. That sounds simple but it will meet with enormous resistance, I would imagine.' Penberthy raises his eyebrow in query.

'Mike, we hear lots of talk, rhetoric, hand-wringing, bold statements – but where is the action? It is lip-service – a salve to the public conscience. What they are doing is amoral while still being legal. We don't need more talk or more audits – we need to change the law. And that, actually, is not that complex. It is what parliaments do.'

'Alright.' Penberthy peers, as if satisfied that his quarry has put his thoughts out on air. 'One final question, you've been subjected to some quite personal attacks over the past few weeks, how are you handling that?'

'My goal is to see the standard of courtesies and discussion lifted out of the gutter and onto a higher plane – and I think it is achievable. I've received much more support than negativity – and the voters of Killen thought enough of me to elect me to parliament.'

'Well, Justin, you certainly have views. I can see how and why you have become such a bright star in the current parliamentary scene. Our viewers have had a chance to listen to you now. We will see how they will respond. I thank you for giving me – and us – your time.'

* * * *

Gordon Milne shakes his hand as he emerges from the media room. 'Bloody well done, Justin.'

Justin smiles absently back, his ear cocked to a sound. 'Thanks, Gordon. Do you hear anything?'

'Can't say I do. Probably air conditioning noise.'

'Yes.' Justin switches his focus back to his fellow crossbencher. 'That would be right.'

Chapter 51

Canberra

Sponsored mingle

The venue is the Eastchester Hotel in Braddon, Canberra.

Cabinet ministers appear to be mixing easily with shadow ministers, along with a host of backbenchers, crossbenchers, journalists and the heads of industry. It's the mining companies' opportunity to emphasise all the good that they are doing for Australia, through employment, training and infrastructure investments – despite the depressed state of the unit price for their products.

Justin stands close to Gordon Milne, carefully following Bob and Simon's advice – watch, listen and don't drink.

A subtle multi-media presentation is playing silently on the encircling huge screens – technology in the round. Michelle Beech is there. She smiles in recognition at Justin and moves over to pass some small talk.

'What happens next, Michelle?' Justin asks.

'You get educated on all the benefits of mining – at least from one side of the equation. You enjoy both.' She grins as she keeps moving. 'I'll circulate for a while.'

Images of turquoise sea and red-brown land merge with smiling Aboriginal faces, female dump-truck drivers and grinning drag line operators. Isn't it amazing how happy everyone is? This moves on to the mining towns with children rushing off to school, mothers settling back for a relaxing cold drink under lush tropical trees. Trains, kilometres long, snake through the ancient land to the jetties jutting far out to sea, where conveyor belts carry the valuable minerals to huge ships, juxtaposed with the continual images of turtles splashing playfully on the sparkling water … and the lighter-green reef with shoals of candy-coloured fish darting in a paradise of coral shapes.

'There's the Shadow Manager of Opposition Business,' Gordon gives a head point in the direction. 'I want to catch up with him. Do you want to come too or are you right on your own?'

'You go. I think I'll just keep watching the dynamics for a while longer. I'll catch up with you when the speeches start.'

* * * *

Gordon has scarcely merged into the crowd when a female voice whispers behind him. 'You must be Justin Kipps. I've heard so much about you.'

As he turns to see a stunning woman in her twenties; long dark hair which she flicks provocatively as she says, 'I'm Miranda. I'm with the RT-BMA consortium. How nice to meet you.' Her beaming smile, the aqua-and-tan silk cocktail dress and her welcoming manner are enticing. 'You have made such an impact on staid old Canberra. Oh, well done. But you haven't got a drink – white wine or red? Can't have you drinkless.'

'White please,' he replies by instinct.

'Back in a second. Don't go away.' And she disappears with a *wait-for-me* smile, towards the drinks table.

Within thirty seconds she is back, still smiling. 'So what do you think of the visuals?'

He assumes she is talking about the multi-media. He puts the glass to his lips, smiles, and then asks, 'So what's your role with the consortium?'

'HR. I love working with people. And I get to travel all round Australia with them, sorting out whatever their problems are.'

'Ah, a trouble shooter?'

'You could say that. It might get me into trouble sometimes too.' Almost with a wink. 'Are you here on your own?'

'I'm with Gordon Milne actually. I've arranged to catch up with the Opposition Manager of Business in a minute; but it has been really nice meeting you, Miranda. I hope to see you again after. Thanks for the drink.'

'Don't forget to drink it, then.' She gives an alluring smile and seems disappointed as Justin moves off into the crowd.

Bob and Simon's advice flashes through his mind followed by an image of himself trouserless in a corridor somewhere. Mind you, Miranda wouldn't be too hard to wake up beside.

He places the glass, untouched, on the table and keeps moving in search of new faces. A group of Liberal backbenchers are in a huddle. He remembers them coming up to congratulate him after his maiden speech.

With jocular jibes, they welcome him. 'Of course you can join us. What took you so long to realise?' He settles into a chat about the social circuit in Canberra.

'This is a city of circuits – London, State, Capital.'

'But this circuit can be more fun.' One of them gives a distinctive nudge and wink. 'No need to be stuck on the outer, just because you are on the crossbench. I think you're really a closet Liberal. Are you sure you're not?'

The laughter almost drowns the crump of someone falling hard to the ground and the sound of tinkling glass. Someone seems to have fainted at the drinks table. White-coated waiters rush to give support to the man who is repeating, 'Sorry. Gone all dizzy.'

Justin glances around to look for the aqua-and-tan dress but she is nowhere to be seen.

Anyway, with perfect timing the guest speaker arrives at the podium. His South African accent, Justin supposes, is intended to give a global credibility to the praise he is heaping on the Australian operations.

Then, his voice takes on a tone of dramatic dread; that the only thing that could change the steady waterfall of wealth to Australia would be if government regulations took away the flexibility to respond sympathetically to local needs.

Justin shakes his head in disbelief and mutters, 'Pathetic, rather than sympathetic.' But the others don't appear to have picked up his words. 'Got to keep circulating, fellows.'

He smiles farewell to the backbenchers and carries on round the room, looking partly for Gordon or whatever might catch his eye.

A Greens member who sat near him in the House is looking green in disgust at the speech. As Justin arrives, he asks, 'Why do we come to this rubbish?'

Kipps shrugs. 'To be seen. Free hospitality and then a taxi home.'

'Yeh. I think I've seen and heard about enough. Catch you later, Justin. You must have a stronger stomach than I have, to keep taking in all of this.'

And as if by magic, a woman's voice sounds from behind him – not Miranda but a more mature voice. He turns to see a woman in dark business dress, slim, jewelled and coiffed to impress. 'You wouldn't be Justin Kipps, would you? I'm so pleased to meet you in person.'

She might have been late thirties or even forty but she has a ready expensive smile for him. *Oh*, he thinks, *this must be what it's like to be important.* She is still talking, 'How are you finding Canberra? It can be a hard place to get to know initially.'

'Oh, I'm getting out and about a bit now. There are always good people to meet, I find. I didn't catch your name.'

'Natasha. Natasha de Marco. Multiple ancestry.' She laughs easily. 'I'm with the Italian embassy. Been here two years. That was a brilliant maiden speech you made. Well done. Do you find it a bit noisy here? We could escape out on the verandah, if you like, and chat. Goodness, you don't even have a drink.'

'I'm fine, Natasha. I'm just drinking in the atmosphere.'

She pouts as if disappointed. 'I'm not trying to mother you – only to be helpful, friendly. Can't I get you a drink?'

'You are helpful and friendly and it has been nice to meet you. Perhaps I'll see you again if the embassy attends many of these functions. I see my friend, Gordon, beckoning me. Have a pleasant evening.'

'Twice in half-an-hour, Gordon. Two very different types. Natasha and Miranda. Bob's advice was good.'

Gordon looks at him in askance.

'That man who fainted near the drinks table. I'd just placed my untouched glass there – given to me by a delightful Miranda in an aqua dress. I'm guessing that a mickey had been placed in the glass. The classy older lady wanted to get me a drink too.'

'Can you see either of them around now?'

As Justin scans the room, he shakes his head slowly. 'Not a sign. Maybe they weren't after me – just anyone.'

'That is naivety talking. This needs to be reported to the federal police. It's a serious offence to try to compromise a parliamentarian. Mind you, some of them don't need much help.' At least they both manage a grin. 'There will be an AFP man here, somewhere. They have to be around the Cabinet ministers.'

* * * *

Ten minutes later, they are in the hotel manager's office as the security tape is being played on the large monitor.

'That's Miranda.' Justin rises and points to a long-haired woman on the screen.

The AFP sergeant zooms in and saves the image. 'Good. What about the other one?'

Several minutes later, as the tapes play quickly on the screen, the elegant Natasha can be seen entering the room and scanning around; looking every bit like a confident embassy attaché. 'Stop. There.'

'This one?' The sergeant zooms in again and saves the image. 'Thank you. We'll get back to you on this. Are you heading home now?'

'Absolutely. Enough of being stalked for one evening.'

Chapter 52

Canberra

Peter Connell

There is a bite in Malcolm McGlashan's tone as he asks, 'What do you know about a drink spiking at the mining consortium function, Peter?'

'Nothing, Malcolm,' Connell replies. 'Who was the target?'

'Apparently, it was Justin Kipps.'

'Naw. We haven't touched anything to do with him since the Pieter Goosens business – and we had nothing to do with that either – well, nothing, directly.'

'So who was it, Peter? The AFP have identified two women hired from *High Class,* an escort agency in Fyshwick. People need official passes to get in to these functions.'

'Lively bait, at least. Someone in the promotional gig would have supplied the passes. Who has Kipps upset? Mining, business, religious interests?'

'Indeed. Who hasn't he upset? I'll have to meet with him. He's too much of a loose cannon … and he should be one of us, anyway. He fits the profile.'

'We've had nothing to do with women spiking his drinks, anyway. Absolutely not. We don't do that type of honey trap, Malcolm. I'm disappointed that you would think that. We just do detailed research into people's backgrounds. You should be looking at others … Gareth Dawes, for example. He works for the other side. No scruples.'

'Dawes, eh? I've heard his name on the grapevine. Okay, Peter. Sorry. But we need to woo Kipps, not fight with him.'

Chapter 53

Canberra

Rejection

To say that he is miffed is to underestimate the level of Kipps' *pissed-off-ness*. He has applied to be on the Speaker's Panel and the Procedures Committee – and has missed out on both.

Instead, he's been given Tax and Revenue, with the possibility of being on the Economics committee at a later date. *Might as well have me sucking eggs.*

The Honourable Speaker, Bruce Holt, has granted him some time in his ultra-plush chambers – designed to impress and intimidate. His manner is gently patronising. 'The Speaker's Panel needs people with significant parliamentary procedural experience, Mr Kipps. They help keep me on the straight and narrow with regard to the fine points of standing orders, protocols and the administration of the House. That's their role. Some stand in for me when the deputies are unavailable. It does need a thorough awareness of correct procedure.'

Kipps is politely sweet. 'I understand. I also applied to be on the Procedures Committee. Instead, I've been given Tax and Revenue.'

'The Procedures Committee is in really high demand and you have only been for a few weeks. I'm sure you appreciate the position. But I understood that you're very interested in Tax and Revenue. Isn't it part of your platform?'

'Indeed, it is. And I'm sure I'll find ways to contribute to the committee. My interest in being on the Procedures Committee is to learn about the fine points.'

'I'll bear that in mind for discussion when the committees have a vacancy.'

'Thank you. I also have a question about the standard operation of Question Time.' He watches the Speaker's owl-like eyes failing to look wise. 'Why is it that the main televised part of parliament is so often a cacophony of ill-mannered hectoring across the chamber?'

'Question Time has always been a boisterous session. Both sides tend to go hard at each other. We have to be careful not to deny free speech, don't we?' He gives a patronising smile.

'Mr Speaker, as I understand standing orders, you can warn and then dismiss members for a period of time, if they call out abusive comments.'

'There are gradations. Offensive comments must be withdrawn. If I tossed out all the interjectors, there would be no Opposition left to ask questions.' He grins at his observation.

Kipps responds. 'Perhaps, one of the reasons that political debate is held in such low esteem by the public comes from that extraordinary poor performance for a gathering of such national prestige. Shouldn't this chamber be the exemplar of debating performance?'

The patient forced smile returns. 'I understand your enthusiasm for changing things. You're young and you are new to the chamber. I suggest you take a little time to learn the established ways of the House.'

'I'll take your suggestion on board. If I wanted to see the procedures improved, what would be the best approach?'

'Usually, you would need the agreement of the main parties. They make most use of the questions and answers. Perhaps, you should have a meeting with the Leader of the House and the Manager of Opposition Business.'

'Thank you for your assistance.'

And Justin leaves with a very different plan in mind.

Chapter 54

Canberra
AFP office

Gordon and Justin sit quietly in the AFP office in Parliament House as the sergeant relays the results of their enquiries.

'Both Miranda and Natasha are highly paid prostitutes who have on occasion worked out of the *High Class* brothel in Fyshwick. Clearly, neither has worked in HR of a mining company nor for the Italian embassy. The guest at the party who collapsed at the table had imbibed a drug from a glass of wine.

'Following your description of the chronology, Mr Kipps, we would have to assume that the drug was intended for you. It appears that a room on the ground floor had been booked for the ladies' use.

'I assume that it was a sting to get you into a compromising position. Clearly, that is illegal. The women have skipped town. We'll pursue them. They'll turn up somewhere and we'll prosecute where we can – using the circumstantial evidence.'

'Who were they working for?'

'Not established. But they were hired by someone intending to manipulate you in some way. We will need to wait until we can interview them. And, even then …' He raises his upturned palms at the uncertainty of getting definitive information. 'My advice for you is to continue to anticipate repeats of such situations. You appear to be a threat to someone or some people who have money enough to set up that exercise. We will keep you under close watch to try to pre-empt problems arising.'

Chapter 55

Canberra

Malcolm McGlashan

'A casual friendly meeting to touch base,' is the way Malcolm McGlashan describes his invitation for Justin to visit the Liberal director's office in Barton.

Kipps is happy to accept.

A slim, well-groomed man, perhaps aged in his late thirties, wearing a white shirt, dress trousers and blue tie welcomes him. 'I am Liam Driscoll, Mr Kipps. I'm Mr McGlashan's deputy. Please come through and meet the federal director of the party.'

'I really think you are one of us.' McGlashan smiles in greeting and invites him to join him and Liam in a pot of tea.

Justin settles into a comfortable armchair for his *friendly meeting* with the two Liberal officers. 'I'm very Independent, Malcolm. My family would affirm that for you.'

'Your father is a company accountant and your mother was an executive secretary. Bastions of golf and bridge clubs. You were a debating champion at school. You are one of us.'

Justin ignores how the director might know that information. 'Your party only gave me fourth preference on your ticket.'

'It was *our* seat. You took it.'

Liam Driscoll smiles politely at his boss's humour but he is clearly present to listen to the new Member for Killen.

'The electors gave it to me. They were unhappy – but not with Don Finucane. He seems like a good man. They are unhappy about how politics works, here in Canberra.'

'I hear you. We got the message from Killen. What would it take for you to come over to us?'

'You want the list? I've just met with the Speaker to ask why I didn't get on any committee to do with parliamentary procedures. He told me to sit down and bide my time. Yet, the quality of Question Time and debate is woeful. I have pledged to the people in Killen to shine a light into a whole range of practices which do politics no credit. So, can you pull any strings to allow me to debate the standards of chamber behaviour?'

'Mmm.'

'Then, another thing – it seems to me it's not rocket science for the parliament of a sovereign country to pass laws that would make it a criminal offence for multinationals to shed assets offshore to avoid paying tax. It's a bit rich for the Treasurer to cry crocodile tears about declining revenue flow and the need for all other countries to come to the party. The parliament could legislate on this at the next session. It would be in place by the end of the financial year. It wouldn't even be a broken promise.'

Liam, the deputy director, is having trouble controlling an incredulous expression.

But Malcolm is all charm and grace. 'Mmm. It would have a huge reaction, though.'

'The question is whether or not your sponsors are more important than the nation.'

'What else?'

'Let's start small and just go with these two.'

Malcolm glances at his deputy, who rises as his boss says, 'I'll arrange a meeting with Hetty Fry. She is the Prime Minister's chief of staff. She has the PM's ear. Let's see what her view is. Good to meet with you, Justin.'

Chapter 56

Sydney
Dai Evans

Every television and radio station is covering it.

Dai Evans has called a press conference to apologise to Michelle Beech and his listeners; and to Justin Kipps.

Insiders are saying that this is part of the out-of-court settlement of the legal case. The barristers and ACMA – the Australian Communications and Media Authority – had apparently demanded it – or Evans could take his chances with the judicial process.

But no-one can actually believe that Dai Evans would really eat humble pie. He has never done so in the past.

'I want to give a sincere apology to Michelle Beech, to you our listeners and to … Ju–Jus–Justin Kipps. The information I used on my talk-back show was incorrect. In future, I'll be careful to abide by the directions of my radio station with respect to verifying facts and not being cavalier with interpretations.

'I really don't know what came over me. Perhaps, it was misguided frustration with the way the country might be going.' He gulps. 'I am sorry. There, I've said it.'

He looks at the camera, perhaps expecting some acknowledgement of his magnanimity. Receiving none, he announces, 'And, as a gesture of good faith, I'll donate $250,000 to three charities of Michelle Beech's choice.'

As Justin watches the screen, he can't help but wonder at how Dai Evans could even consider projecting himself as a victim – but that is how he's trying to come across. Blind Freddy can see that the fine is no spontaneous gesture of atonement but a requirement of the threatened court settlement.

Nevertheless, it might pull his head in for a month or so. The money would be a drop in the ocean to him.

Chapter 57

It has all the appearances of a friendly meeting of colleagues. Senior Sergeant George Buckley has driven across from AFP Headquarters in the Edmund Barton Building to have a chat with Detective Sergeant Sarah Power in her Belconnen office. They have known each other for several years from previous postings and courses.

But George Buckley gets straight to the point.

'Sarah, are you aware that your detective constable has been watching people that might have been involved in the Desmond Wilson case?'

'When?'

'Over the past few weeks … since the case was transferred over to us.'

'How do you know, George?'

'We've seen his Mitsubishi Lancer and we have photographic evidence.'

'Really. When has this been happening? He's either been on holiday or working with me.'

'Oh, this is happening in his time off. In the evenings. Just sitting in his car observing. That's not illegal – just very unwise in the circumstances. Sarah, this has the potential to be a very sensitive case. Warn your man off, please. He could be getting in the way of stake-outs and operations.'

'I'll certainly speak with him … and explain the rules. I don't suppose there is anything you're able to share with me about progress with the case, confidentially? Luke Dexter and I were very close to it at the time.'

'There is nothing that I can share, Sarah, except to strongly request that your constable desist his surveillance activities immediately … lest more severe action be precipitated.'

* * * *

After the AFP man leaves, Sarah Power sits back to reflect. She's surprised at the allegation – but not really disappointed. She likes Luke Dexter's fire, his commitment to a moral society, and he has lots of potential as an analytical detective. He has a good ability to link clues into hypotheses based on evidence … and he has an aversion to any hint of manipulating the processes of justice.

She likes too that she can see many of her own characteristics mirrored in him. The reason that she's kept her discreet USB copy of their observations at Desmond Wilson's apartment is because she has an uneasy feeling about the whole business. Why does someone who is, to all intents and purposes a strong-man enforcer, have actual, or good counterfeit, access passes to select private parties?

Why has someone funded his apartment, car and accessories through a courier company in Fyshwick? What was he expected to do in return?

Why was he murdered and tossed over the Scrivener Dam? And, if it was a woman who did the deed, what sort of woman has the physical and emotional ability to carry that out?

If ASIO is involved, should she be thinking there are dangerous agents from other countries involved?

She's had a relaxing festive season break with her most recent, steady companion in life – Greg Edwards, a partner in a Canberra legal firm. A few years older than her, Greg has an unflappable nature and a sense of confidentiality that Sarah admires and feels comfortable with. Some of his work revolves round witness protection – the legal representation under the Witness Protection

Act – but his more public profile is in corporate crime … fraud, in particular.

But more than all that, and as well as the physical attraction, Greg gives her a sanctuary environment where he understands her need to unwind and be distracted from the responsibilities of her work.

Now, she is wondering about Luke Dexter's support environment. She knows he plays tennis and will start orienteering when the weather cools a bit. But, apart from that, he likes reading and music. He has never mentioned a partner.

In the business of criminal investigations, all detectives need *to fix their own oxygen masks* before trying to help others.

Chapter 58

Canberra

Labor Party

Doug Henderson is the head of Labor Party administrative presence in Canberra. Ironically, the office is in Sydney Avenue – but there has to be levity somewhere in the place.

Gordon Milne has set up the informal meeting for Justin.

'We got you elected,' is Henderson's opening gambit. 'You got in on Labor preferences.'

'And so I should have. You need me to shake things up here,' is Kipps' brash reply.

The grins are a reasonable start. 'What can we do for you?' Henderson asks.

'I'm new to town, Doug, and I have lots of way-out ideas – some will be practical, others will be for wonderland. I'm not a Labor man but we share common ground around many social justice issues – *the fair go*, free universities, Medicare and accessible disability care, for example.

'But it seems to me that politics is just two rams bashing heads together – and nothing for the good of the country is getting done. I want to tidy up Question Time and get some quality debate going at other times. So, first, I'm looking for Labor support if I bring a private member's Bill.'

Doug Henderson shivers as if to clear his head but keeps listening.

'Then, I'm looking for a new way to appoint Cabinet ministers. We've bloody nearly got a hung parliament again – hung by incompetence. Yet, you have at least four of the best Cabinet ministers sitting cooling their heels on the Opposition benches. Why couldn't we have a system where the government chooses the best people for the Cabinet, irrespective of their party allegiances?'

'You're right. This is not just wonderland. You need to be in an asylum.'

'Doug, they do that in the United States – a very different system, I know, but at least it gets the best financier in charge of the budget and a qualified military person as defence minister or its equivalent. Why can't something different work here?'

'Pheew! Where do I start? In the Labor Party, caucus chooses who will be in Cabinet and the Prime Minister doles out the portfolios.'

'Well, how brilliant is that, Doug? You'll get a plumber in charge of farms, an electrician overseeing the Treasury and a union man running defence.'

'Don't be too harsh. The Lib system might look cleaner but it isn't. The men behind McGlashan instruct him on who will be Cabinet ministers. And, do you think they'd share anything with us? Pig's bum. Then there's Cabinet confidentiality. How could one of our people not disclose to caucus that Cabinet has decided to close a shipyard? It can't work.'

'Well, what about an Independent being a Cabinet minister, if he or she was properly qualified? That would rule out most of your objections.'

'In theory, hypothetically, it could work. But could you honestly see an ambitious Liberal, or one of ours I suppose, giving up a chance to be a minister to let an Independent take the spot? Dream on!'

'I don't think there should be a barrier to that, Doug. That would be discrimination.'

'I'm speaking about the real world, Justin.'

'Well, perhaps the real world needs to be less about personal ambition and more about the country's best leadership. So,' Justin grins at his stunned host, 'will you support me to tidy up the rules around political debate?'

'In principle. We would need to see the fine print. But less obstructionism would be an improvement.'

'Absolutely, Doug. Don't give up on the other thought either.'

Chapter 59

Canberra

Power and Dexter

It is just after 6 am. Both Sarah Power and Luke Dexter are having an early start to work with the promise of an early knock-off time. Ostensibly, they are finishing off paperwork and taking time to talk … *to fix their own oxygen masks* … before the demands of the day take over.

'Luke, have you let that Desmond Wilson business go now? It has been quite a few weeks since we handed that over to the AFP.'

'Why do you ask, Sarah? Is it still on your mind?'

'You'll recall that I gave you a clear instruction that we were off the case?'

'Sarah, spell out what is concerning you.'

'Have you been involved in surveillance of the people or places in that case?'

'I may have driven around a few spots – a bit like Adla Bello's excuse for driving late at night to help her get to sleep. It's been in my time off. I've neither used nor accessed any police resources. I'm just an interested citizen.'

'Well, your interest has been noticed by our AFP colleagues. They've noted your car and they have photographs of you watching. You could be compromising their operations either by warning potential suspects or getting in the way of the surveillance that they are clearly also carrying out … in line with their officially endorsed brief.'

Luke Dexter says nothing. He watches calmly, waiting for his detective sergeant's next comment.

'I had a visit from the AFP requesting in strong terms that you cease your observing activities.'

'I see.' Luke pauses. 'Have I being doing anything illegal? Or have I been in breach of police protocol?'

'No, to the former. Yes, to the latter. The case has been passed to the AFP.'

'So, if I was a journalist or a private investigator I would just be carrying out a normal role.'

'But, Luke, you are not a private citizen, nor a journalist nor a private investigator. You have had access to police information which has given you an unusual interest in the case.'

Luke sits still again. 'I see.' There's another long pause of more than a minute. 'We both know that there's something wrong with the case. I will back off, out of respect for you … but I hope this case will be resolved in accordance with the laws and practices of this land.'

It's Sarah Power's turn to sit quietly, before saying, 'Thank you, Luke. You could be right. I trust our AFP colleagues but, clearly, there are other influences at play. Our police roles can at times be different from our instincts. We know nothing more officially. Did you see anything different from that?'

Luke Dexter smiles and pauses. 'Sarah, I read widely – history, non-fiction analyses of the secret world of spies … right back to Roman times. Cicero had an interesting technique in the Roman Senate to avoid appearing to say anything official. So I won't tell you that I followed Adla Bello to a rendezvous in Fyshwick where she, along with another woman and two men, left to visit a very private residence behind high hedges in Forrest. They were not dressed as caterers.

'And I won't tell you that a car left that same party some three hours later and I followed it all the way back to the Russian Embassy.

'Nor will I tell you that I've observed that same Fyshwick *catering* vehicle more than once engaged with similar activities involving multiple people from the US embassy, the European Union Delegation and the Kenyan High Commission ... in the time since we've been taken off the case.'

Sarah Power grins at her detective's way of expressing himself. 'And you're not telling me that you could think they were embassy staff, are you?'

'I'm not telling you that ... nor that they could just as easily be privileged visitors of embassies, to be looked after just like Leo Clarke had to look after Desmond Wilson. No, I am not telling you that ... or that there are others in this business – not just Adla Bello and Leo Clarke. There's at least one other group that is *catering* for these visitors. But I can't watch them all. I can tell you that some of the *caterers* seem to come from a place called *High Class* in Fyshwick. I won't tell you that it's an escort agency – with multi-ethnic services.'

Sarah laughs this time. 'Good. I'm pleased you're not telling me that.'

'Indeed, I certainly won't tell you how I followed the legendary caterer, Mario, in either of his two vehicles – a black Mercedes or a dark-brown Nissan Navara ute – or give you their registration number plates.

'And I won't tell you that Stephanie Taylor seems to have gone to ground. There's been no activity that I've noticed around her Lyneham home.

'So I wouldn't tell you that it's no wonder that ASIO might be interested. As to why, I couldn't possibly surmise.'

He pauses to note that Sarah Power's expression has become very serious, before he says, 'Alright. I won't waste my spare time wondering about the case. But I'll keep my powder dry just in case something should come to light in another case at a future date.'

'A wise move, Luke. And I'm glad you didn't tell me if you observed anything.' She breaks into a grin again. 'Now back to the present.' Her phone is beeping and she looks at the screen 'Right! So much for the paperwork and time to chat – we're on the move. We have a burglary, just in, with the owner tied up and abused; over on the southside – in Hughes. Uniforms are on their way there. That'll keep our brains busy along with all the other cases on the books. Let's go. You drive.'

Chapter 60

Brisbane

Janet

It's a relief for Justin to drive back into Brisbane from Canberra after two months of sitting days in parliament. A chance to catch up with all the people who had supported him in winning Killen – and to return as promised, to a range of groups, to give feedback on what he had found in Canberra.

But it doesn't take long for the first disappointment to bite. The phone call to Janet is deflating.

'I want to move on, Justin.' She is matter-of-fact. 'You're living in a different world from where we were.'

'I haven't changed.'

'Then maybe I have. I'm a uni student with another year to go. I need someone near me, beside me; happy and positive; to talk to – not a person away in Canberra. And I don't want the notoriety that comes from being close to high-level politics. It scares me.'

He pauses to absorb both the information and the tone. 'Okay. Fair enough. I'm afraid I'm committed to Canberra for at least a couple of years. Naturally, I respect your view. I'm sorry. I really am. It's been great while it lasted. Thanks for that.'

'I'll still support the cause, Justin. You're a good man … and I really like you. I just need to move on – for me.'

'Okay. I understand. I respect your wish. Take care. Give my regards to your parents for me – and I'll see you around.'

Understanding is one thing; emotion is another.

It's dawning on Justin that political partners must be a special breed – the long absences and the playing second-fiddle to the needs of the electorate; the public commodity when it suits, the necessary social appendage for community functions, the sense of completeness for the image makers. Clearly, that's not for everyone.

* * * *

Frank's reaction is immediate. 'Someone has got to her.'

'No, Frank. I believe her. Sad though it is, this is just the normal cycle of relationships. Things have moved on, for her.'

'Have it your way – but I think someone has sowed a seed. Along the lines of *Do you want to be pestered because you are Justin's friend?* She'll remember the stalking, the shock jocks, and think that none of that is worth it. Sorry, mate. I thought you were both a good item in the making. But, as you say, it's time for you to move on.'

'Yeh. Right. So what is pressing on the agenda back here?'

'Lots of requests to meet with you. Everyone wants a piece of the new Member for Killen. Maybe the hardest one will the people from the Bible Belt. They want a *discussion group* – their words – around your secular Australia ideas.'

Justin shrugs in agreement. 'I said I would go back to them, if I was elected. Let's do it – and soon. Bite the bullet. I need a distraction. Catch them before they have too much time to get organised.'

'Oh, they'll always be organised. That's what they've been doing since you went to Canberra. My advice is not to go to any of these functions alone. You are the elected member now. You can't afford to be misrepresented, without anyone able to speak in your defence.'

'We'll record the thing on the phone.'

'Mate, you still need someone physically with you – *they* need to know that you have someone there, who can say, *No, this is what was said*, and back up any recording. Now, that sort of shindig is not my scene – high passions and no rational answers that would satisfy them. Normally, I would have suggested Janet but now ...'

'Zoe?'

'Naw. She's given enough pro bono to the cause. She has her own work to think about. Karen Porter has been doing some good things with us, recently. She's keen and she's got a good legal brain, logical, fair … What do think?'

'Yes. She was in at the start. Would she want to sit through that argy bargy?'

'Maybe she would. Her father's a barrister, remember. She's probably starting out on the same trajectory. I can ask her for you?'

Chapter 61

Brisbane
Bible Belt

The notion of a secular society seems to have caused consternation in the Bible Belt. What is the place of religion – Christian religion in particular – in the current political space?

Karen Porter agrees to accompany Justin into the lion's den – indeed she seems to be relishing the prospect. Dressed like a businesswoman, with her neat dark hair, blue eyes, shoulder bag, high heels and dark suit – she looks like a high-quality, in-control adornment for the new Member for Killen.

There are about fifty in the group, seated in a semi-circle with a place for Justin, facing them at the focal point. Karen sits discreetly on the end of a front row as the discussion starts with the preliminaries of needing to know where Christianity sits in Justin's representative thinking.

Eventually, a Bible-holding lady in the front row decides to ask the question that they've all been waiting for.

'Mr Kipps, I don't know if you are an atheist or an agnostic – but you certainly talk the language of the secularist. I have the view, perhaps like many in the room, that secularists suffer from self-delusion. They seem to think – you among them – that if religion vacates the space in political life or they remove religion from social discourse, then some benign vacuum will have been created where everything will be just and fair. Is that your position?'

Justin glances across at Karen, who has a trace of a questioning grin behind her distractingly well-designed glasses. She tactfully chooses to look down at her notebook as if waiting to jot down the main points of the reply.

'Thank you for the question and your perspective.' Justin's mellow tones still seem to have their effect – or maybe this audience is just used to listening intently. 'No, that is not what I am arguing. I accept that religion has a valuable role in some people's lives – perhaps for many people. It's a normal human need.

'A thinking person is always trying to find ways to explain the complexities of the universe in which we live; to fill the gaps which science has yet to find theories to test.

'To me, the religions of the world appear very diverse and, to an outsider looking in, some can appear quite weird.

'As a member of parliament and as a person, I respect everyone's right to believe in the religion of their choice. Indeed, a strong faith may well be a contributor to the mental health of many.

'So, be clear, I respect your right to follow your faith. But there are many faiths in Australia ... even in this electorate. At the last census, sixty-one per cent of the whole population identified as being part of the umbrella of Christianity.

'My argument is that government policy shouldn't be decided because of someone's – or anyone's – infallible interpretation of an ancient theological text. That denies the rights of the rest of the population and their choice to doubt.

'Christianity has been in a favoured position of privilege in the deliberations of Australia since Federation; and possibly long before. In 1911, ninety-six per cent of the census still identified as being broadly Christian. But, in other parts of the world, Islam or Hinduism or Buddhism held sway, as similarly privileged groups. They still do.

'So, to your question of creating *a benign vacuum*, I think you said. I am not suggesting that people of religion should have no say in the politics of the land. Everyone is entitled to have a view and to make it heard, in a democracy. All that I am saying is that government legislation must be determined on the basis of reasoning and testable evidence. Make your case, argue the point, persuade others – by all means – but neither the argument nor the justification can be what the Bible says or the Quran says or the Torah says or any other tenet of the range of faiths.'

Justin pauses to search the intense eyes of his audience, to ensure that his points have been understood. Satisfied, he continues:

'Discussions of ethics and morality are always fraught. I have no problem with people of religious conviction being significant parts of every ethical debate, but they have to argue it logically. That's all. For example, is all life sacred?

'Why?

'Are all people born equal? Patently they are not.

'Is euthanasia an honourable choice for a terminally-ill person to die with dignity – or should the deceased's friends and relatives be left behind as social pariahs, accused of complicity in murder?

'Is abortion the right of a woman to decide? Whose choice, then, is it to conceive?

'Is a long life better than a shorter life with quality?

'Is it right that the rate of mothers dying in childbirth is over three hundred times higher in Central Africa than in Australia?'

Justin's eyes scan every woman in the room, in particular, as his quiet questions keep coming.

'Is it right to put replacement parts, like hearts, into some people, to give them a longer life? What is the basis for deciding who should get priority?

'Is it right to wage a war against criminals who enslave, rape, torture and murder others – sometimes in the name of religion? Where has God been in any or all of these decisions?'

The Bible-holding lady looks around the group for someone else to answer. A balding man takes up the discussion.

'You have made a lot of points there, Mr Kipps. Perhaps our view is the way that Christ suggested would be a good moral position for the nation – the course we have chosen to follow. We have ideas to offer for government directions.'

'I agree with you,' Justin replies quickly. 'Your ideas are welcome. And, not surprisingly, the other faiths make similar points and claims. Is that alright with you all? Because I meet with them too – and ask them the same questions.'

The uncomfortable shuffling is broken. 'Our way has stood the test of time. It is a proven way of peace.'

'Sir, I'm a history graduate. All religions claim that; and yet over the centuries, different doctrines of Christianity have been used as the excuse for conflict, abuse, torture and death – not least in the Inquisitions. Likewise, at different points in history, other peaceful religions have been hi-jacked by criminal gangs who want to be in power over others. I wouldn't insult your clear intelligence by cataloguing even the most recent examples.

'But your suggestion of a test is an excellent one – not necessarily time, but perhaps a caring, responsible way to move forward as a society.'

'So,' the balding man is back asking the questions. 'Do you want religions to compete for political recognition?'

'No, I don't. I want ideas to be debated – particularly in how they could be absorbed into the laws of the land. Think back to the ethical questions that I've just mentioned.'

A lady with pale-blue eyes and fair hair asserts, 'But there have to be some absolutes. *Thou shalt not kill* comes from the Ten Commandments – Christian writings. What's wrong with that?'

'Nothing. It is the law of the land, except in certain medical-ethical situations such as people on life support or when police or the defence forces have to defend the innocent. My point is that the idea should be argued on its merit – not because it's part of this religion's text. If the concept is good, it can stand logical scrutiny.'

A man at the back asks, 'You mentioned *all life is sacred*. That has been part of United Nations Human Rights Declarations and Declarations of Independence, for centuries. Clearly, many civilised countries have seen the idea as good, for a long time?'

'Indeed. But what does that mean?'

'Are you joking? It means that all life is sacred.'

'That's what I wanted to establish. So you include *all* life – cattle at the abattoir, fish caught in nets, vegetables and grains. The definition of life can be broad – and for some that is what is meant.'

'You are splitting hairs. It means human life.'

'How sacred then is the high mortality rate of mothers in childbirth through much of the developing world? The African woman doesn't always see a pregnancy as a matter for joy but rather as another likely foot in the grave. There are a lot of shades of grey in all these ethical questions, aren't there?'

'But we are talking about general principles for living properly.'

'Exactly, and the laws of the land should reflect general principles, rather than specific doctrines. As I have indicated, the twenty per cent of the Australian population who follow religions other than Christianity also have their own specific beliefs. I have heard them tell me – but the laws need to cater for you all.

'Likewise, another twenty per cent follow no religion. They would not want to be bound by the specifics of your beliefs; or any other groups who have registered as a religion – and some of them have bizarre suggestions. So the laws need to be general principles which try not to impinge on most religious freedoms, while disallowing those for which no rational argument can be forwarded.

'For example, in some cultures, women have far fewer rights than here in Australia. You couldn't use the Bible to reject that argument – nor indeed many other religious texts – because there are many biblical references to the inferior position of women. No! The improvements in the emancipation of women in our society have been argued logically on the grounds of equality: think of the right to vote, the right to work, to have equal pay, to have maternity leave, the right not to be abused or raped in marriage. These are not religious rights.

'Likewise, discussions on the concept of marriage mean different things to particular groups – and have evolved through history. Traditionally, from my history studies, it was an alliance – an economic transaction and arrangements between families with dominant and subservient roles – honour and obey.

'In modern society, such relationships are more commonly about love, about choosing one's own partner … and in many forms. Churches choose to have such ceremonies witnessed and pledged before God – but huge numbers of others are conducted in secular ceremonies by marriage celebrants – civil unions.

'Perhaps the question to ask is about general principles. Does a different interpretation of marriage devalue your concept of marriage or your practices? Why *should* any one group presume to know what is best for everyone else?

'If you think that, argue the case and accept the general principles of law on a logical decision of what is best for an inclusive tolerant society.'

The Bible-carrying woman then asks, 'So, will you represent *our* views in parliament?'

'Absolutely – along with the arguments from every other religious group in Killen. Then parliament will make its collective decisions based on testable evidence and reason. Now, the argument that I heard here earlier, that particular practices have stood the test of time; that is tangible evidence, documented – not necessarily to the exclusion of other arguments, however, but still sound evidence.'

The woman nods, as if tumblers are falling into place.

The man at the back casts his eye round a now quietened group. He has the bearing of someone in charge, as he responds. 'Okay. I think we get you now. Perhaps we should break for a cuppa and mingle with Mr Kipps and his friend Ms Porter.

'While we are all together, can I just say *thank you* to Mr Kipps. You promised that you would come back to us and you have. I think we see the process you're suggesting – where you're coming from, as a member of parliament – and how we can express our views.'

* * * *

Karen gives a conceding grin in the car going back to her home. 'You handled that better than I expected, Justin. I thought there would have been fireworks but there is something about the way you speak to people, in groups like that, that seems to defuse the tension.'

Justin grins back. 'I actually like these types of discussions. They all have strong personal beliefs; but they're not stupid. Given a bit of space to think, they get the bigger picture – even if it is a bit unpalatable at times for them. None of this conscience stuff is easy for anyone. Maybe your legal brain can get your head round the subtleties of drafting legislation to keep most people happy – and still be about *a fair go.*'

'You're an interesting man, Justin. You seem to have come a long way in a few months.'

Chapter 62

Brisbane

Jack Carew

Graham is picked, coming off the bench, for the A-team at the league ground and Justin has arrived to see his friend in action.

Immediately recognised, however, one of the Board members invites him up to the exclusive verandah for a better view and the chance for a few select constituents to have his ear. This seems to be how life now has to be for him – blending the watching of his friend play football with the full-time job of a politician. Maybe Janet has been closer to the mark than he wishes to admit.

'Jack Carew, Justin,' the American thrusts out a large hand. 'Real pleased to meet you. The Club Board has been looking after me tremendously since I arrived. Chance to see your type of football – mad to be charging at each other without any decent padding.'

Justin takes the intake of breath as the opportunity for him to speak.

'Pleased to meet you too, Mr Carew. What are doing over here …?'

'Naw, call me Jack, Justin. I'm vice president of Galveston Enterprises,' he announces and seems to think it necessary to add, 'Named after my home town. We're in oil, gas, pipelines, tankers. I'm really here to talk transport logistics and gas development with my good friends at the port here in Brisbane and some others up the coastline.'

'Very good. And I'm glad you've had the chance to get a break here at the football.'

'Jeez, yes, Justin. Your Board chair at this club is also on the Board at the port. It has all worked well.' He pauses. 'I hope you don't mind me saying but you seem mighty young to be representing the people in Congress – sorry, your parliament.'

'You wouldn't have been the first to say that, Jack. Our system allows any adult to apply as a candidate. Then it needs a majority of the people to elect him or her to Canberra.'

'Well, that's a mighty fine achievement. It couldn't happen in our country. You just couldn't afford the campaign costs.' He stops and looks at the flow of play on the field. 'Your players don't get much time to rest out there. It just keeps going all the time.'

'That's why we have the replacements on the bench. See number 14? He's a friend of mine. He should be getting his first chance to play at this level later in the game.'

'But you've hardly any people on the bench.'

'Multi-skilled fit people, Jack.'

'You Aussies. You are different.' He pauses again and lowers his loud voice to a whisper. 'I wondered if I might have a quiet word in your ear while we sit here?'

'Sure.'

'My people tell me that you're on a bandwagon to hit companies like mine for extra tax. Would that be right?'

'If you mean that I'm advocating for companies to pay a fair level of tax on their profits earned in this country, then you're right.'

'Well, you see Justin, you're a long way away from anywhere, here in Australia. One of the benefits of trading down here is that companies are allowed to spread their profits across all the international branches of their corporations. It's all quite legal.'

'Oh, I know it's legal, Jack. I don't know that it's very ethical however – which is why I'm proposing to get the laws changed to prevent that happening.'

'Naw, Justin, you're young.' His shakes his big bear head in disbelief. 'You probably don't understand how international business works. My task – my first duty – as a Board member is to look after the interests of my shareholders – the people who have invested in our companies–'

Justin holds up his hand to interrupt the flow. 'Oh, I understand that, Jack. I have a degree in economics. It's just that with you looking after your shareholders, you are dissing the lives of all these people down below us there.' He points at the cheering crowd. 'See them? Their lives are being screwed harder and harder to make your wealthy investors even wealthier.'

'But that's the way of the world, Justin. We are just one huge supermarket of trading goods – and some people have to manage the business, take the risks, plan the future; while others work at the checkouts or filling the orders. That's how the world works.'

'I agree. That's how it is working. But it's not sustainable – either from a global economic stance or from a social viewpoint. You would live in a big Galveston mansion, wouldn't you, Jack?'

'Oh, I have a few – busy life: Galveston, Bahamas, New York, Paris, you know.'

'I'd guessed.' Justin is smiling, although he surmises that the American might be thinking that it is a gesture of support. How wrong could the big Yank be? 'These people, cheering down there, Jack … they don't have multiple homes or even own their first homes – and when you shift your tax requirements offshore, they have to pay more to maintain this government's revenue. They can't afford it – and they are subsidising the lifestyle of you and your shareholders.'

'Justin, there will always be people who worked hard for a mansion and those who will rent trailers. I never stop working. Never have. It's our ethic–'

Justin raises his hand again. 'Look, Graham is coming out now.'

'He's your friend, eh? Where's he from?'

'New South Wales.'

It takes less than a minute before, 'Hey, he's not bad.' Graham has just taken the ball as second receiver, side-stepped two large forwards and sent the ball swinging out to the winger.

'Yes. He's come a long way. We met at university. Graham grew up in poverty – not of his choosing – and he is making his way forward with energy and talent.'

'Good on him, Justin. That's exactly what I was saying. Hard work is the way to go.'

Graham has the ball again and his deceptively fast footwork flashes him past two defenders, over the line for a try and a giant leap into the air in joy.

'Hey! That's just magic,' Jack shouts. 'How'd he do that? That's crazily good.'

Justin smiles in reply. 'Jack, back to your tax. Where I'm coming from, if you pay the correct tax on the money you earn in Australia, then more Grahams will be able to contribute to this land.'

'But it must have been Graham's hard work that got him here. That's ma point.'

'And mine is, your mansions are not needed by your shareholders. Be content with sufficiency. Don't condemn more people here to trailer parks, as you put it.'

'But – *you're* still not getting it, Justin – that's the way the world is. Take away the legal tax minimisation then the companies will go where they can get what they want.'

'No. With all respect, that is how the world has been. You are an astute man, Jack. The mining companies will not walk away from their investment and their ready supply of resources. If they did, the Australian coal, iron and gas would just stay in the ground for some company to mine in the future. Is that what you think will happen with the world population expanding? The changes are coming. The days of plundering with impunity – because that's what this is, if you don't pay fair tax – these times are fast coming to an end. If you can't see that, you'll be like the French aristocracy before the revolution.' Justin likes that line – it always seems to pull people up short. 'That didn't end too prettily for those who weren't watching. Do you want to be in the start of the change; to have an influence? If you don't, you'll be shut out – not the other way round.

The Australian public will not allow the Grahams of this world to be paying the bills that you should be paying.'

'Well, you sure are a straight shooter, Justin. We like that in Texas. We know where we stand, at least. But you're not in charge here.' He grins across his overly chubby cheeks and then he winks. 'An Independent is not in government.'

'As I said, Jack, you're not a silly man. You've done your homework on me. You know they were all saying the same thing before I stood for parliament – but they don't say that now. I shine a light onto dodgy practices – and I share it on social media. These *legal* tax minimisation schemes are on their way out – and pretty fast as the rorts become common knowledge around the world. You know as well as I do that company directors work within the framework of community expectations. You blow that, you blow it all. Do you want me to give you a list going back decades of when huge multinationals have ignored public opinion? Like you said, if America is a supermarket and your public stops buying, then you make no money. Right?'

'Your Graham is on the ball again.' Jack points to another slicing run.

'He won't be just on the bench next week. Smart selectors can see when change has to come.'

'It's been good listening to you, Justin. I think we'll have to agree to differ though – but that's just business. I hope your assessment of the future is wrong – but, in case it's not, here's my card. I have influence. Call me if you need.'

'No problem. Too easy. Let's enjoy the game now.'

'You are different.'

'So I'm told.'

Chapter 63

Canberra

Burglary

The burglary is at the house of a Gareth Dawes in the suburb of Hughes. The uniformed patrol meets Detective Sergeant Sarah Power and Detective Constable Luke Dexter as they arrive at the scene. There's an ambulance team on site looking after a shaken-up crying lady and, in an adjacent room, the owner is getting wounds to his torso dressed.

The uniformed senior constable explains, 'We were called to a burglary with the owner injured and tied up. The call came from a cleaner at 6 am. That's her over there – Alice Fox. She cleans here, twice a week. She has her own key and individual pass-code to the security system.'

Sarah Power looks over to a female constable helping the woman with a glass of water and comforting words.

The uniformed constable continues. 'We found the owner in the living room. He'd been tied with gaffer tape and gagged. The cleaner cut him free. He was partially undressed and in pain from burns to his stomach and even lower. He's pretty exhausted from his ordeal. He's been trying to free himself for hours. He hasn't told us much. We called you at Criminal Investigations immediately.'

'Thanks. Forensics?'

'We put a call into the station to warn them they'd be needed … it's early … and a call for medical help. The rest is waiting your assessment.'

'Okay. Thanks. We'll contact forensics and let them know what we need.' Sarah nods to Luke Dexter, who has his phone at the ready. 'Can we meet the owner now please?'

They go into the living room where ambulance officers are attending to the needs of a man in his forties to early fifties, black hair with a fashionable dart of grey above the ears. His shirt is unbuttoned and the fly of his trousers is also open as the ambulance people apply dressings down the middle of his torso. He has dressings on his wrists and cream around his mouth and on his cheeks.

Sarah does the introductions as the ambulance team step back. She asks the injured man, 'Can you tell us who you are and what happened?'

The man is clearly very tired and in pain. 'Gareth Dawes. This is my place.' He gasps and winces at a pain under the dressings. 'Got mugged in the driveway and forced in here. About 10 o'clock last night. I was coming back from a meeting. There were at least three of them – they blindfolded me and tied me up. They wanted the combination for the safe and the keys to the filing cabinet which I keep in the safe.'

Tears are flowing from his eyes. 'They burned my guts with cigarettes and told me they'd keep burning down until my genitals were gone.' He slumps lower. 'I had to tell them. I imagine they've cleaned out the safe and the filing cabinet. They left me gagged and bound. I've been here all fucking night just wearing myself out trying to get out of the gaffer tape. Alice came in on her key and found me and phoned you.'

'Thanks, Mr Dawes. Can you tell us what was in the safe?'

'Just business stuff.'

'What business are you in?'

'Research. Investigations. I am licensed in NSW but operate here.'

'Any jewels or money in the safe?'

'Some. Not much.'

'We'll need a list of what's missing … in time. Did you know any of the men – they were all men, were they?'

'It was late. They had balaclavas and then they blindfolded me.'

'What about their voices?'

'Definitely male. One had a bit of an accent – you know, European.'

'Did they speak English all the time?'

'The one giving the instructions did.'

'Did they mention any names?'

'I don't think so.'

'You have a security system here?'

'Yes. Two. But I had to switch the main one off when they brought me in.'

'Where did you do that?'

'Key pad at the door.'

'Do you have sensors or CCTV in here?'

'Yes.' He points to the open office door. 'All linked into the main system – even remote viewing. But they smashed it with a hammer. I heard them laughing as they did it. I don't know if anything can be retrieved.'

'You said two systems?'

'The other one only has outside cameras.'

'Did they smash it too?'

His eyes brighten. 'Maybe not. It's in the wardrobe in my bedroom. I'm getting dizz …' He faints backwards almost as he says the words.

Sarah calls the ambos in. 'He's out. He needs to get to hospital. Thanks. The cleaner too – just give us a minute with her.'

And to Luke. 'Let's speak to Alice now. Are forensics on their way?'

At Luke's affirming nod, Sarah sits beside the sobbing woman. 'Hi Alice. I'm Detective Sergeant Sarah Power. We're sorry you have arrived to such a scene. When did you get here?'

'I clean for Mr Dawes twice a week. I come at six in the morning. I don't usually disturb him, unless he is up and about. It was such a shock to see him all tied up and writhing. I pulled the tape off his mouth – he was all burnt and undressed. I called 000. Mr Dawes asked me to cut the tape on his wrists and ankles. He is in so much pain.'

'Thanks, Alice. Did everything look normal outside when you arrived?'

'Yes. I didn't notice anything unusual. I just came in quietly like I usually do.'

'Have you worked for Mr Dawes for long?'

'Two years now, two mornings a week. He is a good man. Always pays. Always polite.'

Sarah nods. 'Did you go anywhere else in the house?'

'Oh no. Mr Dawes managed to get to the office door but he screamed and fell in the doorway. He's in a lot pain. So sad. They were so cruel to him.'

'Thanks, Alice. The ambulance will take you with Mr Dawes to the hospital now – to check that you are okay. Do you have anyone who can meet you there?'

'My daughter. Can I ring her now? I didn't want to do the wrong thing.'

* * * *

Gloved and with cover-alls on their feet, Sarah and Luke move slowly through the quiet house, observing and taking photographs.

In the office, the safe door stands open and the filing cabinet, key still in the lock, has empty drawers slid open. In a recess built into the wall unit – it would have been concealed behind a sliding panel normally – the remnants of the master security unit appears smashed as Gareth Dawes has described.

The forensics unit arrive just as the detectives prepare to move upstairs. After they are briefed, Sarah and Luke take the technical specialist up to the bedroom. There in the wardrobe, under hanging garments, is an apparently intact second security system with a small monitor attached. Presumably, Gareth Dawes could check on outside visitors from the safety of his bedroom.

The technician nods that it appears to work.

'Try 10 pm last night.'

The screen bursts into green pictures showing the mugging just as Dawes had described. Three, presumably men, hooded and prepared, had immobilised the arriving Dawes in seconds and bundled him inside the house.

'Go back 30 minutes, please. See if we can see them arriving.'

As the images flicker by on fast backward, a ute arrives in the street at 9.42 pm. Then, after watching for a few seconds, it enters the driveway to disgorge three dark shapes with their faces already hooded.

Then the ute backs out and pulls away up the street.

'Okay. That's how they arrived. Can you zoom with this set-up?'

'A little, maybe,' the technician replies.

'I'm after the make of the ute along with the registration and/or any shots of the driver's face.'

The technician plays with the controls.

'Bingo! There's the registration plate.' He points. 'It's a Nissan Navara ute. I know the model. The driver isn't clear.'

Sarah Power turns to her companion. 'Luke, run a check on that rego, please.' With thanks to the technician, she and Luke head downstairs.

'Sarah, the ute is registered to a Mario Nuessle. Address in Fyshwick.' He looks at his sergeant with a meaningful nod. 'I know this address and this ute ... from before.'

She swallows. 'Right. This is a new case – not the old one. Let's report in and wrap up here with forensics and the uniforms. Then, we'll head off to see this Mario.'

Chapter 64

Brisbane

Giles

It seems to Justin that old Giles has hit the nail on the head.

The new parliamentarian is visiting one of his benefactors at his Manly house, overlooking the brilliant blue of Moreton Bay with the sand hills of Stradbroke Island behind and darting sails cutting across the wide stretches of water.

'They can't pick you,' the old man had said. 'They're waiting to see you fall over – a flash in the pan, like so many before. But you're not like so many before, Justin. You are different because you can argue from basic philosophical logic. Like we did with our maths in the old days – when you could demonstrate a mathematic challenge by a first principle proof; that foundation stops you getting confused by false distracters. My business was mathematics and civil engineering – big projects, national level. I've had a lot to do with federal politicians over time.'

So, Justin is being very attentive. He is hearing a dispassionate perspective on himself, and on politics, from someone he respects.

Giles explains further. 'Justin, from the first time you spoke at the Rotary meeting, I noticed it. And my later observations have confirmed – when you argue, people actually listen because you are not spouting ideology but rationality – common sense without all the double-talk. Very few have that ability and I've never met anyone who had it at your age.'

A hell of a compliment but Justin is only too well aware of his frailties. He is constantly running on adrenalin inside, even if his voice and body seem in control. And in all honesty, his bravery in taking on challenges is more about naivety than calculated courage.

He didn't know that he is supposed to be intimidated by Jack Carew's money and influence, or by party leaders with their hard-earned war wounds, or by the traditional interests in the corridors of power. Armed with no preconceived baggage, he can just breeze through, oblivious to all the not-so-subtle hints that he should back off. Old Giles seems to appreciate that his protégé is listening carefully – and without interruption.

'My advice is to hit them fast and hard. Don't let them settle. What you're trying to do has to be done – it's different; and it's up there in terms of national significance with the Snowy Mountains Scheme, with Whitlam's throwing off the shackles of old world thinking, and Keating's recession that we had to have, as well as Howard's gun laws and the plain packaging for cigarettes. They changed attitudes and they all met great resistance. You have the ability to get to a public before the armies of the powerful can mount their expensive indoctrination campaigns.'

Justin sits quietly, chin resting in the cleft of forefinger and thumb, before he asks, 'Giles, why are you helping me like this?'

The pause is long. Giles appears to be looking at a long landscape painting on his wall. Eventually, he turns to face the young man. His eyes are glistening and moist.

'Guilt, Justin.' Another long pause as he flicks his remaining strands of hair back from his brow. 'A conscience is a terrible thing when you get old. I am a widower. My children, grandchildren and great-grandchildren are interstate and overseas. I live on my own, with just some home-help for the chores.' He slows again as if collecting how he wants to word his comment. 'We – our generation – should have called out all this behaviour years ago. But it didn't happen because we didn't have your courage – and maybe not the means. We didn't have the freedom that the Internet has brought, perhaps. But that's just an excuse.

'There it is, Justin – guilt. So many things we looked at and didn't see; so many things we just accepted and didn't challenge. I benefited then – no mistake. I worked hard for it but, really, I was too focused on the projects in hand to look up and see what was happening in the world around me. I – we – were doing alright.

'But I could do the maths. I could see the population explosion building, with no logical end in sight, and I passed it up as too hard. Same with all the crazy stock market speculation. Really, we were all just tired after the world wars – we wanted to enjoy the fruits of the peace; and we did well, very well. It has been a good life – in this lovely spot.' He casts his hand to show the window view.

'But who needs all this wealth at my time in life? If I can help you a little to fight the battle we deferred to you, then that's a good thing. You're helping me, much more than I'm helping you, Justin. Guilt. It's a bastard.'

And then he gives Justin his considered tips to change his world.

Chapter 65

Canberra

Greens

Justin thinks that he might have grown up by five years in the short time he has been back in Killen. If he had realised earlier how much he hadn't known at the time, he would never even have stood for election – and he certainly wouldn't have had the brash confidence to have held such robust arguments with people old enough to be his parents or grandparents.

Now, back in Canberra, he has a whole new world to master – a world of compromise deals, aggressive competitiveness, dog eat dog, cat scratch cat, party machines, brinkmanship and media mischief – kite flying among the reporting – all about power and egos. How guileless has he been?

'Unworldly,' they all told him – Malcolm McGlashan, Doug Henderson, Jack Carew at the head of a long, long list. And yet ... and yet, they have been unfailingly polite – all of them; except Dai Evans; and it was his dummy spit that had started the whole conveyor belt that is currently carrying him along.

Old Giles probably picked it best of all. They're wary – maybe being patient, seeing his time out by courteous obstruction and delay.

How salutary the old man's advice has been. Kipps could only thank him for his support and, particularly, for giving him the tactics which he is intending to follow diligently over the next few weeks. Even on his morning head-clearing walk, Giles' wise words pass through his mind, keeping his train on the main track, preventing him from slipping off into an easier siding.

* * * *

Gordon Milne seems to have lost none of his enthusiasm. He has set up a meeting for them both with the administrative leader of the Greens in Canberra, Frances Grant, at her office over in the suburb of Turner.

The Greens are a Senate force, rather than in the House of Reps, but their support in both places could be crucial. Justin has always subliminally realised that it would be the party heads who he would need to persuade, the advisers – before trying to tackle the vulnerabilities of the elected officials – and that has been Giles' advice too. Keeping the powder dry and staying out of the line of direct fire – remaining the unconventional and unpredictable adversary.

There are two items on the agenda with Frances Grant. One is to amend the standing orders around debates and questions; to bring the procedures into the electronic technological age, and to entrench the highest expectations of behaviour for politicians in all circumstances. Justin's pitch is that politicians have to set themselves as exemplars of honesty, integrity and courtesy beyond the currently accepted norm. That would cover everything from Question Time, to lifting the quality of debate, to transparent use of expenses, to open consideration of requests for abnormal travel or study tours.

To Justin, in the pub test, the current practices are seen to be an offensive insult to the intelligence of the general public.

Frances Grant's response is, 'Great intention. But, you are trying to domesticate feral animals. You might be able to give them the veneer but, underneath, the wild beast's instinct will be to compete. They are, by nature, street fighters.' And she waves him to continue.

The second Bill is to outlaw *any* asset shifting by multi-national companies such as engaging in clever invoicing from overseas subsidiaries; or other attempts to avoid lawful Australian taxation assessments of the profits earned in this country.

Having heard the second pitch, Frances gives a tolerant smile.

'There are one hundred and fifty-one members of the House of Representatives. At the moment, you are outnumbered by one hundred and fifty to one.'

'One hundred and forty-nine,' Gordon corrects.

'I admire your passion and aspiration, both of you,' Frances continues, 'but this is a hard road to get any traction on. Alright. My first suggestion for your opening pitch is to sit down with the Clerk of the Chamber. He knows all the protocols and the standing orders. There is a Procedures Committee which looks at the operations of the House.'

'I know,' Justin says. 'I didn't get selected for it. I have met with the Speaker to express my disappointment. But ... it's all part of making sure that they have had the chance to improve.'

Frances Grant sits back surprised. 'Is this your strategy – to talk to everyone and then blame them for not taking action?'

'No. I'm consulting; and asking everyone as a courtesy – more like warning that the waves of change are coming. No, it won't be about blame – but it will be about change.'

'Right.' Grant is still surprised. 'Now, I think you'll find that there'll be other conventions – rules even – that financial Bills will have to be presented by the *Treasurer* to the House and then to the Senate. So getting any changes to corporate tax laws will be probably be like knocking down the Great Wall of China with a toy hammer.'

'Yes, I realise that.' Justin speaks patiently and quietly. 'Frances, at some stage in the future, I suspect that I will speak in the parliament – a notice of intention to present the Bill that the government will have already refused to present – despite the protestations. At that point, I expect that the advertising campaign from the globals will saturate the media. And then the actual debate will take place. I just want you to be aware so that you're prepared with your senators to rectify the sensible revenue stream to Australia, to be paid by those who can afford it most.'

'Justin, you are certainly different. Maybe, we're all a bit jaded by life in this town. We've been fighting these battles for years – and the Democrats before us – and we have not achieved what you, as an Independent, are proposing. But I will ensure that our team is briefed to support your foray into the phalanxes of the enemy.' She laughs at her descriptive analogy. 'I wish you well – but you'll need more than good wishes, I think.'

Justin gives her an appreciative smile and a handshake. 'On the other hand …'

Chapter 66

Canberra

Hetty Fry

Malcolm McGlashan had been as good as his word as he introduces the two Independents formally to Hetty Fry, the Prime Minister's chief of staff ... and he remains as part of the conversation.

Justin maintains his polite self-control as, simultaneously, he takes in the ambience of being in the Prime Ministerial suite and meeting this apparently powerful person.

Ms Fry is a stunning woman – perhaps in her late forties, striking auburn-red hair, expensive-looking emerald shirt under an equally well-cut dark business suit, finishing with low heels, discreet jewellery, designer glasses and a radiant welcoming smile.

But something isn't right to Justin's way of thinking. He was expecting a frazzled lady, struggling with multi-tasking the plethora of Ministerial demands among the chaos of risk management. Yet, her desk is neat, well organised – an appearance of calm efficiency. Bookshelves, cabinet doors, filing drawers and the wide-screen monitor perhaps conceal the complexity of the busyness of her role.

Justin explains his concerns about global corporations being able to dodge a fair tax payment – legally – because their high-powered accountancy firms shed resources across other arms of their international businesses – ending up in tax havens.

'The government is working to see changes there, too,' she replies patiently. 'However, there are lots more complexities to this business than your concise overview would suggest.'

'Do you mean a legacy of deals and concessions made by past governments?'

She smiles. The smile could be interpreted as cynicism but, somehow, the lady has enough charm to allay such a thought. 'Indeed, Mr Kipps – along with commitments made in other contexts by this government and others. There are international trade agreements, for example, and diplomatic flow-ons which complicate the matter considerably.'

'So what is the solution?'

'The Treasurer and the Cabinet are engaged in a strategy to gain international cooperation to solve this very problem. It has been discussed at the G20. All the relevant finance ministers are making commitments for change. I know the PM certainly has strong hopes that progress will be made soon.'

Justin nods and then asks, 'Pardon my naivety but would it help if I, as an Independent member, were to put it on the table as a private member's Bill?'

'How might you think that would help?'

'To take the pressure off the government. The Opposition really only opposes for the sake of it. If it came from me, it puts the issue on the agenda without setting up usual adversarial competition. Just a thought?'

Hetty Fry glances at Malcolm McGlashan. It is quick, like a begrudging acknowledgement but with a query – and the expression is not lost on Kipps, or perhaps Gordon Milne.

'It's a thought, Mr Kipps. I can certainly pass your idea on. Perhaps a question to the Treasurer at Question Time might be an appropriate start to easing into the matter.' She gives him another smile which indicates that particular topic is concluded. 'Was there something else you want me to know about?'

'Yes, thank you. One more. I was elected on a platform to return respect and dignity to parliament, particularly where the general public can see politicians on televised broadcasts. I was unsuccessful in getting onto the Procedures Committee. I've spoken with the Speaker and I intend to talk with the Clerk of the Chamber about where tweaks could be made to the current standing orders – about the interruptions and hectoring comments which aren't allowed in any other debating forum. I've debated at state and national levels – and such behaviour is not allowed at any of them. How can I progress this agenda?'

Again, a glance at McGlashan and a smile for Justin and Gordon. 'You don't tackle anything easy, do you? The 43rd Parliament made some changes to speaking times when the Independents held the balance of power in that hung parliament. That was seen as an improvement. However, change always meets strong resistance. That is why the orders are standing – they are long-standing. Politicians from all persuasions have always accepted that the House and the Senate are places where robust discussions would be held.' She pauses to await a response.

Justin takes his time. 'I've heard that term, *robust*, a lot. It's possible to be tough without being rude and disrespectful, though.' He pauses. 'I suppose, if I can't get on the committee to advise on procedural change, that it would need the support of the *Prime Minister* to influence the agenda, perhaps?'

She grins. 'I can certainly advise him of that suggestion too – and I will, Mr Kipps. The whole parliament would have to vote to accept such changes, though. That's not just the will of the Prime Minister.'

'Could I raise that as a private member's suggestion in the House?'

'You would have to get it on the Notice Paper and that is usually very crowded with government business. As I say, I'll draw it to the PM's attention.'

As they shake hands on leaving Hetty Fry's office, Justin notices yet another glance between her and Malcolm McGlashan. He's not sure what it is or even if he just imagined it. Perhaps it only meant that she has carried out her agreement with the head of the party to have met with the Independents.

* * * *

McGlashan parts from Justin and Gordon in the main hall. 'Good that you had the chance to express your views to Hetty. Glad I could have been of assistance.' His smile is broad. 'Maybe something will come of it. Now, if you'll excuse me, I have some other people to meet here.'

* * * *

'What did you think, Gordon?'

'I think we have just been dropped into a neat circular file. She was just doing a favour for McGlashan.'

'Did you notice her glances at him?'

'Not really. That's just business. She has to look after the administrative wing of the party.'

And then Justin notices the rumbling is back. Clearly, Gordon is not showing any overt signs. It is just him. What is it?

* * * *

Following the tactical plan, Justin updates his manifesto blog.

The Manifesto. **Economic Security – 1e**

The Tax Minimisation Industry or 'How to screw the plebs, legally'.

Without even touching on the issues of long-standing industry subsidies, rebates, fuel exemptions and super-profits, if the global corporations just paid the standard tax on what they earned in this country in a year, an extra $8 to $10 billion, at minimum, would be paid per year as government revenue on *your* Australian-owned assets that the multinationals use to generate profits.

It is just arithmetic!

That might only be the tip of the iceberg.

One-third of the biggest companies operating in Australia are paying less than ten per cent in corporate tax – and the law says that they can.

270

The rate is supposed to be up to thirty per cent. Some of the biggest corporations actually pay zero tax.

Fifty-seven per cent of all the ASX200 companies have subsidiaries in tax havens. They are supposed to be Australia-based.

Small business gets none of those chances at perks.

Pay-As-You-Go employees can claim negative-gearing expenses, self-education and private transport – and that is about all.

The spin says that the wealthy pay most of Australia's tax income – but as a percentage of individual income, the poorer groups in Australia pay the highest proportion of their incomes, in tax.

Where is the fair go?

Global corporates can artificially inflate their debt loading to minimise their tax assessment and shift former losses forward to apply to current profit, so as to depress their liability. If the private citizen tried that, he or she would be facing a criminal prosecution – jail.

Not only does Australian law make it legal for companies to off-load assets to offshore subsidiaries – but they protect the confidentiality of such arrangements; even to elected members of parliament. So, no-one can actually get all the numbers to apply the arithmetic.

As I say, this $8–10 billion is probably only the tip of the iceberg – and an iceberg is 90% below water.

The laws have to be tightened and new ones have to plug the loopholes in the current practices.

Chapter 67

Power and Dexter

'This is the same address that Adla Bello came to,' Luke Dexter says to Sarah Power in their car in Fyshwick.

'It's just an anonymous warehouse with a roller door and an entrance into the office,' Power says as she looks further. 'Laneway down the side. Perhaps he lives at the back? Let's see if he's up yet. No signs of activity.'

* * * *

'Alright, I'm coming,' is the response to Dexter's repeated knocking on the office door.

It opens. A solid man, about 175 cm tall with black swept-over hair, stares at the two figures outside who are holding up police badges.

'Detective Sergeant Power and Detective Constable Dexter, Criminal Investigation Branch, ACT Policing. Mr Mario Nuessle?' At the man's nod. 'May we come in, please?'

'What for?' the puzzled man replies.

'May we come in, please?'

'Do you have a warrant?'

'I can get one within minutes. Do you want this conversation conducted in the street?'

'Come in.'

They enter an office which looks out into a warehouse with racks of carpet and fabric on the far side wall. Three vehicles are parked on the concrete floor near the rear wall – a fork lift, a black Mercedes and a dark-brown Nissan Navara utility.

'What business do you conduct here?' Power asks. 'You have no signs on the outside walls.'

'We distribute carpets and fabrics from central Asia around the territory and interstate. Online wholesale orders. Silk Road Carpets.'

'From where in central Asia?'

'Turkey, Iran, Turkmenistan, Uzbekistan.'

'Are you from central Asia?'

'No, I'm Swiss. Italian mother. German father. Why are you here?'

'Can you account for your movements yesterday evening between 8 pm and dawn?'

'I was here – at home. My quarters are at the back.' He points. 'I was watching DVDs – French ones, good quality.'

'Can anyone confirm that?'

'No. I am the caretaker here. I live on my own. What's this all about?'

'Vehicles. Do you own these vehicles in the warehouse?'

Nuessle seems to relax visibly. 'I own the ute – not the Merc. The business owns the fork lift.'

'Who owns the Merc?'

'A courier service, two streets way. It's just kept here.'

'Whose courier service? Who runs it?'

'A Leo Clarke is the manager. I think it's based interstate. Why?'

'Was the ute out last evening?'

'No. I was here. I told you.'

'You didn't lend the ute to anyone?'

'No.'

'Okay, Mr Nuessle. Open the warehouse door, please.'

'Open it?' The man shakes his head, confused, but moves to comply.

As the door opens, a marked police car drives in and uniformed police emerge with a warrant to inspect.

'Mario Nuessle,' DS Power says. 'I have strong reason to suspect that one of these vehicles was used to commit a crime last night. Accordingly, as of 8.28 am, I am placing you under arrest. You will be taken from here to the Central Police Station where I will speak to you later today. Please hand over your keys to the building and to the cars. Constable, over to you.'

On cue, Luke Dexter reads him his rights.

* * * *

Power and Dexter, wearing gloves and shoe overalls, carefully move around the warehouse and the office, looking for any anomalies. The forensic van arrives and the team are directed to examine and take samples from the cars.

Using Nuessle's keys, the detectives enter the quarters at the rear, which turns out to be a spacious two-bedroom apartment with teak furnishing, good carpets, a large screen TV and an open multiple-DVD box of a French detective series – with Disc One in the player.

'Not what I was expecting,' Dexter says. 'This is pretty comfortable for a caretaker's quarters.'

Sarah Power nods in agreement. 'Yes. Very comfortable. We'll let forensics go through it. Until Gareth Dawes can tell us what we are looking for from his safe and filing cabinet, we have other priorities.'

'Sarge, you picked up the connection to the courier service … the Merc and Adla Bello. Does this mean we can investigate again?'

'Let's just move forward very carefully. I'll phone our superintendent in a minute or two to let him know what we've found. He will let the AFP know, as a courtesy, that we are working on this burglary case. And Luke, we'll work *only* on this case, for the moment – keeping our powder dry, as you suggested earlier.'

Chapter 68

Canberra

Dai Evans

Dai Evans' voice has a slight quiver as he announces, 'Listeners, this is Dai Evans. My guest today is Independent Federal MP for Killen, Mr Justin Kipps. We are coming to you today from our Canberra studio, rather than Sydney. I encourage you all to stay tuned. It promises to be an interesting conversation to discuss his latest blog post. Welcome, Justin Kipps.'

'Thank you, Dai.'

'Now before we start, please allow me to clear the air on a few matters. First, it was you, Justin, who asked for this interview, not vice versa.'

'That is correct, Dai.'

'Second, as this is the first time I've met you in person and it's well-known that I apologised publicly to you at a press conference over some of the comments that I made rashly and erroneously as it turned out, may I take this opportunity to apologise to you, in person.'

'Thank you, Dai. That is both accepted and appreciated.'

'Good. Now to the reason you'd indicated you wanted this interview; it's about your latest blog on what you call economic security. So let me not put words in your mouth. Would you tell us what your concern is, please?'

'Certainly, Dai. The government has been telling us consistently that our revenue is in decline and that cuts must be made to a range of services. Yet you are paying your proper taxes, Dai, as am I; and so would your listeners be; even if it grates a bit at times. If we didn't pay we would be charged with fraud and face a potential criminal charge. Am I right?'

'You're certainly right on that, Justin. I pay a lot of tax which I don't begrudge, not a cent of it because, thanks to the listeners and my sponsors, I earn the income. Please go on.'

'Perhaps some listeners would be amazed to learn that hundreds of the richest companies who operate in Australia do not pay the required corporate tax of up to thirty per cent – and there is no court action against them. Indeed some huge companies pay zero tax because they shift their profits offshore to tax havens.

'At a conservative estimate, just doing the arithmetic, that amounts to eight to ten billion dollars *per year* – to use the resources that are owned collectively by the Australian people, you, me and your listeners; and – wait for it – it's legal, perfectly legal for those companies to avoid paying. You have to ask how that could be.'

'Indeed, Justin. You are telling us that it's legal for the mega-rich to pay less tax than the rest of us have to pay – and some of them actually pay sweet zero. Please explain to our listeners how that could be.'

'Global companies get their offshore subsidiaries to charge them inflated prices for services, so the tax liability on profit is written down. In local business, that would be seen as fiddling your invoices. But there is no law against it for multinationals.

'So, if I'm following you, Justin, the Australian company has reduced its taxable income and the tax is paid in the country where the subsidiary is based?'

'Spot on, Dai. And those countries are low-tax places, the havens – usually small nations like islands whose expenditure is negligible. And Australia gets nothing or next to nothing paid in tax.'

'I think I'm with you. And those tax havens make lots of small amounts of tax revenue. I'd bet they would benefit in many other ways from having all those subsidiaries on their patch.'

'Indeed, Dai. I'm sure you are with me – as would be most of your listeners. Clever accountancy companies – some of them Australian – specialise in legal tax minimisation; claiming deductions for research and infrastructure development, for example, or past losses being moved into the current year to cancel out the actual annual profits. In Australia, the current laws allow all this to happen.'

'I'm sure my listeners will be right across the unfairness of what you're describing. But you're not the government, Justin. What can you do?'

'But wait there's more.'

'No, there can't be. There can't be! Enough. I can feel my outrage rising.'

'Australian law also protects the confidentiality of all those transactions so that neither I nor you can actually get an accurate handle on exactly what numbers are involved. I suggested on my blog that this could just be the tip of the iceberg, which is ninety per cent submerged. If that were to be so, potentially we could be talking about one hundred billion in lost revenue per year.'

'One hundred billion! Can you prove that?'

'It is ten times ten billion – the tip of the iceberg. If that's not absolutely accurate, then let them publish the secret files to prove me wrong. Even ten billion for one year would fund the Commonwealth commitment to schools for two years. That's how much difference this can make.'

'Justin, these are huge numbers. You're an economics graduate, I know. Can you put it into context for our listeners?'

'I'll try. Total taxation receipts in any given year are around twenty per cent of this country's Gross Domestic Product – that comes to something between 350 billion to 400 billion in any given year. Do you have that number in your mind – 350 to 400 billion in one year?

'Remember, that take is without the big companies paying their fair share. So, if their commitment was ten billion, that's what the rest of us wouldn't have to contribute. That's a lot of health care and disability care. Lots of road infrastructure. It would pay for lots of nurses, doctors and teachers. And that's just with ten billion.

'Now project it upwards to the one hundred billion mark. That would be a quarter of the annual revenue. Then the much-talked-about deficit is paid down and all the services are still able to be provided. It's just arithmetic.'

'So why is it not being done? You're a member of parliament, Justin Kipps.'

'As many have pointed out, I am an Independent member, new on the scene. I am not the government. We're told that for any of this to happen, we need international commercial agreements on tax havens. That seems to be quite illogical to me. We are a sovereign nation. *We* make the laws which apply to companies who operate in this country. How hard is this to do?'

'Well, I can't argue with you. All of us have to follow the laws of the land. But what if these companies pull out of here? Then our tax take will be zero.'

'So what's different, Dai? That's what some of them are currently paying – sweet zero for using the country's resources to make billions for themselves. Those billions go back to the company shareholders overseas and to the senior executives multi-million dollar salaries, plus bonuses. They're living well on the sacrifices made by the ordinary people in Australia.'

'But if they do pull out, won't it mean sacrificing jobs?'

'I would just about guarantee that the same companies that are ripping us off, legally, will be preparing an advertising blitz as they are listening to your program. They will tell you how the economy will collapse without them; how they will pull out of Australia; how so many jobs will be lost.'

'And you're saying that won't happen? You are predicting the future?'

Justin's quiet laugh carries over the airwaves. 'As many have pointed out, I'm the young amateur trying to play in the A-league, and I'm an Independent and I have no numbers to change legislation. So no, Dai, I don't predict the future.

'What I can say, though, is that if our resources that are not mined by companies who won't pay the proper tax, then those resources will stay in the ground, safe for a later time; and all the infrastructure will stay too – their investment, their means for bringing out their wealth. Are they going to walk away from that?

'Companies who are selling services into the Australian market do so at exorbitant prices – think of music, movies, online buying – because they know that this market will pay. They won't want to lose their slice of that golden goose just to be pig-headed about a small percentage of their huge profits in tax. They will pay their tax to get the seventy per cent of what they currently take in profit.

'They might take some enterprises out of the country to try to prove their scare campaign. But once the laws have changed, the company accountants will do the arithmetic again – and the business will still be here; except that they will be paying their proper taxes to Australia instead of filtering to their shareholders.'

'So what do you need, Justin Kipps?'

'I need the public to be educated about the rort that is being played on Australian taxpayers and consumers. I need everyone to challenge the argument that nothing can be done about it. That's codswallop.'

'My listeners might have stronger words to describe it.'

'Their call. But, in my view, all that it will take to change this system is for the parliament to enact new laws to stop all those loopholes and collect a fair slice of revenue to pay down debt. As you so wisely note, Dai, this needs to come from the government. I can put it on the agenda and keep pushing it. But it needs commentators like you, and electors like your listeners, to demand their government to get this stupidity sorted out satisfactorily.'

'Very good, Justin Kipps. We need to go to a commercial break now. When we return, can we talk about what other issues you are keen to raise in parliament?'

* * * *

'Welcome back. While we've been on the break, our team has been flooded by messages – text, tweet and website feedback – about your ideas, Justin. And I can tell you that you've hit a nerve there. The vast majority have been very supportive. We'll have helpful contacts on the website after the show is over – so that all listeners can know how to go about helping. Now, what else is on your busy agenda, Justin Kipps?'

'I want to see parliament bring its quality of debate and courtesy into the twenty-first century – to get rid of the abuse and the long boring speeches which say nothing. You understand this, Dai. *You* have to get your message across in the limited broadcast time. I don't think parliament cuts through because it's a lot of suits taking too long to get to the point.

'And on top of that, there are rude interruptions with half-smart comments. We should be above that. Politicians should be setting an example of clear speaking and honest dealing.'

Evans laughs. 'Listeners, I can scarcely believe that I am sitting here with a man in his early twenties who is advocating for traditional manners and speech. Am I hearing you correctly?'

'Yes, you are, Dai. It's my belief that we get the type of behaviour we are prepared to ignore. If we want it to stop, then your listeners have to rail against the stupid comments, the put-downs, the rudeness …'

Evans coughs. 'I may not always have been the best role model myself. It could be the pot calling the kettle black.'

'But, to your credit, Dai, you have acknowledged that. Learning is a journey not a destination.'

'Well put. Very well put. So, why can't you get those things changed in parliament?'

'Parliament has to vote on changes to standing orders. A Procedures Committee advises the House. I'm not on that committee but I have made representations to the Speaker and the parties in the House. It needs them to hear what the public want. I am happy to give suggestions. Debating happens in forums all over the country, without all the interruptions. This acceptance of the unacceptable has just crept up on us like a virus.'

'Good for you, Justin. Here's another cause for our listeners. Now while you're here I have a couple more questions for you. Can you give me your view on foreigners buying up houses, farms and businesses, seemingly without any restrictions? You couldn't go and buy in their countries. As a member of parliament, what is your view on that?'

'Dai, I'm no expert on that topic. I try not to give off-the-cuff opinions on matters that are outside my experience.'

'But you will vote on such matters. You are a member of parliament.'

'Indeed. And if it comes before parliament I'll do my research as you have done and get public service briefings before coming to an opinion. I think one of the weaknesses of the public debate at the moment, is the plethora of everyone giving ill-informed opinions – the chat-show format. It's especially important that people in public office don't engage in that type of speculation.'

'Right.' Evans' gulp can be heard on air. 'That is certainly a different view. Let's try one that you've written about. You advocated that religion should have no bearing on parliamentary decision making. Are you going to ban *The Lord's Prayer?*'

'Take a step back, Dai. I have put the position that all legislation should be based on reasoning, with evidence that can be tested. People of religion can put their case like anyone else in a democratic society. If it can stand the test I've just mentioned then, irrespective of its source, it can be part of the debate.

'I have the view that everything is subject to doubt, unless it can be proved by evidence and testing. That is the scientific and philosophical method – a sounder basis for legislation than reverting to interpreting a theological reference or referring to the dogma of any particular religion.'

'So, do you want to ban *The Lord's Prayer?*'

'I have to avoid your gotchya questions, Dai. In a secular society, it strikes me as passing strange that the prayer of a particular belief should be invoked in preference to any others. The practice is a legacy from a time when ninety-six per cent of Australia professed to follow a Christian religion. Now twenty per cent follow other faiths and another twenty per cent follow no religion.

'I took an affirmation when I was sworn-in. That's on the public record. Like most things in a democracy, it would take a majority to change a standing procedure. That one is not as important to me as common courtesies and high-quality concise arguments in debates.'

'Alright, Justin Kipps. Thank you for coming on the show and giving our listeners the chance to hear your views. I must confess that you appear to be a significantly better informed man than I had thought at an earlier time.'

'And I return the compliment, Dai. Thank you to your listeners.'

* * * *

'Well, keep the feedback rolling in, folks. As I told Justin, you're telling me that you're passionate to change the tax laws. The website now has the contact details of the Treasurer, the Prime Minister and the Finance Minister among others – but contact your local member as well.

'You're also in strong support of improving the quality of parliamentary debate – getting rid of the obvious lies and double-talk as well as the rudeness.

'I must admit that Justin Kipps seems to have highlighted the main issue – we have whinged about it for years but, by accepting it, it has grown like an unchecked illness. So now we need to inundate the politicians with demands for change – and that they listen to young Mr Kipps' ideas. Yes, John from Penrith what do you have to say?'

'Dai, I think young Kipps is alright. I think I actually understand what he is saying about revenue and global corporations. He could explain a difficult subject without just repeating jargon. And Dai, he has some bottle – to ask to come on your show after the roasting you gave him last year and this. He stood up to be counted and politely argued his case, told us what he wanted us to do and stayed well-mannered throughout the whole business.'

'Well, I have to agree with you, John. I found him a respectful and courteous young man with a good intellect. As I said on the show and as I apologised, I got him wrong. There are still a lot of big issues that the government has to deal with and he has only been in parliament for months, not years. I think his quiet measured voice can get the message across. Anyway, over to you now, John, and all the other listeners. For my part, I'll try to get the Prime Minister on here so that he can tell us how he views young Kipps' suggestions.'

Chapter 69

Canberra

Trust

Social media has lit up. *The Voice of Australia* clearly is heard by a large audience. Electorate offices are inundated with emails, texts, tweets and website queries.

* * * *

Justin has sorted out some arrangements for his Canberra support staff. A system is already in place – the Independents share a range of research assistants to read proposed legislation and to offer advice, particularly regarding the fine print.

Gordon Milne has agreed to share his chief of staff, Blair Adie, with Kipps, with the new Independent contributing to his payment, with bonuses for extra advice.

The new Member for Killen is having trouble getting his head around employing staff and paying from expense accounts. Despite having an accountant father, Justin has spent much of his life as an employee or a poor student – not an employer. His parents trained all of their children in budgeting, earning their own money, expecting no handouts for doing nothing – albeit with a backstop of assistance for special opportunities. Habits of frugality and financial discipline are hard to shake.

Very regular phone calls home to his former executive secretary mother are proving invaluable. He can ask the naïve questions which only his mother could understand as being appropriate. She is listening to a son, not the Member for Killen.

His dad too is the stable sounding board for his often way-out financial questions. It is one thing to have had the theoretical knowledge from an economics degree, but another to not have had the experience of life and work. His father's unquestioning love and tolerance for explaining all the subtleties that Justin doesn't know, is proving to be a rock pier to stop him from being swamped by the waves of doubt.

Harry and Jenny are good stabilisers too; but that's a very different teenage banter.

The reasons that Janet had given him for moving on are still niggling at him – mainly because she is right. Any friend of a politician is a target – even if it's only benign interest – but still someone whose privacy would be viewed as a peripheral piece of public property. Not an easy scenario; and Janet is a significant emotional loss for Kipps, too. Her company lifted and energised him. Who can Justin trust?

After the episode with Miranda and Natasha at the consortium party, how can he tell whether a person is interested in him or his position or is just trying to lure him into some trap?

He keeps busy – daily phone calls back to Frank to check on emerging issues in the electorate give him the stability of his known world. They have a receptionist, Carol, in the office and Frank is prepared to always be on call – that, he argues would equate to the three days a week he was being paid for.

Apart from that, the volunteers are always willing to give time and energy; listening, reading and responding on the email and text trees. Karen Porter has set up a simple database where queries can be recorded and dealt with. Justin can access that from Canberra – so he keeps across that flow of incoming concerns ... and praise, it's fair to say. The electors seem happy that he's being heard in Canberra – particularly about keeping the tax issues front and centre.

Justin is always wary at meetings. He works hard to never let it show on his mask of confident professionalism, but underneath, he is processing anticipated agenda items at a rapid speed – it's better than his mother's bridge club for keeping the brain alert. Indeed, his personal self-control is a daily exercise of mind training, carried out on his morning walks and, in front of a full length mirror as he practises his arguments, rebuttals and tactics for the day ahead.

He attends functions, mainly with Gordon – and sometimes with Blair Adie, who is proving to be a wise adviser. Blair was a newspaper editor and his lived-in face inspires confidence that his advice is coming from the hard knocks of experience.

And Justin calls Giles on most evenings, partly to maintain his confidence and direction; but also because he knows Giles lives alone. Being in Canberra, sharing a house and working, but still being essentially alone, Justin has an empathy for the old man who is helping plan out his strategy. It seems to be working quietly – but it won't be long before it will have to explode with a ferocity, not anticipated by those complacent ones who are born to rule.

Chapter 70

Canberra
Media

Despite being almost Budget Week, every news channel, webpage and newspaper front page is taken up with reaction to Justin's contribution on the Dai Evans' show. Commentators each want to show the quality of their insider credentials; and the reactions on social media are going viral again.

The Prime Minister is clearly cautious in every doorstop opportunity – he looks nervous, waiting for the trap questions. While the government can get its Bills through the House without needing to cosy up to the Greens or Independents, the numbers are still tight. Justin's win in Killen has effectively taken a Lib number out and put it with the Opposition, in terms of guarantees. If that scenario were to happen again, through an unforeseen circumstance, then anticipated support and alliances could easily be strained.

* * * *

Justin is at a musical – on his own – at the Canberra Theatre Centre. Lost in the anonymity of the crowd, he feels a peace floating over him. The staging, the music and general artistic feel of the audience transports his soul and lightens his thinking.

Leaving the theatre in his car on the way back to the share house, he takes a detour through a suburb called Ainslie for no other reason than he got in a wrong lane, again – that's Canberra for you – and headed north. Still, a new suburb is all part of his learning and familiarisation with the city, so he nudges the Commodore along tree-lined streets and avenues, checking street names against his sat nav, the most modern part of his car.

He drives slowly through the wide roads of the leafy Ainslie suburb, savouring the tranquillity and thinking that Canberra is a much more attractive place than people generally seem to acknowledge – when he passes a blue car, stopped, waiting to exit from a plush, exclusive-looking driveway. He notices, in passing, the driver's face while it looks to the right, checking for a break in the light traffic.

The coincidence of what he has seen doesn't register until his Commodore has covered another hundred metres – the driver of the dark-blue car had auburn-red hair albeit partly hidden by the angle.

He turns, drives back and notes the address from the sat nav. Coincidence? The more he thinks about it, the more he's sure he knows who he has just seen.

* * * *

'Where does Hetty Fry live, Gordon?'

'That's not public knowledge. Blair might know.'

Justin shows Gordon the address. 'Does anyone important live there?'

'Search me. I have a feeling that Hetty might live south of here – Red Hill way, maybe. But Ainslie? Political people don't publish addresses. Blair is more across that stuff than I am.'

'Mmm. Thanks.'

* * * *

Sticking to Giles' tactical advice, Justin resists asking any questions in the chamber or making any more speeches.

But he starts to embrace the media throng at the door.

An astute smiling journalist asks, 'Haven't you just stirred up the hornet's nest and now you're sitting low watching everybody running for cover?' She thrusts her microphone closer.

'I have asked legitimate questions,' Justin pleads with a grin, 'on my website, through the media – social as well as mainstream. It's the public asking the questions now. Something is not right, not fair. That's what it seems. Isn't that what they're saying? The people employ us all. It is for the government to address these laws, is it not?'

'But you could ask the questions in parliament?'

'I would prefer to wait until we amend the standing orders to stop the political theatre of Question Time. If I ask a question, I expect a respectful, straight answer. Do you think that would happen?'

'Isn't that what it's for?'

'Absolutely. Do you think that's what happens now? I would want a concise accurate answer – no more than thirty seconds – but I suspect I'd get a filibuster of repetitive rhetoric to fill up the minutes, leaving us all none the wiser. I don't think I want to encourage that. Do you? Believe me, I'm quietly talking about these matters in the corridors and meeting rooms.'

'So, can the taxation laws be changed?'

'All laws can be changed, provided they fit within the principles of the Constitution – and a majority of parliamentarians agree across both chambers. That's the simple message which is cutting through with the public. Of course, laws can be changed – even despite all the screaming and wailing of vested interests. The sky will not fall in, tomorrow.

'Global company Board members see their first duty towards their shareholders – that's fine, that's why people invest. But Australia is not one of those shareholders. You – we – don't figure in their priorities so they don't need to look after you or us. That's why so many in the general population are making all this noise now to say, *Enough is enough – indeed way past enough!*'

'Why don't you put up a private member's Bill?'

'That's always an option. My preference is for the government, the Treasurer, to get the kudos for changing things. He's a capable man, pulling the levers on all the financial settings for the government – a figure on the world stage. He deserves the credit for putting the laws in place. This is not about me. This is about you – all of you.'

Chapter 71

Canberra

Sam Sendoza

Treasurer Sam Sendoza wants a meeting.

Senator Nick Rathie is there in the room first, to welcome Justin Kipps and Gordon Milne to the Ministerial office. Rathie is lean, with a tall man's shoulder stoop – the less charitable might suggest that this enables him always to talk down to people. He's a long-term politician, assertive, unfailingly courteous albeit with a primary schoolmaster's manner.

The Treasurer arrives late, bursting through the door with no sense of any need for explanation or apology – a bull of a man, big shoulders, florid face, greying curly hair; substantial paunch rolling over the pin-stripe suit trousers. His distracted eyes and the dumping of bundled folders on the desktop might have hinted at a mind having trouble adjusting to this meeting – but he is clearly annoyed. Sweat is beading on his forehead and upper lip.

He glances at his senator, before he focuses his eyes on the two Independents, who are politely waiting to acknowledge the Treasurer and be welcomed.

Instead, Sendoza opens with, 'Next week, I will bring down the Commonwealth Budget to address the pay-down of inherited debt, the cutting of administrivia and double-handling, the staying ahead of world financial fluctuations, meeting the government's election promises and handling the diplomatic tensions of evolving international trade deals. It's complex – very bloody complex – high-powered and challenging, involving all of Treasury and most of the staff in every other department – an army of dedicated people working flat out – and what is the bloody media talking about? You – Justin Kipps – your bright ideas about some simplistic way to stop global corporations accessing tax havens.

'How fucking naïve can you be? To lob in here at twenty-one or twenty-two – whatever age you are – with an economics degree from Queensland, for God's sake; trying to tell professional financiers, bankers, economists, diplomats and ministers how to suck eggs? Where the fuck do you get off?'

While Gordon burrs a little, Justin just quietly sits down, uninvited, with his usual appearance of zen – and he gestures to Milne to do the same.

But the Treasurer is rocking on his feet. 'You go on talk-back radio, stir up Dai Evans and his listeners and then they mobilise social media. Every politician's office and email across the land is clogged with these inane inquiries about closing the loopholes and finding 100 billion dollars in revenue to fund every dream on the planet – *one hundred billion*, for fuck's sake. Did you pluck that number out of your arse? Or from the underwater part of the iceberg you rave about?

'You are an idiot, Kipps. You come down here with half an idea, and then assume everyone in the place is a crook, useless, bone idle, stupid or on the take. You have no idea of the protocols or conventions of parliament or how to draft complex Bills and yet here you are, floating around carefree, dropping your ignorant bombs – to make work for me and Nick.

'If you were in our party or any party, you would be drop-kicked over the flagpole on the top of this building. At the moment, I think I can almost report you for abuse of office, with a good chance of getting you sent back to Queensland with your tail firmly lodged between your legs. Nick, what have you to say?'

Rathie has the calmer voice of maturity. 'Gentlemen, this is clearly a very tense time for the Treasurer – budget time always is – the demand of the media, the crossing of t's and dotting of i's – I'm sure you understand. What we need you to do, as a matter of some urgency, is to quell this frenzy you've created. I need to tell you that the Prime Minister is far from happy. This can't turn out well for you. So …?' He turns his open palms toward the two Independents, in askance.

Justin looks peacefully back. 'Finished?'

The Treasurer hasn't left his feet. He glowers, face turning puce, as if about to carry out physical violence. 'Finished, you ask?' The volume is probably carrying far. An office door closes noisily along the corridor. 'I tell you, *you* will be fucking finished – maybe before we leave this room.'

Justin hasn't moved and his expression hasn't changed. 'Did you want me to call the medical team or are you going to sit down, Mr Sendoza?'

Rathie motions to the Treasurer to sit, while offering him a gulp of water. The large glass is devoured in two swallows as he grabs a handful of tissues to mop his brow and face.

'Treasurer,' Justin Kipps begins in his usual serene measured style, 'if this is your usual style of conducting a meeting, it is *you* rather, than I, who should be concerned about his continued presence in this place.

'Since my maiden speech, and in my manifesto, I have been regularly flagging my concerns about corporate tax avoidance and – I might add – the standard of parliamentary behaviour. And I advise you, in front of your two colleagues, that I don't intend it to accept it any further.'

Gordon Milne looks concerned as Big Sam reddens, like a volcano pleading to burst – but the wise old Rathie has placed his arm on the Treasurer's arm. He speaks for Sam Sendoza. 'Mr Kipps, the Treasurer is upset that you have not accorded him the courtesy of waiting for a meeting with him, before going public – and causing all this embarrassing furore at budget time, of all times.'

Justin's soft voice asks, 'How much easier would it be to balance the budget with even twenty per cent corporate tax being paid on gross profit by all corporates, no matter what their circumstances? How much easier would it be to sell your undoubtedly unpopular balance-sheet measures if you could say that the rectifying legislation would be presented to both Houses before the end of this calendar year – to tidy up all the legal lurks and perks from past governments – not even from this one? You are blameless. How much political capital would that gain you as you head to the next federal election?'

'It can't be done,' Sendoza clasps his head with both hands. 'There are signed trade deals which give concessions, subsidies, legitimate deductions against profits. That was why the companies came here in the first place – the compensation to be paid for reneging on contractual arrangements would far outweigh any advantages. And they would take their businesses to a more accommodating country.'

'Says who?'

'Says I,' he roars.

'So you have done the reviews and the cost-benefit analyses? You have checked to see that any legislative changes would be in accord with the parliament's constitutional authority? You have checked to see if any would be deemed to be contractual reneging?'

'Kipps. We don't need to. We have been in this business a long time. We know how the land lies.'

'With respect, hearing the words *Business* and *Lies* in adjacent sentences doesn't fill me with any confidence.' He pauses while the Treasurer tries to recall what he has just said. 'In effect, you have not done the studies or investigations. You're operating on gut instinct. Just trotting out the old rhetoric for public consumption. *Tell it often enough and the people will believe and accept.* Is that the plan?' He slows again to look into angry eyes. 'But I don't accept it.'

Rathie responds. 'Well, have you done your homework on what this legislation might look like?'

'No, I haven't. And I'll tell you why not. Since I've arrived in this place, people have consistently told me I'm young, no-one will listen to me, I'm an Independent, and it's the government that proposes financial legislation. In essence, I don't know anything. I don't exist – just barely tolerated; at least until now.

'Yet, what I *have* done is create a climate for you all to look really good in the eyes of the electorate – although I grant you that a few of your sponsors might be less than impressed. I'm doing you a favour. And you are ungrateful.

'Look, the government has access to the taxation office – I don't. It is a *secret deals* business – protecting the confidentiality of those who are benefiting at everyone else's expense. As far as legislation is concerned, the fundamental paragraphs should insist that income generated in this country will be subject to Australian corporate tax at thirty per cent … or another competitive tax rate that parliament can agree on. It will no longer be legal to use subsidiaries to invoice Australian businesses from tax havens with the express purpose of avoiding due tax. It will no longer be legal to artificially inflate costs or debt by using the arms of an international corporation to avoid tax. Claims for deductions for research or infrastructure replacement will meet the same taxation tests as for all small businesses in Australia.

'So, you sell your budget to Australia on the second Tuesday of the month – and sugarcoat the pill with a commitment to the above measures and timetable. You'll be seen as saviours, instead of pariahs.'

Sendoza slams his hand hard onto the desk top. 'Rubbish. I haven't got time for these student ideas. The PM will have to get involved now. This has gone too far.'

'As you wish, Treasurer. I hope you can manage a calmer time in the days ahead.'

Sam Sendoza walks the few paces over to stand directly in front of Kipps who rises to face him, relaxed and almost smiling.

Face millimetres from Kipps, the Treasurer breathes, 'I will not forget this meeting and the havoc you've caused.'

'Nor will I, Mr Sendoza. But I hope it will lead to something productive, both in terms of future budgets as well as the way we deal with each other in a professional context.'

Sendoza steps back, looks him in the eye and points his finger. 'I will not be responsible for my actions if you continue on this path ...'

'Oh, you will, Treasurer. This whole conversation has been recorded.'

The outrush from the Treasurer's nostrils would make a bull's snort look like a zephyr. 'That's illegal. You can't use it unless you declare it at the start of the meeting. Isn't that right, Nick?' as he looks at Rathie's nod. 'It can't be used as evidence in a court or a tribunal.'

'But *you* know that we have it. That's all I'm saying. You know what was said here today – and how. So do we.'

'Hand over the recording'

'No, I'm sorry. I won't be doing that.'

'I think we'll need to call security. This was a confidential meeting.'

'And it still is. As an elected member of parliament, I have no intention of handing over any recording unless it is in front of a range of witnesses. Then I will play it to them all.'

The Treasurer turns and storms out of the room, while Nick Rathie notes, 'I think you'll be hearing from the Prime Minister's office fairly soon.' And he follows his colleague through the same door.

As they leave, Milne turns to Justin. 'Pheew! How did you stay so cool through that?'

'Political acting. They're all doing it. So can we. A successful meeting and some progress made, eh?'

Chapter 72

Canberra

Malcolm McGlashan

'Hetty lives in Red Hill,' Blair Adie confirms. 'But the address you have is where Malcolm McGlashan lives.'

'He'd live there with his family, I suppose?'

'I think his family is in Melbourne. They still have children in high school and maybe uni. Malcolm would just be here on his own – only while parliament is sitting. The house rental or mortgage will be claimed somewhere for expenses or tax. Same for the gardener, cleaner and so on.'

'Okay. It's all learning for me. Now, this corporate tax business is hotting up big time. I need to speak with Malcolm McGlashan again to sniff the air of where the party is going to stand on it. I'm guessing that the PM will be beckoning us soon. So, can you set up a short meeting today with McGlashan and accompany me to their headquarters, for most of the meeting at least. Fifteen to twenty minutes tops – the agenda is for us to understand the Lib position on tax haven laws. We need a way forward.'

'Done.'

* * * *

As Justin enters Malcolm McGlashan's office, he exchanges polite smiles with the deputy director, Liam Driscoll, who is just leaving.

'Malcolm, I think we need to get a positive way forward so that the budget is set in a clear context. What is the Liberal grassroots position on these tax havens?'

'Positive context? Absolutely. Our position? We want them stamped out. This Treasurer and previous ones have tried to get international cooperation to get full disclosure from the havens.'

'And that hasn't happened?'

'No.'

'So you are stymied?'

'We never stop trying.'

'Let me put it another way. Are you more committed to the saturation advertising of your sponsors or to actually changing the tax lurks?'

He gives the shrug of a man caught between a rock and a hard place. 'It's not as simple as you've been presenting on the radio and social media.'

'It is, Malcolm. It really is. I think it needs your intervention with the Prime Minister to explain how easy it would be and what an electoral boon it could be for you all. He'll listen very carefully to you.'

'The Prime Minister doesn't have to answer to me.' He glances uncomfortably at Blair Adie's wizened, watching face.

'But he does listen. As does Hetty, his chief of staff.' The flicker in his eyes is enough to confirm it for Justin.

Justin turns to Blair. 'I wonder if you could give Malcolm and me two or three minutes on our own, please.'

Adie is surprised but he rises and exits. McGlashan looks similarly puzzled.

'Malcolm, I have a recording of a meeting with the Treasurer and Senator Rathie with me and Gordon Milne. He was in blistering form. I'm sure you understand what I'm saying.' He pauses and emphasises. 'I *need* you to intervene positively with the Prime Minister.'

McGlashan sits thinking, watching this new parliamentarian.

'While you're pondering that, Malcolm – another thing. I was drifting along in my car the other day ... in the suburb of Ainslie.'

The sudden alert expression in McGlashan's eyes is proof enough to Justin that there's a deep enough relationship that the organisational leader of the party would not want to be disclosed.

McGlashan stares and draws in a deep breath. How much does this young Queensland politician know? He asks very quietly, 'Are you trying to blackmail me?'

'I am trying to help you – to do something positive for the nation, to make you and the Prime Minister both look good to the electorate. Admittedly, you may lose some bark with your sponsors along the way ... but you will come out smelling of roses with everyone else – that's a huge voting majority. Who do you most want to win over?'

'That's a lot of money you are asking us to forego.'

'It's in the national interest ... and, even more definitely, in yours.'

McGlashan sighs as he ponders whether to risk confronting this new unpredictable member or to change the political habits of a lifetime in order to protect the security of his family life.

Justin pre-empts his thoughts. 'I've no interest in damaging your private life ... but I need you to put your national interest before your own. You know enough about me now to trust both my word and my resolve.'

* * * *

Six minutes later, Justin beckons Blair Adie back in.

'Blair, Malcolm is keen to help us with the Prime Minister. Do you have the copy of that draft Bill, so that the Prime Minister has some bare bones to discuss with the Treasurer – a skeleton almost ... for the Cabinet.'

* * * *

On the way back to Parliament House, Blair asks, 'What did you do back there to turn McGlashan? He looked like he'd seen a ghost.'

299

'He has a hard task ahead. He has to explain to his multi-million dollar sponsors that the golden goose is going to stop laying so prolifically. I imagine they'll be less than impressed. But I just explained the importance of such legislation to everyone in the nation and that it would save the Treasurer from all the backlash. Oh, and I personalised the benefits too.'

Adie looks across from his driver's seat, shakes his head slowly but says nothing.

Chapter 73

The Central Police Station has the main watch house for the city.

'A couple of hours in the cells will either make Mr Nuessle belligerent or compliant. Let's see which he is … and who his lawyer is,' Sarah Power says to Luke.

* * * *

Sarah and Luke check that the recording gear in the interview room is operating correctly. At a knock, a policeman ushers in Mario Nuessle, with the female duty lawyer at the station.

'You don't want your private lawyer, Mr Nuessle?'

'I'm happy with this lady,' Nuessle replies.

'Okay.' Sarah smiles at the lawyer. 'Are you ready to tell us the truth about last night … and where the ute was?'

'Is this a traffic offence? You said you're Criminal Investigations.'

'Do you still stand by your earlier claim that you were at home watching DVDs all night?'

'That's what I did?'

'A French detective series, I think you said. Was it good?'

'Very good. I like to practise my French.'

'So you were watching that series from when?'

'Nine o'clock until I went to bed after midnight.'

'Three hours or more. And no-one borrowed your ute?'

'Not that I know of. I was out back.'

'But you are the caretaker. You would have heard a vehicle going out through a noisy roller door.' Sarah stops and waits. Nuessle looks at his lawyer and shrugs.

Sarah Power says, 'Your ute was spotted at a burglary in Hughes last night from 9.42 pm onwards. Do you still claim to know nothing?'

'I don't know how that could be. There must be a mistake'

Luke Dexter steps forward and places a print of a screen-shot of the vehicle in the driveway of the Hughes house with a time and date stamp on it. 'Your ute. Your registration – which brought us to your door this morning. Do you want us to show the zoom of the driver?'

'I was home last night.'

Sarah takes over. 'Yes. Watching the French detective series all night. Explain why only Disc One is in the player? That would last less than an hour.' She waits. 'Mario, you're lying to us. Forensics will tie you in to the ute and burglary. Tell us about what happened.'

Nuessle sits silent with his head down.

'We have video of you letting three masked men off at the house at 9.42 pm. They waited for the owner to arrive – then they mugged him, forced him to disable the security system ... and then they tortured him until he opened the safe. Mario, the man is in hospital with serious burns to his torso. What were these men after?'

Nuessle's body tenses and relaxes. 'They'll kill me.'

'Not if we take them out of circulation first.'

'You don't understand. This is much bigger than you think.' He looks across to his lawyer, who sits impassive, watching him.

'We know much more than you think,' Sarah continues. 'We know about the parties ... the lot. Whose house was it?'

Nuessle gives a huge sigh. 'Gareth Dawes. He runs one of the dirt teams – getting stuff to compromise people. Photos. Honey traps. Set-ups. Background dirt to blackmail. That sort of stuff.'

'Who? Politicians?'

'No. More the advisers, the lobbyists, the influencers … people who try to stay in the background. Someone has been annoyed.'

'Who were the masked men?'

'Hard men from interstate. Dawes must have something on their people. They wanted it and anything else they might find in the safe. Then, they'll use that too against others. They are too powerful. You can't beat them. I'm dead.'

'So tell us what happened.'

'I got the call that three men needed to be driven to that Hughes address and then brought back to the warehouse.'

'A call from whom?'

'Leo Clarke at the courier company. But he isn't the boss. He just passes on messages.'

'So, you drove them there and then what?'

'I had to circle back round every five minutes until I could see a light flash. It took over half-an-hour and then I picked them up with all their bags of gear. They left in another car that had been parked in the warehouse.'

'What kind of car?'

'I think it was one of those Subarus. Grey. I was just glad to see them gone. I went out back and put on my DVD.'

'Names, Mario. You've mentioned Leo Clarke. What were the men called?'

'No names to me. They were Mediterranean or Balkan? Slav, maybe?'

'Did you see their faces?'

'Yes. When they arrived. Hard. Beards and moustaches. Big. Heavy set. In dark clothes. Black ski hats. Only one man spoke to me, giving the instructions. You don't argue with men like that.'

'Names, Mario. You're in this business up to your neck. What other names do you know apart from Dawes and Clarke?'

'Can you protect me?'

'I'm the police. Prosecutors can make leniency deals. In special cases, witnesses can get protection. I can't promise you that. My concern is to get these people caught and out of circulation. That will protect you best. Names, Mario.'

He looks at the lawyer who shrugs towards him.

'There was a Des here a few weeks ago.'

'What was his job?'

'He was an enforcer and protector ... from Melbourne. Protecting girls and blokes who go to the parties. Keeping them in line too. But look what happened to him. He got tossed over the dam wall. What chance do I have?'

'What sort of parties?'

'Private jobs. Entertaining guests of all persuasions. Collecting information.'

'Why is that so dangerous?'

'They are often embassy people or their friends, guests ... you know. Their information is usually sensitive. About deals or their agencies.'

'Okay. Who else?'

'Apart from Dawes and Clarke, I heard them mention a Peter. I also saw a note with the name, Jakob, written on it – Jakob with a K. Clarke mentioned an Ivan. That's about it. They're internationals with lots of money and muscle. I'm just a simple caretaker.'

'What do they have on *you*, Mario?'

He sighs again and glances over to the lawyer before saying, 'I've been part of their actions in the past – as a driver to different crimes but, forced to be in other things ... you understand. I am paid well. But they have video of me – so that I can be the patsy if they fall under suspicion. That's all out the window now. Here I am ... caught and fucked. I'm a dead man walking.'

'Mario, do you supply the girls for parties too?'

He looks again to the lawyer.

'Only answer if you want to,' she says.

Mario nods and ponders for a few seconds.

'Alright. This could be to do with a Turkmen ... from Turkmenistan. He supplies us with carpet but ... he also gets entertained.'

'Why do you suggest him?'

'He stays at the Russian Embassy. Turkmenistan has no embassy in Canberra.'

'Is there anything else about the man that you would mention him?'

'Just the timing. I don't know much. The night before Des went over the dam, the Turkmen was with two of our girls. They were unusually agitated when they came back. I asked them if they had been knocked around but they said, no … nothing like that. Then the next day, Des is found dead and one of the girls disappears. That's all.'

'Do these girls have names?'

'Adla Bello and Steph Taylor.'

'Which one went missing?'

'Steph. But the Turkmen came back again and asked for Adla, more than once. That all seemed to go well. So, I don't know. I don't know much.'

'Well, think some more on it. Do you have addresses for those women?'

'On my phone. It's been handed in.'

'We'll get it checked, with your permission.' She looks at the lawyer who replies, 'Signed permission.'

'Of course.'

Chapter 74

Canberra
Prime Minister

'Thank you for sparing us some time in your very busy schedule, Prime Minister,' Justin says as Hetty Fry ushers the two Independents into the Prime Minister's elegantly appointed office.

'You have been making your voices heard,' the PM comments. 'Malcolm has been good, in getting Hetty to reschedule to give us some time together. I have the draft Bill – courtesy of Malcolm. Please be seated, both of you.' He holds up the copy of the draft as they all take their seats and Hetty closes the door to her office, soundlessly. 'Talk to me about it.'

Gordon smiles as Justin takes up the case. 'As you appreciate, I'm new to parliament. Drafting a Bill which would get through both Houses would be something for the expertise of *your* team. But the essence is that we – Australia – need to see your strong leadership on this matter. As you have so often acknowledged, we are a sovereign country. We decide what happens in our land. We can't be held to ransom by foreign corporations.

'And, Prime Minister, that is actually what social media is saying ... and Dai Evans on the radio and the vast majority of political commentators. You are on the right side of the people. This is an absolute vote winner for you.

'The tax havens are little islands and tiny countries that will go broke if they disclose their financial dealings with global corporations. That is never going to happen; but this issue won't go away. It will be a festering sore as we head towards the next election and for however long this crazily favoured treatment continues. But you can change all that, Prime Minister.

'It is Australian accounting companies that have developed the asset shifting to a fine art – read Australian tax dodging – because it is legal. It's write-offs, write downs and inflated asset shifting to subsidiaries, among others.

'What this Bill does is to simply make it illegal for any corporation to avoid tax on profits generated in Australia by using any of those methods that I have just mentioned.

'My estimate, on simple arithmetic, is that you will get an extra ten billion a year in revenue, in the next financial year – but I invite you to get Treasury to check. I am guessing; but I think it may five or ten times that figure in potential annual revenue from all the globals, the service ones in particular – and that is even more important when mineral prices are dropping for the others. That is *annual* revenue, Prime Minister – just to emphasise.

'So there's the nation's deficit paid back, sidelined projects are back on track and the austerity measures are lifted – and all leading into the next election. And you are a national hero for ever more.'

The Prime Minister is grinning as he listens. He looks at Malcolm McGlashan in query. 'Why haven't my advisers said that this was possible? Many of these corporates have been extremely generous supporters of our party, you realise, but Malcolm says the party will be behind the Bill – they'll do the hard yards to explain the issues to their international Boards. I thought that would be the major barrier but he says he will handle it. Sam Sendoza says he'll live with it too, if we can tidy up the sales pitch, before his budget speech.'

'Prime Minister, I'm no media person but my sense is that the ordinary citizens will respond well if the Treasurer announces that he will be presenting legislation to parliament in the second half of the year – that the government has listened to the people and will act to help them. Giving out that early timeline is very important – it allows the public to trust that it will actually happen.

'Then, I think your Cabinet ministers will need to get around the corporates as well – a true team effort supporting Malcolm and the party machine; to show all the multinationals that, even after this legislation, they will still have a very reliable supply, market and a fair profit; well above breaking even. Malcolm knows the arguments. And a few words from the experienced ones will allay most fears.'

The Prime Minister is silent, head dipping slowly as he strokes his nose between forefinger and thumb. 'Yes,' he announces eventually. 'Yes, put that way, I think it is do-able. Having the party machine to do the backroom negotiations will make the difference – and Malcolm is confident that he can make that happen. Yes. Just the circuit-breaker we need.' And he stands up.

Rising in time with him, Justin smiles. 'Well done, Prime Minister. Great decision. I'll look forward to doing my bit on social media to support the government's action. We all will,' with a glance at Gordon, his quiet supportive witness. 'Thank you for your time in your busy day.'

'No. Thank *you* for bringing this to my attention. You should be joining our party; the two of you. We could do with your initiative and ideas.'

* * * *

Hetty Fry shows them both out with a bright, if not warm, smile.

In the corridor Gordon asks, 'Did we actually do that?'

'Maybe we did. We make a good team, Gordon. It changes the dynamic when they are faced with two MPs who can attest to what was said. Thank you. More work to do though.'

Chapter 75

Canberra

Budget reaction

The Treasurer presents his budget with its planned ideological messages of restraint. The groans of a nation can be sensed with every word that he utters.

But, something is different in the way that Sam Sendoza is speaking. Even the most cynical can feel that the usual aggression in his voice has mellowed.

Where is the accustomed hubris in the tone – the victor berating the vanquished? That has gone.

It all becomes clear when, in a quiet tone, he explains that the dire news of austere tightening on social expenditure might be ameliorated, sooner rather than later, when his proposed new legislation – regarding removing the legal loopholes for global corporations – might be passed through parliament in the second part of the year.

There has been no mention of this plan in the budget papers; nor in the leaks beforehand. The news columnists have been taken by surprise; their prepared headlines, predicting doom and more gloom, will need to be changed – and fast. Phones light up and keyboards clatter.

It's as if someone has thrown open thick curtains and hope has returned.

The mass media is swamped with commentators lauding the Treasurer's plan for the new legislation.

How good it is that the government has listened to the people. Yes, the country can live with some short-term pain because soon billions will be flowing back into the coffers. The wave of positivity drowns out the usual fear-mongers, who are still peddling their single-strand melodies of how this will cause the demise of Australia's survival among the world's economies.

The subsequent opinion polls indicate a bounce for the government, when most pre-budget predictions have been expecting a humiliating drubbing. Backbenchers can smile again. There is promise for the future.

Talk-back radio welcomes the move.

Even, the multinationals must have sensed the bi-partisan support for the tax reform at their expense because their saturation advertising quickly melts away with only a few over-the-shoulder hints that the government had better get this right or they would all leave the country. But no-one in the mainstream believes them anymore.

Only the occasional *leaked unnamed source* suggests that McGlashan and the party machine are being shredded and humiliated in the international boardrooms but they are sticking to their lines. Liam Driscoll and the federal secretariat are flat out dealing with responses to the aggrieved. The juggernaut of affirmation rolls on with praise being heaped on the government for the boldness of its move.

The Treasurer's confidence has returned, if not the bravado. He gives multiple media interviews with a quiet surety in the direction forward. He fields questions on the detail of the new legislation with the assurance that everything will be made available to the press and the public, before the finished proposals are to be presented to parliament – soon – after the winter break, in the August sitting.

The Prime Minister extols the virtues of the Treasurer. Even the Opposition focuses on the new laws. The actual budget seems redundant in most people's minds – everyone is future-focused.

* * * *

In the quiet yet public corridor behind the green chamber, as the members disperse to offices, Sam Sendoza clearly has been waiting for Justin Kipps to emerge with Gordon Milne.

'A word please, Justin,' as he moves away from his group. 'On your own, if you wouldn't mind, Gordon, please.' And he smiles to allay fears of his intentions.

Justin nods that it's okay and Milne joins the last runnels of politicians heading away, albeit with a glance back at his colleague.

Kipps stands toe to toe with a smiling Sendoza.

'I want to apologise to you,' the Treasurer says quietly and stops suddenly. 'You're not recording this are you?'

'Only if you want me to?' Justin grins slightly.

'No. No. Enough of that.' He laughs uncomfortably. 'I was out of line in my office. I want to apologise. I could blame the pressure, my own frustration with the budget … a whole range of things, but I was out of line. I said a lot that I shouldn't have said. And ironically, it was you – who is the new bloke on the block and half my age – who showed the maturity. And even more ironically, the plan you suggested was right and it has raised my stocks no end. So I'm both very grateful and apologetic.'

'No worries, Treasurer. All good.'

'Call me, Sam.' He pauses. 'You should really be with us in the Libs. You're one of us.'

'Sam,' Justin smirks. 'I thank you for your apology. But think on this, if I had been in the Libs, you would have drop-kicked me over the flagpole and you would now be getting lambasted everywhere for your cruel budget.'

'Aw, come on now, Justin.' The laughing Sam pats Justin on the shoulder and his expression changes to contrite. 'Seriously, I am sorry and very grateful. Thank you.'

'Enjoy your day, Sam.'

'And you, Justin,' as he turns with a spring in his step.

* * * *

The bevy of journalists has been focusing on the big names for several days.

Justin has been careful to dodge the pack, as he chooses to arrive in a huddle with many others – all part of Giles' strategy.

Two weeks after the budget, one journalist bails him up with, 'All this corporate tax control was your idea originally, Mr Kipps. It was you talking to Dai Evans that put it up in lights, wasn't it?'

Justin replies with his now-accustomed disarming smile, 'Oh, I think you will find that many people had been talking about it, long before me. You should give the Treasurer credit. He's the one who will present the legislation to parliament in August. Credit where credit is due. He will have to appease a lot of his party's sponsors. The public is very happy with him.'

'So, is there any chance his promise will be watered down?'

'I think you should give the Treasurer and the Prime Minister credit for making this bold move in the nation's interest. We'll see the detail in due course and I would expect they'll deliver what they have indicated.'

'Promises have been broken before.'

'At some point, we have to move beyond the legacy of past mistakes. As you'd be aware, I'm very keen to see the quality of debate and the way politicians are regarded in the community, to be at the highest end of respect – earned by the manner in which we conduct ourselves not by titles of office.'

'Wow. Did I hear you correctly?'

'You have it recorded. I'm suggesting that, instead of harking back to things done badly in the past, you might look forward to a new era of politicians being regarded with trust and respect, because that is the way we will act and behave. In that context, be patient and wait for the detail of the Treasurer's legislation. Have a good day, all.'

* * * *

Justin drafts an email to Malcolm McGlashan.

Thank you for all you are doing. You are a bigger and more socially conscious man than most people would realise.

I know you are losing a lot of bark over this business – and you have been true to your word.

312

You can be assured that I, also, will be true to my commitment – and I salute you.

In half-an hour, he received a cryptic reply.

To paraphrase Dickens, Tis a far greater thing I do, than I have ever done.

Chapter 76

Canberra

Gareth Dawes

'Mr Dawes, what was in the safe and the filing cabinet?'

Sarah Power and Luke Dexter are sitting at Gareth Dawes' bedside in the Canberra Hospital.

'Just business. Investigation reports.'

'Mr Dawes. We have arrested the driver of the vehicle who brought your kidnappers to your house. He has given us some information. We need to know what stolen property we're looking for.'

'They'll have destroyed it by now. Don't you worry about it.'

'No. I don't think it will be destroyed. There'll be something in there that is very valuable to your attackers. Something your investigators have turned up.'

'I'm not making a complaint, Sergeant. I will deal with it when I get out of here.'

'So, do you know who attacked you?'

'I don't need the police.'

'You needed us earlier when you were attacked. Either you've deliberately set up a sting on someone or you've accidentally come into possession of very sensitive material. And these burglars were tasked to recover it … without regard that your genitalia might have been burned away. Stop this obstruction and let us get these people.'

Chapter 77

Brisbane

Reunion

'Welcome home. You must be exhausted.' Justin has scarcely nosed the Commodore into the driveway when his mother is wrapping him in a hug, a smile and a kiss. 'I'm so proud of you, son. Come in. Come in to the house.'

'Yes, Mum. Hello to you too. Good to be here. I'm fine. You know I love these long drives. Time to think and take in the scenery. Hi Dad,' he calls to his father who is blithely leaning against the patio post – leaving the stage to his wife, Sally, as husbands and fathers do.

'Need a hand carrying things?' Howard Kipps asks. 'Harry is here somewhere too.'

On cue, the floppy-haired brother arrives with, 'Hey, Honourable Bro. At your service. What's up?'

The men carry in the bags as a grinning Jenny hovers around her big brother, waiting for him to get a break from her mother's grasp.

The July winter break. It's good to be back in the family home – a place of peace, love and trust – a sanctuary after all the Machiavellian scheming of Canberra.

* * * *

Ever-reliable and thoughtful Frank has organised a reunion meeting at the coffee shop on the esplanade where the whole conveyor belt of politics had really started, not even a year before. Has everything happened in just a few months? It's hard to believe.

Hugs and handshakes all round – a little careful with Janet; and fairly formal with Brandon and Karen.

'Who would have thought that so much could have happened like this?' Zoe gushes, with a surprisingly almost-girlish pride. 'That's the pinnacle of event planning, getting someone elected to parliament – and it just seems to have happened.'

'A lot of good work from you all,' Justin replies modestly. 'And a terrific team of volunteers. Any success for me is your success.'

'So what's it like down there?' Graham asks. 'Do you need me down there for protection, a bit of body guarding?'

'I need you down there to go to the footy with. When you get a weekend off, I'll fly you down and we'll be off to watch the Raiders in action.'

'Haven't you got any mates down there?'

'Sure. But no-one quite like you, Graham.'

'You're on, then,' McGrady replies.

A quiet Brandon Jones concedes. 'You seemed to have achieved a hell of a lot since you've been there – stirring up the media and getting the Treasurer to put up legislation to control the corporates with their tax minimisation. That's quite a coup.'

'The Treasurer and the Prime Minister deserve the credit. They're the government; they will present it all to parliament in the next session. That took a lot of doing, on their parts. As you would know, Brandon, these globals are major sponsors of the party – but the government has put the nation's interest first.'

'So you have met the PM and the Treasurer?' Karen Porter sounds genuinely impressed.

Justin nods. 'We've had a couple of meetings.'

'That's fantastic. What are they like?'

'Probably a bit better than they appear on TV. But enough of me, what's happening back here?'

'Same old, same old.' Frank grins. 'The office is working well – lots of queries. Carol is really good at reception – she's mature.' He smiles. 'A foil for us all. She worked in a state electoral office previously – might have been for Bulimba. She knows the language to use and she sweet-talks any complainers.'

'I must get in to see her, Frank. We talk on the phone but a chat over a cuppa would be good. What chance is there to put on a few beers and platters for all the volunteers? I have money now.'

'I'm sure that Darryl over at The Green Man would be happy to accommodate that.'

'And Zoe? How's your business going?'

'Yes, pretty good, Justin. Keeping my head above water. If you need me to organise a Stones concert in Canberra, then give me a call. Do you have a media person down there?'

'Yeh. His name is Blair Adie – old newspaper man; lots of contacts, probably older than my dad with lots of home-spun advice. I share him with Gordon Milne, another Independent from Victoria. We have been tic-tacking on most issues. That part has been good.'

'So, is there a social life down there?' Brandon asks.

'It must exist, Brandon. But unfortunately, if you're a member of parliament, you seem to have a target painted on you. You can't really trust who anyone is or who they claim to be. No-one seems to be innocent. They all have an angle – and it's always all to do with politics. So, if any of you want a trip to the seat of government, I'll make you welcome.'

'But you'd be pretty flat out, most of the time,' Frank says.

'Never too busy for any of you. That's true, though. Everything's new to me – protocols, contacts, networks, connections. Lots of time spent meeting people and lots of nervous energy being used to keep up appearances – looking as if I know what I should be doing. As you would all realise, they never stop reminding me that I'm the young one who knows no-one and nothing – fair game for all the old hands.'

'You've done very well,' Janet's voice is quiet – indeed it has been the first time she has spoken beyond the welcome. 'We're all very proud of you and what you've achieved.'

'Thank you, Janet. It's been rapid learning and it's good to be back here, where it's safe and down-to-earth. I want to just be normal for a week or two.'

'Come and see us at netball, then,' Karen suggests. 'Lots of ordinariness there.'

Zoe nods in agreement, willing Kipps to agree.

'I'll do that. I have my wheels. I'm independent. And I'll get over to watch Graham too – first team now, mate. Well done!' He slaps McGrady on the shoulder. 'I'll be glued to your play – from down on the hill this time – none of the *up on the Board verandah*.' He pauses as he thinks of Jack Carew. It was the big American's innocent comment that had given him the key to changing the tax legislation. The world is not just some huge supermarket. It doesn't need to be the way of the world for many to be destined to only stack shelves while others buy more homes in the Bahamas. 'It's good to be back.'

* * * *

It could have been coincidence but as they disperse, Justin and Janet seem to be heading in the same direction while the others head the opposite way, to their transport.

'I was just going to walk along the esplanade for a bit – to smell the ozone in the air.' Justin's words are spoken as a statement, perhaps as an offer.

'I'll walk with you for a bit, if you like,' Janet says, with some reserve. 'I'm parked a fair way up. I just wanted to walk and clear my mind before catching up with everyone again.'

'How's the study?'

'Yeh. Okay. I'll be ready to go to work though, when I get through this year. Somehow it's dragging a bit.'

'You know, you were right, Janet – about being associated with politicians. It is no life – under the spotlight. Whatever happens at the next election, the longest I'll stay down there is two terms. It's not a real lifestyle – it's a crazy artificial bubble. You're well out of it.'

'Maybe. But it's the way it is. Do you have a girlfriend down there?'

'No. Like I said, you can't tell who to trust. What about you, back here?'

'No. I'm concentrating on my studies. I miss our times – you know, bumping into each other for coffee, just the chats about the world … and the philosophy of life.' She laughs at some memory. 'I'm still a volunteer with your team, though. Frank is good at keeping us all in the loop. Karen seems to be doing a lot around the office. I think she's keen on the politico-legal scene. Mind you, Frank doesn't seem quite the same this year. I think we're all missing your arguments – your drive.'

'Ah well, Frank has Zoe to keep him occupied.'

'Yeh, but she seems to be a bit different too. Distracted, you know. The cause is less important than it was to her, I think. It must be hard keeping a business going – and she's too independent to work for anyone.'

'Nothing wrong with *Independents*.'

It raises a smile.

'Maybe it's just her being a few years older than us. We're still carefree students. She has to be responsible.'

'I'm having to be very responsible now, too.'

'Yes, I don't envy you, Justin. But I'm very proud of what you're doing. My parents send their regards.'

'They're good people. Pass my best back.' He stops to look out over the bay as three large birds cruise by. 'Marvellous birds, those pelicans. You know, Canberra is a much prettier city than people give it credit for. But I haven't seen pelicans there. Swans and ducks, though.'

Janet is smiling. 'So what's the next project?'

'To get Question Time and debate sorted – a bit of respect. Most of the people there are really good, smart people. I've no idea why they resort to such pathetic speeches. It really is juvenile.'

'It might be hard to change that. Habits, you know.'

'Well, I'm learning slowly. I'll keep chipping away. We're only about a year to eighteen months away from another general election. Maybe I can appeal to their better intentions. You know, none of them would speak to their mothers like they do in the chamber and the corridors.'

'You stay with it, Justin. Keep in touch with me – even from down there. Here's my car.' She pauses by a parked little car and looks into his eyes. 'We can always talk on the phone.'

'I'd like that, Janet.' He stops as she unlocks a red Hyundai, while giving him a shy, proud smile.

'Mum sponsored me for this.' She point at the car and gives him a wry grin as she shakes her head slowly. 'Justin, I do miss you – but I just can't handle this politics thing.'

'I understand … and I respect your view. We're platonic friends – free agents who can share ideas and a phone call or two.'

'I'd like that.' She reaches over and kisses his cheek.

Chapter 78

Brisbane

Giles and the team

'You handled that very well,' Giles acknowledges with a knowing smile. He sips at his glass of red while watching the lights flickering over Moreton Bay as they slowly replace the daylight. 'Good that Malcolm was so amenable.'

'He had a choice, Giles. So many innocent explanations he could have used ... so I give him credit. He has fronted all these corporate Boards ... and held his ground consistently. That takes some bottle to cop that.'

'Okay. As you say, *his call.* What about he rest of the time down there? How is that?'

'I know I don't want to do it for the rest of my life. It's lonely, Giles. Sorry, I didn't mean that to sound the way it came out.'

'No problem. I understand living alone. Mine is through choice – but I'm no longer young and needing lots of relationships. At my age, cerebral activities are my sport. Your activities have been very stimulating for my mind, Justin – a new lease of mental cogitation. Perhaps you'll meet someone down there who'll strike a chord.'

Kipps shakes his head at the old man. 'Giles, at the first cocktail party I went to, two hookers tried to spike my drink. They had me lined up to be compromised. How do I know who to trust? Gordon Milne is a good bloke. We seem to be on the same wavelength. Blair Adie has a dry humour and gives sound advice. We

Independents share the research assistants. That's the work side. And your tactics and phone advice are invaluable. We wouldn't have turned the Prime Minister and Malcolm McGlashan without it. The next part of the strategy will be very interesting too. I'll just have to stay celibate down there. Too much to lose any other way.'

Giles toasts him with red wine.

'No wonder you'll be glad to give it away before too long. But, at the moment, look on it as your monastery years – there's too much important work to be done. And I'm loving having someone to share the fruits of my accumulated frustrations with politicians.'

'Easy for you, Giles.'

* * * *

Darryl Hope is his usual ebullient host personality.

'Platters and beers are never a problem, Justin. This hotel is on the map now, thanks to you. Flat out keeping up with the trade. How many are coming?'

'I think Frank invited all the volunteers. Hopefully they will be in their tee-shirts because old Giles wants a photograph – just to prove that they still have them all.'

* * * *

There are one hundred and forty people for the photograph – all in yellow tee-shirts, proclaiming *Vote 1 Justin Kipps. Independent for Killen.*

Justin feels at ease with the team. After his short speech of thanks, he answers all the questions about how Canberra works and what his own working space is like.

'Small and shared. It's handy to have been a poor student for so long. Mind you, the Speaker's suite is huge – able to cater for visits of dignitaries for elaborate meals and meetings. Same with the Prime Minister's offices – and that all links through to the Cabinet room and party meeting areas. It's been designed with a lot of thought – huge and really well-appointed. But, poor Independent members, like me? We share staff, office space and the challenges of making ourselves heard.'

'You seem to be doing that alright so far, Justin.'

'Been a bit lucky, really. Lots to learn. But it's your volunteering, with Frank and Carol, that is looking after business here and giving me head-space to concentrate on the agendas down there. It really is a team effort.'

He smiles at his office receptionist, in yellow tee-shirt, standing beside mine-host, Darryl, to bring a bit of older perspective to the scene.

* * * *

Carol Carey would be his mother's age and has that unflappability that Frank noticed when he appointed her.

'You're really no trouble at all, Justin,' she says. 'Not after where I have worked – in the office of a state Cabinet minister who wanted to drive through the portfolio agendas and to be at every school function, every fete *and* to visit kids who were sick. And then there were those who complained to me about the challenges of public transport, schools and hospitals – nitty-gritty things with no easy answers.

'With you, there are no federal bureaucrats pestering the office. Karen's database keeps track of all queries. Frank has this team of tech-savvy volunteers getting all the answers out. So really, I'm just thanking people in the electorate for all the praise to be passed on to the Member for Killen, with the occasional need for representation from refugee families, citizenship queries or environmental protection for the bay. You know all about that – and we've been able to handle most of it quite easily over the phone. Your manifesto seems to have covered most of their policy questions. So you're an easy elected boss to work for.'

Justin could only shrug and smile in appreciation. 'Frank says that you're something special in the way you handle the office. That's my impression too. So thanks.'

Chapter 79

Brisbane

Sport relationships

The touch grounds at Whites Hill are full of colourful teams, flowing back and forward over half-a-dozen fields under floodlights.

Harry plays A-grade on one night a week but on this night, it's social play – mixed, men and women. Justin watches his speedy muscled younger brother, loose hair flowing, as he darts, stops, splits, wraps and puts his female members through gaps to touch down. Impressive.

On a neighbouring field, younger sister, Jenny, is a fast winger, standing out on the painted line, drawing the defence out so that gaps can appear in the centre. As soon as the defenders move back in, the ball is spun out to her on the wing and she whizzes very quickly down the line to touch down.

The skill, speed and sportsmanship are impressive – but what Justin notices most is the laughter. That's what he has been missing in Canberra – laughter, the sense of fun and team work.

He stands absorbed until he hears, 'I said you should come to watch us at netball.'

Karen Porter stands right behind him in a tracksuit top over her Velcro touch outfit.

'I intend to come to netball.' He glances at her clothing as he turns to see her grin. 'But this is family. Harry and Jenny are out there. You're not a netballer only then, Karen?'

She laughs at his surprise. 'I'm on next. I have to keep in shape. Studying the law doesn't keep muscles toned. We have a C-grade mixed team tonight. I play B-grade with the women on Tuesdays. No, this is part of getting some healthy fitness into Frank. You know Frank as well as anyone. Between lectures, coffee, office, fast food and the computer, he has forgotten how to keep himself healthy.'

Justin grins in surprise. 'Well done. He scarcely ran the length of himself when we were sharing a house together.'

'Exactly. Not good for someone who needs to keep his brain sharp for exams and to keep an overview on the electoral issues. He used to play touch at school and first-year uni. He has the skills. He's just rusty and out of nick. He'll be here soon.'

As if to prove the point, as the hooter sounds for half-time, up rocks Frank looking ready enough for a run.

'Good on you, mate. I didn't even know that you played touch.'

'It's been a while. We get to substitute on and off a lot. Naw, Karen shamed me into it. I won't be able to walk tomorrow but I am getting fitter.'

'Well, I'll stop and watch your game too.'

As Frank and Karen jog to warm up with their other team members, Justin looks for Zoe. But maybe it is her evening in the netball team.

* * * *

Sitting on the hill at the footy is a joy. He can see Graham search the grassy mound for him as the teams run out. A wave and returned recognition.

The opposition are from the Gold Coast – it will be a tough match.

Justin glances up at the Board verandah and wonders if Jack Carew is up there again. Some day, he will thank him for putting the corporate tax issue into a clear perspective. He said that all the world is a giant supermarket and all the populations are just customers to be sold whatever the store has on its shelves.

He had even asserted, without any hesitation, that the only beneficiaries are the shareholders with their mansions in Galveston, Bahamas, Paris and wherever – while all the punters sitting on the hill beside him are being screwed even further to fund an exorbitant overseas lifestyle.

That was the turning point.

Be content with sufficiency. With the population burgeoning, why do the few need to be greedy? Not only did Jack Carew's flamboyant persuasion motivate Justin to pursue the matter with vigour, but it also gave him the market arguments to get the agenda moving. It is the nation's interest versus rich sponsors pulling the strings of the politicians. A sad joke, if it weren't so true.

And there's Graham slicing through the defence again. How he's improved with the confidence of some success. He's been a stalwart mate to Justin back in the student union campaigns – a salt-of-the-earth bloke.

Justin wants to represent the Grahams of the world in Canberra – hard workers who are carving their own paths. He can't wait to get him down to Canberra. Raiders versus Sea Eagles will be a good game.

Chapter 80

Brisbane and Canberra

The winter break is over before he'd even realised how fast the time was passing – relaxing with family and friends, walking on the esplanade and up the rugged paths of Mount Gravatt and Toohey Forest, even visiting the netball over on the northside at Downie Park.

Karen Porter had been there alright – fit and capable. He didn't see Zoe on the night he was there.

* * * *

Back in Canberra, it seems as if he has never left.

Gordon and Blair are their usual cheery selves. They have a first draft of the proposed corporate tax legislation in their possession – but the small group of research assistants have found a few flaws; little changes which could mean a lot, farther down the track.

'Maybe the PM is trying to pull a swifty on us,' Gordon suggests. 'The sponsors will be right up his ribs. It wouldn't take much to shake his resolve,'

With a deep breath, Justin knows he is back in the fray.

Hetty Fry agrees to put him through to the Prime Minister on the phone. The pleasantries are as warm as before, until Justin raises the concerns in the fine print of the proposed legislation.

A defensive PM is back in rhetoric mode. 'Well, we're hopeful that we'll get the legislation through both Houses with minimal obstruction.'

'With respect, Prime Minister, hope is not a strategy. Might I suggest to you that the modifications that we'd agreed on in the last session need to be reinstated.'

'Justin,' he hesitates, as if trying to avoid comment, 'while we've been on winter break, there has been significant resistance to some of the fine points.'

'From the corporates who will have to pay the fair tax?'

'Yes ... but they are our sponsors too.'

'Prime Minister, I was elected to parliament on the smell of an oily rag and a few policies which challenged unfairness. Money shouldn't be the issue. We're not prostitutes. I would suggest that your party doesn't need to be indebted to companies who will profit at the expense of the Australian people.'

'The changes are very small.'

'Prime Minister, is it worth risking the significant bounce in the polls which you have gained because all sides of politics have been behind the whole change agenda? They are not behind just some of it with a few fine point changes. It would be very courageous of you to alienate the voting public, mass media and social media because of a bit of pressure from companies. If we lose the trust of the people over this, we won't ever get it back again. All they'll remember is how the politicians dudded them – again. You are the leader, Prime Minister. This is a time for leadership in the nation's interest. I look forward to seeing the next proposal drafted as we'd all agreed. Doesn't Malcolm McGlashan suggest that too?'

'He does. The pressure is not coming from the party.'

'But it is Malcolm who has been wearing all the flak so far – on behalf of the party and the nation. I exhort you to hold the line. Present the legislation that the Australian public expects.'

'Mmm.'

* * * *

'My oldies would never have dreamed of me being here.' Graham McGrady is staring around the majesty of the Great Hall at

Parliament House. 'Or, that my good friend, roughly my age, is a member of parliament.'

* * * *

The Raiders put up a valiant fight out at the stadium to just lose in the last few minutes to the powerful skill of the Sea Eagles.

'They're good, Justin. Fast and skilful … and tough. That's what I have to build – my toughness. I have it between the ears but I have to work on my strength. And I will. This visit has been inspirational. Thanks. You really are a brother – *Bunji* is what we say for a brother – among my mother's mob, but all my mates use it.'

* * * *

Graham meets with Gordon and Blair.

He listens in to the discussions about the legislation.

'Fascinating, all this back and forward over the fine tuning for the legislation.'

Blair is poring over everything; and checking with one of the researchers as he goes. 'The original requirements have been reinstated in this version,' he advises with a satisfied grin. 'The word is that the PM himself overruled any changes being suggested.'

Gordon gives a respectful nod to Justin. 'Worth the phone call, eh?'

As Graham gets his head around the way the global corporations have been bounced in frank discussions, he observes, 'This must have been what it was like when the Native Title Act came in. Company executives who would never have spoken to any Murris or Kooris had to sit down under a tree and negotiate. Lots of time and learning.'

Chapter 81

Canberra

Courier Company

When DS Power and DC Dexter arrive at the courier company, the secretary looks just as surprised as she had been on their previous visit.

This time they are accompanied by two uniformed policemen.

'We would like a word with Mr Clarke please,' Sarah says.

'Right away,' the secretary replies. But Mr Clarke, presumably, must have heard and is already emerging from his office … looking in puzzlement at the visitors, particularly the police uniforms.

He is a thin man with reading glasses on his nose, dressed in a long-sleeved designer shirt, long trousers and leather shoes.

'Mr Clarke, DS Power and DC Dexter from Criminal Investigation, ACT Policing. We would like a word, please … in your office.'

The uniformed men take position in the outer office as Sarah motions for Clarke to sit.

'Mr Clarke, we spoke on the phone previously about the death of Desmond Wilson and you explained how your company provided an apartment, car and wardrobe for him.' Clarke's eyes are wide. 'We're here on another matter which may or may not be related. Do you know a Mario Nuessle?'

Leo Clarke does not speak initially. 'What is this about?'

'Please answer my question.'

'I don't know. Should I know him?'

'Mr Clarke, you have only seconds to answer my questions accurately and quickly or I'll place you under arrest and you'll answer the questions in the watch house. Understood?'

He nods and wrings his hands. 'I have met Mario Nuessle. Yes. He's a caretaker at a carpet distributor, two streets over.'

'Mr Nuessle is helping us with our enquiries about a burglary. Do you know what I'm referring to?'

'No. I'm an honest businessman.'

'Does your business own a black Mercedes which is garaged in Mario Nuessle's warehouse?'

'Yes. But it's like I told you before with Desmond Wilson's Audi. I'm instructed to lease cars for guests' use.'

'And what is the Mercedes used for?'

Leo Clarke's head drops.

'Is it to transport women to parties, to entertain?'

'I don't know what to say.'

'In that case, you will please accompany the uniformed police officers to Central Police Station where we'll continue our conversation. Detective Constable Dexter, please read Mr Clarke his rights.'

Chapter 82

Canberra

Mary Owens

Mary Owens is the leader of the Federal Opposition in the House. Justin has reverted to his tactic of getting the introduction through Doug Henderson in the party machine.

'You've been making your mark, Mr Kipps,' Owens says in welcome. 'That was a big call to get the government to change the tax laws. I'm not quite sure how you did it – but you are certainly a hit with social media. What can we do for you?'

Doug, Gordon, Justin and Mary are present in the Opposition leader's office for this conversation.

'In the shell of a nut, I want to improve the public perception of politicians.'

It is more of a gasp than a laugh from Mary Owens as she looks at Doug Henderson. His raises eyebrows at her as if to say, 'You should listen to the new man.'

And Justin continues. 'I want to improve behaviour; the way we speak to each other and to the media. The juvenile points-scoring in debates – why should every speech, question or answer bag *those opposite*? Why have we been schooled into that type of speaking as being the norm? Is it from a media looking for a short-grab headline? We sound and look like puppets – frankly, like children who are hurling petty abuse across a playground. My electors in Killen, old and young, seldom fail to shake their heads in dismay at the antics, when they are dealing with their own serious situations in life.'

Mary Owens pays close attention. 'And your solution?'

'Part of it would be in the time allowed in standing orders for questions, answers and debates. But I don't have the detail of how those things can be changed. I can't get on the Procedures Committee and the Speaker gave me the flick.'

She smiles. 'He would. Not just you – that adds to our frustration. But we have people on that committee.'

'But it's not just the rules – it's about not accepting poor behaviour, slack answers, goading questions and parrot-style answers.'

'That's the Speaker's job. We have no control over him.'

Justin is quiet and thinking. 'Okay,' he says eventually, 'can you get *your* side to lift its own game? No more heckling. No more rising to the bait. No more being ejected under Rule 94a. When you speak to the media, no more bagging the government as people. Stick with pointing out flaws in their policy position or delivery. If they choose to bag your people, they will be left smiling at the wind … met by silent reproach … no more nudges, nods and winks. Could we start with that?'

Mary Owens grins. 'You want me to put choker leads on them all? That's a hard ask – because the government is so bloody frustrating, so far up themselves.'

'I imagine the government feels that about your side, too.' He looks at Owens intensely. 'We have allowed this to happen – because we've accepted it for far too long. It's not acceptable out among the battlers. It wouldn't be acceptable in any organised debate and, yet, parliament is supposed to be the exemplar of high-level legislative discussion. Fiery union meetings are better controlled than this place.'

Doug Henderson nods. 'Yes, most of them probably are.'

'And so, when this doesn't work? What then?' Owens asks.

'If your team does that – no reaction to goading comments; serious disappointed expressions when any answer or debate tries to score points by mocking or abuse – then it will be noticed by the media. Same at the doorstop interviews. Never mention *those opposite*, merely speak about what good policy should look like. By ignoring poor behaviour, it will gradually be picked up by the watching press.'

Mary Owens and Doug Henderson exchange doubtful glances.

Gordon adds, 'As Independents who rarely speak in parliament, we can highlight the contrast – quietly, just suggestions – and social media will pick it up.'

'In honesty,' Justin intervenes, 'we need to get the tax laws passed through both Houses as the first priority. This behaviour thing is more a slow burn. Once the laws have passed, if there has been no improvement, I'll go on Dai Evans and stir it up if need be.'

Mary Owens slowly nods her head. 'Yes, I imagine you would.' Another pause. 'What you're saying is right – it's just whether or not your tactic will actually work.'

'What can we lose by trying – by starting – now in the August sittings? All it needs is for the mocking smiles and catcalls to go from your side and be replaced by disapproving dead-pan expressions. It's a bit like when a comedian cracks a joke and there's dead silence from the audience. He knows he has stiffed. The other side will know it too. Let's start in both the Houses. My bet is that the media will pick it up within a week.'

'So all our comments are serious? No smiles? No reaction? We could try it. They'll be asking us within a day what's going on.'

'And you reply that you expect a higher standard than has been happening,'

Gordon adds. 'Once the behaviour has started to change, it will be easier to get the standing orders amended to reflect the practice – the horse before the cart.'

'Worth a try?' Justin asks.

Mary Owens looks at her party organiser.

'He got the tax changes to happen. Why not?' Henderson replies.

'Mmm. I'll talk quietly to them at the caucus meeting. Nothing in writing. It will leak to the press anyway. That will give us a chance to explain that we're trying to lift the standard. Yes, worth a try.'

'It will be remembered at voting time,' Justin adds.

'Maybe. That's a while away yet.'

* * * *

It's back. He hadn't noticed it at all back home on the winter break. But it is back. He knows without looking that there is no thunder outside. What does it mean?

Chapter 83

Canberra
The start of change

It takes only a day for the change in approach to be noticed by the media and another day for it to be confirmed.

The image of Cabinet ministers trying to cajole and prod for laughs is fast falling flat when only one side of the chamber is responding with programmed jocularity while the other remains silent and serious.

From the PM to the whole front bench, there is puzzlement as they are left trying to jolly their own side up to respond.

* * * *

'Mary Owens, what's happening in parliament?' The press are excited and confused.

'We expect a standard of seriousness and decorum in our parliament,' the Opposition leader replies. 'We're setting an example.'

'But you've been some of the worst offenders in the past.'

'We've drawn a line – as a collective group we've had enough. We have important legislation to deal with, not least the new corporate tax laws for which the Treasurer deserves credit in bringing forward. Tidying up our revenue gives us a way into the tasks of the future.'

'But you've blocked revenue measures in the past.'

'We will continue to block ideological screwing of the most vulnerable in society but we want to return balance to the policy settings for the years ahead.'

* * * *

'Prime Minister, what's happening in parliament?'

He gives a dismissive grin to the media questioning. 'Those opposite are just playing games. It's a stunt. Leopards don't change their spots. They're still the profligate spenders of public money. They are not earners. They don't generate anything other than debt and deficit. This is just another of their distractions from their usual poor performance and lack of good policy.'

'Aren't they supporting your government's new Bill to rein in the corporate tax minimisation?'

'And so they should. That's an initiative that the Treasurer has been working on for a long time. You can always be sure that the country will be better off with our side of politics. Ha! Ha!'

'So will you be following Labor's lead with better manners at Question Time and in debates?'

'It's just a stunt. Let's see how long they keep it up.'

* * * *

Dai Evans has been revelling in his return of prestige. It seems to have given him confidence as he addresses the Prime Minister on his morning show.

'Prime Minister, we've all noticed the change in manners from the Opposition both in the House and the Senate. But you call it a stunt. Why is that?'

'Let's just see how long it lasts, Dai. It won't be long before they are back to their rude objectionable stone-walling. Remember, we are the adults in the parliament. They're just trying to be on their best behaviour for a few days for effect.'

Evans voice is very measured. 'Far be it from me to present myself as a paragon of good manners, but Mary Owens said they have drawn a line; that they will no longer accept some of the puerile grandstanding that has passed for debate and answering in times gone by. There has not been a single member call out from that side of the House. They are showing your side of politics up, aren't they?'

'Well, Dai. It's always good to see courteous behaviour in public life. No-one would argue with that. Let's just see if it continues.'

'Well, it might, if your side of politics were to do the same. How many more times will a front bencher from your side be left with only the *canned laughter* being worked from your own side by the Whips? Next, you'll have someone stand up with signs saying, *Clap* and *Cheer*. It's not a good look, Prime Minister. Your bounce in the polls might be short-lived.'

Chapter 84

Canberra

Janet

'I've noticed the change in the Opposition's behaviour,' Janet agrees over the phone. 'It's such a change. Is that your good work, Justin?'

'It's Mary Owens and Doug Henderson – he looks after the Labor Party machine in Canberra. They bit the bullet to make a change.'

'But that was your next priority. What did you do?'

'Oh, Gordon and I might have made a suggestion or two. We're starting to get some better contacts now. So, how are things with you – last semester now?'

'Yes, if I don't do honours, it will be. The course advisers are at me to stay on for another year – but I think I want to get out and start earning. What do you think?'

'No right answers there. Do you have an employer lined up? Would honours help you get a better job? Cassidy's were going to employ me. Maybe they'll have an opportunity for you.'

'Yes, we'll see. I'm not sure that the economics we're doing just now is all that relevant to the future. I like your ideas of sustainable growth but that's a different model from the constant input of resources.'

'It still needs constant inputs, but they are from renewables and recyclables. That in itself creates new jobs. But it takes a mind shift – at least at a national level. The real challenge will come with the constant increase in population. I don't have any smart ideas about that, apart from education. But we can't even get the education right here. It would be even harder in lands where the bulk of the population are illiterate. All they can learn is what they are told or what they can see others doing – and that priority wouldn't be about limiting population growth. Getting change to happen is all about thinking differently, though.'

'Okay. There's not much chance of that at the moment,'

'Yeh, but you never know.'

'There you go again.' She gives a quick laugh. 'You're an Independent. You can persuade, but you can't be the government unless you join a party.'

'Maybe not … But, state parliaments before have had Cabinet ministers from other parties. A hung parliament would make it almost essential.'

'But then you'd have to be the Prime Minister to make things happen at that level. We've never had an Independent prime minister?'

'Not in this country but it has probably happened overseas. You never know what the future will hold.'

'A good thought – another positive one. Thanks. I've got to fly, Justin. Always good to chat. Stay safe down there.'

Chapter 85

'Giles, we just suggested it to Mary Owens and she just upped and ran with it. Hardly a complaint. I don't understand.'

The old man chuckles over the phone. 'Firstly, she has probably been waiting for years for someone to suggest it. They all have. The success comes from having the party machine there too, in the room with you at the same time; that makes a difference because they have to keep all the factions informed and sweet. It's a grubby business, politics, at heart. But, more than that, they're wary of you.'

'Me?'

'You. You who, at twenty-one, were able to articulate a political manifesto on a blog and speak intelligently to it without having to shout at people or bully your way through. Now a year older, you're even more intimidating to the political animals who haven't been used to that. You, who have a following on social media to die for.' He waves his hand over the Skype screen to indicate how technology is enabling them to have their current video conversation on their computers. 'This would have been unbelievable only a few years ago. Now, we can all access it. That's what I mean. It's a foreign world to most of their generation. They can't afford to get you offside or having a go at them on social media. Yes. Justin you are powerful because others are according you that power.'

Kipps shakes his head as he disagrees. 'But I wouldn't do that. I wouldn't use Twitter and Facebook to attack them. I want to challenge their thinking – not intimidate them.' He peers at old Giles on the screen, as if to get him to understand the accidental nature of his supposed power. 'I couldn't do that – social media is not controlled by individuals. It was Dai Evans and Pieter Goosens who inflated that image.'

Giles chortles. 'Like I said. They don't realise how it actually works. They are politicians – used to bowing to influential backers and whichever polls might flag that they could stay in power. For all their bluster and confidence, they are just weather vanes turning to align with majority opinion on any current issues. Alternatively, they need to be persuaded by a mass of money and power to swim against the tide. Either way, you're the unpredictable force with a good logical mind, which they can neither understand nor control.'

'I'm not forgetting the tactical skills of an old gentleman up in Moreton Bay's Manly whose strategic advice is second to none.'

Justin feels good as he sees the hint of a modest smile on the old man's face. 'We do what we can. You are keeping me young and alert, Mr Kipps.'

Chapter 86

Canberra

Kipps

'Blair has told me that he wants to cut back on his days.' Gordon is serious but still upbeat as he passes on the advice. 'He has a book he wants to write and other projects beyond politics.'

'How much cut-back time?' Justin asks.

'By half. Do you know anyone who is interested in working with the media for us?'

'Someone we can trust, you mean? No. I'm the clean-skin down here. When does this need to happen?'

'Soon-ish, he says. Sane work in this city has a short life-span. He's happy to train someone in what he knows; his systems, share his contacts – that sort of thing.'

'Yes, easier said than done. It's more than media contacts; there would be a fair bit of setting up our meeting schedules and the like.'

'Yep. Well, keep your eyes and ears open, Justin.'

'Will do, but don't hold your breath.'

* * * *

The tax legislation seems to be passing through the House – first and second readings. It is expected to clear the House in the week. Then up to the Senate, where no obstacles are expected.

The manners are improving. Mary Owens is clearly setting the standard and the Opposition members appear stony-faced as they savour the squirming on the government benches. The bombast is being toned down progressively. Clearly there is no mileage to be gained when no-one reacts to them with anything other than bored, disdainful looks.

The Prime Minister is trying to claim the high moral ground of having shamed *those opposite* into better behaviour – but even his own side is having trouble with that line.

* * * *

Hetty Fry calls Justin to advise him that the PM and Malcolm McGlashan would like a meeting as soon as possible.

Adhering to Frank's policy of never attending a political meeting alone, he responds with, 'Will it be alright if Gordon Milne accompanies me?'

Someone must have been in the background, because Ms Fry relays, 'That will be fine.'

The meeting time is set for the afternoon.

Chapter 87

'Come in. Have a seat both of you.' The PM seems at once delighted and nervous. McGlashan is his usual courteous self, but strained it seems, to Justin's eye.

Tea and delicate biscuits have already been set out on the low table as the two Independents settle into the comfortable leather of the informal setting.

'An interesting maiden speech you gave in the House. Sorry, I wasn't there for it – but ... you understand. I've read the transcript. Malcolm and I have been having a chat about it. You're never short of innovative ideas. I told you, you both should join our party,' he adds with a jocular laugh. 'We need people like you.'

Justin smiles back while Gordon remains stoically polite.

Having not had a bite at his suggestion, the PM continues. 'You hit the nail on the head about university education when you said that the old Labor government mismanaged all of those programs – endless drain on community resources, is that what you called it? – and you would be right. But you have an idea for making it pay. Am I getting it?' He glances across at McGlashan.

Justin is slow to reply, taking time to sip his tea, before speaking. 'It's a pity that you have so many demands on your time, Prime Minister, because I suspect it might have come across more clearly in the telling, rather than the reading.' He pauses again to catch

Malcolm McGlashan's eye. 'If you are talking, *highlights*, my first point was that sending price signals gives a message about the reverence to money rather than the importance of the learning. Indeed, I was making a second point that not all the world should be seen as a huge supermarket relying on an ever-hungry consumer market.'

The PM holds his hands out, palms upwards and shrugs to his party head as if to query if he has missed the point; but Justin continues.

'Then, I gave my one example of my own university co-payment debt and spoke about how parts of the university system should be free.'

A sparkle returns to the PM's face. 'Exactly, Justin. That's Liberal policy. An elite system with lots of bursaries for the disadvantaged bright students to get into uni.'

'With respect, PM, that is not what I'm saying. I am arguing that key university courses should *only* be accessible on merit and that Australian citizens with that merit should be able to enrol free of any charges.'

'That's pretty well what I was saying, wasn't it? Bursaries for the clever Australian students on merit.'

Justin smiles. 'Perhaps that's why I shouldn't be in your party, Prime Minister. My position is that no-one should *buy* their way into the selected courses. The *only* way should be by merit. But that wouldn't apply to *all* courses.'

McGlashan interjects, 'Perhaps you should talk about those particular courses for the Prime Minister and then that might lead into how a minister might manage that scenario.'

Gordon offers to pour more tea and Justin nods his thanks to the party head for the advice. In return, his expression seems both appreciative and relieved.

'Certainly, Malcolm. I'm proposing that key subjects should be identified as being in the national interest and they should be offered free, on merit, to Australian students. I'm thinking of mathematics, science, English, philosophy – for the logical thinking process leading to law – international languages from all trading partners;

and the Arts – for the cultural uplift of the nation's narrative. The others can be fee-paying and, for overseas students, they *all* certainly would be.'

The Prime Minister grins. 'No economics courses in that priority list, Mr Kipps?'

'The new economics research hasn't been written yet. The universities maybe haven't had the time, with all the money-making agendas.'

The PM is unfazed or just doesn't get it. 'What about medicine, then?'

'Science is the basis of that.'

'Mmm. But would they have to pay to do the final years of medicine?'

'Prime Minister, this is all debatable and will be dependent on government priorities of the time, as well as the fiscal state of the nation. But I would see the government contribution as providing access to the base degrees, bachelor degrees, free of charge, in those key areas. If people want to specialise in economics, they can pay fees. If another wants to continue into medicine or into a Master's degree, then they could pay or be eligible for competitive transparent bursaries – but always on merit. The standards mustn't drop or all credibility goes out the window.'

'What about teaching? You'll need lots of teachers for this new education wave?'

'Perhaps potential teachers should do their academic discipline first, before specialising in teaching – just like the medical specialities. I would doubt that school education in its present form is the way of the future in a technological age. Like twentieth-century economics, the world will need to move into a new century in the way we educate our young.'

'Okay. Like I said, you are full of innovative ideas. So how do we manage that concept, within budget?'

Kipps gives a broad smile. 'You should have me managing that portfolio. Why don't you take me into your Cabinet?'

'You'd have to join the party. I've asked you already – and you have refused. It is collective decision making in Cabinet – no independence there.'

'Why not? Why is there this need for blind following? You accept split decisions by the High Court – that's not challenged. Let a variety of views be aired.'

'You *are* different. What would it take for you to join the party?'

Gordon drops an aside. 'A start would be to formalise changes to the standing orders to acknowledge the new order of mannerly behaviour in the chambers.'

A rat gleam comes into the PM's eye. 'Not impossible, Gordon.'

'And policing the time-filling speeches that could be delivered in an eighth of the time?' Milne continues. 'And give cross-benchers more slots to raise their matters on behalf of their electorates?'

The PM turns to McGlashan with a grin. 'They are running a hard bargaining line.'

Justin brings the focus back. 'Seriously, Prime Minister, there's no reason why the best people for portfolios shouldn't be appointed, irrespective of party allegiances or having no affiliations.'

'Now, you're being silly. That couldn't work.'

'Let's make it even sillier then. There is no logical reason why the Prime Minister couldn't be an Independent. It's a managerial role, a director role – leadership – keeping a policy agenda moving. As long as there are enough members willing to support the agenda, it would be within the constitutional guidelines.'

The PM laughs at McGlashan again. 'Now, he's after *my* job. Give them a sniff and they want the whole cheese. You're right. It is a sillier idea – ludicrous even. So back to the main point, how do we supervise access to education and balance the budget?'

'The starting point should be school education with linked resourcing to the needs of the child rather than the school. What schools have now, they don't lose. No point in retrospectives – that only creates aggravation and long-remembered acrimony. But, the resourcing support goes with the student, from the line onwards.'

'That happens now,' the PM says.

'That's my next point. The criteria for allocating need must be policed, managed like an astute business. No more special deals for particular schools or systems or everyone will soon find dodgy ways to get round the criteria. It's the same with health and disability. Management is about being hard-nosed – but not insensitive.'

'And universities? How do they turn a dollar?'

'They can have as many non-core offerings as they can afford to run; and extra places for overseas students – as long as all the meritorious local students are placed first. It's not about constant expansion, Prime Minister – rather it is about *sustained quality*. Now ... training is not the same as university learning. The two ideas have been conflated in recent years in an attempt to give status to all – and, in the end, the process has trended more toward mediocrity than excellence.

'I'm guessing, but I would think a lot of medical student training would and should be in working hospitals rather than universities – it is training, rather than philosophy. A lot of surgical technique might actually be better learned in abattoirs, for those dealing daily with the rawness of operations, wounds and accidents. We need to sort out the needs from the bullshit and the beige-ness of our current outlook.

'So, what I'm stressing to you is that value is not about money. Education is not the same as training – or vice versa. There are intellectual planes of research and understanding which should be the province of universities. Sadly, much of what currently happens today in universities is really just training to do jobs. Generally, people are unaware of the distinction.

'By all means, train the doctors, nurses, lawyers, engineers, architects, teachers and theatre producers but, beyond the base degree, the training and qualifying should be delivered by professional organisations or in the workplace.

'This is the fault of long-term political leadership allowing this beige situation to develop. It's the result of rewarding the lobbyists rather than engaging in serious strategic planning. We need a victory of vision over short-term pragmatism – and it certainly needs to be managed well.'

Even Malcolm McGlashan is grinning. 'I think you are right, Prime Minister. We need them in our party room.'

'They might be too much trouble for us.' the PM laughs. 'But seriously, you've given us a lot to think about. Would you be prepared to be on a committee to investigate some ideas about this? Maybe even to chair it – since you think it's all so easy?'

'As long as I'm not too young for you,' Justin jibes. 'And the committee is for all parties and non-parties – not just *bi*-partisan. Yes, I would be interested in getting a coherent plan for debate – a shared manifesto even.'

Chapter 88

Canberra

Zoe

The phone call is a surprise.

'Hi, Justin, it's Zoe McAllister. Have you got time to speak?'

'Always have time for constituents,' he jokes, before sensing that the call might be more serious – because there is a pause.

'This is hard to ask, Justin. Would you have any work for me down there in Canberra? I need to get out of Brisbane.'

'Why? What about Frank?'

'That's over!' A long pause. 'He's moved in with Karen Porter. I should have seen it coming. She was around the office all the time, fiddling with the database; then playing touch in the same team. Clearly, more fiddling and touching going on than I'd realised. My fault too. I've been trying to keep the business afloat here but I need a clean break. I can do media-type work – that and planning events; anything in that line. I know it's a big ask – but I thought I should check with you, for old times' sake.'

'I'm sorry, Zoe. I didn't realise either. I actually may have something but I'll have to speak to a few people first. I'll get back to you on that. Not too long. One other thing, though – Frank is still my friend; he is still employed by the electoral office … I'll be dealing with him regularly. Is that going to be a problem for you?'

'It's life, Justin. I need some space away from it. I don't dislike Frank – or indeed Karen Porter. I just want to be able to breathe again without it in my face all the time. Alright?'

'Sure.'

* * * *

'Frank? How are things?'

'Have you just had a phone call?'

'Mmm.'

'To be expected. Tension is a bit high here – but still dignified. It had to happen. Not her fault. I had grown away. She was off in her own world. Karen is a stunner who is interested in me. We click.'

'Yes, I can imagine. Your life is your life, Frank. Are you still happy working with the electoral office? You're not going off to open your own legal business with her?'

'We both have degrees to finish first – but, in the long-term, who knows? We have that shared interest.'

'Frank, part of Zoe's phone call was to see if there were any work opportunities down here.'

'Right. Okay. Yes. She told me she would be leaving town. I didn't know she would head to Canberra, though.'

'I may have an opportunity for her – working with Gordon and me, in the office here. Will that be a problem for you?'

'Not the best situation, mate; but I'll live with it. Like I said, it wasn't her fault. She did nothing wrong. If I was a better sort of bastard, I'd be wishing her well. But I'm still a bit raw today. Tomorrow might well be better. No, mate, if you've got an opportunity for her, that's a good thing – but preferably as long as I don't have to deal with her – at least not for a few months … or years. Zoe and I can be professionally polite. I'm sure of that. We've just grown apart – that's the guts of it. She's into yoga and zen and massage and relaxology. And I'm fit again without any of that, thanks to Karen.'

'Got ya.'

* * * *

'Gordon, I may have someone that we could look at for Blair's part-time role.'

Milne is astute. He can feel the way the words are used. 'I sense a catch.'

'She's a friend.'

'That's not the catch.'

'No, she was on my election committee. She's been running her own business in Brisbane – events management, media liaison. Independent mind. Easy personality.'

'I'm waiting for the catch.'

'She's my electoral office manager's ex.'

'Oh. How recent ex?'

'Very recent ex.'

'Have you spoken to him?'

'Yes. Just did. He says he can handle it. His fault, he says. They grew apart. His view. He has moved in with another woman, who was also involved in the campaign planning.'

'Very tight. Almost within the family. And how is this ex – emotionally? Does she have a name?'

'Zoe McAllister. She'll be hurting. She's the one who was wronged … and she asked me about opportunities. But she's a smart professional woman, used to working in business. Do you want to interview her?'

'Do we want to interview anyone? Don't know that we want to go to open adverts; we could have lots of the enemy applying. Let's talk to Blair. See if he has anyone else in the pipeline. He's been looking for the right type of person. He understands the challenges of the position.'

'At least we know Zoe's past. She comes without any of the Canberra baggage.'

'Very good point.'

Chapter 89

Canberra

Adla Bello

Luke Dexter has recovered the addresses for Adla Bello and Stephanie Taylor from Mario's phone, along with the phone numbers and addresses for a score of other women and men. He also has found a phone number for a Peter Connell ... and he wonders if that is the Peter on Desmond Wilson's Post-It note.

* * * *

Sarah and Luke drive over to Adla's apartment in Bruce and phone her from there, just in case she might choose to disappear. But, in a dispirited voice, she agrees to speak with them.

* * * *

The detectives sit down in Adla Bello's living room, with the same African shield display on the wall.

Sarah says, 'Adla, we've been speaking with Mario Nuessle. He's given us quite a lot of information. When we spoke before, you told us that on the evening when Desmond Wilson died, you'd been out driving to tire yourself out. You also told us that you worked in catering. Perhaps you meant a different definition of catering from the normal.'

Adla sucks her bottom lip.

'Tell us about the man from Turkmenistan, please. Do you know his name?'

Adla sighs and looks round the room. 'Look. I don't want to be involved. There is bad business going on.'

'You *are* involved. Just tell us the truth and we can take the bad people out of circulation.'

She sucks in several deep breaths. 'Can I trust you?'

'We are the police. One way or another, you'll need to answer our questions eventually.'

She rolls her lips as she exhales. 'His name is Ahmed. Steph and I were sent to a house to entertain him and others. It was the usual stuff and we were both lying back on the bed with him between us and he started to rant about the arrogance of Australians – how they look down on anyone who isn't white, how they couldn't understand how someone of colour could be smarter than them.'

'Is Ahmed coloured?'

'Well, he's not pale white. He said he really liked my skin … which is why he has asked for me twice more. He's a stroker.'

'Okay. Go on.'

'Well, he went on about how he had a degree in computing from a university in Ashgabat – that's the capital of Turkmenistan – and that he was a specialist in tiny computers. He had a name for it.'

'Do you mean like microchips?' Sarah asks.

She shakes her head until Luke says, 'Like nano technology … or quantum physics?'

'That sounds about right? So then he goes on about how he can infiltrate these nano bits in computers, if that's what they are … hack into them and make them do what he wants. He said that he could copy the data and even make them explode, if he wanted to. That he and his team were very good at it – that there were really clever people in Turkmenistan.'

'Go on.'

'And he was staying at the Russian Embassy. Well, all of that freaked Steph out. She wanted to tell someone … to warn them like. We have all these terror threats and we're told to look out for anything unusual.

'Anyway, I calmed her down and we got back to Mario's place and then we went home. But she phoned me after midnight, even more agitated. She'd phoned Peter to tell him.'

'Who is Peter?'

'Oh, alright. You gather that we're on the game ... but to look after selected clients – usually guests of businesses. Our job is to keep the clients happy and talking. We listen for any dirt around politics or connections with politicians. We actually hear a fair bit ... and we pass the gossip on to Peter. He decides if it is useful or not. We get bonus payments sometimes ... so it can be worth it.'

'Who is Peter?'

'Peter Connell. He's an investigator really – doing research into people's backgrounds.'

'And honey traps?'

'Blackmail? No, not with us anyway. That's more Gareth Dawes' line. He gathers sensation for others in the city. It's an industry here.'

'Go on. She told Peter that she needed to tell someone.'

'He said that it was to stop with him. She wasn't happy with that. Now, I didn't know it until then that Steph had a contact in the intelligence organisation and that she passed information to him as well ... for bonuses, you know.'

'Do you mean ASIO?'

'Yeh. I think so. So, I think she told Peter that. Anyway, she phoned me all agitated and said that she was going to tell this intelligence person and had arranged to meet him at the Yarralumla boat ramp, you know, on the south side of the lake, near Government House and the golf course. She wanted proper government protection if she told him. It was about one in the morning that she told me this ... and the man would be waiting for her at the boat ramp.

'Then she phoned me again, just a little later, to say that Des Wilson had called her, to stop her going. He was a hard man up

356

from Melbourne. He came on quite a few of our jobs. Protection, Peter said.'

'Fine. What happened then?'

'She said that Wilson was driving over to meet her … to stop her. She said, *Fuck that*. That she was heading out in her car, planning to go past the zoo and over the dam to meet the intelligence man.

'So I thought, this can't end well. So, I got dressed and started driving. I couldn't see them but I followed the route I thought she must take. As I reached the zoo car park, I saw a quick flash of light like someone opening and closing a car door. So I waited to turn right and drove in to check.

'The black Audi was there right beside Steph's blue Camry. I couldn't see them but I could hear her shouting on the walkway over the bridge. So I got out my umbrella,' She grins. 'It has a steel knob on the end. I keep it in the car for safety.'

Sarah and Luke exchange a glance but Adla is continuing. 'I got onto the walkway and Wilson was bashing Steph on the ground. She got up and ran a bit further along. She was screaming. He was punching her and bending her back over the railing. It's a long drop.

'I came up behind him and clobbered him on the back of the head with the base of the umbrella – to stop him – and he dropped like a bag of spuds.

'But Steph was furious, screaming at him. She had been fair beaten up, blood dripping out of her nose and her ear – he had ripped her earring out. Yes, the earring you showed me was one of mine. I lent them to Steph. Sorry. It was the wrong time to tell you – my mind was so confused.'

Adla wrings her hands and sighs loudly. She dabs at her eye, sucks at her lower lip and takes a deep breath.

'So, back to the walkway,' she continues. 'Steph went through his pockets to take his phone, wallet and keys and started heaving him up against the railing. The railing is quite low. I tried to stop her, to pull her away but she was real fired up, hissing – the strength of an elephant. She flipped him over the edge with a huge scream, like revenge … and then she realised what had happened. We kinda both collapsed, drained, sitting down on the walkway, trying to settle – crying with the emotion of it all.

'I helped her back to her car but she wanted to clean her finger-prints from the Audi and then I followed her car back to her place – to see that she was safe.

'I patched up her torn ear lobe with a Band-Aid and put ice on her bruised face. She had a few swollen eggs on her head and some little cuts. Band aids again.

'I took the SIM card out of Wilson's phone, split it up and put his wallet and keys in separate plastic bags and I dropped them into skips and different rubbish bins behind shops. They'll be in landfill now.'

Sarah and Luke nod. 'And then what?'

'I called her in the morning to see how she was. With her bashed face, she wouldn't be working for days at least. She said that she was going to ground – not to worry. She had people to support her. And that's the last I heard from her.'

She let out a huge sigh and looked at the two detectives.

'So she didn't catch up with the man at Yarralumla?'

'Not that night anyway. Maybe he was the support she talked about.'

'You could have told us this when we first met, Adla.'

'I was scared. I'm still scared. There are some hard people behind this business that we're in. Mario is a mouse. He's just the driver.

'There's Leo Clarke. He's a manager of a courier company. But he isn't calling the shots. He's just taking the bookings and organis-ing Mario to make sure we can get to places. There's competition in this business. We're not the only ones. Dawes has quite a few and he's a trap merchant.'

'You say you met with Ahmed on two more occasions. Is that right?' To the nod. 'Did he talk any more about the nano-computers?'

'He brags a bit about all sorts of things … like how the gas fields in Turkmenistan will go ahead when the Chinese come in with their *belt* – like the old Silk Road. He raves a lot. I couldn't follow him. But I told Leo what he said. He was to pass it on to Peter … but I heard no more.'

'Does Ahmed only meet with you?'

'Oh no. There are others from Fyshwick who host parties – legit parties. Ahmed brags about others being there too.'

'Like who?'

'Other nationalities … guests from embassies.'

'Could these parties be run by Gareth Dawes?'

'Easily. I'm sure he does. We hear the word. There's lots of talk in our game.'

* * * *

Back in the car, Luke Dexter gives an earnest look at his detective sergeant. 'I'd be prepared to bet that Ahmed has talked about some sensitive deal around China and Russia … or about nano-computers or deals with countries … and he has been compromised … by Gareth Dawes.'

'And Ivan has found out about it,' suggests Sarah, 'and sent Jakob to get the evidence.' She pauses. 'But how did Ivan know?'

'The grapevine?' Luke offers. 'Blackmail gone wrong?'

Sarah smiles – perhaps a light-bulb moment. 'Ivan might be working both groups.'

'How would that work?'

'Ivan is just a name at the moment. He could be Russian or Panamanian or Turkmen or from none of these places – the name just distracts. He could be the controller of Connell *and* Dawes.'

'No wonder ASIO is involved.'

'Okay. Gently, gently is the name of the game. We still have to clear up the attack on Dawes … without getting shuffled out of the investigation.'

Chapter 90

Canberra

Progress

Newspaper and website headlines herald that the tax legislation has passed both chambers of the parliament. Lots of brownie points are being directed to the Treasurer, for his management of a very difficult situation.

The Prime Minister has also given his tacit approval to changes in the standing orders to reflect the new more efficient way of operating. He initiates a multi-party committee of MPs to investigate, report and recommend the detail of the changes to parliament. Gordon Milne is an Independent voice appointed to this team and the Clerk will eventually be charged with the responsibility for creating a draft in intelligible language for the committee to reconsider.

Justin is starting to feel more comfortable in Canberra. For some reason, the image of Jack Carew flashes often through Kipps' mind – the big American speaking about hard work and making your own luck; but it has been his abhorrent portrayal of the world as a supermarket battleground that has been the abiding backdrop to a lot of Justin's recent thinking. It needs to be so much more than deals and trade.

Nevertheless, *The Manifesto* agenda items are moving in the right direction as Justin picks up his mobile to chat with Giles on the progress so far.

* * * *

Zoe is Blair Adie's pick of the potential aspirants … and absolutely on merit.

It appears, also, that she might be able to access extra work – event planning with a theatre; booking live acts from the touring circuits. She hasn't been putting total reliance on Justin clearly. Good on her – independence.

'I didn't want to be bored down here,' she announces on the first day as she is introduced eventually to Gordon. 'Being busy leaves no time to get distracted. Life is too short but the sun is shining again for me.'

After that introductory meeting, Justin scarcely sees her as she trains with Blair.

For his part, Blair declares that he is impressed. 'She's a good fit, Justin.' The craggy face breaks into a grin with, 'Fast learner – and has views of her own too.'

Two weeks later, she is sitting in the chamber gallery watching the proceedings and personalities – and being noticed; shoulder-length blonde hair, neat business suit, shapely and confident.

'I appreciate the start, Justin,' she advises in the corridor. 'This is an interesting place. Blair seems like a good man. He certainly knows the business down here. I'll be flat out learning all that I should from him before he goes off on his next adventure.'

'How's the theatre gig going?'

'Good. Hard to balance everything just at the moment – but give it a month or so.'

Chapter 91

Canberra

Dealing with the Brisbane office

It had to happen, Justin supposes.

Carol Carey has phoned to discuss some electoral office politics … and her concerns about Karen and Frank.

'I've been around offices like these since I left school, Justin. You need to have a word with them, at the very least,' the Killen receptionist advises. 'They do good work, in their own ways. They're not rude. I don't dislike them. Maybe you will understand it better if I put it this way – there are too many animals on heat around the office and I'm not one of them.' Justin can almost hear the silent chortle over the line. '*They* don't notice, but others do. I know Frank is your close friend. Perhaps, best to hear it from a friend – but soon, please.'

* * * *

Justin runs a few opening lines through his mind and they all sound like a preface for bad news – like, *Frank, we've been friends for a long time.*

In the end, he phones to ask Frank how the office is going.

'Good, I think. Karen is spending a bit of time there – the database, you know.'

'Frank, Carol's there – in the office. She can handle data input. Is the program not working?'

'Naw. Karen keeps it going well.'

'You're missing my point, Frank. Would it keep working from day to day if Karen was away doing her studies?'

There's a pause. 'You're not very subtle, old mate.'

'Maybe. But you two are not being subtle enough either. Eh?'

'You could be right. But … I've never been happier, Justin. This is cloud nine.'

'Frank, could you just keep the bloody clouds away from the electoral office then? For me? Let Carol get on with the work she does best – and the constituents can be dealt with the way they should. Really, your role of overseeing can be done mainly from a distance. Indeed, if either you or Karen need to go there, do so separately. We're all adults – even if your hormones are in overactive mode.'

'Okay. I didn't realise. Honestly, I didn't. How's Zoe settling in with you?'

'She seems to have a new lease of life, Frank. I don't see her much, as yet. She's been training with Blair Adie. Plenty of variety for her here, though. Very busy.'

'Yeh, that's good. Life moves on.'

'Now Frank, did you hear anything of what I just said to you or is your nose still at forty-five degrees, following the scent?'

'Time you got back to work solving the problems of the nation. Don't worry about here. We won't let you down.'

Chapter 92

Canberra

Power and Dexter

'Right, Luke, we have Mario Nuessle and Leo Clarke in temporary custody and an understanding from Adla Bello about what actually happened on the night that Desmond Wilson died. But, I empha-sise, we are not on that older case – that is with the AFP. Our case is about the burglary and the assault on Gareth Dawes.'

Luke Dexter sits impassive in the driver's seat, listening without comment, as his sergeant explains her thinking some more.

'I need to get back to Belconnen and talk this all through with the superintendent. He will advise the AFP and, by implication, ASIO – although ASIO probably knows so much more about it than we do.

'We're now in the politics of policing. We're not in competition. It would be the task of the AFP to follow up on the Turkmen's alleged threat and any interstate criminal connections. Our job is at the grass-roots level of policing. The world of spies is way beyond our remit. We need to be very careful here, Luke. I'll keep the superintendent informed. No freelance observations now. Are you clear on that?'

'I hear you. I'll follow your lead, Sarah.'

'We still have Dawes attacked by three thugs, one of whom might have the name Jakob. We still have Leo Clarke to interview … and then all the pieces have to fit together for credible prosecu-tion cases for the courts and justice.'

Luke Dexter says, 'Okay. That's our business, Sarah – the law and justice for the wronged, not matter whether they are saints or sinners.' He pauses. 'The challenge is to keep moving forward on the right path.'

'Yes, Luke, but remember Barry Cotter's words too. This is a bubble of a place with people intoxicated by the illusion of power. That tests many people's notions of right and wrong.'

Dexter replies. 'Fine. As long as, at the end of the day, the policing component is to keep the streets safe for ordinary people to conduct their legal business.'

'Okay. We still have to find Stephanie Taylor – just to know that she's safe and hasn't fallen victim to someone else. She may even be in witness protection for all we know.'

Sarah smiles and shrugs at Dexter's questioning look.

* * * *

Leo Clarke is ushered into the watch-house interview room, with a duty lawyer to advise him.

After the preliminaries from Luke Dexter, Sarah Power gets straight to the point. 'Mr Clarke, you sent a team of heavies, led by a man called Jakob to Mario Nuessle's warehouse. Correct?'

'Is that what Mario said?'

'I'm asking the questions. And that team was driven by Mario to a house in Hughes where the owner was assaulted and robbed. You gave the instruction for that to happen. Is that correct?'

Clarke looks at the duty lawyer. 'Do I have to answer that?'

The lawyer says, 'My client reserves his right not to answer that question.'

'Let me be clear then, Mr Clarke. We have testimony and evidence with which we *will* charge you with involvement in the assault and robbery at Hughes. When you reach court, the judge can take into account your cooperation, or lack of it. Potentially, you are facing a significant prison sentence unless there are mitigating factors. Ponder that and talk to your lawyer.'

'I would like some time with my client alone,' the lawyer says.

Five minutes later, Clarke and the lawyer are returned to the interview room by a constable. The lawyer says, 'My client would like to make a short statement and is prepared to answer some questions.'

Clarke sits, squeezing the fingers of each hand and pursing his lips.

'I was relaying instructions to Mario Nuessle from Ivan. It was not my decision. I was not in charge.' He pauses and looks up.

'Who is Ivan?' Sarah Power asks.

'He represents our parent group of companies. I'm told that represents a Panamanian company called Bollen Investments.'

'Describe Ivan.'

'Never met him. It's all phone calls and messages.'

'Accent?'

'Foreign. I'm not a linguist.'

'How do you know that the instructions are not a scam?'

'Code words come to the courier service.'

'How?'

'Packages. That's our business.'

'Really?'

'Yes. He has to give the code word.' Clarke looks surprised. 'Ivan controls the money ... and the company. That's how the parent set-up works.'

Sarah looks across at Luke Dexter, her eyes suggesting a vindication of a theory. 'What sort of code words?'

'This month, it is *Amador*. Last month it was *Armenia*.'

'And you don't meet the bosses of this parent company?'

'Look. I run the courier company. We are paid. There are questions you don't ask. These are hard people. If we do what we're told, everything runs smoothly.'

'Alright. Your business operation is a matter for others and at another time. I'm interested in this particular robbery at Hughes. Who is Jakob?'

'He's known as Jakob the Pole. He's not a man to argue with. Ivan sends him.'

'Have you met him before?'

'Once. Certain people come up from Melbourne and I'm required to look after whatever they need. Jakob has been here before.'

'And that's what you did with the incident in question?'

'Yes. I'm an employee.' He looks at his lawyer who remains impassive.

'And Gareth Dawes?'

'Low life.'

'Why?'

'He is a dirt digger ... blackmailer ... sets traps.'

'You knew that Jakob and his team were going to his house in Hughes.'

'Yes.'

'Why was that?'

'He had some stuff on one of Ivan's people. Jakob was told to take the lot.'

'And they did that?'

'That's what I understand. They didn't come back to my depot.'

'What else does Ivan ask you to do?'

'Deliver parcels. That's what we do.'

'What sort of parcels?'

'All sorts. We don't need to know as long as the sender signs the safety declaration.'

'What checks do your run on your packages?'

'The required checks. We've had no problems.'

'So anything could actually be in the packages?'

'We have to trust the sender.' He gives a tired shrug. 'That's the system.'

'So what happened to the material taken from Gareth Dawes's safe and filing cabinet?'

'I don't know. We weren't required to send it on. The team didn't come back to the depot.'

* * * *

With the interview over, Luke Dexter gives a sympathetic grin to Sarah Power. 'That was like boxing while being hobbled. You got a lot of information without mentioning Desmond Wilson or Peter Connell who are both out of our remit. Where do we go from here?'

Sarah returns a patient smile. 'We have a victim who won't co-operate. We have other agendas spinning around our heads. But a crime has been committed. We have some of the culprits, so we do our reports for the prosecutor and we keep the boss informed. And we wait patiently. It always seems to be an important virtue in tricky situations like this one.'

Chapter 93

Canberra

The bombshell

Time has just flown. The last sitting week has arrived.

It's been a year since Kipps' election to represent Killen – and he is just starting to feel as if he belongs in the Canberra bear pit.

There have been many achievements: the passing of the corporate tax legislation and the changes to the standing orders. Justin is now chairing an all-party committee to address the direction of education into the future.

He loves the stimulation of chairing the committee – the bouncing of ideas, the optimism. This is what Kipps savours about the political scene – the ability to mix with clever people, to tease out concepts and perceptions, and to convince the majority to make it all happen. Creativity and logical justification are being used to challenge the certainty of doubt. This is gold!

Justin's mind is absorbed in this whole futures adventure when he returns to earth with a jolt. Blair brings the news.

The inside word is – an early election.

The PM has been impressed with the national opinion polling on his achievements. They're being received very favourably out in the electorates. Two Liberal members are in ill-health. If they were to fall over, the safe voting margin in the House would be gone.

His plan, Blair suggests, is to catch the Opposition napping – to strike while the stars are aligned in his favour. The leak has come from the party office. Forewarned is forearmed but no-one should let on that they know.

'Protect our sources at all costs,' Blair advises. He doesn't know if Labor or the Greens know but Gordon and Justin need to quietly organise themselves.

Zoe will look after the Canberra office as the campaign develops. Blair will bow out to write his books. That is the logical succession plan.

Justin will head back to Killen for the Christmas break – to Frank, Karen and Carol. Without being obvious, he will initiate some forward planning, some meetings in the community – to keep his feet on the ground.

Chapter 94

Brisbane

Giles

Darryl Hope at The Green Man Hotel is high on Kipps' list for an early visit – to show his appreciation and to set the scene for activity in the new year.

Janet has told him she's going to take up a position with Cassidys. Smart move, he thinks. She's happy with her start on a career path but, somehow, her vitality seems to be a bit jaded.

Her language is about what might happen when Kipps finishes his political adventure – and yet she isn't to know that it's all about to crank up again; potentially for a new three-year term, if he's re-elected. For all that, when they talk on the phone or when they're near each other, the scents, the sounds of her voice, the sight of her smile… Ah, whatever – they are platonic friends. It was her choice. That's what they'd agreed. No strings. Free agents.

But, in the main agenda of elections, Giles is the key. He is ageing fast – waiting for the Queen's telegram is no incentive for him. So, Justin will make him an urgent point of call.

* * * *

'This is the actual Notice Paper from the passing of the Standing Order amendments.' Justin hands the document over to the old man, on his Manly verandah. 'Signed personally by the Prime Minister and Mary Owens. That is real political history. What else could I give to the man who has everything?'

Giles grins. 'Very good. Thank you. Another success. It would mean even more to me if you would sign it too, Justin. You were the quiet initiator of it all.'

'Happy to sign.' And he scrawls his moniker on a vacant space.

'Thank you. You're keeping me young. So,' he taps his nose to acknowledge the secrecy, 'we can expect an election announcement sooner rather than later. Good. That'll give us some strategies to plan. I have some thoughts.'

'Your wise words have made the difference so far, Giles. You're my oracle.'

'Mmm.' The old man carries on, ignoring the compliment as if it hasn't been heard. 'I'm guessing that it would be the first Saturday in March, maybe the second – depending on the political logistics. I'd better hang around long enough for that, eh? I have an idea or two for you to think about – especially with the way they all seem to be ceding the higher ground to you over recent matters.'

'Big ideas I can work with. The political tactics you've suggested have all worked. The strategy gives it a context.'

'Absolutely. When the going gets tough, we always test our plans against first principles – the engineer's mantra. And this whole business is sweet revenge, Justin. After a lifetime of being on the receiving end of Canberra's numbing power games, it's good to send a bit of their own back up the pipeline.'

Justin laughs aloud. 'You look too sweet and innocent for revenge. Anyway, this one will be a general election plus a half-Senate ballot. I'm thinking I'll stick to my tried and proven approach of local area meetings in the electorate, and keeping up the social media. Much harder to get traction on a national stage. An Independent can't run on policies that can't be implemented as a government. They all want to vote for a completely programmed and costed strategy, and the leader who can implement it.'

The wily Giles has a twinkle in his rejuvenated eye. 'On the other hand ...'

Chapter 95

Brisbane

Summer break

The summer break has a totally different feel for Justin Kipps. He is back in his parent's home – the comforts, the love, reinforcement and security – but he is also a piece of public property.

Festive season meetings and parties are places to be seen for a returning politician – questions to be asked; answers to be given; pats on the back. Even the whingers are polite. He seems to have been spared the aggressive confrontationists that other parliamentary members had mentioned. Perhaps, it's something about his manner? Maybe, he isn't attuned to their barbs?

The consensus wherever he goes seems to be that he's doing alright – he's been heard in the halls of Canberra and many of the changes that he flagged in the original manifesto have come to pass. All the Killen electors know who made it happen, no matter who claimed the credit – because it is never Kipps who does that. But, they'd heard him and read about the ideas in his manifesto long before he arrived in Canberra.

His priority visits on this trip home are mainly the aged care homes – to sing a carol with them and listen to wiser words than he often hears elsewhere.

He may be young – twenty-three very soon – but with Giles' tactics, along with listening rather than talking, he is gaining a degree of confidence in the direction forward.

That doesn't mean he's without doubt and, as his father regularly tells him, that's not a bad thing – humility not hubris. It is the way he's been brought up.

Yet, he seems to have aged faster than his peers, with the experience down south. He is clearly the man in charge of the future year's electoral direction in Killen – there's a quiet authority about him on his return.

Frank declares that he is happiest when he can defer to instructions – the willing lieutenant. He is happy for Kipps to call the shots – he has been anyway for a long time, quietly, tactfully. Other interests are now consuming a lot of Frank's waking energy. He's studying again, part-time. He and Karen appear to have mellowed gently into an image of discretion. Carol has had her independence re-established at the office.

People treat Kipps with a respectful admiration, which he is finding a little strange to accept. Perhaps, it comes with the status, the role – and it's certainly better than being put down as a too-young lightweight – but he hopes it's because of what he has achieved in the past year.

The volunteer team has grown to over four hundred. While the original model tee-shirt is the badge of honour for foundation members, Giles has donated five hundred more with his new logo: *Vote 1 Justin Kipps. Killen's voice in Canberra.*

Darryl Hope plans to host a pre-Christmas function for all the volunteers when, as he explains, a host of local businesses suddenly want to be associated with the occasion – financially.

Clearly, Kipps is a good drawcard – fame by association.

'I only told them I was going to do it, at the Chamber of Commerce meeting,' Darryl clarified. 'I wasn't even sure if many of *your* people would turn up – being in the busy period – but in the end I've had to dedicate the big room. And the businesses approached me, wanting to donate – I didn't push it – just to have their logos on banners as sponsors. This is not part of your campaign donations, Justin – this is towards The Green Man Hotel. The banners even say... *Proud sponsors of The Green Man Hotel, campaign hosts for Justin*

Kipps, the Member for Killen. It doesn't cost any of us – and the volunteers get a tee-shirt and a good night for nothing.'

'Okay, Darryl,' Kipps replies. 'I'll declare it on the register anyway – although I'm sure it's well within guidelines. The volunteers will earn it all back anyway whenever the Prime Minister chooses to call an election.'

'Any whispers when?'

'His call. Sometime in the next ten months. The last time it was in September – but no harm in being ready earlier.'

'The big parties are starting to advertise now.'

'Darryl, let's just keep the theme of having fun. The volunteers all want to be part of a group which can make a difference. It's people power – mainly young people power. It's so good to see teenagers and early twenties talking about the direction of the country … and indeed the world.'

'You've made a difference, Justin. This community is zinging now.'

'Still a long way to go – and your ready help is giving us a base, a place to focus, where we can cater for several hundred at a time.'

'This is what I mean. Business is zinging. What will your platform be this time around?'

'Patience, my friend. All will be revealed …'

* * * *

In the end, nearly four hundred happy volunteers turn up.

Karen, Carol, Graham and Frank are flat out distributing tee-shirts. Janet doesn't attend.

Justin gives a short speech on life in Canberra and encourages them to be ready to keep democracy vibrant.

Their exuberance is infectious. He can't help but be carried along on their wave of excitement. Yet, they are saying it's him – Justin – who is creating all this momentum.

He doesn't get it… and he has his prescient sense again.

Chapter 96

Brisbane

Breaking news

'Are you going to have a rest, Justin?' Sally Kipps asks. 'You've hardly stopped since you've been back.'

'You should see me down in Canberra, Mum.' He kisses her cheek. 'Seriously, I expect things will be very busy on the national stage when I get back there – so I've got to do the hard yards here, now, visiting people in Killen while I can. They'll get little enough attention later.'

'Isn't that what Carol and Frank do?'

'Yes. And they do it well. All the queries are logged. That was Karen Porter's work. I access the database from Canberra. They all get replies in due course – volunteers do a lot of it – and they seem to love doing it. That's all smooth – but the voters actually want to see me in person. And, honestly, I learn from listening to them.'

'And Zoe McAllister is looking after your office in Canberra?'

'Yes, for me and Gordon Milne. She was just assisting Blair Adie earlier but she'll be on her own now, with only the research assistants who we all share when legislation Bills are coming through.'

'How is she getting on? I was disappointed when she and Frank broke up.'

'It's life, Mum. She's doing fine. There's lots of openings for her talents in Canberra.'

'Have you seen Janet Chou, this time back?'

'Mum, I'm grown up now. I believe she's on holiday in Taiwan.'

'Okay, Mothers are allowed to worry about their sons. You have achieved a lot down there. Even the bridge club ladies talk in glowing terms about you. That's nice for me to hear. Howard and I have been very lucky with our children.' She pecks him on the cheek. 'You're good, decent young people.'

Justin laughs. 'I think the jury's still out on Harry. Only joking, Mum.'

* * * *

After three more visits to Giles, Justin is ready to head back to Canberra – aiming to be down in the week before the Australia Day holiday.

Zoe has managed to get him booked in as guest speaker at the National Press Club – their first speaker of the new year – the benefits of having a staffer on site with experience in event organising and the media. Gordon is planning to be back too. He might be one of the few friendly faces in the audience.

* * * *

Breaking News.

The Prime Minister announces surprise election date.

'Well, there you go,' Kipps mutters at the car radio as he enjoys the peace of the long drive south. 'Blair's source was right after all.'

The headline is on every web page and in every news broadcast.

All the preparatory efforts might well pay dividends in the weeks ahead.

And the date?

So predictable. Even old Giles had suggested it.

Maybe, just maybe, the Prime Minister is as smart as his polling suggests ... but then? Maybe, he thought everyone has been lost in the festive season cheer?

Surely, the business of government is too important for that.

Chapter 97

Canberra

National Press Club

Justin has just driven the Commodore to the Canberra share house to be greeted by a new sense of political excitement. It's in the air – the adrenalin that feeds the political machine; endorphins, testosterone … whatever it is, everyone is sensing it. There is busyness around, in the way people walk; on radio and television; phones are beeping with texts … energy.

The election is to be on the second Saturday in March. It is what Canberra lives for – the **raison d'être.**

'What's the gossip, Zoe?' he asks on the mobile. She is already at Parliament House.

'The PM seems to think he'll catch the Opposition unprepared. And he's travelling well in the polls. It's his call. Apparently, he could have waited for months – a tactical gamble, eh?'

'Mmm. Very courageous. It will be interesting to see how it pans out over the next few weeks. Everything is still right for the Press Club next week?'

'All in place. I've even scored a seat in the audience. Maybe they don't think you will draw a crowd?'

'Some people you just can't help. Let's hope they don't bump me off the agenda to let the PM get first shot at the press. Can we catch up tomorrow and run through everything? Gordon should be here by Friday. Do you have plans for the Australia Day weekend?'

'*Summer Sounds*. Jazz and blues on the grass at the Botanical Gardens on the weekend. Australia Day? I'll probably watch the ceremony at Commonwealth Park, since I'm down here. I've never seen it live before. There's the Australia Day Awards at the Federation Mall on the day before. What's your fancy?'

'You never stop being busy, do you? I'll think about it. See you tomorrow.'

* * * *

Jazz in the Gardens, awards at the Federation Mall and relaxing in Commonwealth Park on Australia Day. Zoe is easy company.

They do it all.

Gordon joins them for the jazz – the novelty of the ceremonies is taking second place to him getting his campaign rolling at home. His systems are more practised than Justin's.

No-one recognises Kipps or Zoe at the events – two young people with big hats casually enjoying the atmosphere. It's like therapy after the constant attention in Killen.

* * * *

'Ladies and gentlemen of the National Press Club

'Thank you for the opportunity to speak with you so soon after the Prime Minister has announced the general election date.

'I wish to address the concept of *the national interest* and pose the hypothetical question, *Why shouldn't an unaligned cross-bencher be Prime Minister of this country?*

'Many of you might remember that, prior to being elected the Member for Killen, I published my manifesto – my set of policy principles – on a website. They were pretty rough and ready – as Dai Evans suggested, undergraduate piffle – but fundamentally they struck a chord as a set of principles and indeed, some of them have since been enacted into law and brought changes to parliamentary standing orders.

'So, *the national interest* ... starting with people – meaningful work for as many as possible, particularly in the *renewable* industries and the transition processes that will be needed over a decade or so. That will take a major mind shift in public attitudes. So, what type of work?

'Non-polluting transport – electric cars and trucks; rechargeable at home or at service points across the land. Sustainable energy production, particularly solar power stored in rechargeable batteries at each house. That is where the research needs to go – battery technology, perhaps lithium ferric phosphate cells – to take the strain off transmitting current over a network of poles and wires.

'Fast, clean, safe public transport as the main mass-transit mode, with urban design to reflect that priority. This is about *the national interest*, clearly encompassing international imperatives that I will address later.

'A vision would plan for everyone to feel a sense of worth – partly through employment and partly from belonging to a community, a nation and a planet. This plan would emphasise a contentment with sufficiency, enough to meet needs – and before you start, I'm not advocating communism, nor overpowering government control, but rather just a mindset away from insatiable greed, away from the price-signalling that the only sense of value or worth is measured by money or possessions. Rather, **value might more appropriately be about dignity, caring, compassion and a social conscience**.

'The plan would advocate a scientific ordered approach to decision making, based on evidence – not gut instinct nor irrational belief.

'It would share a strategic vision of broad direction-setting brush strokes with the concept of *national interest* being understood through the education system – a focus on thinking-skills, not job training. Schools would build expertise in basic understandings while universities would be confirmed as research and learning venues where theses could be promulgated, tested and peer reviewed through professional networks.

'Skill building, for employment, should be supported by business and professional institutes of specific job-based training, whether that be for plumbing, medicine, the law, or aeronautics. The plan would be to prepare the workforce for twenty years ahead and beyond – where Australia will need a degree of national independence in its energy sources, food supply, manufacturing, research and development. The emphasis would be on program management within budgets, as well as budget management itself to create savings for difficult times ahead … for protecting the vital organs of the nation.

'The positivity of the vision will carry the vast majority of our people along. But this is not about blind hope. This will be **a definite plan** with performance checkpoints, deliverables which can be measured. And the legislation would reflect those priorities – easing unnecessary barriers but not abdicating the government's strong role in the regulation of aberrant behaviour.

'At an international scale, the platform is about population control, climate change and renewable industries. There are currently many tens of millions who are refugees or displaced, many more millions in slavery and there is a plethora of crimes against humanity across the globe. Australia's role would be to advocate on the world stage.

'So, in essence, the vision is about putting settings in place which are so well understood and shared that there will be a long-term national commitment. Such is the nature of the time scale – decades to change energy supply systems or manufacturing industries into a renewable mode – that businesses need certainty. The mindset needs to be adopted and so engrained that, for a future government to attempt to change direction in a fickle way, would be akin to unravelling the Snowy Mountains Scheme of the 1950s.

'So, if that is some of the vision, **let me ask why couldn't a cross-bencher be Prime Minister?** Why, indeed, does the leader have to be the expert on everything? Why shouldn't we encourage free-thinking Independents to be part of our Cabinet, rather than be locked into the strictures of the two-party system?

'There are many talented politicians across the whole parliament. Why shouldn't the best be picked, irrespective of allegiance?

'The Prime Minister's role is to manage, direct and lead a team of the most capable in the parliament. Why not enlist the best? Why couldn't they be Independents?

'Let me conclude by saying that I have not mentioned the electorate of Killen specifically in this talk. I tend to communicate with them directly, as often as possible and face-to-face.

'This talk has been about *the national interest* – about the bigger picture of what each of us can do for our society. It is the antithesis of greed and power games. It is about a new mindset.

'Thank you.'

* * * *

A curly-haired man rises in the front row at the invitation of the chairperson.

'Question from Andrew McDade of the West Australian – Mr Kipps, you are not offering new railways, infrastructure, tax concessions nor great gifts for marginal seats … Why not?'

Kipps takes a second or two before replying gently. 'Andrew, this is about a fundamental change in national thinking. It's not about pork-barrelling or indeed huge electioneering budgets from the apparently powerful to the needy. The *apparently powerful* are actually quite weak – they are bribing for votes, after all.

'My push is for grassroots movements – for educated people to be making informed decisions about the future for us all.

'Hope for the better is not a strategy. There needs to be an understanding of the stages to get there – for their continued progress, long after all of us have gone.

'This is a bigger picture – aiming for a change in thinking; being content with sufficiency, having meaningful work to give a sense of worth, belonging, independence and time for the enjoyment of life. It's about building awareness and capacity in the population, the notion that a valid meaning of life is to help others pursue their sense of happiness too.'

'Michelle?' from the chairperson.

'A question from Michelle Beech, Canberra Freelance. Hello again, Mr Kipps. Can I ask you to assume that there is a hung parliament after the coming election and by popular acclaim you become Prime Minister, what process will you follow then?'

'Michelle, thank you for picking up the challenges in my talk. My instinct is to try to use the expertise of all the parliament – otherwise it would be discriminatory and not based on merit. I would seek a generic prioritisation of projects. Each party has aspects of policy which are worthy – but none is omnipotent nor omniscient. The test should be: *Where does it sit in the national interest?*

'It is a management-cum-directorship role, primarily – and ideally it shouldn't be a partisan appointment.'

Chapter 98

Canberra

Planning for post-election

The meeting is held in Malcolm McGlashan's board room in Barton – mainly because it has the convenience of space, plush appointments and ease of location. It is intended to be confidential – visitors arriving in vehicles which are driven discreetly under the building into a secure car park.

Justin and Gordon have gathered with McGlashan; his deputy, Liam Driscoll; Doug Henderson from Labor and Frances Grant from the Greens, each with a staffer to take notes. In truth, the agenda is an offshoot from Justin's Press Club address. While none will admit it publicly, they are wary and here to discuss post-election options – in case there is no clear majority.

Could there be a compromise of allowing an Independent into Cabinet? Could there be an Opposition member in Cabinet? But this is not part of the tribal culture of the two-party system.

Henderson queries, 'How could there ever be agreement in a Cabinet when, politically, ministers would be poles apart in ideology? And Cabinet solidarity? What about that? Surely that is part of the process.'

'It always has been,' McGlashan affirms. 'Both here and in Westminster. I don't see any workable way round that.'

'So, we are looking at shared policies then?' Grant asks. 'Where we can compromise?'

Henderson and McGlashan nod while looking over to the Independents. 'You don't really have costed policies, do you?' McGlashan looks almost smug.

Kipps responds calmly, ignoring the question. 'Why couldn't there be a process for majority decisions in Cabinet? Do you really think this solidarity charade is accepted by the public? Wouldn't it be more honest if we accepted minority disagreement without the Cabinet member having to resign? We accept it from the High Court. It's ridiculous that we can't accept disagreement and doubt in Cabinet.'

Gordon doesn't let the stunned participants recover when he adds, 'Those who disagree shouldn't have to front the media. Let the majority do that – it's their position, after all. When the Cabinet papers are released in thirty years' time, the public will know that there were disagreements. We know that from previous Cabinet disclosures. So, why the masquerade?'

'It's politics,' McGlashan replies.

'Then perhaps it's time we stopped treating the public as if they were ignorant children,' Kipps suggests. 'The government back-bench politicians would thank you. They wouldn't have to come up with weak lies and double-talk to cover what is only rational doubt about policy. That shouldn't be some crime against protocol among free-thinking people.'

'That's only an issue for you and us, Justin,' Frances Grant acknowledges. 'The major parties don't allow free thinking.'

'Our conference wouldn't accept an arrangement like that,' Henderson agrees. 'We have direction setting from our democratic processes. The representatives must follow those directives of the national conference.'

'Look, Justin,' McGlashan's tone and hand gesture show his frustration. 'We have a system that works. It has worked for centuries here and overseas. A Cabinet full of independent thinkers would get nothing done. No policy direction, no clarity – just a hotchpotch of arguments.'

Kipps smiles. 'So your alternative will be to go back to the polls? Aren't we here trying to find alternatives to that multi-million dollar credibility fiasco?'

Gordon Milne suggests, 'Can we at least look at the shared policies – so that you can run them past your party organisations?'

Kipps launches straight in. 'Balancing the books – any problem? Borders – temporary protection for genuine asylum seekers?'

Frances Grant interjects. 'Surely we need to address the issues that the rest of the world is agreeing on – climate change, renewable energy generation?'

'This won't be easy.' Malcolm McGlashan is clearly uncomfortable. 'The whole point is that our policies are different. We are offering the voters a choice – different viewpoints. Even on big issues, we're poles apart – policies on trade, workplace practices, generation of jobs, getting some growth back into the economy, small government.'

Justin laughs. '*Same old, same old*. If we can't agree on the broad issues, what chance do we have about assisted suicide, medical ethics, population control, excessive accumulation of wealth in the hands of a few. Malcolm, if there is a hung parliament after this election, the party organisations will be critical in resolving it all.'

'This is never going to work,' Doug Henderson growls. 'We're all too fixed in our ways.'

Gordon's tone is angry and sarcastic when he says, 'So, we should get the politicians to sort it out on the day? Is that what you're saying? With you and the party machines feeling totally left out? Because someone with have to sort it out?'

'I'll tell you,' McGlashan asserts. 'I'm advocating a strong Liberal win, just as we and the Prime Minister expect. This type of doom and gloom chat is not something that should be discussed seriously in the lead-up to an election. We're all focused on the positives. We are geared up to win.'

Kipps smiles again – thinking of how he'd had the same scenario being painted to him by old Giles weeks before. 'Well, there's not much compromise here in the competitive bear pit. The Aboriginal people advocate finding some harmony. They appeared to live in sync with their environment in this land and, perhaps, with themselves. We have some weeks to go in the campaign process. Always happy to talk again, should you change your minds.'

* * * *

'What a waste of time that was.' Gordon is not in a tolerant mood as they descend in the lift to the car park.

A man is waiting to enter the lift as the doors open – dark, lank hair, eyes shaded by thick brows, giving him a distinctive appearance. In a neat dark suit and with a forced smile of acknowledgement, he enters the lift as the Independents exit.

Ten paces further on, Gordon stops. 'I knew I recognised him. He's Peter Connell – the dirt squad investigator.'

'Who?'

'Peter Connell. Euphemistically called a researcher into people's pasts and presents. He digs dirt – usually one step removed from actually stalking people. I bet he was behind the photos of you at the Brisbane café, which set off Pieter Goosens' rant.'

'Really?'

'Remember what he looks like – and which lift you've just seen him enter.'

Chapter 99

Canberra
Dai Evans and the PM

'Welcome, listeners. Dai Evans here, for our morning show. This is a big day. Coming on shortly will be the Prime Minister in person. Stay tuned. He'll be here after a few messages from our sponsors.

* * * *

'Prime Minister, thank you for giving your time today for our listeners. Now, you are cruising in the polls, after a long time battling along – and you've called an early election. That was a surprise to many. What is your thinking?'

'Well, good to be here with you and your listeners, Dai. As you say, we've successfully overcome a number of very difficult challenges recently – great achievements for the people of Australia – not least, shaming those opposite into good parliamentary behaviour, which we have now formalised into new standing orders.'

'Prime Minister, perhaps your greatest recent success has been the removal of the tax minimisation loopholes for global corporations.'

'Absolutely, Dai. I couldn't agree more. That will add billions to the nation's revenue stream, in otherwise very difficult times – because, as you and your listeners would know well, commodity prices are dropping worldwide. As a country we earn less in these times. This extra income means that the hard but responsible measures which the Treasurer announced in the budget can be progressively withdrawn. The winners are the people of Australia.'

'And, Prime Minister, this money will still flow in the new financial year?'

'That's exactly right, Dai. And may I publicly thank Sam Sendoza, our Treasurer, for his hard work in getting the legislation so efficiently through both houses of the parliament – no easy feat.'

'And have any of these global companies pulled out of Australia – as their advertisements suggested they would?'

'No. They haven't, Dai. That hasn't been easy either. That's the beauty of our great government team – a lot of tremendous work has gone on behind the scenes to persuade them of the benefits of continuing to do business in Australia and of looking after our people here, as good global citizens.'

'So, their shareholders are no longer their top priorities, Prime Minister? The dollar is not the most important priority for them anymore?'

The PM's chortle is clearly heard over the air-waves. 'It wasn't a simple task to get them to see the challenge through Australian eyes – a lot of work has gone on behind the scenes. They are doing the right thing by Australia.'

'So that, and riding high in the polls, is why you are going to this early election?'

'Not entirely, Dai. We wanted to take all our optimistic policies to the people, before the next budget – so that we would have a mandate for this very positive forward direction.'

'Now, Prime Minister, most of these international companies are long-time sponsors of your party and it has been your party officials, led by Malcolm McGlashan, who have actually turned their attitudes around. Am I not right?'

'Aw. Not quite, Dai. Malcolm has done a fine job but it's always a team effort.'

'And isn't it true that both these major achievements that you have referred to were originally put forward by the Independent MP, Justin Kipps? Haven't you stolen his ideas and taken credit for them?'

The chortle is more embarrassed. 'Lots of us have been discussing these ideas for years, Dai – as you would know.'

'But until Justin Kipps put them up in lights – with practical suggestions of how to implement them – nothing happened. You were all in the pockets of big business, PM. Kipps shamed you into acting, didn't he?'

'That's a bit unfair, Dai. As your intelligent listeners would understand, it takes a government to push finance Bills through parliament. It takes a government to change the tone of debate through the standing orders.'

'Prime Minister, it was Mary Owens and the Opposition who stopped the childish wise-cracking in Question Time. They froze you out; and rejected the half-smart mocking comments from your side. Didn't they?'

'Dai, we all had a part to play and I'm sure that the standard of debate is much improved now.'

'So, you've decided to go to the polls in March to catch your opponents off guard after the summer break? Is that right? To capitalise on your bounce in the polls?'

'It's the same preparation for everyone. The Electoral Act is fair to all, Dai. We look forward to hearing all the costed policies from all the parties. The public never get general elections wrong.'

'I'll remind you of that on the second weekend in March, Prime Minister. What about the Independents? Would you consider Justin Kipp's idea to the Press Club that the best people should be in the Cabinet – not just those from one party?'

'Dai, your listeners would know that the only way to get stable progressive government in parliament is to vote for the Liberal–National Coalition on the second Saturday in March.'

'So no place for talented Independents in the Cabinet?'

'The only way to get good reliable government with fully-costed programs is to vote for the government. No other alternative will give the people that.'

'Well, thank you, Prime Minister, for coming on our program and giving our listeners the chance to hear you answer the hard questions.'

'Always a pleasure to be with you, Dai.'

* * * *

Zoe McAllister has a smirk. 'Insider talk says there was a major blue between the Prime Minister and Dai Evans after this morning's program. Almost came to blows.'

'My, you have good antennae, Zoe.' Gordon looks at Justin for endorsement, as he speaks in appreciation of their media adviser. 'Is it likely to become a media story?'

'The word is that Hetty Fry calmed the PM down and got him out of the situation. But he was apparently ropable – using words like *ambushed, you're one of us, Evans* and *traitor act*. I expect the media will have enough stories just with the PM's on-air answers – they were bad enough. Their risk-averse editors will steer clear of antagonising the party with side issues at election time.'

'Trouble in the tent,' Justin agrees with a grin. He licks his forefinger and points in the air. Silently, he gives another round to old Giles.

Chapter 100

Canberra

Mike Penberthy

All the television channels want to cover it – potentially the most hard-hitting interview of the campaign. Mike Penberthy is going to ask Justin Kipps the hard questions. The advertising announces that there will be no place for the young Independent to hide. Everyone should tune in.

* * * *

The ominous, bespectacled Penberthy looks like a storm cloud as, clipboard on his knee, he faces the almost-slight, yet self-assured, youthfulness of Justin Kipps.

'Mr Kipps,' the unsmiling Penberthy opens with his first salvo. 'You have no costed policies – indeed you don't actually have any detailed policies. Only motherhood statements, broad brush strokes – a manifesto, as you put it yourself. And yet you float the notion that you could be a Cabinet minister – perhaps, as you also imply innocently, even Prime Minister. Isn't this just populist rubbish? At best, you can only hope to get re-elected in Killen.'

Kipps smiles and, as is his custom, takes his time to answer. 'I'm not putting a complete costed program forward. That will be a task for *after* the government is formed. How often have electors voted for a series of *fully-costed* programs only for the newly elected party to throw their arms in the air in mock horror. *It's so much worse than we expected.* And then they renege on their pre-election promises and pull completely new rabbits out of the hat.

'So, rather than setting inflexibly rigid promises, I am putting forward *a process* to the voters of Killen – but, more broadly, to the whole Australian electorate.

'I'm committed to putting a negotiated program in place within sixty days of government being formed, with costings based on transparent figures and a clear rationale – a budget to achieve the results with performance checkpoints along the way for monitoring, and key indicators to measure the eventual annual performance. That's a process that can continue into the future, irrespective of who is elected to parliament, rather than the traditional pork-barrelling, insincere promises and deceit.

'And I hold the firm view that the Cabinet should include the best people, with the expertise, to lead the country into a new age. Among those *best people* could indeed be Independents.'

Penberthy's expression doesn't change. 'You have also floated the notion that economic growth is a model for the past century, not the twenty-first century.'

'Not quite, Mike. What I said is the current notion of growth is based on an infinite supply of *new* resources – and that is not a sustainable model. The Keynesian model where governments can promote and stimulate economic growth is still based on past-century thinking. And Free Market champions are no better with their arguments that governments don't create wealth, people do.

'Those models are based on a world where a growing population could keep providing more tax payers who would then use their discretional income to purchase from the supermarket of unnecessary *must-haves*. One of the catches comes when the new people don't have jobs, therefore don't earn income, don't buy, and don't pay tax. Instead of increasing the productive market, they have become dependent on government support.

'It has kept advertisers, marketers and salespeople in business for centuries. But that was when there was endless booty to plunder and cheap labour to be enslaved. That's the old colonial model – and it has followed its exponential curve to have the same amount of wealth held by the world's ninety wealthiest people as have the four billion of the world's poorest – that is half the population of the planet, Mike. Can you honestly say that's the way forward in the twenty-first century?'

Penberthy sits in his familiar Buddha pose and asks, 'Do you have a model that is not past-century then, Mr Kipps?'

'Yes, I do – in the broad brush strokes that you seek to demean. The new model is based on the assumptions that the world's fossil and mineral resources are finite and that the planet's natural systems are under strain from human intervention, including exponential population expansion. The new model is based on reusable, renewable and recyclable resources – *they* are the inputs to the model.

'The changed mindset is that, as people, we need to be content with sufficiency. There is no necessity for greedy accumulations of wealth. That mindset can also understand the meaning of *value* in other ways than as a function of money. Other ways – principles really – such as caring for others, sharing happiness in human interaction, and the joy of artistic invigoration rather than collecting material possessions. So the new economic models are about sustainable sufficiency rather than being based on unsustainable growth – more like natural ecosystems actually.'

'But, Mr Kipps, you have no detail. You can't run a government on these generalised motherhood statements.'

Kipps grins again at the way Penberthy asks his questions without seeming to ask directly – just leaving the statement hanging. 'Several points, Mike. First, the world's brains have not been focused on these motherhood principles, as you put it. That is a product of leadership failure on a grand scale, worldwide, for decades. When they do, the detailed models will emerge.

'Secondly, the scientific community is flagging significant changes to the world climate. Viewers of television see populations wearing face masks because they have no clean air. Starvation and polluted water plague many continents, and the world population which is now at 7.6 billion is projected to be 8 billion in 2025. In 1950, it was 2.5 billion. That is a major part of the problem.

'If you use the analogy in my maiden speech of a train moving along a track, with many sidings going off to nowhere, everyone watching and listening can see that the track we're on is heading to rapid deterioration – it must come to a head at some point. But, it's an enormous challenge. What can one person do to make a difference? Is it just easier to hope that it doesn't all go to shit in our lifetimes? Or that some great overseeing deity will at least save the chosen ones?

'Mike, I think the Australian public are smart enough to see through the spin, the lies, the broken promises – fuelled by a lack of vision and supported by vested power groups, still only looking for short-term gain.

'The starting points are to move as fast as possible to renewable energy sources – that will take one to two decades at best – but it does generate sustainable jobs on the way. Then the research into battery technology needs to get power storage attached directly to solar panels or windmills on every house. Suddenly, the challenge of maintaining inefficient poles and wires has been significantly reduced. That reduces the costs to treat water and to power the industries which create the jobs.

'Recycling and regenerating must become the major source of materials for manufacturing industries and Australia must train its skilled developers of clean-energy transport, telecommunications, construction and food producing. It is a major change in philosophy which will progressively take decades to implement.

'There's a start for you, Mike. How much more could be formulated with the nation's best brains working on it? The great value of process over sham-costed programs is that the process is based on rational principles which everyone can understand – even if some will not admit to it, usually because they are losing their power bases.'

'Alright, Mr Kipps. Can I move to your suggestions of population control. Isn't this so much pie in the sky?'

'Not easy, I grant you, Mike.' And Justin takes his customary pause. 'Logic would again suggest that with infant survival rates improving dramatically and life expectancy increasing by decades – through fine medical support – the need has surely gone to have huge families in the hope that some might survive. This is about attitude change.'

Penberthy raises his hand. 'Before we get off into your philosophy on this one. Let me point out that you are part of a family that has produced more surviving children than the original parents. Doesn't that just highlight the moral dilemma – not in my back yard? How would you respond if your sister hadn't been born?'

'Ah, Mike. Overly emotive. Clearly when someone is born, they can't be unborn. The question is not about killing people off, it's about how many are conceived in the first place. We have the means to control that aspect.

'Take the emotion of personalities out of it and make the issue something more bland; like building a levee bank to protect a town from floodwaters. We have the means to do it. There are costs; financial and human. If we didn't do it because of the price to be paid, a government would be accused of irresponsibility.

'Hard moral questions are easy to play for a sensational headline – perhaps that makes for good TV – and the questions are invariably asked by the people who don't have to take any responsibility for either the way forward or the end result.

'The Chinese government has been the only national government to have a one-child policy and the results are there to see in the population pyramid, now forty years or more on. The massive growth has slowed dramatically and will continue to slow – probably with more humanity than at the start, given that they now allow a second child. Other countries with large populations have other more specific programs of education and birth control.

'Mike, one way or another, the population growth will slow – hopefully before the regenerative powers of the planet have been suffocated. Famine and disease are rife in the poorest countries. Wars are happening elsewhere; either for contested space or for power games. History shows a pattern of genocides – sanitised with terms like ethnic cleansing – and that is still happening.

'The challenge is great. But like most journeys, it starts with one person and one step, followed by others joining. It's about educating for another way – and not retreating into the shell of denial.'

Penberthy gives his first nod of the interview. 'Alright. Final question. Under what circumstance, if you are elected by the voters in Killen, could you make a difference on the national or international stage?'

'I think voters can see by the recent tax minimisation legislation and the standing orders improvements that some Independents like me can influence the national agenda. I serve currently on an education committee – indeed, I chair it. Our education processes were devised in previous centuries and haven't been changed to meet modern needs because of too many vested interests – not least, its child-caring capacity. There are strategies to move this agenda forward in ways that the public will welcome.

'But, my next priority will be to push the notion that the best parliamentarians should be in Cabinet, regardless of party allegiance or lack of it.'

'Thank you for this interview, Mr Justin Kipps. I wish you well with convincing the electorate.'

* * * *

'Well done, Justin. It came over well,' Gordon praises him and Zoe smiles.

'That's good. We'll see what the wider reaction is.'

'It'll be a lot better than the PM is getting,' Zoe concedes. 'After Dai Evans gave him that touch up, he'll be lying bruised and battered in casualty. No-one has come in to support him since – the whole flow has been negative so far.'

'Remember, they build you up and they knock you down,' Kipps notes sagely.

'Pleased it has gone well for you, though, Justin.' Gordon gathers his gear into his briefcase, in a hurry. 'We need all the backers we can get. Now, I've got to fly – electoral business to deal with.' And he leaves with a wry grin.

Justin looks at the still smiling Zoe. 'Do you hear rumbling?'

She listens. 'No. Just the normal sounds.'

'Mmm.' He frowns. 'This has happened to me before – I can hear something. I've put it down to tension or my mind anticipating some stressful event.'

'Have you tried massage?'

'It's in my head, Zoe.'

'Heads can be massaged. Even hairdressers do that. Will you let me show you?'

He grins, patiently. 'I'll try anything once.'

'Where is the rumbling?'

He laughs. 'Inside my ears. Where you normally hear things?'

She is unfazed. 'Heard in the ears … or sensed, deeper in.'

It is at that point that Justin takes the offer for more than a gimmick. 'You're right. It is sensed. Okay, give it a go.'

He lies back in the office chair, with her behind and above him.

'This is not the ideal situation for any therapy,' she advises, 'but we might see if it makes any difference.'

Her fingers are strong but gentle. They move in circular motions, above the ears, to the sides of the brow, over the scalp and back to the brow.

'Any difference?' she whispers.

'Yes. Very peaceful. It's feeling better by the second. Thank you.'

'This is part of the relaxology that I practise. It works for me too. Yoga. Stretching. Massages with aromatic blends. It takes away tensions. Goodness, how much tension have you been subjected too, recently?'

'Just the usual amount.'

And she continues working his forehead.

'What about your neck muscles?' she asks.

'Try that.'

Her fingers knead gently into his knotted neck muscles.

'That's good too, Zoe.'

'Justin, your muscles are as tight as a drum skin. If you like, I have all the gear back at my little apartment. I reckon I could take months of tension out of you in an hour or so. Only if you want.'

Chapter 101

Canberra

Zoe

Justin is floating on an aromatic magic carpet. Zoe has been right.

Her apartment is a little one bedroom, plus a living area, bathroom and verandah – but all that a hard-working woman would need (or probably be able to afford) in Canberra.

The large high-mattressed bed is doubling as a massage table with towels beneath an old sheet.

Justin lies face down in his underpants while Zoe works delicately over all the knots in his back muscles. The exotic scents of flower blossoms fill the air.

'Is this working for you?' she asks. 'Are your tensions going?'

'It's brilliant, Zoe. I've never had a massage before – never in my life. This is great therapy. How are *you* doing? That must be hard work. All that pressing and rubbing.'

'Might take a short break. But glad it's helping. Do you fancy a wine?'

* * * *

The headlines are beeping on all the mobiles.

Prime Minister accused of stealing Kipps' ideas.

Backbenchers query PM's decision to go to an early election.

Mary Owens calls PM a national disgrace.

Can the PM last to the election?

Justin has hardly looked at Zoe before. She had always been Frank's girl – older and wiser – and taboo.

As he lies sipping his wine, looking at her in her sports bra, glowing from the effort of soothing his tight muscles, he is seeing a confident, independent woman with skills beyond the business image.

And he realises that he's with someone he has known from before the politics – someone he should be able to trust.

'That was good, Zoe. Thank you.'

'You're welcome. Has the rumbling gone?'

'Yes. It has. Maybe it was just natural anxiety.'

'Justin, your back, hamstrings and calves were knotted tight – rock hard. Do you do any exercise? Play sport?'

'Not really, anymore. Just what movement I do in daily living. Been a bit fixated with politics for a while.'

'Then, you need regular massage sessions to keep relaxed, especially through this busy time leading up to the ballot. Probably every couple of days. There are plenty of professional masseurs around.'

'I think your skills are pretty good. We might try this again. I'll need to buy you some more sheets and towels. What are *you* doing to keep fit?'

'There hasn't been time for sport yet. Might look into doing netball or touch later, when its cooler but, for the moment, I just do lots of the exercises I've been telling you about. I could show you those too.'

They both grin as their eyes meet.

He had parked the Commodore in the street about two house blocks along from Zoe's apartment.

A movement causes him to glance across the road. There's a woman on a mobile phone – a normal enough event.

Adrenalin courses through him for no apparent logical reason. It's like a flashback – the uncharacteristic pose and she isn't speaking on the phone; she is videoing. His mind absorbs it all in nano-seconds. He freezes; not looking at her but trying to sort out his thoughts; hand in pocket as if feeling for car keys.

When he glances up, she has moved and is getting into the passenger side of an idling car. The driver's face is familiar; the eyebrows and the lank hair. He is trying to look away, at his visitor; and then the car leaves before Justin can reach his own.

What is that all about?

Chapter 102

Canberra

Ann Fletcher

Ann Fletcher from *Bay News* calls. She is following up on the Mike Penberthy interview.

'How can you be sure that the current economists have got it wrong? I follow your reasoning but you seem to be the only one speaking about a whole new economic model for this century. Can you give me something to work with – for a story?'

'What about some history. In 2007, APEC (Asian-Pacific Economic Cooperation) met in Sydney and stated proudly, *"We are confident that robust economic growth will continue"*. Twelve months later, the Global Financial Crisis hit and the economies collapsed.

'Even John Maynard Keynes, back in 1936, said, *"Practical men, who believe themselves to be quite exempt from any intellectual influence, are usually the slaves of some defunct economist"*.

'The US Federal Reserve and the International Monetary Fund have consistently downgraded US forecasts for the past decade. The current economic forecasts are just hopeful optimism and a belief in old economic models whose time has most probably passed. The Australian Treasury forecasts have been adjusted down again – every time for the past seven years. Do your own research on it because politicians will always spin it to keep the *same old, same old*.

'I've said it before: the stock market is the world's biggest casino. It's not just mum and dad investors trying to support a business or two – the danger is caused by the high-rollers gambling with money that they don't have. That has been a major reason behind most of the recent corporate collapses and, indeed, the Global Financial Crisis back in 2008. With that type of thinking, the next collapse won't be far away.

'But, it's deck-of-cards stuff, Ann. The foundation of current economics is fundamentally flawed. It's based on having infinite resources and the discretionary income of an ever-growing market. They can't predict how their policies will work. They've been getting them wrong everywhere … and very often. Those last-century models don't deliver, in these times.

'We need to get our budget on a realistic footing with sustainable industries providing stimulating jobs for most of the population as they gradually become self-generating energy sources.

'Then we can have some insulation from the world crazies as we work to persuade the international debates on population management and the refreshing of our environment.

'This is not rocket science, Ann. It's just that the rocket scientists have been working on other projects.'

Chapter 103

Canberra

Blackmail

Justin is on his own, near his share house, when a shady-looking man approaches him; clean but shifty.

'The press have a story about you and your media woman.'

'My media woman? And? Why is that a story?'

'Visiting her in her small apartment? That's a story.'

'I'm a single man. Is there something wrong with that?'

'Just giving you advice. They could take the line that you have stolen your best friend's girl.'

'And where is your information coming from?'

'Sources.'

'And what do you want?'

'Social media is giving the government a hard time; the PM, in particular. It would be good if it stopped.'

'And who are you?'

'I have no name.'

'Isn't that convenient? Who do you work for?'

'Just passing on information for a friend.'

'And his name?'

'Just a man I met, who asked me to pass on the intel to you.'

'What did he look like?'

'Just an ordinary bloke.'

'My age or older? Blond or dark? Tall or short? What did he look like?'

'Middle-aged, dark hair starting to go grey. Big eyebrows.'

'That covers about a quarter of the population. And what do you need from me?'

'I just had to make sure I told you. That's all.'

'You've been paid?'

'In advance. In a pub. Didn't I tell you that?'

'And how will the greying man know you have delivered the message?'

'Social media will change. You might appear on it.'

'And your name?'

'Told you – no name.'

'Mind if I take your picture then?'

'Fuck off, you bastard …' and, as he disappears quickly along the street, behind parked cars, Justin stops his recording.

Chapter 104

Canberra

Did you start a rumour today?

'The therapy is working, Zoe. How are you with all this?'

'You could give me a massage in return.' She grins as she speaks. It is the invitation that has been implied and yet never said – until now.

Both in underwear, glowing with perspiration, they breathe the aromatic oils from the permeated sheets and towels supplied by the reliable Kipps. It's only a small step from the shared physical contact of massage for it to transcend into an almost spiritual blending of needy souls.

For Justin, it's as if he's been lifted into a euphoria-fuelled haze of aromas and sensations. Zoe's skills seem to know no bounds of eroticism and Justin is a very willing student; a responder and then an initiator.

When they eventually descend from their mutually frenzied exhilaration, Justin notices that the rumbling has gone. They are surrounded by an aura of peace.

* * * *

By morning, Justin thinks, *Probably shouldn't have done all that.* But another inner thought sees a shady man, a woman with a phone-camera and the bushy eyebrows of that Connell bloke.

'Up them! Up them all! We're just being healthy and honest – and no-one will tarnish that.'

* * * *

The story breaks on a sensational Sydney talk-back show, but not with Dai Evans. It's nothing definite – just a suggestion that Justin Kipps is not all the sweetness and light that he paints himself to be.

After he and Zoe discuss it, he tells Gordon – they all work together after all.

'Probably not wise to be cavorting with an employee, Kippsy. There's a bonking ban between bosses and staff in Canberra, after all – for Cabinet ministers, really. But hey … you have no ties and she's quite a lady. Keep it under control.'

Then Justin phones Frank.

After a stunned silence, his mate blurts out a half-laughing, 'You randy dog, Justin. In a way, I'm jealous – because I couldn't keep it working for us. In another way, I'm happy for her – she's a good woman – and for you, me old mate. You old dog, you.'

'So you don't have any problems?'

'Naw, I wish you well. I'm fine in my own world, with Karen.'

'Do you see Janet at all?'

'Oh yes, around you know; sometimes. She's not very active here really since you left. Why? Was something still going on between you two?'

'No, Frank. She called it off, remember? Didn't like the politics. We have talked on the phone from time to time – but not much recently, either. No, I just wondered.'

'So, no problem then. Are you expecting this story to go big? We haven't heard about it up here – it's just a grubby Sydney shock jock. I know who he is. They call his radio station – Dysart FM. Acronym for *Did You Start A Rumour Today*. Just grubs, they are. I actually doubt that mainstream would touch it. That station does this all the time – flying a kite to see if they can get a publicity bite. And who would be game to spread spurious rumours about you on social media? You have a lot of fans, mate.'

Justin almost laughs. 'Good to know there are some troops in my corner for a change because I always get the impression down here that the enemies of our legislation are just rolling over fairly quietly with a *we are waiting our moment* gleam in their eyes.' He pauses to get back on track. 'So, I don't know if it will get bigger. I've given the federal police a recording of a man who approached me in Canberra. I think I know who might be behind it all – they are just creating a distraction from their own problems by maligning me – fallaciously, I might add. I, and we, have done nothing wrong.'

'She works for you, mate. That's the bit. Conflict of interest.'

'Technically, only. Zoe works *with* me. Gordon and I share her payment – but this is not a boss-servant relationship, in any traditional sense. She is not an employee really – more a free-agent, paid for the work she does for us out of parliamentary expenses, which is hardly even my money. There is no power relationship between us. She's a good friend from my pre-politics era. She does work for theatre events in Canberra, as well as what she does for us. She's not dependent on me. We're just one set of the people she contracts for. No-one would boss Zoe around. You understand that.'

'Okay – I get you. Don't get too defensive. I'm only flagging how others might choose to see it. But no problems with me. I'm guessing your mother will be the next phone call.'

'Yep. And then old Giles over in Manly. He'll have perspective, too.'

* * * *

'What do you mean? Freelancers released a story, Peter, and you know nothing about it?' Malcolm McGlashan is quietly furious with Connell. 'Have you any idea what problems you're creating with these unauthorised forays into your dark arts?'

'They're always unauthorised, Malcolm.' Peter Connell chortles on the other end of the phone. 'He'll be off your back, now.'

'You bloody fool. He was never on our backs. He was almost one of us.' McGlashan growls. 'So this *is* your team's work? I'll find out anyway; you can be sure. Come clean with me.'

'Of course. All we did was take a photograph or two of him leaving a particular address. Guilt does the rest.'

'Except that he has nothing to be guilty about. You're a cretin.'

* * * *

McGlashan makes two phone calls.

The first is to Hetty Fry on her personal mobile.

The second is to the Australian Federal Police. 'I want to talk with you about a man called Peter Connell.'

Chapter 105

Brisbane

Election night

The election is close and Justin flies back up to Killen. It seems that the story from the Sydney shock jock hasn't achieved any public traction in Brisbane. Those who do know, think Justin's reputation has been enhanced – he's more mortal, has human needs and flaws.

Graham McGrady thinks it's all brilliant. 'Terrific woman, Zoe. Always liked her.'

And Justin only wants to concentrate on the jobs to be done by the volunteers.

Darryl Hope has given them a small meeting room – with the big one to be available when the ballots are on. His only request is for a couple of meetings with Justin speaking, to draw the crowds from far and wide.

No problem for Justin. This is an accustomed routine after over a year in the role – but he still gets nervous, despite his projection of an ultra-calm image with the quiet tone of his voice.

Giles doesn't seem in the least fazed by Justin's new relationship or the failed scandal. 'Half your luck,' is his only comment before they begin discussing tactics.

* * * *

Janet turns up at one of the meetings.

'I wasn't sure if you would still volunteer for these gigs,' Justin says.

'I told you I would still work for the cause. You've achieved a lot, Justin. We're all very proud of you. And here, I'm just one in the crowd.'

'I'm pleased that you're happy, Janet.' She gives no indication of having heard of his Canberra relationship.

'You haven't phoned much, Justin. You must be very busy.'

'Yes, I get tired from all the meetings. It's hard to get time just to think.'

'I wouldn't mind talking to you a bit more, after the election is over. I've enrolled for a research Masters in economics – but I'll still be working with Cassidy's. I approached the uni with the idea of doing some work around your ideas of a new economic model for this century. I've even met my likely supervisor.'

'And how did he react to your proposal?'

'He's a she. She thinks it has potential. She's interested too.'

'You can be the first of our public intellectual brains to apply their minds to the task. That's good, Janet.'

'Well, let's get through the election first and, if you're back in Canberra, we'll see how things are placed after that three years is over. I might even be well into my doctorate by then. Cassidy's is working out fine, too. They are good people. Keeping my feet on the ground.'

He replies, 'Keep in touch, then.' He has a strange sense of being flawed as a person. And yet, what has he done wrong? He didn't choose this path.

Rather, ever since he posted *The Manifesto* on his blog, it was the southern shock jocks who stirred up social media and carried him along on this path to a political career – albeit, a short-term one.

* * * *

The night of the election is more restrained than previously – at least from Justin's viewpoint. Frank, Karen and Graham are power-houses in terms of organising the volunteers.

Justin gains thirty-nine per cent of the primary vote, which after preferences comes out at fifty-nine per cent – a substantial margin; an increase and a clear mandate to represent the electorate. The talk this time round is all about *the process* for government, for Cabinet, for vision.

* * * *

In Canberra, at the close of the night's counting, the Liberal–National Coalition have sixty-five seats, Labor have sixty-three. The Greens have nine. And the Independents have ten – with four undecided.

ABC psephologist, Laurie Black, is prepared to give the undecided seats to the Independent candidates, although it could be a week before the final declaration is made. A governing party needs to have control of seventy-six seats to pass supply; the financial Bills. Neither major party can do that, even with the support of the Greens.

They will need to have some Independents on-side.

The PM advises that he will carry on in a caretaker role until the final results are declared and then he will resign the leadership – with an immediate move to the back bench. He will accept no Ministerial position. Sam Sendoza gives the same declaration.

The talk among the television commentators is about who could form a government and who could be the leader.

As Mike Penberthy puts it, in his accustomed droll manner, 'Perhaps, Justin Kipps and his process will get a chance to be tested.'

And no-one is quite sure whether it is a question or a statement.

* * * *

An AFP superintendent phones to advise Justin Kipps that a Peter Connell has been taken into custody for questioning.

'We've identified a number of his customers and targets – you were most probably one of his targets. We have a catalogue of possible charges against him. Potentially, he could be facing up to ten years, so he will plea bargain and we would expect to net lots of others – many small employees, perhaps, but we are very interested in the corruption at higher levels.'

'So this Connell will be out of my hair now?'

'*He* will be. But you shouldn't assume that there aren't others out there – all with similar agendas. That's part of the task of your security detail's brief – to be on the watch for them.'

'Thanks. I appreciate your good work.'

Quite a night.

Chapter 106

Canberra

To form a government

The scene is the House of Representatives meeting room, set up for a round-table discussion. There have been corridor huddles going on for days but the nub of the problem is that neither of the main political parties can muster the numbers to form a government.

Almost in despair, the party leaders have answered the call of Justin Kipps.

Around the table are Malcolm McGlashan, his deputy, Liam Driscoll, the chief of staff to the PM, Hetty Fry, and their leader-elect in the parliament, Dr Judith Holmes, an experienced and clever Liberal from South Australia. Kipps is there, in the control chair, with Zoe McAllister on one side and Gordon Milne on the other. Mary Owens and Doug Henderson are representing the Australian Labor Party, and they have two advisers called Tony and Roberta to assist them. Frances Grant is there from the Greens with former CSIRO science director, Dr Jane McClure as the leader of the parliamentary wing. They have a man called Nathan advising them.

The group is also capably served by the Clerks from both chambers to answer questions on protocol, with a secretarial assistant to record official minutes.

Justin opens. 'Ladies and Gentlemen, Australia expects that we can overcome many of our philosophical and ideological differences – put them to one side and produce some good government

415

for the nation. It would appear that neither of the large parties has been able to secure the numbers to govern. That is in no small part, I admit, due to the thirteen Independent members elected to the House.

'My take on that is that the people want no more of *same old, same old* – and I'm also sure they don't want another expensive election.

'In the lead-up to the ballot, I proposed a different model – asking the question as to why the most talented from each political group should not make up the Cabinet of a new cooperative government.' Old Giles has told Justin to concentrate on the flattery. *Brush their egos*, he'd said. 'That's what I put on the table first today. I'm prepared to chair such a group but I'm not putting myself up for the same style of chair or leader as prime ministers have been in the past.

'Clearly, I've just turned twenty-three. There are people in this room old enough to be my parents and perhaps grandparents. I respect your experience and your sensitivities, but what I bring to this impasse are several proven independent skills of debating, negotiating and of developing processes based on principles.

'They could form a basis for our cooperation in finding common ground. Do you want me to stop or should I explain my ideas further?'

There's a silence as everyone looks at their neighbour like a querying Mexican wave.

Mary Owens breaks the impasse. 'We have sixty-three votes in Labor. We could make a bond with Jane in the Greens – that is nine more: seventy-two. We need four more from the Independents. Would we have that, Justin and Gordon?'

Gordon answers. 'I'm sure you and we could get it as long as we're talking about the process that Justin flagged before the election – agreement on principles, not reinventing the wheel, the best brains in the parliament on the same team – and working towards a vision.'

'And whose vision would that be?' Malcolm asks.

'The test,' Justin answers, 'should be: *Is it in the national interest?* Followed up with: contentment with sufficiency, who is disadvantaged or advantaged? Nothing is ever perfectly neat but it needs to be honest and transparent.'

'Remind us of the process?' Doug Henderson asks.

'The policies evolve from the planks of economic security, physical security and social security. It's also a move toward our national independence by fostering renewable energy generation; innovative engineering designs for the industries of the future; and meaningful employment for the vast majority of our people. Any proposed policies would go out to experienced committees to refine. Then, I would want to know that we'll operate with integrity to change the current mindset. That's the challenge I've been thinking about a lot recently.

'I would propose to you – and the people – that we form an Independent National Corruption Commission (INCC), based in Canberra as an independent body, with significant statutory powers, a range of investigative powers and public hearings to expose corrupt matters that are systemic around the conduct of government.

'Although it has been talked about for years, it hasn't really got beyond ineffective tokenism. This INCC would be new and it would shine some sunlight into dodgy and criminal behaviour that has been ingrained into the psyche of those in power.

'Under my original process suggestion, Doug, we are effectively in caretaker mode until we sort out our new direction – so the business of government can continue as it has been doing. After thirty days, we should be able to present our raft of reasonably refined agreed policies, in development, to the people.

'After sixty days, we should have a budget in place to maintain services and to gently move the agenda forward. The policies would be out for public comment and adjustment before that – and on-going. However, as a government, we will be back on the main track with a sense of direction, openness and purpose.

'We would then audit our revenue – that could influence policy development even further. I'm particularly interested in discrepancies between pre-tax profit, say from large organisations like the banks, and what is actually paid in tax.

'Likewise, we need a thorough examination of current expenditure. As Gordon said, this is about moving forward carefully with a new model, towards a vision. It's not about throwing out what works, nor trying to reinvent the wheel.'

More silent looks – broken eventually by Dr Jane McClure. 'You are at least offering a practical situation out of the impasse, Mr Kipps. I thank you for that. The devil will be in the detail, however. Since you have clearly thought about process and probity – which I don't actually mind on the surface – did you have any ideas of what a cooperative Cabinet might look like? That might indicate your priorities to us in a different way – in a method that my questioning mind might find some answers.'

Justin takes his time. 'I've thought about portfolios and even about the people who might fill them – but that would be for negotiation with you and your teams. This would just be as a guide for further thinking.' He looks at Dr McClure and the Liberal leader, Dr Judith Holmes, both clever women who he would particularly need to persuade on the merits of his proposal, once again using the old skills of argument that he much prefers to a wheeling and dealing approach.

'Here is a type of overview of *a* proposal. Nineteen in the main Cabinet – another eight in the Outer Ministry. Cabinet would have fourteen from the House and five from the Senate. Twelve male and five female, but selected on expertise not on gender. Outer Ministry – four each from each gender. That is where your balance will come from in the future.

'In the Cabinet, of the nineteen, there would be five Liberal, three National, seven Labor, two Green and two Independent. Outer Ministry – two Liberal, two Labor and four Independent, reflecting the experience and the need for developing professionally.'

'What about the state split?' asks McGlashan, pen in hand.

'Cabinet – four from NSW, three from Queensland. Victoria would have three, as would South Australia. Two for Western

Australia. One for the ACT and the Northern Territory. They're all covered.'

McGlashan has not lifted his head through Justin's explanation. He now asks, 'And the breakdown for the Outer Ministry?'

'Two for Victoria. One each for the rest, except ACT.'

'Mmm.' Frances Grant acquiesces. 'I think there's some potential there. You've given every region and every party a fair go. We could live with that.' And she glances sideways at McGlashan. 'You've even included the Lib-Nats, who wouldn't ever get the numbers on their own – that's a magnanimity that they'd never have shown to us.'

'No jibes, please, Frances. Neither could any other party on their own, without Independent support. This is about a new way of working.'

'Alright.' Mary Owens appears positive. 'So you have portfolios in mind too?'

* * * *

Mike Penberthy shakes his head as he answers Laurie Black's question on a national television commentary panel.

'I never thought I would see this in my lifetime. That a twenty-three-year-old in his second term would be elected Prime Minister by so many experienced and battle-hardened politicians. I never thought that could happen.'

Black appears to be similarly impressed, and yet logical, as his left-brained approach usually is. 'It's all about the numbers, Mike. It's all arithmetic.'

'It is that, Laurie, but it's a lot more too. Kipps has managed to install an agreed process – a totally new arrangement which seems to me to be the antithesis of everything that's gone before. He has done that apparently just by persuading others as to the rationality of his arguments. And he has imbued a refreshing sense of integrity among crusty old pollies. Early days, I know, Laurie. He has to deliver; but this is such an interesting and historic swearing-in of a Cabinet.'

Michelle Beech expresses similar sentiments in print as she publishes the table of the sworn-in Ministry. She writes about the balance, the mix of male and female, experienced and inexperienced, the spread across states and territories – not to mention bringing the expertise of all the parties into a blend of a commitment to the nation's interest.

The Cabinet

Prime Minister	Justin Kipps (Ind – Qld)
Jobs Development, Skills Training and Workplace Relations	Mary Owens (Lab – NSW) Deputy Prime Minister
Treasurer	Dr Judith Holmes (Lib – S Aust) Second Deputy Prime Minister
Trade	Sen Nick Rathie (Lib – Vic) Leader in the Senate
Science and Innovation Research	Dr Jane McClure (Greens – S Aust)
Transition to Sustainable Energy	Sen Dr Rachael Adamson (Greens – NT)
Foreign Affairs	Sen Albert Richardson (Lab – Qld)
Industry and Small Business	Samuel Blackburn (Lib – W Aust)
The Arts	William Gaskin (Lab – ACT)
Border Protection, Customs and Immigration	Barbara Freeman (Nat – NT)
Defence	Paul Rowland (Lab – S Aust)
Regional Development	Gordon Milne (Ind – Vic)
Attorney General	Sen Philip Cartwright (Lab – Tas)

Infrastructure and Communications	Ronald Vittorio (Lab – Qld)
Education	Prof Thomas Coppock (Lab – Vic)
Health	Dr Valerie Johnstone (Lib – NSW)
Social Services	Sheila Duncan (Lib – NSW)
Agriculture, Water and Fisheries	Vernon Karlsson (Nat – NSW)
Disability Services, Mental Health and Ageing	Dr Brian Cathcart (Nat – W Aust)

The Outer Ministry

Veterans' Affairs	Sen Gary Wilson (Ind – NSW)
Aboriginal and Torres Strait Islander Development	Sen Vilma Anderson (Ind – NT)
Finance	Nicholas Senden (Lab – S Aust)
Housing, Homelessness and Emergency Services	Marjorie Lister (Ind – Tas)
Sport	Sen Gregory Hitchen (Ind – Vic)
Justice	Natalie Papasavas (Lib – Qld)
Defence Materiel	Sen Florence Tasker (Lib – Vic)
Community Services	Gary Thompson (Lab – W Aust)

How he did it is beyond my understanding, but I salute that young Justin Kipps, Beech writes.

And a public, hungry for a new way – for hope – hang on every word.

Beech's insights are in demand on television too, in the thirst to understand what is actually happening in this new political order.

Suddenly, the wise old heads are more important than the off-the-cuff opinion pushers – as *insiders* often appear to be on endless commentary teams – even marvelling over such innovations as the new parliamentary seating plans.

The Cabinet sits to the right of the Speaker as usual; but the front bench is now made up of all parties and Independents.

All the other seating is mixed and matched, seemingly without rhyme nor reason. But Kipps has suggested a new logic: opposites beside each other – and the result has been no shouting out; they can whisper their grizzles to their neighbours.

Anyone can ask a question but there are to be no more Dorothy Dixers, nor effusive collegial sham-praise.

Ministers are answering the questions within the three-minute maximum. No formulaic question patterns are allowed, no filibustering – the discussions are concise, reasoned statements of fact or clarification of argument.

'Isn't that what Kipps was arguing for, right at the start?' Michelle Beech notes.

Chapter 107

Canberra

Peter Connell

'Luke, we have permission to interview Peter Connell with regard to the Gareth Dawes burglary. The AFP and perhaps ASIO will listen in … and may close the interview if we go into their diplomatic territory. That will be their call.

'Connell is working on a plea deal. If he's been dabbling in international blackmail, he could be facing a life sentence under the anti-terrorism laws. Not very likely to happen, but he couldn't be sure … and can't take the risk. He must tell us the truth or face the consequences. He will have a skilled lawyer with him.'

'So we can't ask about Desmond Wilson or Stephanie Taylor?'

'Absolutely not.'

'Here we go again – trying to run while hobbled. I'll leave the questioning to you, Sarah.'

* * * *

'Mr Connell, you are subject to a plea deal. We have permission to question you with regard to a burglary and assault in the suburb of Hughes. The same plea deal rules apply here. We require the truth. Do you understand?'

Connell looks at his lawyer. 'Yes'

'You run an investigation agency. Investigating what?'

'It's generally background on politicians and their associates. Research mainly, for political parties and for media. We do some surveillance and other investigative work for insurance claims.'

'Thank you. Do you know a Leo Clarke?'

'Yes. He manages a courier service in Fyshwick.'

'What is your association with him?'

'Just that. He carries parcels when required.'

'Gareth Dawes. Do you know him?'

'Yes.' He scowls. 'He claims to be in the business of gathering background on personalities or events. Our company deals discreetly. His doesn't.'

'What do you mean by that?'

'He runs honey traps. No ethics. No integrity.'

'Are you aware that his house was burgled and that he was assaulted?'

'Yes.'

'What was your involvement in that affair?'

He looks at his lawyer who says, 'My client denies involvement in that affair.'

'Do you know why his house was burgled? I remind you of the requirement not to withhold information.'

He looks again at the lawyer who meets him with a stare that suggests that this matter has already been discussed between them.

Eventually he says, 'I understand that he had sensitive information on one of our clients – information that he might use to blackmail. He has no class.'

'So did you give the order for the burglary?'

'No.' A glance at his lawyer suggests a lack of confidence in his reply.

'Do you know a man called, Jakob … spelt with a k not a c?'

'I have heard the name.'

'Do you know him?'

'I believe he is Jakob the Pole, from Melbourne. I don't believe I've ever met him.' He looks again at his lawyer.

'Who gave the order for Jakob and his team to burgle Gareth Dawes house?'

'It wasn't me.'

'But you knew it would happen?'

Silence.

Sarah says, 'Jakob came from Leo Clarke in a grey Subaru, to a warehouse run by Mario Nuessle. Nuessle then drove the hit team to Dawes' house in a Nissan Navara. Who told Clarke to send them?'

'It wasn't me.'

'I remind you again of your plea arrangement. Do not withhold information that you know.'

He looks again at the lawyer. 'I suspect that it might have been a man called Ivan.'

'Have you dealt with the man called Ivan?'

Another look at his lawyer, who shakes her head.

'I think that is protected information, at the moment,' Connell recites, as a memorised pat line.

'Okay. So the material which was taken from Dawes. It was to be sent to Ivan?'

'I believe so.'

'How did Ivan know about the material?'

Connell looks again at his lawyer who answers for his client, 'I think that is also protected information, for the moment.'

'Can Leo Clarke take messages or instructions from Ivan?'

'I wouldn't think so. I wouldn't know, though. There are code words.'

'Alright. So your testimony is that this burglary and assault has resulted from a message from Ivan. If Clarke didn't take the message, did you advise Leo Clarke how it was to happen?'

'Not in so many words. I just alerted him to expect company from Melbourne. No details.'

'Then, Jakob and his team arrive from Melbourne. Clarke arranges transport. Mario Nuessle drives them to the house and back. Then the team disappears with the material in a Subaru. That's how it happened?'

'Yes. Probably.'

'Thank you for your time.'

* * * *

'Well, we didn't get interrupted by ASIO or the AFP,' Luke Dexter says. 'Have we solved this burglary then?'

'We have Connell's recorded answers. That will be for others to check later. We don't have Jakob or the other heavies. We don't have whatever was stolen – but whatever it was seems to be sensitive enough to be *protected information*. We have done what is possible in our ACT Policing jurisdiction. I think we can wrap up our reports on this business now and get on with our other cases.'

Dexter smiles. 'Well, we have two dirt-digging agencies out of business. That can't be too bad. Maybe if the new Prime Minister gets his way there will be much less demand for that sort of entrapment.'

'I hope so, Luke. He certainly seems to be making things happen. And, as we all now know, his name is Justin Kipps, not Kipper like Barry Cotter suggested.'

Dexter smiles and then asks, 'And the death of Desmond Wilson?'

'That's not our case, Luke. Nor is Adla Bello or Stephanie Taylor. Our colleagues will handle it. We've passed that on. That's the process.'

'I hear you. But a man is dead.'

'The coroner will hold an inquest in due course. Generally, coroners' hearings are held in public but this one won't be. I expect that they will invoke *'special circumstances of national security'* and place legal restrictions on media reporting. That is all covered in the ACT Coroners Act.'

'But if it was a murder by Stephanie Taylor?'

'The coroner will decide if there is sufficient evidence to proceed to a prosecution … or whether extenuating circumstances apply.'

'So an official record of the coroner's report will be filed for examination in the future? The public will know what happened?'

'Definitely filed, Luke … but under a restricted classification. It will be on the record but as part of *protected information.*'

'Okay. I suppose I can live with that. As you say, we need to trust that due process will be followed. At least, we've achieved our part.'

'Yes. ASIO will keep tabs and the AFP is across it. Trust them, Luke … and move on.'

'So,' Dexter grins, 'we can perhaps get a life beyond trying to solve murders and mysteries all the time.'

'That's it – work-life balance. A skill of policing is being able to turn up to police for another day. We don't need people burning out. Have you taken up your orienteering yet?'

'As it happens, I have – on the occasional weekends when I'm free. And it's great. Lots of fit, friendly people and a challenging sport.'

Sarah Power closes her folder with a grin, as Luke adds, 'One last thing on this, Sarah. I've been thinking about the code names that Leo Clarke mentioned – *Amador* is in Panama, at the southern entrance to the Panama Canal. That is a straightforward connection to the alleged shell company.

'Now, *Armenia.* I was looking for an Asian-Armenian connection with Turkmenistan or with the name Ivan. It sounds Russian. But, I found that Armenia is also the name of a place, a small city, in Colombia – coffee country but with a significant cocaine connection – major cartel leaders came from there.

'Ivan and his mates, whoever they are, may well be kingpins around running these escort-cum-investigation agencies to get dirt on politicians. Perhaps there's a Russian connection, especially with Ahmed, the Turkmen, staying at the Russian Embassy. And then, there is mention of the Chinese *belt*? But maybe, it's not about any of that at all. Maybe there's a different, simpler, slant to it – money, drugs and power – from Colombia and Panama.'

Sarah Power just smiles. 'That is ASIO's job. It's out of our jurisdiction now. Go and run through the bush with a map and compass to clear your mind of all the scenarios.'

* * * *

That evening, Sarah removes the USB from the second drawer in her study and wipes it clean. 'I don't think I need this insurance against a cover-up, now,' she says to no-one, as she gives a wry smile. She hopes the new PM's integrity processes can reduce the suspicion that dodgy official behaviour might be happening under a diplomatic veil of secrecy.

Chapter 108

Canberra

PM Kipps

Prime Minister Justin Kipps is a low-key leader – perhaps the lowest ever seen. He usually defers to his ministers, with the comment, 'They know most about their portfolios.'

Indeed, Kipps seems to devote most of his early attention to getting the Independent National Corruption Commission (INCC) up and running as the top priority.

The INCC is not a law court. Its role is to investigate and expose the corruption that some might see as the systemic *modus operandi* around the conduct of the federal government and their public service in Canberra.

At a lesser level, parliament approves that INCC will have a watching audit brief over the use of parliamentary expenses, applications for study or travel leave, disclosure of financial interests, disclosure of diary meetings, and donations to political parties from individuals – or, in a more secretive manner, to associates of politicians.

INCC powers include the ability to: initiate their own investigations; compel witnesses; conduct surveillance and telephone intercepts; compel the disclosure of documentary evidence including metadata; obtain warrants to search and to enter properties with proper authorisation; and **to conduct public hearings**. But confidentiality is paramount until such times as investigated evidence confirms that a public hearing might be in *the national interest*.

PM Kipps warns, 'It needs to be shaped well so that its remit does not suck in the innocents. We're really after a cultural change where people – as a matter of instinct – will operate legally, ethically and morally in the best interests of the people and the nation.'

* * * *

The footnote, which could have easily missed if Zoe's eye had not been scanning the court reports in the Sydney papers, stated: *Two former employees of Canberra's High Class Gentlemen's Club have been remanded in custody after a long pursuit by the Australian Federal Police. They are being charged under the Criminal Code for threatening acts against a member of parliament.*

'So they got Miranda and Natasha eventually,' Kipps observes. 'Can you check with the AFP, please, to see who they were working for?'

'What's your guess?' Zoe asks.

'Peter Connell, perhaps? But taking orders from powerful people much higher up – and maybe not even political puppeteers. There are bigger players in the game.' For some reason, he pictures Jack Carew in his mind – a symptom of an alien culture, perhaps.

* * * *

Ann Fletcher phones looking for a story on the local Member for Killen.

'Many people have been commenting on the Independent National Corruption Commission, the INCC. *Long overdue* is what I'm hearing most. Do you have a comment, Justin?'

'Sure, Ann. I'm happy to give you a response about the fight against corruption, the source of which is probably endemic in our culture – the frontier independence, the resistance to authority. But it's only a small step from there to twisting honest behaviour into greedy unethical practices. We have to take that temptation off the table.

'My hope is that the INCC will shine a public light and be more of a deterrent rather than a crime fighter. We need a strong community that can look after itself, independent of tempting pressures.'

Ann responds carefully. 'Some of your critics say that you talk too much about moral behaviour.' She must have been watching Mike Penberthy's technique.

'Critics never changed anything for the better, Ann. I want a change to moral behaviour, without exuding morality. It has to be internalised; part of our nature.

'I have no intention of trying to be a preacher. But the opposite of morality is unprincipled selfishness. I'm just swinging the pendulum back a little. We need the energy focused for the nation's good.'

Chapter 109

Canberra

Government operates

Dr Judith Holmes delivers a budget without any pre-budget leaks to soften the public. She doubts whether the press actually need to be *locked up*, to read the budget papers in advance and to prepare their stories.

'I would actually prefer that you sit in the gallery and listen to what I have to say,' she says to the assembled media throng. 'It won't be earth-shattering nor will it be long. Essentially, it's the nation's financial statement, some Treasury projections which may or may not be on the mark, and a way forward for the next six months to a year. But we will do the *lock-up* for those who want it – probably for the last time, though. We are now in a new way of operating.'

* * * *

'Ladies and Gentlemen,' the new Treasurer begins. 'Australia is not broke but nor is its revenue stream very strong. Commodity prices fluctuate – indeed they have been hard to predict over some years. At the moment they are declining, which reduces the country's income from that area.

'Part of the funding in this initial budget is for the Australian Taxation Office to police the rules that currently exist, particularly around pre-tax profit and actual tax payments. New money is allocated for INCC, the Independent National Corruption

Commission, to run constant audits of any slack or corrupt processes within government. At the next budget, I want to be able to report to you that we've tightened the robustness of the revenue systems.

'In terms of expenditure, all existing programs are being maintained. The new cooperative government is working hard to reach fundamental agreements on principles and projects which meet the test of being in the nation's best interest.

'Over the next six months, Treasury will run audits over all programs to ensure that they are value for money.

'As the Prime Minister has indicated, the cooperative government sees its main priority as being to transition towards renewable power sources with industries based on recyclables and re-usables. That is a long-term program, continuing over many decades, to secure the nation's present and its future.

'It involves significant scientific research, particularly around the next generation of photo-voltaic cells and high-capacity home-storage battery systems. If you will pardon the pun, that could be the circuit-breaker to kick-start those innovative scientific programs. But transition from old ways to new ways is a journey – a long-term investment in a cleaner, more sustainable future.

'Other priorities, such as investment in education will be assessed over the next few months. It is not just about money but more a philosophy concerning what schools should be doing and how they should do it, given the new technology platforms; what universities are and should be; what processes should be available for trade and professional skilling and gaining qualifications. We are sadly, to channel Prime Minister Kipps, still working on last century's models.

'The proposals will be floated to the public for comment before any changes to the current budgetary allocations are made.'

'So, in essence, this is not an emergency. There is money to pay the country's bills. We are monitoring trading figures, international commodity fluctuations and we are tightening up our systems to ensure that everyone pays their fair tax.

'The budget figures are now on the website for analysis and for comment to me or to your local member. Thank you.'

* * * *

The Lodge is the venue for official Prime Ministerial functions in Canberra.

It is far too grand for a man who lived in a share house with Frank Willis before embarking on this parliamentary experience. But his AFP security men emphasise that it is easier to protect him within *The Lodge* walls.

It actually takes several phone calls to his parents and to old Giles to convince Justin that he won't be compromising his integrity by sleeping and living in a few of the private rooms, in the house provided for him by the nation – which is why his trusted advisor, Zoe McAllister, arrives regularly for his essential massage therapy. Then, his guard always melts away to a suitably discreet distance and graciously accepts if the masseuse is still there in the morning.

It seems to be the only treatment needed for the rumbling that he still senses from time to time, sometimes more sharply than ever before – then it completely goes again. Of the choice of alternative remedies, Zoe's is the most pleasurable option for Justin.

Chapter 110

Canberra

Blindness

'I can't see out of my right eye.' Justin sits up in bed. It's the first time that the pressure hasn't gone following extended massage therapy.

Zoe leans over, wakening fast beside him in bed. 'What about the left eye?'

'It works.'

'Headache?'

'Pretty bad – but inside; right inside. You won't get at it by massage, I wouldn't think.'

'You need to see a doctor. I've been trying to tell you that. Relaxology can only help in some ways. You can't drive yourself relentlessly without things breaking down a bit.'

'I don't like doctors.'

'You might not have a choice. You can't see out of your eye.' He nods slowly as her fingers work his forehead. 'Any effect?'

'I don't think so.'

'Right. Let's get dressed. We'll call the doctor. You may have to go to hospital for scans. Something's definitely not right.'

He winces. 'Okay. That was a fair jolt just then. This is new.'

* * * *

The next day's headlines run with *Prime Minister admitted to hospital for tests.*

The day after, it is *Prime Minister to remain in hospital for several days. Mary Owens is acting PM.*

Then, *The business of cooperative policy development continues as the PM is said to be having problems with his eyesight.*

* * * *

Sally and Howard Kipps smile wanly at the police security detail as they enter Justin's hospital room.

They're permitted fifteen minutes to chat with him, from his left side; only about Harry, Jenny and things back in Brisbane – on the doctors' advice.

It seems strange to Justin that his father is holding his mother so tightly round her shoulders. He almost never does that – and his mother's eyes are red. She's been crying. But he can't even focus clearly with his left eye.

'It's alright, Mum. Don't worry. I'm not in pain. I'm being well looked after. The Cabinet know their priorities. I'm not worrying about work. Mary Owens is leading them well. She calls in most days to keep me informed.' As his mother squeezes his hand really hard, he says, 'Mum, I love you. You know that. Please don't worry.'

'I'll try not to, son.'

Two senior doctors arrive to take up positions within the PM's range of vision. They seem to know Howard and Sally already, because they give a cursory smile to each – as if to encourage.

'This rumbling you've been sensing, Prime Minister,' the first doctor asks, 'how long has it been happening – just to confirm?'

'Really badly, with pain? Only in the last couple of months. But I've sensed it probably for years. I just thought it was a premonition or anxiety before some event where I had to perform.'

They beam up the MRI scans on the screen as the elder doctor says, 'Justin, in simple terms, you have a brain tumour and more recently some bleeding. That's what has caused the loss of sight and the sharp pains – but this has probably been developing for years.' His mother wails and bursts into tears. 'We have explained this to your parents.'

Justin's one eye looks in surprise and possible annoyance that his parents have been told before him. And then it twigs; he understands why. He nods very slowly before saying, 'And there's no cure?' There is a resignation in the question and a better appreciation of his parents' distress now.

'Not given where it is, Justin.' And the sad doctor lets it sink in.

His mother is lying across him, hugging and crying. His father stands stiff, resolute, pursing his lips every few seconds in a vain attempt to contain his emotion.

'Bummer!' Justin calls out and then he cuddles his parents, as the flood gates open in his father's eyes. 'Bum, Bum, Bummer!'

After a long pause, as the doctors sit patiently like statues, Justin asks, 'What next? What will happen next? You're saying that nothing can be done?'

'Nothing that would make a difference. It's very advanced, very malignant and growing fast. Any attempts to attack it would fail and just end up delaying the inevitable.'

'I think I like your honesty, Doctor. How long before the inevitable, as you put it?'

'Not long. Days. Maybe a week or two. Your sight will be gone soon and your medication will need to be increased to control the pain.'

Another long pause. 'We have explored options back near your home for secure hospital care – for you. There's a private hospital near your parents' home. They can accommodate you. What do you need to do here immediately – because we want to fly you to Brisbane tonight or tomorrow, with a security detail and your parents. You are still the Prime Minister, Sir.'

'Bummer. Okay. Zoe and then Gordon are the priorities to advise. I suppose the Cabinet will need to be told. Maybe just let Mary Owens come first.' He grins wryly. 'I've never had to do this before.'

'I'll let your security know – and Ms McAllister and Mr Milne, first.'

In the end, it's a surprising crew that files past his bed, after Gordon.

Zoe stays – not willing to leave him alone. Mary is first, then Judith and all the Independents. They are fighting to be strong for him while he merely smiles and asks them to carry on the good fight.

Then Malcolm and Hetty arrive.

'Thank you for your trust and confidentiality,' Hetty whispers as she kisses his cheek.

Frances Grant and Doug Henderson. 'It's good of you to drop by.' He gets their empathy and sympathy from their expressions because they can't find their words. He's trying to help them not to suffer for him.

Then it is quiet for a while. His parents are away helping with arrangements, keeping busy. He talks to Harry and Jenny on the phone – that cheers him. The prospect of flying home is looking good – if you pardon the pun on his eyesight.

Suddenly, a lady's mature face peeks round the door – Michelle Beech … and, just behind her, the ponderous presence of Mike Penberthy.

'I'll miss you, Justin Kipps.' Michelle smiles at him with the ageless compassionate expression of the caring. 'You've been a breath of fresh air to us all.'

Penberthy says slowly, 'You've changed this place forever. I can't think how to thank you, young man, except to salute you.' He stands his huge frame to attention and snaps a crisp salute. 'Puckapunyal and Vietnam – but we never forget how to show respect.' His eyes are moist. 'Thank you, our Prime Minister, *Sir.*'

* * * *

Zoe still holds his hand after the room goes quiet again.

'How soon?' Justin asks.

'Onto the plane in a few hours. Then to Brisbane. I'm coming too.'

Chapter 111

Brisbane
Old friends

The room in the Carina Private Hospital has everything necessary, including space for visitors, chairs and even a fold-out cot. The security detail is always a discreet presence.

Justin had been sedated for the flight and, as he starts to sense consciousness, Harry's voice raises him from the deeps. 'I hope you can hear me, big brother. Dad said for me to tell you jokes and Mum said to read you poetry. I realise you can't see. But we're all here: Mum, Dad, Jen and Zoe. There's others who want to come – but you probably need a rest – Kipps by name, kip by nature.'

'Can't you shut it, Harry, please?' Justin manages to mumble through the fog of coming out of the haze.

'Told you he couldn't sleep through my patter,' Harry responds. 'Welcome back, Bro. Sorry it has to be like this.' Then his voice breaks. 'Fuckin' proud of you, mate.' And he dissolves into a teary silent hug with his big brother.

'Can you see out of your left eye?' Jenny asks quietly.

'I can see you, my beautiful sister,' and she clings to him too.

* * * *

'How long?' Howard Kipps asks the specialist.

'He's comfortable. Maybe a couple more days that he'll be able to communicate with people. Then progressively, he will go to sleep.'

'Okay. There are people who will desperately want to see him – and all I want to do is to hug him myself, for as long as I can. Nobody said that being a parent would be this hard, Doc. It's not supposed to be this way. He's only just turned twenty-three.'

'And he is the Prime Minister of the country. What an achievement!'

'But I'm his dad and he's our son. That's so much more important.'

* * * *

Harry becomes the guardian for his brother, to let his parents and Zoe try to get some rest.

Justin manages to be awake for a visit from a distraught Graham. 'This puts everything into perspective, Brother. So sad. Mate, you are a true *Bunji*. I'll carry on the cause – you see if I don't.'

His tearful exit is followed by Carol Carey – a gentle presence with a small posy of flowers, from an old lady at the Shady Rest home. 'She said you were as good as your word. And that you might remember the old woman in the wheelchair.' This draws a tired smile from the patient.

Frank and Karen bring regards from Darryl and the volunteers – but his old house mate is too tongue-tied so they smile through tears and both hold his hand. 'It's okay,' Justin says, comforting Frank. 'It's all okay, Frank. I understand.'

Janet arrives. 'I'm so, so sorry, Justin. I wish I'd understood better. I'll always treasure what we had together. I'll see your economics model through to fruition. I promise you that. It will be the Kipps Economic Ecosystem – the model for the future. Thank you for everything.'

* * * *

'Getting tired, Harry. Maybe you should get Mum, Dad, Jenny and Zoe, eh?'

The words have only just left his mouth when a wheelchair appears round the door – Old Giles, walking stick between his legs, being rolled in by Darryl Hope.

'You were supposed to be doing this to me, Justin,' Giles gives his familiar smile. 'Can you hear me?' He stands up, supported on the stick. 'You were perfect – Justin Kipps, Prime Minister of Australia. Amazingly perfect. The process will continue successfully after all of us have gone. It will be your legacy. So sorry to see you like this.'

'Thanks for coming, Giles. I owe you more than I could ever repay.'

'Justin, you've brought me so much joy to my final years – and made the country a better place, at the same time.'

'Likewise, Giles. Sorry, I have no energy – the drugs, you know.'

'I brought you something, Justin.' He holds up a yellow tee-shirt to Kipps' left eye. 'It reads, *Justin Kipps. Number 1. We are all better for knowing him!*'

* * * *

When it finally happens, he has a peaceful smile on his face.

The family hugs him and kiss his still warm face.

Pride in his civic achievements means nothing at this moment. A son, brother, a lover and friend has left the mortal land – and the pain is palpable.

Chapter 112

Brisbane

Respect

The funeral ceremony is private – family only; but Zoe manages an invitation.

Mary Owens announces that a national memorial service will be held at the Brisbane Convention Centre, in a week's time – flags will be at half-mast and she asks that the nation should pause for a minute's silence at noon on that day.

* * * *

The memorial ceremony is a *who's who* of national identities and Killen supporters.

The eulogies flow, soaring statements amid choirs and orchestral music. Parts of Justin Kipp's speeches are played and the audience watches videos of him persuading and coaxing with his gentle smile.

At noon, the thousands in the hall stand for a minute's silence.

Outside, across the nation, television cameras record shoppers stopping in malls, cars pulling over and government workers assembling, sombre, outside their offices in silent respect. Shopping malls stand silent.

Even television commentators stop their chatter.

A nation has paused in reverent respect.

Suddenly, after a silent minute of reflection, fighter jets roar over the Convention Centre in Brisbane and Parliament House in Canberra – then the nation quietly resumes its labours.

In the hall, five hundred solemn Killen volunteers in their new tee-shirts resume their seats, beside the hundreds of other assembled mourners.

'What else would I do with my money?' old Giles is heard to say from his wheelchair. 'These will become collector items. This is a man who changed the direction of a nation – almost accidentally.'

* * * *

Dai Evans, *The Voice of Australia*, is given the last word as he takes to the Convention Centre stage.

'Perhaps like many, I didn't understand Justin Kipps when he came to our attention with his manifesto.

'I, more than anyone, am thoroughly ashamed of the reaction that I had at the time. Perhaps we'd just come to accept the downward spiral of the world as we knew it then. We'd been duped into thinking that was normal.

'And then Justin Kipps arrived; a bright star to show us a way forward. Bit by bit, he fed us another way – just by using his quiet logical arguments. And we all followed. Perhaps, social media helped. The support and advice of millions on Twitter and Facebook didn't seem to restrict him. They were as transfixed by his message, as all Australians came to be.

'He was the greatest of persuaders. I have never personally known the like – and he has changed the Australia from what we were becoming into a new and promising nation and a world-leading exemplar.

'And he did it by the age of twenty-three. The brightest of comets who burned so brightly – but he has not burned out; the luminosity of his wake will lighten our world for generations to come. That is the national legacy of this great young man – and we are now custodians of the path that he has set for us.

'Rest in Peace, O shining light!'

The new cooperative government carries on with Mary Owens and Judith Holmes leading the way with new standards of behaviour and ethics.

It seems to have gone unnoticed by most, except Michelle Beech, that the country is actually now being run very capably by two women of very different political persuasions working really well together.

Public polling gives the thumbs-up to the new way of creating government policies; gently, in consultation with the people. The transition to the new Cabinet process has been seamless and the old aggressive faction-ridden politics of the past has become history; the fare of comedic satirists.

A by-election is held in Killen and a woman is elected as the new member – Zoe McAllister, former chief adviser to Justin Kipps; a professional woman, steeped in the thinking of her predecessor.

A whole phalanx of volunteers have led her to victory, headed by an A-grade footballer as campaign manager. Graham McGrady had mobilised his teams, as he had promised his *Bunji*, armed with his past experience in the Kipps' campaigns and a quiet acknowledgement of an old man from down Manly way, who was giving them very good advice.

Social media has taken on a new significance in how politicians communicate with their electorates and Karen Porter is fast becoming the guru consultant, in her new legal partnership – Porter and Willis.

* * * *

An impassioned, yet calm, Sally Kipps sits with Howard in the specialist's rooms. They are seeking clarity – a kind of closure.

'Doctor, did politics kill my boy?' she asks, through moist eyes.

The specialist's voice sounds almost Justin-like with its serene gravitas. 'According to what he told us, he was sensing the rumbling before all this political business began. Could it have helped if he had gone to doctors earlier? Perhaps. Most likely not, though. It was a particularly malignant tumour in a very inaccessible place. And would he have wanted to miss out on Canberra? Not to be part of changing a whole direction? Just to receive treatment earlier?

'From what I've seen of him, I suspect he might have chosen life quality over length of time on the planet. There are no right answers, Mrs Kipps. Your consolation has to be the time we all had, knowing him, what he stood for, and how he enriched the lives of everyone he met. He will live on in the fondness we feel for him and the legacy of his new political process.'

Sally Kipps smiles. 'Ah, yes – *The Manifesto*.'

Chapter 113

Canberra

Power and Buckley

AFP Senior Sergeant George Buckley says, 'We meet again, Sarah. It's amazing how so many paths all lead to a similar point. Our respective superintendents have shared all the information now.'

'Yes, George,' Sarah Power replies. 'The dirt squads of Peter Connell and Gareth Dawes seemed to overlap with their targets and people. Dawes was using brothel prostitutes to compromise people with political influence. Connell had this select stable of women and men to cater for all and any tastes of entertainment, with Leo Clarke organising the logistics of it all – that was his main occupation after all, managing a transport service.'

George Buckley grins. 'Yes and we are checking a drug involvement with that company also – all sorts of things could be in those packages. But this goes interstate ... and to Border Protection, as well. There's certainly a Melbourne organised crime link with muscle, international funding and an agenda to manipulate politics. We're also on the track of a man known as Jakob the Pole.

'Then there is the financial connection with international money laundering and deals from Panama and who knows where else. ASIO and our own international intelligence agents are working on that. And, at a corporate level, there is serious mismanagement of a company in allowing foreign interference to effectively control the operation of an Australian business, allowing it to be a front for other things – illegal things. So that has been referred to the Australian Securities and Investment Commission to see how it slipped through their processes.'

Sarah Power nods. 'So, back here, Leo Clarke and Mario Nuessle were relatively small cogs. Even Desmond Wilson was just muscle.'

'But with some organisation behind him,' Buckley says. 'The security passes that you found in his flat were stolen and cleverly amended. The theft of such high-powered clearances is a constant challenge for us – keeping ahead of the counterfeiters who then let nasty people into protected places, to foment their mischief.

'And Ivan?'

'Ah, Ivan. The name, Ivan, is interesting. Very possibly it covers multiple identities. No-one admits to ever having met him or seen him – he is identified by the code of the month. Sometimes a verbal instruction is given by phone or relayed by a known conduit with the right password. Sometime it's a written message.

'But we have made another very useful arrest, based on plea information from Peter Connell and a follow-up meeting with Gareth Dawes.

'It's been confirmed that Dawes organised two prostitutes from *High Society Escorts* to try to compromise Justin Kipps at an Eastchester Hotel function. Dawes has been charged with that offence. But the instruction came from Ivan – the code word was correct. And it was relayed to Dawes over the phone by Liam Driscoll, the deputy director to Malcolm McGlashan, the Liberal Party federal director … although Dawes didn't know his identity from the call.'

'Wow! The plot thickens.'

'It appears that Driscoll was a mole in party headquarters relaying potential targets back to Ivan and he was also a conduit for Ivan's messages to both Connell and Dawes. Indeed, Connell admits to irregularly visiting Driscoll at the Liberal Party Headquarters, unbeknown to McGlashan.

'While McGlashan certainly used Connell's agency to run background investigations and interference, he never used Dawes – scarcely knew of him. Driscoll was the person who contacted Dawes when Ivan required it. It appears that McGlashan was completely unaware of the clandestine network which involved his deputy.

'Didn't anyone recognise Driscoll's voice?'

'Connell knew who he was but just as a gatekeeper relaying information from Ivan. Neither Dawes nor Leo Clarke knew Driscoll personally. Driscoll is apparently quite adept at imitating a range of accents. The code word, not the voice, identified him as a messenger from Ivan.

'Ivan was manipulating Driscoll and, through him, Ivan controlled both Dawes and Connell, as well as their investigative networks. Our enquiries are on-going.'

'Amazing! Now I don't suppose Driscoll could actually *be* Ivan, then?'

'Unlikely. He's a puppet, like so many others. Our working hypothesis is that Ivan is a name used by agents working for certain foreign countries and/or for organised international crime, operating by some mutual arrangement. Whoever they are – and I'm sure we will find out in time – they are seeking to compromise decision makers in Canberra and to collect all sorts of intelligence through pillow talk. Their agenda is probably around quiet power and money … but possibly also to cause social disruption and maybe even regime change. It is serious stuff!'

'Right! Okay! And how did they compromise Driscoll to do their dirty work?'

'The usual. According to him, they gave him offers that he couldn't refuse. They had an explicit movie of him in action at a discreet sting party, followed up by a visit from Melbourne hard men – perhaps Jakob and his team. And then they sweetened the deal with regular financial payments. Carrot and stick.'

'Sounds like a similar technique that was used on Mario Nuessle. And Driscoll has confessed to all this?'

'Oh yes. He has lots of information that he wants to share as part of a plea to vanish with a cover story, a new identity and witness protection. It will keep our team busy for many weeks yet.'

'Goodness. Can that be done? An absent deputy director will be noticed.'

'Only McGlashan knows he's in custody. For others, he's away on personal leave. Then, there will be a story of a job offer overseas and Driscoll will disappear. If the info pulls in enough of the bad guys, most things can apparently be done. That's way above our pay grade though, in the secret world of spies.'

'Right! And Adla Bello, George?'

'One of many – living in a dangerous world. Their protection rarely comes from the minders. More often it's from the solidarity of the workers, looking out for each other.'

'And Stephanie Taylor seems to have been working for more than one master.'

'ASIO has all types of snitches and listeners.'

'So is she alright, George? In witness protection? Or just running scared?'

George smiles and shrugs. 'We're back under the security blanket again, Sarah. You could guess that she has moved on, safely.'

'George, do you realise that my detective constable, Luke Dexter, actually connected a lot of the dots to resolve this case, at our level? He gave the challenge significant thought in his own time. He's a very capable police officer.'

'I accept that. He is on our radar as someone to promote rapidly through the ranks. And I'm thankful that he didn't accidentally get in the way of any of our surveillance.'

'And George, what of Ahmed from Turkmenistan?'

'Well, Ahmed might have been on the money with the general Australian attitude of dismissing the abilities of people from countries that they know bugger all about. But, I can assure you we take these people very seriously in the current climate. The intelligence agencies are checking carefully into his alleged cosy intimate chats. We don't underestimate any of them, or their alleged talents.

'Ahmed made a big mistake, though, in allowing his own gratification to compromise himself. But we aren't blameless either in enabling the Connells and Dawes to tease them with such pleasurable offers that are so hard to refuse.

'You could also reasonably assume, Sarah, that Connell has given us a whole list of his clients from embassy connections who can now be on ASIO and AFP watch lists. It has been a very productive wrap-up of present and potential crime.'

* * * *

Back home, sharing a red wine with Greg Edwards, her lawyer partner of the moment, Sarah says, 'It was a moving memorial ceremony for the late prime minister today, Greg. So young, too.'

'Yes. He's certainly a loss to our community but he achieved much more than most people do in a very long life. We just need to be grateful.'

'I think the country is. So many seemed to stop for the minute's silent reflection today.'

'Let's hope that his legacy is carried on now.'

Sarah tells him of the satisfactory resolution of the convoluted dirt digger case, which has been in her consciousness for over a year.

'It seems to have been a complicated one. It's always good to be able to draw a line under a challenge.'

She smiles over her glass. 'We have to trust that ASIO is across all the big issues. Greg, have you ever heard of the missing lady, Stephanie Taylor?'

He grins back, through his veil of witness protection confidentiality. 'I haven't seen her name in any corporate crime files. So what would I know?' He raises his open palms in the smiling shrug of pretend ignorance.

Author's Note
and Acknowledgements

To you, the readers loyal and new, I hope you have enjoyed this tale and that it resonated from your own perspectives. Your regular encouraging feedback is what keeps the stories flowing. Thank you.

Consider: When the world can seem to be going downhill fast and 'the news broadcasts' are dire, you have to realise that within the younger generations there are very many highly capable people who can see through the indoctrinating baggage of the past, who have a world-view beyond self, who can use the technology of the future in ways that we, older ones, cannot even yet imagine.

I have met many of them in my working life. They have talent, moral integrity, optimism and respect – so necessary to be exemplar family, business and community leaders.

They are the hope and inspiration for the future – alert educated young minds who visualise things as they can be and are not content just to settle for *same old, same old* – just because it was deemed appropriate for the contexts of generations gone by.

They are the *Justin Kipps* for the years ahead, leading in all fields of human endeavour, frequently living without fanfare – under the radar of sensational media celebrity but making a huge difference to all of those around them. And they may just reform the way politics works, too.

I am very positive for the years ahead in a global world of social consciousness and an appreciation of the importance of balance in all the ecosystems of the Earth – including Man's surviving place in it all.

Thank you to Patrice Shaw (psediting.com.au) for her careful editing as well as her challenging suggestions for writing improvement.

Thanks also to Kirsty Ogden (epiphanyediting.com.au) for her eye-catching cover design and clear page layouts. Kirsty's assistance in the world of publishing enables me to concentrate on writing the stories.

Patrice and Kirsty together deserve a lot of the credit for the success of my books – and they do it all with a gentle grace.

I thank my wife, Brenda, and my extended family for giving me the love, space and encouragement to write my stories. My brother, Lewis, has helped with all my stories. Our shared history has been a catalyst for many of the writing ideas.

Finally, this book is written for you, the reader, to savour. So, I trust that you have settled back and relished getting lost in optimistic adventure.

www.ingramcontent.com/pod-product-compliance
Lightning Source LLC
Chambersburg PA
CBHW071634260626
47170CB00001B/100